"FINE IMAGINATIVE ACTION!"
—*The Columbus Dispatch*

Laurelin saw Igon fall. "Igon! Igon!" The words were rent from her throat in horror, but the Prince moved not, his blood welling up to run in scarlet rivulets in the snow. Screaming in rage she snatched up a dagger and hurled herself in front of the fallen Prince to protect him from the mad Ghulen. And she sat in the snow and wept. . . .

BOOK TWO OF THE IRON TOWER TRILOGY

SHADOWS OF DOOM

DENNIS L. McKIERNAN

A SIGNET BOOK
NEW AMERICAN LIBRARY

This is an authorized reprint of a hardcover edition published by Doubleday and Company, Inc.

SIGNET TRADEMARK REG. U.S. PAT. OFF. AND FOREIGN COUNTRIES
REGISTERED TRADEMARK—MARCA REGISTRADA
HECHO EN CHICAGO, U.S.A.

SIGNET, SIGNET CLASSIC, MENTOR, PLUME, MERIDIAN AND NAL BOOKS are published by New American Library, 1633 Broadway, New York, New York 10019

First Signet Printing, September, 1985

1 2 3 4 5 6 7 8 9

PRINTED IN THE UNITED STATES OF AMERICA

To my own Merrilee:
Martha Lee

And to Laurelin:
Tina

And the ichor and the thees and thous
are respectfully dedicated to
Ursula K. Le Guin

CONTENTS

SYNOPSIS

This is the second part of The Iron Tower.

The first part, *The Dark Tide*, told of unsettled times in the Boskydells, where the Wee Folk—the Warrows—prepared for trouble. Amid rumors of Wolves and of mysterious disappearances, of War and of dark Evil looming to the far north, five young-buccen Warrows—Tuck, Danner, Hob, Tarpy, and their guide Patrel—set forth from Woody Hollow to join the Thornwalker company guarding Spindle Ford. On the way, the buccen were attacked by evil, Wolf-like Vulgs, and Hob was slain.

Surviving to carry the word that Vulgs were in the Bosky, the four remaining buccen continued on to Spindle Ford, where they took up their Thornwalker duties in Patrel's squad. Some days later, as a Kingsman came sounding the High King's call to War, Tarpy was killed during another Vulg attack.

Swearing vengeance, Tuck, Danner, and Patrel, and two squads of Warrows set forth from the Boskydells to answer the muster at Challerain Keep.

Upon arriving at the strongholt, they learned of the Dimmendark, a spectral Shadowlight to the north, where the Sun did not shine and Adon's Ban did not rule; hence, evil Modru's vile creatures—Vulgs, Rūcks, Hlōks, Ogrus, Ghûls, Hèlsteeds—roamed free.

The Warrows were assigned Castle-ward duties, and Tuck became friends with Princess Laurelin, betrothed of High King Aurion's elder son, Prince Galen, absent from the castle on a mission into the Dimmendark.

Tuck, Danner, and Patrel were invited to Laurelin's birthday feast. At the height of the celebration a wounded warrior came bearing news that the dreadful pall of the Dimmendark had started moving southward toward the Keep. The Winter War had begun.

The next day Princess Laurelin departed Challerain Keep, heading south on the last waggon train of refugees. She was escorted by the King's younger son, Prince Igon, who was traveling to Pellar to hasten the King's Host northward.

The Dimmendark soon swept over the Keep and beyond. The spectral Shadowlight baffled eyesight: Men saw at most two miles over open plains and much less in forests and hill country; Elves saw perhaps twice as far as Men; but the strange, jewel-hued eyes of the Warrows, as if seeing by a new color, saw farthest of all, as much as five miles. Hence, the Warrow company was sundered, and the buccen were assigned to various of the King's companies to be their eyes in the Dimmendark.

At last one of Modru's evil Hordes came through the Dimmendark and assaulted the woefully undermanned Keep, overwhelming the defenders. On the final 'Day of combat, Challerain Keep was abandoned by the King's forces as they attempted to break free of the Horde.

Separated from the others during the last desperate battle, Tuck eluded a Rūck patrol by taking refuge in the ancient tomb of Othran the Seer. Weaponless, he discovered in the sarcophagus an elden blade of Atala and a single red arrow for his bow. By happenstance, Prince Galen came to the same tomb. Alone and armed with only the Atalar Blade and the red arrow, the Man and the Warrow fled southward, striking for Stonehill to rendezvous with any other allies who might have survived.

Before reaching Stonehill, Galen and Tuck came upon the slaughtered remains of Laurelin's refugee train, ravaged by Ghûls. Neither Laurelin nor Igon was among the slain. Taking up weapons from the dead, Galen and Tuck followed the Ghûl track, hoping to overtake the Hèlsteed-borne Ghûls and somehow set the Prince and Princess free—if indeed they were captives.

Two 'Darkdays later the Man and Warrow came to the Weiunwood, the site of a three-'Day battle wherein one of Modru's Hordes had been repelled by the Weiunwood Alliance of Men, Elves, and Warrows. From the Captains of the Alliance, Galen and Tuck learned that a party of Ghûls bearing eastward had passed by some six 'Darkdays ago, later followed by a lone rider.

Continuing their pursuit, Tuck and Galen rode eastward too and came at last to the Elven strongholt of Arden Vale. Upon hearing of their mission, the Elven leader, Lord Talarin, led them to a house of healing where they found Prince Igon, wounded and feverish. In a moment of lucidity Igon confirmed that Laurelin was in fact a prisoner of the Ghûls.

In that same moment Elf Lord Gildor arrived at

Arden Vale to tell Galen that Aurion Redeye was dead and that Galen was now High King of all Mithgar.

We left Galen faced with a dilemma: Should he ride north and attempt to rescue his beloved, or south to gather the King's Host and lead them against Modru's Hordes? It was a choice between Love and Duty.

But as *Shadows of Doom* begins, we return to the day when Laurelin departed Challerain Keep.

"The days have now fled, and the 'Darkdays are come upon us."

Gildor Goldbranch
December 22, 4E2018

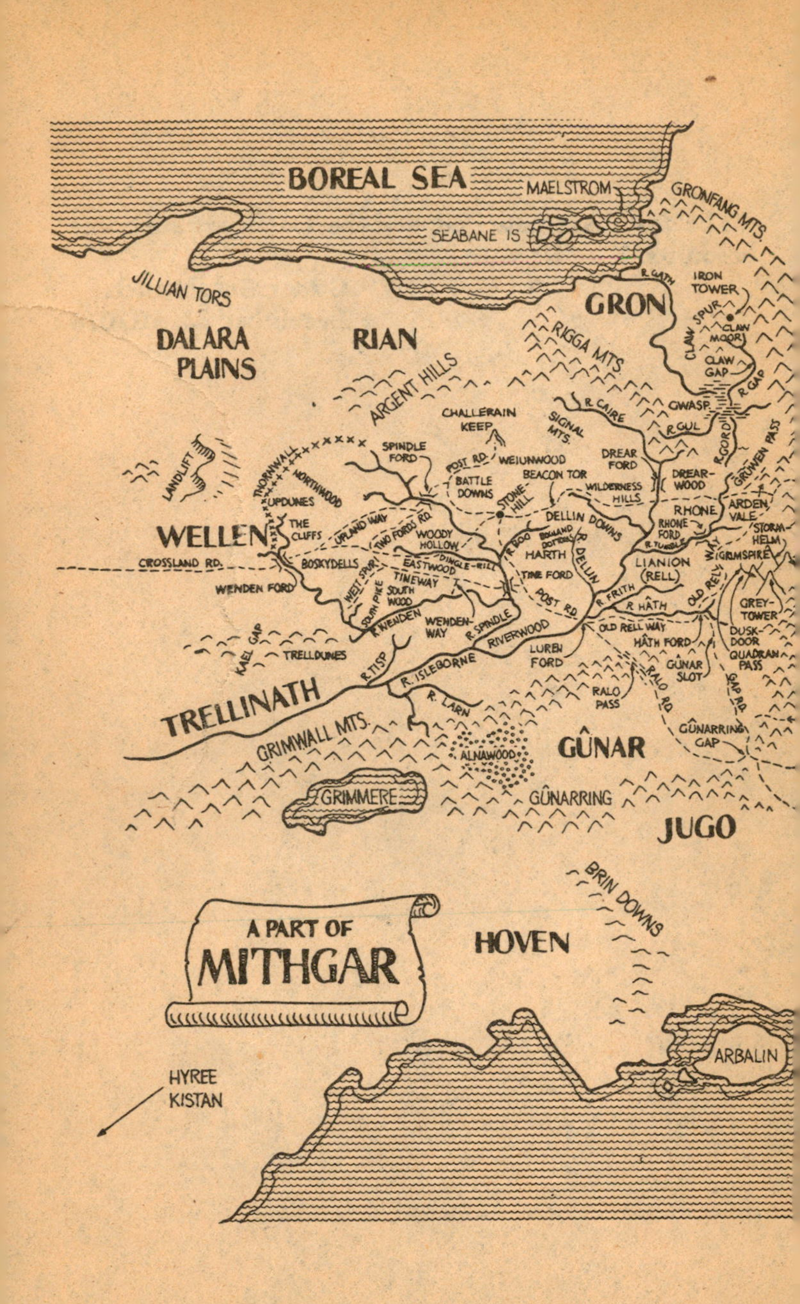
A PART OF
MITHGAR
BOREAL SEA
MAELSTROM
SEABANE IS
GRONFANG MTS.
JILLIAN TORS
DALARA
PLAINS
RIAN
GRON
IRON
TOWER
CLAW SPUR
CLAW
MOOR
CLAW
GAP
R. GAP
RIGGA MTS.
ARGENT HILLS
CHALLERAIN
KEEP
SIGNAL
MTS.
R. CAIRE
GWASP
R. GUL
R. GORD
GRUWEN PASS
LANDLIFT
THORNWALL
NORTHWOOD
SPINDLE
FORD
POST RD.
WEIUNWOOD
BATTLE
DOWNS
BEACON TOR
DREAR
FORD
DREAR-
WOOD
WILDERNESS
HILLS
UPDUNES
STONE-
HILL
DELLIN DOWNS
RHONE
ARDEN
VALE
WELLEN
THE
CLIFFS
UPLAND WAY
TWO FORDS RD.
WOODY
HOLLOW
RHONE
FORD
STORM-
HELM
CROSSLAND RD.
BOSKYDELLS
EASTWOOD
DINGLE-RILL
HARTH
R. DELLIN
LIANION
(RELL)
GRIMSPIRE
WENDEN FORD
TINEWAY
TINE FORD
POST RD.
R. FRITH
OLD RELL WAY
SOUTH
WOOD
R. HÂTH
GREY-
TOWER
R. WENDEN
WENDEN-
WAY
R. SPINDLE
OLD RELL WAY
DUSK-
DOOR
KAEL GAP
TRELLDUNES
RIVERWOOD
LURBI
FORD
HÂTH FORD
QUADRAN
PASS
R. TISP
R. ISLEBORNE
GÛNAR
SLOT
TRELLINATH
R. LARN
RALO
PASS
RALO RD.
GAP RD.
GRIMWALL MTS.
GÛNARRING
GAP
ALNAWOOD
GÛNAR
GRIMMERE
GÛNARRING
JUGO
BRIN DOWNS
HOVEN
ARBALIN
HYREE
KISTAN

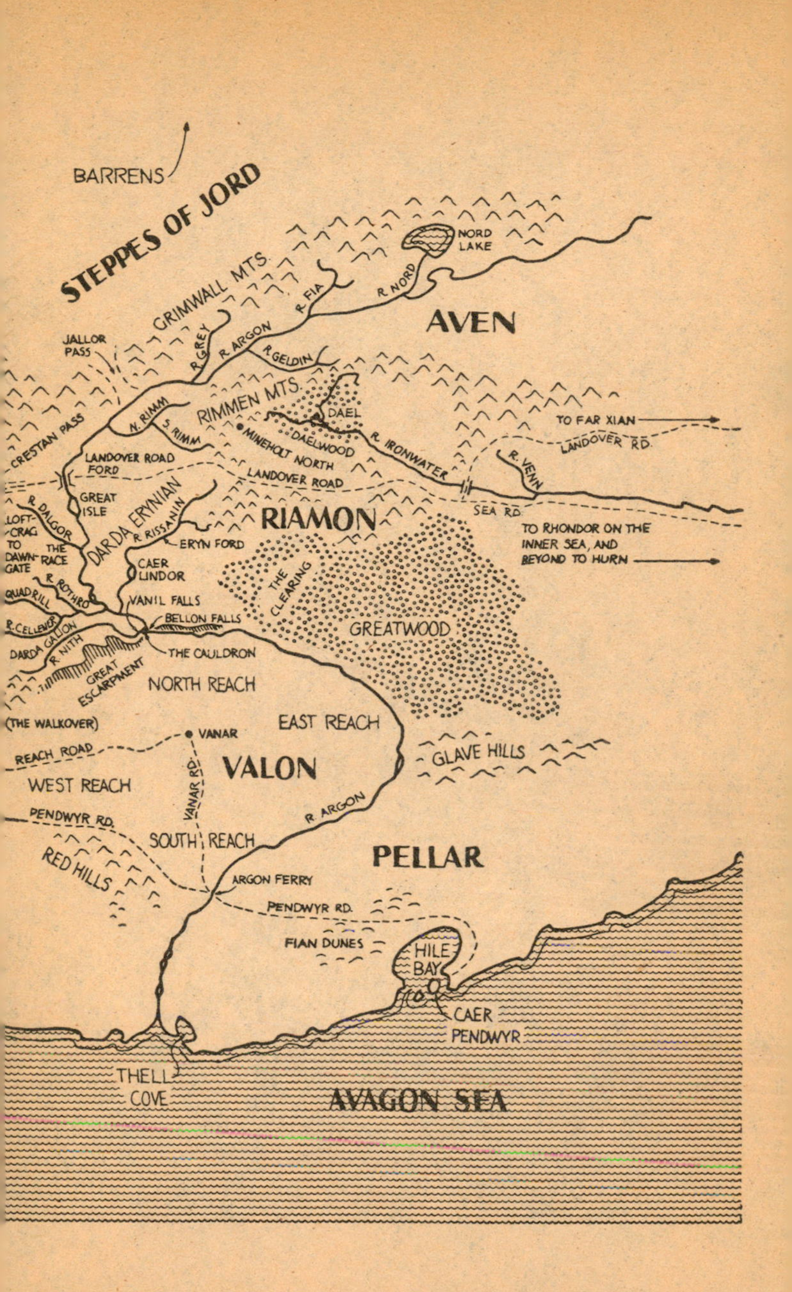
BARRENS
STEPPES OF JORD
GRIMWALL MTS.
NORD LAKE
R. NORD
R. FIA
AVEN
JALLOR PASS
R. GREY
R. ARGON
R. GELDIN
CRESTAN PASS
N. RIMM
S. RIMM
RIMMEN MTS.
DAEL
MINEHOLT NORTH
DAELWOOD
R. IRONWATER
TO FAR XIAN
LANDOVER RD.
R. VENN
LANDOVER ROAD FORD
LANDOVER ROAD
SEA RD.
GREAT ISLE
R. DALGOR
LOFT-CRAG
TO DAWN-GATE
THE RACE
DARDA ERYNIAN
R. RISSANIN
ERYN FORD
RIAMON
TO RHONDOR ON THE INNER SEA, AND BEYOND TO HURN
CAER LINDOR
R. ROTHRO
QUADRILL
VANIL FALLS
THE CLEARING
BELLON FALLS
R. CELLENER
DARDA GALION
R. NITH
THE CAULDRON
GREATWOOD
GREAT ESCARPMENT
NORTH REACH
(THE WALKOVER)
EAST REACH
VANAR
REACH ROAD
GLAVE HILLS
VALON
VANAR RD.
WEST REACH
PENDWYR RD.
R. ARGON
SOUTH REACH
PELLAR
RED HILLS
ARGON FERRY
PENDWYR RD.
FIAN DUNES
HILE BAY
CAER PENDWYR
THELL COVE
AVAGON SEA

CHAPTER 1
CAPTIVE!

Nearly two days ere the Dimmendark came unto Challerain Keep, the Lady Laurelin was borne away south in the last caravan. Slowly, the wagon trundled down from the mount, and the Princess wept silently while her chaperon, Saril, eldest handmatron, chattered about inconsequential trivialities and complained about the discomfort of the wain. What the Princess needed at this moment was to be held and soothed and to have her hair stroked, although even this would not heal a heart in despair, for only time could serve that end. Yet Saril appeared unaware of the weeping damosel's needs, seeming not to sense the quiet anguish of the maiden as she looked with tear-blind eyes out through the open flap and back at the passing hill country—though the handmatron did give over a linen kerchief to the Princess when Laurelin could not find her own.

Onward the wain groaned, last in the line of a hundred waggons, along the south-bearing Post Road. Down through the foothills they wended, and out upon the snowy plains. At last Laurelin's weeping subsided, yet now she knelt upon blankets at the tailboard and looked ever backward toward the Keep and did not speak.

Time passed, and slow miles rolled by to the flap of the canvas cover, the creak and jingle of singletrees and harness, the plod of horse hooves, an occasional command of the driver, and above all the grind of axle and iron-rimmed wheels turning upon the frozen snow.

In midafternoon the train pulled up a long hill, snowy slopes to either side. Laurelin's gaze held still to the north, toward the distant fortress. Finally, her wain topped the crest and started down the far side, and Challerain Keep could be seen no more.

"Oh, Saril, I'm afraid I've made a sodden mess of your kerchief," said Laurelin, turning to her companion and holding forth the crumpled linen for the other to see.

"La, my Lady, worry not," said Saril, reaching forth and taking the cloth. "Oh, my! It *is* wet, isn't it? Why, there must be enough tears in here to last several years." She held it out and away, a thumb and forefinger grasping one corner. "We'd best spread this out, else the cold will freeze it into a lump hard as a rock."

"Well, then, perhaps we just should let it freeze that way," replied Laurelin, attempting a smile. "Then it can be used as a missile in some warrior's sling and flung at Modru."

At the mention of the Enemy in Gron, Saril made a swift gesture with her hand, as if scribing a rune in the air to ward off the presence of the Evil One. "My Lady, I think it best not to mention that name, for I hear that even the speaking of it draws his vileness down upon the speaker as surely as iron is drawn to lodestone."

"Oh, Saril," chided Laurelin, "now 'tis my turn to

say 'La!' for what could he want with Women and children, or the oldsters and the lame?"

"I don't know, my Lady," answered Saril, her matronly features apprehensive, glancing over her shoulder as if someone may have been creeping up from behind, "yet mine own eyes have seen the lodestone reach out with an invisible hand to snatch the iron, and so I know that is true; thuswise there's no reason to believe that the other isn't just as true, too."

"Oh, Saril," responded Laurelin, "just because the one is so, it doesn't mean that the other follows."

"Maybe not, my Lady," answered Saril after a bit, "but just the same, I would not tempt him."

They spoke no more of it, but Saril's words seemed to hang like a silent echo in the thoughts of Laurelin the rest of the day.

Just at sunset, camp was made some twenty-two miles south of Mont Challerain. Although the train had paused several times along the way to tend the horses and stretch the legs and see to other needs, still it was not the same as being out of the waggons and encamped for the night. And now that the train had stopped for the eventide, Laurelin walked the full length of the caravan and back, some two miles in all, speaking to oldsters and young alike, buoying up spirits, and she passed Prince Igon doing the same.

When at last the Princess returned to the fire by her waggon, Saril had prepared a stew over the small blaze. Wounded Haddon sat on a log near the warmth, eating, his arm in a sling but his appetite ravenous, though his features were pale and drawn.

"My Lady," he said, startled by the Princess's sudden appearance from the darkness, struggling to gain his feet, but Laurelin bade him to sit.

"And now, Warrior Haddon," said the Princess, taking up a bowl of stew and a cup of tea and seating herself beside the soldier, "speak to me of my Lord Galen, for I would hear of him."

And long into the night, Haddon told of the forays, skirmishes, and scouting missions that Galen's One Hundred carried forth in the bitter Winternight to the north. And as the warrior spoke, Lord Igon came to the fire to take a meal, and so, too, did Captain Jarriel, ever present at the side of the Prince. Igon's eye sparkled in the firelight as he heard tell of the probing in the Dimmendark to find Modru's Horde:

"Along the Argent Hills we rode, and to the Rigga Mountains," said Haddon, his eyes lost in memory, "but nought did we find: Modru's myrk hid all. North we turned, toward the Boreal Sea, and at last our search bore fruit—though bitter it was—for a vast Horde we found, and it moved south along that dire range, coming down the western margins of the Rigga. From dark clefts and deep holts within those grim crags they came swarming, and their ranks swelled as they marched.

"Vulgs were with them, running their flanks, and we could not raid, for those dark beasts would sense us from afar and give the enemy warning ere we could close with the Spawn. King Aurion named them aright: Modru's curs." Haddon paused as Saril, whose eyes were wide from listening to the tale, refilled the warrior's teacup.

"Messengers were sent to Challerain," continued Haddon, "to tell the King of the Horde."

"None arrived," said Igon grimly, shaking his head.

"Then they were cut down ere they could do so, my Prince," responded Haddon, and he held forth his sling-bound arm: "As the Vulgs slew Boeder, and nearly me, they must have hauled down those sent to carry word to the Keep."

"Prince Igon tells me you spoke of Ghola," said Captain Jarriel.

"Aye," answered the warrior, eyes deep in craggy face lost in reflection. "Ghola there are, and upon Hèlsteed. Many were the times they pursued us, but Lord Galen always gave them the slip, e'en in the snow. Wily is the Prince, clever as a fox. We would wait till 'twas right to strike, when there were no Vulgs about, and when some o' the Spawn would be separated from the Horde. Oh, then we'd lash into those pockets like bolts from Adon's Hammer. Back we'd jump, with Hèlsteeds after, but Lord Galen's black steed would fly to the north and us right behind. Onto the trampled snow we'd ride, our tracks mingling with and lost within the wide wake of the very Horde we'd struck. Along this beaten swath we'd run a ways, soon to slip aside to hide among crags or bracken or hills, and watch the Ghola race by while we were concealed by the very Enemy's own dark myrk."

"Say you that their sight is no better than ours?" Prince Igon seemed surprised. "I had thought that all night-spawn could see well in the dark."

"I don't know how well they can see in ordinary dark, but Lord Galen says that the Shadowlight baffles their eyes as well as ours." Haddon drank the last of his tea. "This I do know: Mine own sight never reached beyond two miles in the Dimmendark, and at that distance I could see but vaguely: the movement of the Horde, many Ghola racing upon Hèlsteeds, and at times a mountain flank: only these could I see from afar. Even things nearby in that shadowy glow held little detail for me; color is lost beyond a few paces." Prince Igon nodded his understanding, for he, too, had spent time in the Winternight.

"I hear that Elven eyes see beyond those of all mortals," said Laurelin. "Perhaps their sight pierces even the shadow of the Dimmendark."

"Mayhap, my Lady," responded Haddon, "yet strange eyes indeed would it take to see afar in that myrk."

Strange eyes. An unbidden image sprang into Laurelin's thoughts, for suddenly she pictured Tuck's wide sapphirine gaze looking into her own, and she wondered about the jewel-eyes of Warrows.

The dawn found the horses being harnessed to the waggons by some, while others ate the last of their breakfasts. Laurelin aided the healer in putting salve and a fresh bandage on Haddon's slashed arm, and the healer pronounced him fit enough to lay his sling aside, "if you treat it gingerly. We cauterized it that night, you know, with a red-hot blade to sear out the poison, or at least to hold off its effects till the Sun rose. It's the burn we're ministering to now, and the healing of the gash, for daylight and Adon's Ban have destroyed the Vulg venom."

Soon all was in readiness, and at the calls of the escort's horns the train got under way once more, continuing on its southerly course along the Post Road, away from Challerain Keep and toward the Battle Downs and Stonehill and beyond.

All day the waggons jostled and jounced over the icy way, and Laurelin found the brief hourly stops a welcome relief from the juddering, swaying wain.

She saw little of Igon, for he along with Captain Jarriel rode at the fore of the train to be first to receive word from the far-ranging horse-borne forward scouts of the caravan escort.

But Saril kept the Princess company, and they whiled away the afternoon hours in conversation, though in the morning they had played *zhon*, a tarot of omens gamed often at court. Yet instead of the pleasant time at cards she had expected, the more they played, the more uneasy Laurelin became; and even though the suit of Suns was filled with nought but bright portents, still her eyes sought only the four of Swords and the Dark Queen, her heart lurching at the turn of each card. At last she bade Saril to lay aside the deck, for Laurelin had lost the joy of the game.

In midafternoon of the next day, as was her wont, Laurelin sat at the rear of the wain peering out through the canvas flap and back at the passing countryside, and rolling hills began to rise up from the prairie as the caravan approached the northernmost margins of the Battle Downs. Many pleasant miles had passed by when suddenly her eye caught the movement of a running horse, and she heard the sound of a horn: it was the rear scout, riding hard to overtake the train. Soon he thundered past, urgent horn ablare, snow flinging from the steed's pounding hooves as he flew southwest toward the lead waggons, and Laurelin's heart thudded in her breast and she wondered at his haste.

Time passed, and again the Princess heard the tattoo of hooves; horses beat past: Igon, Captain Jarriel, and the scout raced north, their cloaks streaming behind as they flew back along the caravan's track. They veered from the Post Road and galloped to the top of a hillock where they reined to a stop. Long they sat without moving, looking to the north, back in the direction of Challerain Keep, now far beyond the horizon. Laurelin gazed at their dark silhouettes shadowed against the afternoon sky, and once more her heart raced, and she felt a deep foreboding. And there was something about the way the trio sat, and then she realized: *How like the ancient wood carvings of the Three Harbingers of Gelvin's Doom they look;* and a grim pall fell upon her breast, for that was a tale most dire.

At last Igon and Jarriel turned and plunged back down the snowy slopes, leaving the rear scout behind upon the hill. The horses cantered toward the slow-moving train, overtaking it swiftly. Jarriel rode on to the fore as Igon drew Rust up to the tailgate of Laurelin's wain. She threw wide the flap and raised her voice above the rumble of axles and wheels: "What is it? What see you to the north?"

"It is the Black Wall, my Lady," said Igon grimly. "It moves south steadily. I deem Challerain Keep to have been engulfed by the Dimmendark, nigh yesternoon, I ween; most assuredly it now lies deep within the grasp of bitter Winternight. Yet the Wall has come on apace, and if nought changes its course, it will o'ertake this train on the morrow.

"Tonight, you and I must go among the folk and prepare them for this black curse, for it will scourge their spirits and sap the fire in their hearts." Igon reined Rust back and to the side, calling, "I must away to set the escort plans." And the great roan plunged forward at Igon's urging.

Laurelin's heart was filled with dread by this news, and she despaired for those left behind at the Keep:

Aurion, Vidron, Gildor, the Warrows, especially Tuck, all of the warriors, and, somewhere, Galen. And the Princess wondered who would comfort her own heart, her own spirit, when the darkness came. And she turned to look at Saril and saw that the matron wept and shook with dread, for she had heard all that Igon said. Laurelin drew Saril unto her and soothed her as a lost child. And Laurelin knew that none would comfort a Princess, for it is common knowledge that royalty feels not the fears nor anguishes of the ordinary folk.

That night, Laurelin's uneasy slumber was filled with desperate dreams of being trapped.

The next day at dawn the Black Wall was plain for all to see, jutting upward on the horizon, seeming to grow taller as it drew closer. Children cried and clung to their mothers, and faces bore stricken looks as the 'Dark stalked southward.

Swiftly camp was broken, and the caravan once more took up the long trek, moving slowly upon the Post Road as it swung westerly along the Battle Downs. And Saril wept because now the road did not run south and away from the approaching Wall. And sweeping toward them out of the north like a great dark wave came the murk of the Evil One, flowing nearer with every passing moment.

Slowly the Sun rose into the sky, climbing toward the zenith, but its golden rays did not stay the advance of the darkness as the morning passed and noon drew nigh; yet so, too, did the evil dark tide, now rearing up into the sky perhaps a mile or more: a great, looming, vile Black Wall. Before it, a boiling cloud of snow swirled, and there came the rumble of wind churning along the base of the dark rampart.

Horses began to shy and skit, and from the wains there rose the cries of children, the sobbing of Women, and the moans of old Men.

Grimly, Laurelin watched the blackness come, her features pale and her lips clamped in a tight line; but her gaze was steady and she flinched not as the Wall drove down upon her. Behind her in the waggon, Saril knelt over double with her face buried in her hands, moaning and rocking in distressed fear, a huddled ball of dread as the 'Dark plowed onward.

Now the train was engulfed in a blinding, driven blizzard, and firm hands were needed to rein rearing horses to as the shrieking white howled about them.

The Sun's light began to fail, swiftly growing dimmer as the 'Dark swept on, fading into black Shadowlight, spectral and glowing.

Then the wave was past, and the wind yowl slowly fell into muteness; the billowing snow began drifting back unto the ground. The caravan now stood in the full Dimmendark, and the grasp of bitter Winternight reached forth to clutch this land. A dread silence fell across the plains and into the Battle Downs, broken only by the solitary wails of those frightened beyond the limits of their courage.

Twenty miles the waggon train went that day, ten in the sunlight, ten in the 'Dark. Camp was made and meals prepared, but the people were without stomach and little food was taken. Laurelin forced herself to eat a full meal, but Saril only picked at her food, her eyes red from weeping. On the other hand, Haddon's appetite seemed unaffected by the Shadowlight, but then he had spent many 'Darkdays within its glow as a member of Galen's One Hundred, and he ate readily;

but his look was grim and wary, for he knew that where fell the Dimmendark, so, too, went creatures of evil.

Igon and Jarriel came to the fire to take their own meal.

Captain Jarriel looked thoughtful as he ate, and soon he broached his concern, his speech that of court parlance: "My Lady, on the morrow I propose to thy wain to train center whither thou will be safer."

"How so, Captain?" Laurelin asked.

"Here at train's end thy wain is greatly exposed," answered Jarriel, setting aside his cup, "manifestly open to attack by hostile foe. I would move thee to where it is more difficult to single thee out, to a place more easily defended."

"But then, Captain," responded the Princess, "someone else would be last and exposed. I cannot ask another to take my place."

"Oh, but you must," moaned Saril, her eyes wide with fear, her hands wringing. "Please, let us move to train center. We'll be safe there."

Laurelin looked with pity upon her frightened handmatron. "Saril, no place is safe from the Evil One: not train's end, center, nor fore. I chose this position to be closer to my beloved Lord Galen, and that reason still holds true."

For a moment no one spoke and the only sounds were the crackle of the fire and the whimpering of Saril. Then rough-hewn Haddon spoke: "My Princess, the Lady Saril is right, but for the wrong reasons, and so, too, is Captain Jarriel. You must move to train center, e'en though it may be no safer from the Enemy in Gron than any other space in this train, nor more easily protected either. Nay, I stand with you on those two reasons, yet still I think that you must move, for something else compels:

"Did you watch the people tonight as you bestrode the length of the caravan? I did, and this is what I saw: Grim were their looks and fell were their spirits ere you went among them. Yet many of the most frightened mustered a wan smile when you came through the Shadowlight. Oh, they be still frightened, yet not as much as before. And that is why you must ride at train center. For you are the gentle heart and bright spirit of the people, and at their heart you should go, as near to as many as you may be; and though you cannot ride in each one's waggon, amid all waggons you can ride. Then all may know that you are among them, and not remote and distant at train's end."

Now Haddon's voice took on the courtly manner: "I will take thy present place at the last of the caravan, but thou must take thy true place amid thine own."

Haddon fell silent, his rush of words at an end. He was a warrior and not of the court, yet no courtier could have spoken more eloquently.

Laurelin looked into the flames of the fire, and tears clung to her lashes, and none said aught. At last she turned to Captain Jarriel and gave a curt nod, for she could not trust her voice, and Jarriel sighed in relief and relaxed, while Saril began rushing about, collecting and stowing things as if the move were to occur instantaneously.

Igon turned to Haddon: "Ai-oi, Warrior Haddon, I must have thee by my side when next we need make treaty with another nation, for thy rough exterior doth conceal a golden tongue."

Laurelin's silver laugh rang out above the campfire, and Igon, Haddon, and Jarriel joined in her mirth, as

Saril stood gaping at the merriment, wondering what anyone could possibly find humorous in this dreadful 'Dark.

But then a warrior of the escort came riding to the fire, leaning down to speak with Captain Jarriel: "Sir, Vulgs lope by in the distant shadow, running south as if to o'ertake the moving edge of the Black Wall. Yet it is thought that some turned back, racing along the track whence they came. If so, what it portends, I cannot say."

Jarriel sprang up and mounted his nearby steed, and Igon vaulted astride Rust, and they rode away from the mealfire and toward the fore of the train, and with them went the messenger.

Laurelin and Haddon sat for long moments more, and little was said by either, the only sound being that of Saril, now sitting in the waggon and muttering in fear as she peered out through the flap of the wain and into the shadowed land nearby.

Laurelin's sleep was broken by the sounds of the camp stirring to wakefulness.

"Come, Saril," said the Princess, shaking her hand-matron by the shoulder, " 'tis time to break our fast, for we shall soon be under way."

Saril groaned, not fully awake: "Is it dawn, my Lady?"

"Nay, Saril," answered Laurelin, "there'll be no dawn this 'Darkday, nor perhaps for many to come."

Saril blenched, and would have hidden 'neath her blanket but Laurelin would not allow it and bade her instead to dress, inwardly despairing of Saril ever gaining a measure of courage to face the Dimmendark.

Soon they descended from the wain to make tea over

the rekindled campblaze, tea to take with their otherwise cold morning meal. Bergil, their driver, harnessed the horses and hitched them to the waggon. Then he came to the fire.

"Ar, my Lady," said Bergil, shuffling his feet in the snow as if to wipe them clean ere stepping through some imaginary door, acutely aware that he was speaking to the Princess instead of to Saril as usual. "When we're done wi' the eatin', I'm to drive us to the middle o' the train. Them was Cap'n Jarriel's direct orders, miss: 'to the middle o' the train,' he said, he did."

At Laurelin's nod, relief washed over Bergil's weathered features, for it was not every day that coachmen dealt face to face with royalty—footmen, now, well that was a different matter altogether, for they often directly helps Lords and Ladies alike, but then footmen are trained to do so, e'en though they answers to the driver.

Bergil took his tea and a portion of the bread and cold venison and hunkered down opposite the fire to eat with the Ladies instead of joining some of his fellow drivers at another fire as he normally did, for they soon would be moving to train center and Bergil had not the time. Haddon, too, came from the next waggon to join them. They sat and ate with little converse, looking out into the spectral 'scape of the surrounding Dimmendark.

No sooner, it seemed, had they finished their meal than through the Shadowlight came riding Igon and Jarriel.

"My Lady Laurelin," asked Igon, "be thou ready to move forward?"

"Yes, Lord Igon." Laurelin stood and smiled down

at Haddon, gesturing him to remain seated. "Another takes my place at train's end."

Igon turned to Jarriel. "Let it be so. Sound the ready."

Jarriel raised a horn to his lips and blew a rising call that echoed down the line of wains and out into the surrounding countryside. *Aroo!* (Prepare!) And from the land nearby came answering cries: *Ahn!* (Ready!) *Ahn! Ahn!* From fore, aft, and north came the answers.

Jarriel waited, yet no call came from the south, from the Battle Downs, dark hills to the leftward of the train. Again he sounded the call, and again all answered but the south guard.

"Sire, something is amiss," said Jarriel to Igon, a grim look upon his face. "The south hillguard answers not. Perhaps . . ."

"Hsst!" shushed Igon, holding up his hand, and in the quiet that followed they could hear the pounding of running hooves—many hooves—hammering upon the hard frozen ground to the south.

"Sound assembly!" Igon shouted, flashing bright sword from scabbard.

Jarriel raised horn to lips: *Ahn! Hahn!* the imperative call split the air as the drum of hooves grew louder. *Ahn! Hahn! Ahn! Hahn!*

And then, bursting through the spectral shadows clutching the sinister hills to the south, erupted the enemy: Ghola upon thundering Hèlsteeds, striking down upon the standing train with shattering violence: cruel barbed spears driven by running Death, slashing tulwars cleaving into innocent flesh, slaughter racing upon cloven hooves, shocking into and through and over Women and children, oldsters and the lame, the ill and wounded, the sundering blades and impaling shafts riving a great bloody swath through the unprepared caravan. Some stood stunned and were cut down like cattle at butcher. Yet others turned to flee and were slain while running: thus did Saril die, clambering to hide in the waggon.

A running Hèlsteed struck Laurelin a glancing blow, and she was whelmed back against the side of the wain, to pitch forward, smashing face down to the ground, her cheek pressed against the snow, her arms scrabbling futilely as she desperately tried to rise while at the same time trying to breathe, but she was unable to, for all the wind had been slammed from her lungs.

Captain Jarriel crashed dead unto the ground beside her, his chest pierced through by a broken-shafted spear. Laurelin tried to reach out to him but could not, for she had no control of her limbs and she could not breathe, and dark motes swirled before her eyes and her sight dimmed.

But at last she drew in a great ragged sob of air, and her lungs began pumping in harsh gasps while tears ran down her face. She heard herself moaning but could not stop.

Crying in anguish, she rose to her hands and knees and looked up to see Haddon lashing with a burning brand at a Ghol on Hèlsteed. And the vile creature's dead black eyes stared from the corpse-white flesh as he slashed the tulwar through Haddon's throat, and the warrior fell slain beside the body of dead Bergil.

Horses in harness plunged wildly and screamed in terror, for the stench of Hèlsteeds was among them. Some ran amok, bolting toward the plains and hills, only to have the wains overturn and throw the horses' legs from under them, or drag them to a halt.

Amid the milling confusion, a knot of warriors fought: Prince Igon upon Rust had rallied a band unto him.

The young Lord's sword hacked and chopped ceaselessly, and others laid about with their steel glaives.

Laurelin saw a Hèlsteed stumble, dropping to the snow, throat gushing black. Yet the pallid Ghol rider rolled free and sprang up to impale a young warrior upon his barbed spear.

Then Igon saw the Princess on hands and knees where she'd been hammered to the ground. "Laurelin!" he cried, and spurred Rust toward her, driving into the foe. But a Ghol on Hèlsteed rode to bar his way, and rage distorted Igon's features beyond recognition. *Shang! Chang!* Sword and tulwar clashed together amid a shower of sparks. *Chank!* The Ghol's blade was shivered into shards; and as the Ghol threw up his arm to ward the blow—*Shunk!*—Igon's steel drove completely through the Ghol's wrist and pallid neck: riven hand and severed head flew wide, while chalky corpse-body toppled into the snow.

Once more Igon drove Rust toward Laurelin, crying out her name, but again Ghola blocked the way, this time attacking in concert. Three, then four, fell upon the youth, and he was hard-pressed; yet Igon's blade hewed into the enemy, driven by fury and desperate strength. Another Ghol fell dead, his skull cloven in twain, and Igon's voice cried out, "For the Lady! For the Lady Laurelin!"

A Ghol on Hèlsteed crashed into Rust, and the great red horse was staggered, yet he kept his War-trained footing and wheeled about for Igon to meet the Gholen foe. Igon's blade swung in a wide arc, driven so hard it hummed; and the sharp steel clove through Gholen armor and sinews, and chopped deep into bone, where it lodged. Furiously, Igon wrenched at the blade, but just as he hauled it free, an enemy tulwar smashed down and sundered his helm, and blood splashed crimson over the youth's face as he crashed to the ground to move no more.

Laurelin saw Igon fall and staggered to her feet at last. "Igon! Igon!" The words were rent from her throat in horror, but the Prince moved not, his blood welling to run in scarlet rivulets and fall adrip to the snow. Screaming in rage she snatched up dead Jarriel's dagger and hurled herself into the mêlée, poniard clutched in her fist, and with a hoarse cry of hatred she plunged the blade to the hilt into the back of the Ghol on foot. Unaffected by the steel lodged deep in his ribcage, the Ghol turned from the battle and smashed her aside with the sweeping haft of his spear.

Laurelin was dashed to the ground, her arm shattered by the blow, the Princess so battered she could no longer stand. And she sat and wept as the Gholen ravers smote the survivors.

Now all the soldiers were slain, and the foe turned to easier game, their swords riving, and the snow ran red with blood. Ghols stalked among the waggons, their dead black eyes looking for the innocent and defenseless, and where they strode, none was spared: no Woman, no child, no oldster, none. Even the struggling horses were slain, trapped in their traces, and some waggons were set afire.

And Laurelin sat in the snow and wept at the horror and waited for them to come and cut her throat.

Another waited also, but this one in anger and defiance: it was Rust! The great roan stood above Igon's fallen form, teeth bared and hooves lashing out at passing Ghola, the War-horse defending his master as he had been trained.

Laurelin saw the horse and exulted, for the Ghola

gave it wide berth. Yet one hefted a spear, preparing to hurl it at the steed. *"Jagga, Rust! Jagga!"* (Hide, Rust! Hide!) Laurelin screamed, the cry torn from the depths of her anguish. The roan whirled and looked at the Princess. *"Jagga!"* came the command again.

Rust sprang forward just as the spear was flung, and the haft glanced off the roan's withers as he thundered forth for the nearby hills hurtling past Laurelin as he fled for the Battle Downs, obeying the War command to hide.

Ghola on Hèlsteeds spurred after him, but the great red horse ran swiftly before them, and the gap widened. "Ya, Rust! Run!" cried Laurelin, "Run!" The words were hurled after the fleeing steed, and Rust ran as if his feet were winged. And Laurelin watched him fly into the Dimmendark, to disappear into the Shadowlight grasping the hills. "Run," she whispered after him, but he was gone.

A corpse-white Ghol bearing a barbed spear stalked up to Laurelin, his red gash of a mouth writhing in anger, his dead black eyes staring soullessly down. Laurelin glared up at him, unable to stand, cradling her broken arm with the other. Her eyes blazed with hatred, and she jerked her head in the direction Rust had flown. "That's one of us you won't get, *Spaunen!*" she spat defiantly, her pale eyes boring triumphantly into his dead black ones.

The Ghol raised his spear, both hands on the shaft, preparing to plunge it through her breast. Laurelin's teeth ground in fury, her eyes flared up at him with unflinching wrath. Back drew the spear for the final thrust.

"Slath!" lashed out a command from behind her, the hissing voice hideous, and Laurelin felt as if vipers

slithered over her spine. The Ghol lowered the shaft, and the Princess turned her head to see a Man upon Hèlsteed. A Naudron he was, one of the folk that roam the northern barrens hunting seal and whale and the antlered beasts of the tundra. Yet when Laurelin looked beyond his yellow-copper skin and into his dark eyes, utter Evil stared malignantly back at her.

"Where is the other, the youth?" The hiss of puff adders filled the air.

"Ghun." The Ghol's voice was dull, flat.

"I said to spare the two of them!" the sibilant voice cried. "But you give me only the Princess." The evil eyes turned upon Laurelin, and she felt as if her skin were crawling, and she wanted to run and hide from this being. Yet she stared back at him and blenched not. "Where is puling Igon?" hissed the serpent voice.

Laurelin's spirit almost broke then, for Igon lay in the snow not twenty feet away. Yet she made no sign.

"Nabba thek!" spat the order, and Ghola dismounted and began moving slowly among the slaughtered, catching the barbs of their spears in the clothing and flesh of the slain, turning them face up, dead eyes staring, mouths agape.

Laurelin looked on in horror. "Leave them alone, *Spaunen!*" she cried. "Leave them alone!" And then her voice lost its strength, sinking to a whisper: "Leave them alone." Still the cruel barbs jabbed and hauled as the faces of the slain were inspected. Laurelin turned to the Naudron and cried, "He's dead! Igon is dead!" Uncontrollable sobbing racked her frame as the horror of the brutal slaughter overwhelmed her at last.

"Dead?" The Naudron's voice was filled with rage. "I commanded that he be spared! All in this party will suffer for disobeying." Evil glared out at the Ghòla, yet still they stalked among the dead.

"Slath!" the puff adder voice commanded. *"Garja ush!"* The Ghola turned from their grisly task, and two came and dragged Laurelin to her feet, the broken bones grinding in her right forearm. Blackness swirled, and the Princess felt her mind falling down a dark tunnel.

Laurelin became aware that icy hands clutched her, and a burning liquid was forced down her throat. Coughing and sputtering, she tried to fend away the leather flask, and agaonizing pain jagged through her right arm, jerking her full awake. Ghola held her. Her right arm from wrist to shoulder was swathed by heavy bindings over a rude splint bent at the elbow. Again the liquid was forced upon her, its fire burning inside her chest and stomach and running into her limbs. She struck away the flask and turned her face aside. Yet once more the Ghola forced the burning drink upon her, roughly grasping her head and wrenching her face upright, pouring until she gagged, spraying the vile liquid wide.

"Ush!" Again Laurelin was hauled to her feet, and she stood weakly, shuddering, swaying. *"Rul durg!"* And the chill hands of the corpse-people rent the clothing from Laurelin till she stood naked before the Naudron. He sat upon the Hèlsteed and his evil eyes gloated. Laurelin felt a great horror and loathing, and the cold was numbing, yet she stood defiantly. Quilted Rukken clothing was flung at her feet, and fleece-lined boots. Ghola forced her to don the garb: filthy it was, and mite-infested, and overlarge upon her, but it was warm. During the dressing the only sound she made

was a gasp through clenched teeth as the right sleeve of the jacket was slit from wrist to shoulder and forced onto her, then roughly wrapped over and bound to the splinted arm.

The Naudron's voice spat and hissed commands in the foul Slûk tongue too rapidly for Laurelin to make out individual words from the guttural, slobbering drool-speech. Then the evil eyes turned upon her as her arm was jerked into a sling. A Hèlsteed was brought forth and Laurelin was hauled astride the hideous beast, and its foul odor was nearly enough to make her retch.

"Now you will be brought to my strongholt," hissed the voice, "where I have a purpose for you to serve."

"Never," said Laurelin, her voice gritting forth. "Never will I serve you. You set yourself on too high a seat."

"I shall remind you of your words, Princess, when it is time for the throne of Mithgar to be mine." Malevolence crawled over the Naudron's gloating features.

"There is one, nay, there are many in Challerain Keep who will thwart that aspiration, *Spaunen!*" Laurelin's voice snapped.

"Pah! Challerain Keep!" the Naudron's voice sneered. "Even now that pile of hovels is aflame, set to the torch by my engines of destruction. Challerain will burn to the ground ere this 'Darkday ends, and there is nothing that Aurion Redeye with his puny force can do to prevent it: nothing! And the fire will sap his will; the strength of his Men will fall into the ashes of its destruction. Then will I strike: my Horde to whelm the gates, to scale the walls, to slay the fools trapped inside."

Laurelin's blood ran chill to hear such words, yet she betrayed no sign of fear, and she said nought.

"We waste time," he hissed, then cried a command to the force of Ghola now arrayed behind: *"Urb schla! Drek!"* Then once more he addressed Laurelin: "We shall speak again, Princess."

And even as Laurelin looked on, the Naudron's features writhed and then fell lax, and the malignant glare was utterly gone, replaced by a witless, vacant, slack-jawed look.

A Ghol rode to take the reins of the Naudron's Hèlsteed to lead the beast, while another took up Laurelin's, and at a sharp bark the Gholen column rode forth, heading east.

Behind, amid strewn and burning waggons and butchered steeds, lay the slaughtered: babes and mothers, the lame, Women, oldsters, soldiers, and youths, sprawled upon blood-soaked snow, some with their unseeing eyes staring at the track of the Gholen column as it disappeared into the Dimmendark; and nought was said by any, for the dead speak not.

Thirty grinding miles the Ghola rode through the Winternight, through the icy Shadowlight grasping the northern hills of the Battle Downs; and the jolting of the Hèlsteed drove shattering agony up Laurelin's arm. At times she nearly swooned, yet still the pounding went on. Her features became gaunt, drawn into haggard lines of pain, and she could no longer hold herself erect. That she did not collapse was perhaps due to the burning liquid forced upon her, for she did not fall, though how not she could not say. And the cruel miles hammered on. At last the column stopped to make camp. Laurelin was hauled down from her mount and she could not stand. She sat in the snow and dully stared as the Ghola took the vacant-eyed Naudron from his 'Steed.

Once more she was forced to drink the burning liquid, and then given a meal. She numbly ate the stale dark bread and thin gruel but touched not the unknown meat. And she sat revulsed, watching the Foul Folk tear voraciously at their own food, all, that is, but the vacuous Naudron, who chewed and slavered with dull-witted sluggishness upon the runny porridge spoon-fed to him by a Ghol.

And as she sat in this camp of ravers, her desperate thought was, *Galen, oh, Galen, where are you?*

Laurelin was kicked awake and given the flask of fiery liquid. Her battered body shrieked with pain: arm in torment, joints aflame, muscles knotted in agony. This time she drank from the flask without being forced, for the vile fluid dulled the harrowing rack.

Once more the Ghola prepared to go on, and Laurelin was given no privacy to take care of her needs. And she felt utterly degraded by the dead black eyes.

On through the Dimmendark they rode, beating steadily eastward, still within the northern margins of the Battle Downs. This time they covered nearly thirty-five miles before making camp.

Laurelin could but barely move when they stopped at last, for the unremitting pain in her arm had grown, thoroughly sapping her energy; and her legs, buttocks, back, and even her feet were tormented beyond telling from the pounding Hèlsteed ride.

Dully, she took her meal, eating without thinking. But then a cold chill fell upon her heart, and without knowing how she knew, Laurelin suddenly became aware that the Evil once more looked upon her: she turned and saw that it was so, for malignancy again glared forth from the Naudron's face.

"Challerain is burned to the ground," gloated the voice. "The first and second walls have fallen to Whelmram and my Horde. Aurion Redeye and his pitiful few retreat up the mount, trapped like rabbits before the serpent."

Dread thudded within Laurelin's breast, yet rage burned there, too. "Why say you this?" she demanded. "Think you that these things you say will cause me fear on your spoken word alone?"

But the Naudron answered not, for now his eyes were blank.

Racked with agony, the stabbing pain pulsing in her arm, Laurelin wondered how long she could endure. Yet she gave no outward sign of her torment, as once more the column bore east, and her mind sought ways she might escape, yet none were forthcoming.

Three leagues they rode, then four, passing through the Shadowlight toward the eastern reaches of the Battle Downs north of Weiunwood. Twelve miles they rode ere an uneasy stirring rippled down the column. Laurelin craned her neck, and ahead, just within the limit of her vision, she saw . . . *Elves! Elves on horses!* Her heart leapt with hope. *Rescue!* But wait: they were not coming this way. Instead, they rode swiftly toward a line of trees to the south; and behind, running on foot, pursued a great force of Yrm in close chase, their harsh yells drifting over the snow. "Wait!" cried Laurelin, but her voice was lost amid the gleeful howls of the Gholen column, gloating to see Elves flee into Weiunwood with Rukha and Lōkha in full cry.

As the Elves disappeared into the winter forest, Laurelin's heart fell into despair and tears rilled down her face. Yet inwardly she raged at herself: *Give them not the satisfaction*, she thought, *not the satisfaction*, and she sat up straight in Hèlsteed saddle and fought to stifle her weeping ere any Ghol could see. And she watched as the first of the yelling Rukha and Lōkha now rushed headlong into the 'Wood, and hundreds upon hundreds of others poured after.

The Gholen column continued eastward, swinging slightly north to pass behind the force of Yrm invading Weiunwood. As they rode, ahead Laurelin could see another band of Ghola sitting still upon Hèlsteed, watching the force disappear into the trees.

The two Gholen columns met and merged, and spoke with flat, dull voices, sounding bereft of life except when one or several would emit bone-chilling howls. Some came to inspect Laurelin, their dead black eyes fixed upon her, and she stared defiantly back at them.

The new force of Ghola numbered nearly one hundred strong, and Laurelin saw that among this band, too, rode a Man: black he was, as if from the Land of Chabba south across the Avagon Sea. And then Laurelin saw that his eyes were vacant, and drool ebbed down his chin, just like the Naudron's. And, also like the Naudron, the Chabbain, too, was led by a Ghol. It was as if neither Man bore any wit or will.

Yet even as she looked, the black face filled with malice, and Evil stared out at her. "The third wall of Challerain Keep now has fallen, as will the last two," hissed the Chabbain; and Laurelin's hand flew to her lips and she gasped in dread, *for it was the same viperous voice she'd heard issue forth from the Naudron's mouth!* But then the ebon face went slack, the eyes emptied out, the Evil was gone. And Laurelin spun to look at the Naudron and saw the same vacant stare. And she shuddered, for now she knew with whom she dealt.

Onward went the column with Laurelin, resuming the trek to the east. And as they rode forth, the Princess looked back at the stationary band of Ghola waiting near the fringes of the Weiunwood. And her eyes were drawn one last time to the Man from Chabba, his dark skin standing out amid the pasty pallidness of the Ghola like a slug among maggots. Shuddering, she turned her gaze to the fore and did not look back again.

Another four leagues they rode before emerging at last from the Battle Downs, and they made camp two leagues beyond upon the open plains. And as Laurelin spooned thin gruel to her mouth with her left hand, her broken arm throbbed in its sling; and pulsing with that pain, her mind kept echoing the hissing words: *"The third wall of Challerain Keep now has fallen, as will the last two."*

The next 'Darkday, the fifth since Laurelin's capture, the Gholen column crossed the plains to camp within sight of a northeast arm of the Weiunwood. Still their track bore eastward, and they had ridden thirty or so miles each of those five 'Darkdays. Yet the Hèlsteeds were not spent, for although they were not as fleet as a good horse, their endurance was greater.

Nay, it was not the tiring of the Hèlsteeds that determined where the column would camp, nor was it the amount of pain that Laurelin could withstand. It was instead the limits of the Naudron that paced the force of Ghola, though how the corpse-people could tell that the vacant-eyed Man needed rest, Laurelin could not say. Yet she did not care how it was done, for she was weary beyond measure when the camp was set.

She had just fallen into exhausted slumber when a Ghol kicked her awake. Opposite the campfire, Evil looked upon her. "The Keep has fallen and is now mine," hissed the puff adder voice. "Your brave Aurion Redeye has fled. And though I now have no eyes to see, I think none shall escape."

Laurelin's pale gaze locked with that of the dark-eyed Naudron's. *"Zūo Hēlan widar iu!"* (To Hèl with you!) she gritted in the old high language of Riamon, and lay back down to sleep, as evil laughter hissed in her ears. But though she lay with her eyes closed, her mind would not let go: *"The Keep has fallen . . . Redeye has fled . . . None shall escape."*

The next trek took Laurelin beyond the margins of the Weiunwood and into the low-set craggy tors of the Signal Mountains. And just ere they stopped to camp, the Naudron's blank eyes suddenly glared with Evil. "They seek to defy me!" the voice shrilly screamed, no longer a sibilant hiss. Laurelin snapped around to see rage upon the features of the Man of the Naud. "The fools of mine Hèlborne Reavers raced straight into their trap! But this ragtag Alliance of Elves, Men, and jewel-eyed runts shall not bar me from conquest. Weiunwood shall fall by my hand!"

Now the voice sank into viperous sibilation: *"Thuggon oog. Laug glog racktu!"* At these festering Slûk words, nearly half of the Ghola turned southwest along the Signal Mountains, while the rest continued to bear eastward, taking Laurelin with them.

As they divided, the voice hissed at the Princess,

"They go to replace those impaled upon the wood. Think not to gloat over this minor setback, for the final victory shall be mine!"

But Laurelin's eyes bore into his, and she smiled fiercely.

Three 'Darkdays later, snow was falling down through the Dimmendark when Laurelin awakened, and their trek began in flakes swirling thickly. The past two 'Darkdays had been spent out upon the open plains, bearing south of east from the Signal Mountains, crossing the land north of the Wilderness Hills. And each of those days had been filled with dull ache for Laurelin, and her mind seemed to haze in and out of awareness: at times her thoughts were preternaturally sharp, at other times sluggish beyond her understanding. Yet she fought to show no sign of weakness and to let no sound of pain pass her thin-drawn lips.

Once more their journey carried them southward, and they had gone nearly ten miles when they came to a high-bluffed river. South they ranged along the wall to come to a low place where there was a frozen ford. Through the swirling snow and across the ice they went, cloven hooves ringing on the surface. As they came to the far side, the snow began to slacken, yet Laurelin knew that their tracks had been covered, and anyone following would have lost the trail. But perhaps this vague feeling that someone came after was only a girlish dream, and whether or not the snow covered their wake, it did not matter.

As they rode into the land beyond the ford, the column turned slightly north of east, and Laurelin noted a strange run of excitement ripple through the Ghola. But she knew not what it portended.

Onward they went, the snow diminishing as they

rode, finally to stop altogether. They came in among dark trees, and Laurelin felt a deep foreboding—from what, she could not say. It was in these woods that they made camp.

As Laurelin was drifting off to an aching sleep, a thought came unbidden to her mind: *It is Last Yule, Year's Start Day, Merrilee's birthday. Where are you now, Sir Tuck?*

Once more the trek resumed, and still the Ghola acted strangely: their flat voices arguing among themselves, their heads turning this way and that as they rode through a wood dismal, a wood from which darkness seemed to flow beyond that of the Shadowlight. And the Ghola appeared to revel in this miasma of dimness and vague dread.

Miles they went among the trees, at last to break into the open: a great clearing. Across the treeless expanse they rode, ten miles or more, to come once again unto the wood. At its very edge they made camp, and still the Ghola spoke, as if the dead debated what course to follow.

And as the campfire was lighted, without warning the evil voice hissed forth: "Why are we here? Why have you not turned north for the pass?"

The dead black eyes turned to the Naudron, and Laurelin sensed fear running among the Ghola, though she knew not why.

"Ah, I see," the sibilant whisper came, "you thought to make the Drearwood into a place of dread as of old."

Drearwood! Of course! That's were we are! thought Laurelin. *And the pass he spoke of is Grūwen Pass.* Then her heart plummeted, and she felt as if she had been struck in the stomach, and her spirit cried out in despair: *Oh, Adon! They bear me to Gron, to Modru himself!* Agony lanced up her arm.

Her thoughts were broken by a shrill scream: "Did I not say that *my* plans come first? Which of you has guided us here instead of toward the pass?"

Black eyes turned briefly toward one of the Ghola standing in the open snow, and his flat voice spoke: *"Glu shtom!"*

"You would stay?" hissed the sibilant voice at him. "You say you would stay?" Now the voice rose in a scream and shrieked, "Then stay!" And for the first time Laurelin saw the Naudron move when the Evil was present: he raised his arm and reached toward the Ghol and his hand made a clutching, squeezing motion, and the Ghol fell, flopping face down into the snow, dead.

The Naudron's arm dropped limply back to his side, the Evil flickering weakly in his eyes: "Thus to all who obey not my will. *Nabbu gla oth.*"

North and east the column rode, passing through five or so miles of Drearwood before coming into the open. Twenty more miles they went, the land rising steadily; and although she could not see afar through the murk of the Dimmendark, Laurelin had been raised in Dael in the ring of the Rimmen Mountains, and she knew that the slant of the land around her bespoke of tall peaks ahead.

They came to a high-faced bluff stretching out beside them, and the Ghola spurred up the pace as they rode alongside the cliff, as if to pass by this place as quickly as possible. Seven more miles they rode at this swift gait along the wall, and the agony jolted and jabbed through Laurelin like hot, lancing flames. And deep breaths hissed through her clenched teeth, but no groans escaped her lips.

Then they were beyond the long butte and the pace slackened, and they came into a stone-walled valley, yet still they did not stop, but rode eighteen miles more, until at last they reached the beginning rise of Grūwen Pass, and mountains loomed upward into the Dimmendark.

Fifty miles they had ridden, and Laurelin knew not when they stopped. Rough hands dragged her down from her mount, and she could not stand, but lay gasping in the snow where they dropped her. Inside her mind she shrieked in agony, but no sound of pain did she make.

Grūwen Pass was nearly thirty-five miles in length, and northward through the long slot the Gholen column rode. Great buttresses of ice-clad stone mounted up perpendicular cliffs into the Shadowlight, and rime glistened along their path. Bitter was the cold of the Winternight, and the irony-grey stone looked black in its light. Hard-frozen snow lay packed in shadowed crannies, and the echoing ring of cloven hooves juddered down the tall rocks.

When they stopped at last to camp, Laurelin was chilled to the marrow, and she could not seem to stop shuddering with the cold. Once more a Ghol brought her the leather flask, and he bruised her lips as she drank, for her left hand was too numb to hold the bottle. Yet the vile, fiery liquid brought a measure of warmth to her veins, and the campblaze made from wood they had borne with them and the hot gruel warmed her even more.

They had ridden the fulll length of the Pass—the slot where the Rigga Mountains met those of the Grimwall and the Gronfangs. And now the column had come down into the wastes of Gron—Modru's Realm of old—and Laurelin despaired, for this Land was dire.

From the edge of the pass, down the length of Grūwen Vale they rode the next 'Darkday, the stone of the valley dropping toward the plains of Gron below. Nothing seemed to grow in this land: no trees, no brush, no grass, no moss—not even lichen clung to the rock. Only ice and stone and snow could be seen about them, and sharp-edged darkness where the Shadowlight fell not.

They camped three leagues beyond the mouth of the vale, out upon the desolate plains of Gron. Though her arm throbbed dreadfully, that was not what caused Laurelin concern: it was instead that now that she was in Gron, a great bitterness clutched at her heart, and she was distressed by its sting.

Two 'Darkdays they rode north through the Winternight across a barren wasteland, and still no sign of life did they see. Laurelin knew that off to the left rose the Rigga Mountains, and to the right the Gronfangs. But they were too distant to see in the Dimmendark, though were the Sun to shine they could have been seen far over the plains. But there was no Sun, only cold Shadowlight, and Laurelin could have wept.

On neither day was there wood for a campfire, but

dead tundra moss made a feeble flame, and Laurelin ate cold gruel for her meals.

At the end of the third 'Darkday upon the plains, the Ghola made camp along the southern edge of the Gwasp, a great swamp squatting in the angle of Gron. This sump was reputed to have midges beyond number and mire beyond depth in the summer, yet now it stood frozen in Winternight, looking to all like a lifeless morass. It was said that in days of yore Agron's entire army had disappeared within the sucking environs; but Agron's unknown fate merely added to the dire legends of the Gwasp, for it *always* had been a place of dread.

All the next 'Darkday they rode along the Gwasp's eastern flank, crossing frozen rills and seeps feeding the great bog, once passing across the ice of a river that descended down from the unseen Gronfangs. When they finally reached the far northern flank of the Great Swamp, they again made camp.

As she ate, Laurelin looked upon the vacant-eyed Naudron. It had been eight 'Darkdays since he had last spoken, and then it was to slay a Ghol; twelve days since he had last spoken to her; thirteen days since she had last said aught, and that was to tell the Evil to go to Hèl; sixteen days since she had been captured: sixteen 'Darkdays since she had last heard a friendly voice; twenty-one days since she had last been happy: at her nineteenth birthday party. When Laurelin slept at last, tears ran silently down her cheeks.

They crossed another frozen river and rode north. Some six hours later they passed close by tall black crags to their left as the column rode through Claw Gap and onto the flats known as Claw Moor, a high, desolate land.

Upon the Moor they rode, going some eighteen miles farther before making camp.

Once more Laurelin was kicked awake; once more the column rode north. Now their pace grew swifter, for they neared their goal. Agony jarred through Laurelin's arm with every stride the Hèlsteed took. They had ridden for hours, and her pain-dulled mind no longer held coherent thoughts. But, unbent, she sat in the saddle, straight as an iron rod, a rod now tempered in the very forge of Hèl. Miles had passed beneath the cloven hooves, nearly thirty-five this 'Darkday alone, nearly six hundred twenty since her capture eighteen 'Darkdays past.

Groggily, she saw black mountains loom up ahead, and in the face of the rock was clutched the towers of a dark fortress. Massive stone tiers buttressed turreted walls, and one central tower stood above all. Laurelin struggled with what she was seeing and suddenly snapped awake, and fear coursed through her, for now she realized that she gazed upon Modru's strongholt: the dreaded Iron Tower.

Across an iron drawbridge above a rocky chasm the column clattered, riding past a great, scaled Troll guarding the gate. Raucous horns blatted, and Lōkha screamed harsh orders as the Hèlsteeds came on, and Rukha leapt forward to winch up an iron portcullis with a great rattle of gears.

Into a stone courtyard the Gholen force rode, and Rukha ran forth snarling and elbowing one another, jostling for position to see and jeer at the prisoner.

To the central Iron Tower they rode and stopped before a great studded door. Laurelin was dragged down from her mount and led up steps to the portal. A leering Rukh hauled it open, and the Princess was shoved stumbling inside. And but one Ghol came after, and the great door boomed shut: *Doom!*

A torchlit hall stood before her. A Rukh thrall scuttled down the passage toward Laurelin and the Ghol and motioned for them to follow, croaking, "Uuh! Uuh!" for he had no tongue.

He led her along the cold black granite hall to another massive door. Fearfully, the Rukh scratched at the panel, then slowly opened the heavy portal, standing back for Laurelin to pass through, and again she was shoved from behind by the Ghol, and the door ponderously swung shut behind her, to slam to with a thunderous *Boom!*

The great room she stumbled into was lighted by flickering, cresseted torches, and there burned a blaze in a gaping stone fireplace; heavy wall hangings and massive furniture burdened the chamber. But none of this did Laurelin see. Instead, her eyes were drawn to the black-cloaked, black-clad figure standing with arms folded across his chest in room center. A Man he seemed, for Man-height he was, yet an immense, vile aura of malignancy exuded from his very being. As to his face, it could not be seen, for he was masked with a hideous iron-beaked helm, like the snouted face of a gargoyle of legend. But from the visor, eyes of evil stared: the same evil eyes she had seen upon the face of the Naudron, the same vileness that had looked forth from the eyes of the Chabbain. Yet no distant puppet was this baneful figure; instead, it seemed the quintessence of utter Evil.

And then the maleficent reptilian voice hissed out at her: "Welcome to my Iron Tower, Princess Laurelin. Though we have spoken many times, we meet face to face at last. *Ssss,* I am Modru."

Malignancy washed through the room, and Laurelin reeled under the impact. A woeful bale, a crushing desolation, reached out to clutch at her spirit, and her heart fell to the nadir of despair.

He stepped forward, and, although inwardly she shrank back, outwardly she did not flinch. And he took her by the hand as he drew her into the room. She wanted to scream in horror, for his very touch made her feel *violated,* as if his essence invaded her and made her unclean, polluted by a hideous corruption.

"Ah, my dear, why do I feel you shrink from me?" his sibilant voice hissed.

"If you feel me shrink from your hand," her clear voice answered, "it is because you are foul to the touch and vile to the eye: an abomination."

"I?" His voice rose in anger, and rage burned in the malignant eyes behind the hideous iron mask. *"I?* You say *I* am foul to the touch, vile to the eye?" Jerking her roughly after, he strode to a black-velvet-covered panel and wrenched her before it; and he stood to one side and ripped away the black cloth. It had covered a great mirror. "Behold, O Beautiful Princess, what an abomination truly is!"

Laurelin gasped at the apparition reflected in the glass: a grimy, gaunt, filthy drudge with a broken arm in a soiled sling stood before her, dressed in foul, stained, quilted, Rukken clothing; she stank of Hèlsteed and of human waste; and there were dark rings under the sunken eyes set deep in her grime-streaked face and dirty, tangled, lice-ridden hair matted down on her unclean head.

Long this haggard wretch stared at herself in the full-length mirror, and then she turned and spat in Modru's face.

CHAPTER 2
GRIMWALL

Tuck looked from Talarin to Gildor to Galen to Igon, the young Prince now asleep, his face flush with the dregs of fever. *South to Pellar or north to Gron? Which way to turn? Rescue the Princess or lead the Host against Modru's minions?* In despair, Tuck put his face in his hands, and tears welled from his sapphirine eyes.

Galen held the red eye-patch in his hands, smoothing out the scarlet tiecords.

"I took the patch so that the *Rûpt* would not defile Aurion King's body," said Gildor.

Galen nodded without speaking or looking up.

Long moments passed, and Igon's breathing lost its ragged edge. "His fever is gone," said the Elven healer. "He has cast off the poison from the enemy blade at last. When he awakens, he will be weak but his mind will be clear; yet it will take a fortnight or more for his full strength to return, and he will bear a scar for the rest of his days."

Galen now turned from his brother and looked up into the face of Talarin: "We are four, perhaps five 'Darkdays behind the band of Ghola fleeing north with the Lady Laurelin. I deem they fly toward Modru's strongholt. Where think you that they would be now?"

Talarin turned to Gildor, and Tuck looked and saw that these two Elves were much alike. "In other times you and your brother Vanidor have been upon the angle of Gron," said Talarin, "even unto Claw Moor and the Iron Tower itself. What say you?"

Gildor thought but a moment. "If they are five true days to the north, then they have come to the Gwasp; if but four instead, then they are one ride short of that morass, Galen King. And in three or four 'Darkdays at most, they will come to the Enemy's fortress."

Galen's voice was bleak: "You confirm my thoughts, Lord Gildor. This, then, is my dilemma: ere we can overtake the Ghola, Laurelin will be locked in Modru's strongholt, and nothing short of a great army—the Host—will e'er break down those dire doors; and even the Host would be hard-pressed to do so. In any event, foul Modru may maim or even slay the Lady ere the Host can throw down his Tower."

"Slay the Lady?" Tuck gasped, jumping to his feet.

"Her life is as nothing to him," answered Gildor.

"Hold, my son," said Talarin, raising a hand in thought. "What you say is true, yet Modru has gone to greath lengths to bring her to him. Perhaps he has a purpose for her."

"Purpose?" cried Tuck.

"Aye," answered Talarin. "Hostage perhaps . . . or worse."

"Worse?" Tuck's voice dropped to a desperate whisper. "Something . . . we must do . . . something."

Galen spoke, setting forth the seed of a perilous plan: "Perhaps a few can succeed where an army would fail. It can be no more than a hand of people: to gain the walls of Modru's holt, to slip unseen within, and to draw her free."

No one spoke for moments, then Gildor broke the silence: "Galen King, such a plan might prevail, though I think it unlikely, for the Iron Tower is a mighty fortress. Yet you have spoken of only half of your quandary: the plight of the Lady Laurelin. The other horn of this dilemma is even sharper: the Realm is beset, for Winternight and Modru's *Spaunen* rave down the Land, and the Host must be led to stop them."

"But Lord Gildor," responded Galen, anguish in his voice, "Pellar lies more than one thousand miles to the south. To journey there and return with the Host will take weeks, months!"

Again long moments fled in silence, and Igon stirred, then opened his eyes. Clear they were now, not wild, and in the yellow lamplight he saw those around him.

"Galen"—Igon's voice was thready, weak—"know you of Laurelin?" At Galen's nod, tears welled in Igon's eyes, and he squeezed them shut, the drops to run down his cheeks. "I did not succeed," he whispered. "I did not succeed. I failed in my sword-oath to see her to safety. And now she is in the Enemy's clutch." The Prince fell silent.

Time stretched, and just as Tuck thought that Igon had gone back to sleep: "They were so many, the Ghola, and they cut us down as if we were but sheep led to the slaughter. I was felled, and knew nought thereafter. Next I remember, Rust stood over me, nudging with his muzzle; how he was spared, I cannot say. So cold, I was so cold, yet I managed to start a fire from a coal still red in the ashes of a smoldering wain."

Again the Prince fell silent a long while, mustering his strength to continue: "Their track was a 'Darkday old, yet I took food and grain and followed. I remember not much of that chase, though it did snow once, and I recall despairing I'd ever find their tracks—yet Rust knew, he knew, and bore me on: Drearwood, perhaps.

"Dead Ghol next to the forest: was he real?

"North from there . . .

"I remember nothing more, Galen, nothing more." Igon's voice had fallen to a faint whisper. "Grūwen Pass . . . Gron . . . Modru Kinstealer . . ." The Prince sank again into unconsciousness, the effort spent to eke out his report exhausting his feeble strength.

The healer turned to Galen: "I do not know where he found the will to speak, for his life ebbs dangerously low. You must leave ere he wakes again, for it drains him beyond his limits to give over his words to you."

"Galen King," said Talarin, "you must eat and bathe and rest, and renew your own strength, for on the morrow you must choose the course you will follow."

As Tuck drifted to sleep, in his mind Talarin's words echoed again and again: *"On the morrow you must choose . . . On the morrow . . ."*

Tuck awakened once to see Galen standing at a window looking out into the Shadowlight: in his hand he held a scarlet eye-patch; at his throat was a golden locket.

Their clothing had been washed clean and dried before a fire as the two slept. Now Tuck and Galen dressed, yet the thoughts of neither dwelled upon the freshness of his garb.

At last Tuck broke the silence: "Sire, perhaps it is

not my place to speak, and the words I am about to say are like to choke me unto death, yet still I must say them, be they right or wrong.

"The Lady Laurelin I hold dear; she stands near the center of my heart, next to my own Merrilee. And I would follow my heart unto the very Iron Tower itself, to batter down the gates or to creep in stealth to win her free. And I will shout with joy if that is the course you choose."

Tears began to stream down Tuck's face. "Yet my head and not my heart tells me that the grasp of Modru strangles the Realm, and a King is needed to lead the Host, to hurl back the Horde, to rescue the Land. And you are King now, none other.

"I think a squad must enter Gron and perhaps even attempt to penetrate the Iron Tower, to bring forth the Lady Laurelin. Yet neither you nor I should ride north with that squad: her fate must be put in the hands of others, for you must go south to lead the Host, and I"—Tuck's voice now broke—"I must go with you to be your eyes."

Tuck turned to the window and looked forth into the Shadowlight, but his vision swam with tears and he saw nought. His voice was now low, and he spoke haltingly: "When we stood at the slaughtered waggon train, you swore an oath as a Prince of the Realm to run these kinstealers unto the ground. But you swore that oath as a Prince; yet again I say, now you are King . . . and a higher duty here calls, and you are honor-bound to answer . . . no matter what your heart cries out to do. Even though it will take . . . weeks . . . months . . . still our course should be south . . . to Pellar . . . to the Host. You must crush Modru Kinstealer, at the last, but crush his Horde ere then, for it lays waste to the Land.

"This, also, I know: were the . . . were the Lady Laurelin able to say, she, too, would urge you south, to save the Realm, for you are King."

Tuck fell silent, his face to the window, and Galen said nought.

There came a knock at the door, and the Elf Lords Talarin and Gildor entered. Talarin spoke: "Galen King, the time has come to choose."

Galen's voice was grim, barely above a whisper. "South. We ride south. For I am King."

A dreadful pall fell upon the hearts of those in the room, and Tuck wept bitter tears.

Long moments fled, then Gildor stepped to Galen's side. "When last I saw your Lady Laurelin," said Gildor, "she bade me to stand by the King and advise him, and I gave my pledge. Now you are King, Galen, and if you will have me in your company, I would ride south with you, for I would not break my word to that young damosel."

Galen simply nodded.

At last they walked down from the guest quarters and joined the Lady Rael seated at a large table. Upon hearing that Gildor would fare with Galen, Rael smiled. "It has ever been so that the High King has accepted one of the Lian Guardians unto his service," said the Elfess, and she reached out to clasp Talarin's and Gildor's hands. "It pleases me that you accept our son, as did Aurion, your father."

Gildor is Talarin's son! thought Tuck, somewhat astonished, looking from one to the other. *No wonder they favor.* Then Tuck's eye glanced from Rael to Gildor: *Yet there is something of Rael in him, too.*

Food was served and they broke their fast. And while they ate, they were joined by another, one who looked to be Gildor's twin. Tuck stared in amazement from one to the other, yet, but for their clothes, he could not tell them apart.

The stranger smiled at the Warrow's confusion, and winked.

"Ah," said Talarin, looking up, "Vanidor." The Lian Lord turned to his guests. "Galen King, Sir Tuck, this is my other son, Vanidor; he is but three 'Darkdays back from abandoned Lianion, the First Land, the domain also known as Rell. He can tell you of the regions to the south, toward your goal of Pellar."

Vanidor bowed to Galen and Tuck, then sat and took a bowl of *dele*, a type of porridge, but like none other Tuck had ever tasted, for it was delicious.

"Lianion falls into darkness," said Vanidor. "Modru's myrk hides all: down the Grimwall it has stalked, reaching nearly unto the Quadran when last I saw, some fifteen 'Darkdays past.

"Your mission is to Pellar, and so you must fare south through Lianion, but not upon the Old Rell Way, for that is the route of the *Rûpt*: Ruch, Lok, Ghûlk, Vulg. They, too, march south along the Grimwall, following the tide of the Dimmendark."

"Crestan Pass, it is near," said Galen. "Can we not take the Crossland Road up and the Landover down to come to the Argon? If unfrozen, we could ride that river south along the marches of Riamon and Valon to Pellar."

"The River Argon is frozen, Galen King," answered Vanidor, "in the north, that is, perhaps unto Bellon

Falls. Even so, you could not cross the Grimwall at Crestan Pass, for it is winter, and the cold is too bitter at those heights. Too, the approaches are held by the *Spaunen*. Nay, your first chance to pass over the Grimwall will be perhaps at Quadran Pass—if it is not snowed in or held also."

"If Quadran Pass is blocked by winter or foe," said Gildor, "then Gûnar Slot will be our next chance, then through Gûnarring Gap to Valon and along Pendwyr Road to Pellar."

"Can the enemy be that far south?" asked Tuck, remembering the maps of the War-council.

"Perhaps; perhaps not," answered Vanidor. "Their goal could be the Quadran, for under those four mountains lies Drimmen-deeve, where rules the Dread! And if the Dimmendark sets that creature free, then Darda Galion will be their target."

At Vanidor's pronouncement, grim looks came upon the visages of Talarin, Gildor, and Rael, for dearly did they love Darda Galion, Land of the Silverlarks, Land where grew the twilight Eld Trees, home now of the Lian. And for a Gargon to be free to rave into that faer sylva would be a dire prospect indeed.

"This, then, is my advice," said Vanidor: "Go south through Arden Vale to come to Lianion. Follow parallel to the Old Rell Way and not upon it, for there go *Spaunen*. You can try to cross the Grimwall at Quadran Pass, and if the way is free, you can fare south through Darda Galion where our Lian kindred will aid you on your way.

"Should the Quadran Pass be held by the foe, or if it is closed by winter snow, then you must turn south once more for Gûnar Slot, or even Ralo Pass beyond, and then to the Gûnarring Gap and on to far Pellar.

Because I know not the mind of the Enemy in Gron, none of these ways over the Grimwall may be open, and how you will ultimately come to Caer Pendwyr I cannot say, yet there you must go, and those are the choices before you."

Galen nodded his understanding, but it was Talarin who spoke next: "Galen King, if I thought it would help, I would send an Elven warrior escort with you. But I think that evil eyes would follow a large force and set a trap, where but two or three might slip south undetected.

"This, too, I say: Aurion King was a beloved friend and we share your loss. And we know you journey southward when your heart cries out, *North*. And though my son has not told you, last night we held counsel and debated our course should you choose north, or south. You have chosen south, and this is now our plan: Vanidor, Duorn, and two you have not met—Flandrena and Varion—will slip into Gron. By stealth they will approach the Iron Tower, and if there be any a way to rescue your Lady Laurelin, they will do so. Else, they will bring word of Modru's forces at his strongholt, so that when the time does come at last, we will know something of the Enemy's strength and disposition. This we will do while you muster the Host."

Galen said nought, but there stood tears in his eyes, and he gripped Vanidor's hand.

"Prince Igon is awake, Galen King," said the healer. "Pray, tax him not."

Galen and Tuck stepped through the door. While Tuck stood at the portal, Galen stepped to the bedside. Igon smiled wanly, the youth pale in the yellow lamplight. Galen spoke: "We now go south, my brother, to gather the Host."

"South? But no!" Igon protested, his voice weak and atremble. "Laurelin is north!" Then he seemed to see the Waerling for the first time. "Sir Tuck, why are you here? Challerain Keep . . . Father . . ." There was a silence, and then Igon asked, "Are you King now, Galen?" At Galen's nod the young Prince wept. "Then it was not a fevered dream as I had hoped. Father is dead." He turned his face to the wall.

The healer made motions to Galen, and the new King took his brother's hand and held it in his own two. "We must go now, Igon. The Horde must be stopped."

Galen loosed Igon's hand and gently stroked the young Prince's hair, then stepped to the door where stood Tuck. Igon turned his face to them. "I understand, Galen. I understand. You are King, and the Host is south." And as Galen and Tuck passed through the door, behind they could hear Igon's quiet weeping.

Now it came time for the parting, and Tuck and Galen stood in the company of Elves. And neither the Dimmendark nor the solemnity of the occasion could dim the fair brightness of the Lian. Beautiful Rael stood with Talarin and at their side was Vanidor. As they stood, three rode up: Duorn, Flandrena, and Varion. With Vanidor they would issue into Gron and attempt to reach the Iron Tower itself. Assembled there, too, were other Elves: warriors in the main: Lian Guardians.

Gildor, Galen, and Tuck stood before Talarin; and the warrior leader of Arden Vale turned and held out his hand, and Rael the Elfess came to stand at her Elf

Lord's side. "Galen King," said Talarin, "ere I bid you and your comrades farewell, I would have my Lady Rael speak, for her words often bear portents."

The gentle voice of the graceful consort fell softly upon their ears: "Galen King, the way before you is arduous, for the Land is fraught with dire peril. Along your path will lie great danger, yet unbidden aid will be found there, too, just as you and others before you found our aid here at the Hidden Stand. Now you and your small companion go forth with my son, and you take all of our blessings with you. Yet hearken: even as you three fare south, four others will bear north." Now Vanidor and his three companions came to stand before golden Rael, too. "And so both of my sons—Gildor Goldbranch and Vanidor Silverbranch—as well as all of us are caught up in events of Modru's making.

"And that is what Evil does: forces us all down dark pathways we otherwise would not have trod. By choice we would not have stepped out upon these courses, vet little or no choice are we given, and our energies are turned aside, turned away from the creation of good and toward the destruction of Evil. Make no mistake, Evil must be crushed, not only to eliminate the suffering Evil causes, but also to atone for the good lost. But if for no other reason, Evil must be destroyed so that we can once more guide our own destinies.

"Until that time, the fates of us all are intertwined, yet the fortune of one weighs heavily upon me. Ever have there been soothsayers in my lineage, and auguries come unannounced at times. Yet this sooth has long been upon me, since the flaming Dragon Star fell, but now seems to be the time to speak it:

"Neither of two Evils must thy strike claim;
Instead smite the Darkness between the same."

At these words Tuck's heart pounded unexpectedly, but he did not know why, and he did not understand the message. And Tuck looked to see that the others were just as puzzled as he by Rael's rede, yet what she said next only added to the mystery: "I know not what it means nor to whom its portent bodes."

Rael moved to the wayfarers and pressed the hand of each, kissing Gildor and Vanidor upon the cheek. And when she stood before Galen, she said, "We will tend young Igon until he has the strength to join you. Hence, fret not upon his state as you fare south, for that would be needless worry." Then she stepped back to Talarin's side and spoke no more, though her eyes were bright.

Now Talarin spoke: "Galen King, should your course be through Darda Galion, bear our greetings to our Lian kindred; they will help you on your way. Unlike Arden Vale, their Realm is wide and their strength is great. Yet this, too, I will say: though my warrior band in Arden is small, still Modru's minions give the Lian wide berth, for they fear us. Yet though the Dimmendark does not grasp this vale as much as it cloaks it, if the *Spaunen* are left unchecked, there will come a time when they will fall upon us, both here and in Darda Galion; and we, too, will drown beneath that dark tide. But ere then, with good fortune, you shall guide the force to shatter Modru's black dreams of power. And now this last: when you need us, we will be at your side."

Now all the wayfarers mounted up, and Tuck was

boosted astride the packhorse to sit before the supplies strapped to a cradle cinched to its back.

Galen upon Jet turned to Vanidor and the three Elven comrades who were to steal into Gron. "My heart goes with you to the holt of Modru Kinstealer. May fortune smile upon you."

Then Galen faced Talarin and Rael and the Elven gathering, and he raised his hand. "Dark days lie behind us, and darker days loom ahead, yet, by my troth, one day the Evil in Gron shall be overthrown and the bright Sun shall shine again down into this deep-cloven vale."

Galen flashed his sword from its scabbard and to the sky and cried to all: *"Cepān wyllan, Lian; wir gān bringan thē Sunna!"* (Keep well, Lian; we go to bring the Sun!)

Gildor, too, raised his sword, as did Vanidor. *"Cianin taegi!"* (Shining days!) cried Gildor. *"Cianin taegi!"* answered Vanidor, and a great shout rang up from all.

And as the sound echoed through the pines, Galen, Gildor, and Tuck started south while Vanidor, Duorn, Flandrena, and Varion set off for the north.

And Tuck on the packhorse being led by Gildor on Fleetfoot spoke quietly under his breath: "May the fair face of Fortune smile upon us all."

South they rode—Gildor, Galen, and Tuck—alongside the frozen Tumble River running through the deep cleft of the vale. Pines covered the valley floor, and craggy stone palisades could be seen rising steeply up into the Shadowlight. Narrow was the vale, at times pinching down to widths less than a furlong from wall to wall, and in these places the river spanned the full vale width. In these narrow gaps, pathways could be seen carven upon the faces of the stone bluffs, but the trio shunned these icy ways, choosing instead to go upon the frozen surface of the river below.

Long they rode down the vale, yet when at last they stopped to make camp, still they were between the high stone walls, for Arden Vale was lengthy. Some thirty-five miles they had ridden south, and Gildor said that perhaps fifteen miles more lay ahead ere they would leave the gorge.

Their supper consisted of Lian wayfarer's food: dried fruit and vegetables, hot tea, and, much to Tuck's delight, mian, a delicious Elven waybread made of oats and honey and several kinds of nuts. "Sure beats crue all hollow," said the Warrow, taking another bite and savoring it.

Tuck prepared to bed down, for he was weary and had the midwatch and so needed sleep. But ere doing so, he reclined against a log by the small campfire and wrote in his diary. Nearby, Galen sat with his back to a tree and gazed at the red eye-patch in his hand.

"Lord Gildor, speak to me of the last hours of my father." Galen's voice was low, nearly a whisper.

Gildor looked upon the Man and then spoke: "When there we stood upon the final parapet of Challerain Keep and chose that last desperate course—to break through the *Rûpt* ring and win free—I felt a deep foreboding, and this I said to thy sire: 'Beware, Aurion King, for beyond yon gate I sense a great Evil lurks, an Evil beyond the Horde at our door, and I deem it bodes ill for you.' Little did I know that at the north gate of the first wall would we be met by Ghûlka led by Modru."

"*Modru?*" cried Tuck, sitting bolt upright with a start.

"Aye, Modru," answered Gildor. "It was he who taunted the King before the sundered gates."

"But that was a Man!" exclaimed Tuck. "The Man from Hyree! Modru's emissary!"

" 'Twas Evil Modru who spoke at the north gate," answered Gildor, but ere he could say more, Tuck interrupted.

"Then Danner slew him." Tuck's fist smacked into palm. "Danner's arrow struck him full in the forehead, crashing into his brain; he was dead even as he pitched backward off his Hèlsteed."

"Nay, Wee One," answered Gildor, holding up a hand to forestall Tuck's protests. "It was only one of Modru's puppets that was slain. Did I not say that Modru uses hideous powers to command his Horde? This, then, is one of them: though the Evil One sits afar in his Iron Tower, still he can look out upon distant scenes through the eyes of his emissaries, listen through their ears, speak through their mouths, and at times slay through their hands. None knows how far he can reach out to *possess* his pawns, but his power is great. Yet perhaps it diminishes with distance.

"Nay, it was not the Evil One himself slain by Danner's arrow, though I think Modru felt the unexpected blow. Yet, at the most, Danner's bolt has but delayed Modru's plans: for Danner slew the puppet, and now Modru has lost his eyes and ears, his mouth and hands at Challerain Keep—though another pawn by now must have been sent to take the place of the one slain, for Modru will not long allow the Horde to sit idle at the mount."

Tuck shuddered at the thought of the Evil One *possessing* another; and now the Warrow understood why the emissary's slack face writhed and became evil when Aurion and Tuck came to parley: *It was Modru "taking over."* And Tuck thought he knew, too, why the emissary did not join in that treacherous fight upon the parley field: *If the hideous power diminishes with distance, it just might be that Modru back in Gron could not control the Hyranan well enough to engage in combat upon the fields of distant Challerain.*

Tuck's speculations were interrupted by Gildor speaking: "Galen King, thy sire won through the north gate after you and your band broke the Ghûlka ring. Yet he was sorely beset, and had taken many wounds. But still he fought with the strength of many. At the last he was surrounded, and pierced through by Ghûlken spear. Even with the lance in him, he slew two more foe ere he fell forward to Wildwind's back."

Gildor drew both his sword and long-knife and thrust them out before him. Each held a blade-jewel, one blood-red, the other ocean-blue, and they glinted in the firelight. "Even with these two blades, Bale and Bane, still I could not win to his side in time to save him. Yet the scarlet fire of Bale and the cobalt blaze of Bane drove the Ghûlka back, for they fear these weapons forged long ago in Lost Duellin, forged to battle evils such as they. When they fled, I caught up Wildwind's reins and rode free of the mêlée.

"On a nearby slope, I eased Aurion King to the ground. He said but one thing ere he died: 'Tell Galen . . . Igon . . . I chose freedom.' Then he was gone. What he meant, I do not know."

Tuck sat with tears in his eyes. "I know the pith of his words," said the Warrow. "When the emissary

. . . when Modru met us on the field to parley, he offered to spare the King's life in return for the surrender of all of us into slavery. But the King said, 'Pah! Say this to your vile Lord Modru: Aurion Redeye chooses freedom!' "

For long moments no word was said, and the only sound was the crackle of the fire. At last, Gildor stirred. "I cut loose the eye-patch so that none would know him or defile his body, and so that Modru would not know that Aurion King had been slain. Then I laid his sword beside him and composed his hands over his breast, and remounted Fleetfoot to return to the fray.

"But Vidron at the head of a band had broken free and raced eastward. Catching up Wildwind's reins, I followed.

"East we ran through the foothills, with Ghûlka hard on our trail. But Hèlsteed has not the speed of horse, and we finally escaped their clutch.

"Far to the east through the Dimmendark we had fled, unto the Signal Mountains, but now we circled southward, heading for the rendezvous to join with any others who might have broken free. Our course swung just to the north of the Weiunwood, and while Vidron bore on west and south, riding for the Battle Downs and Stonehill beyond, I turned aside into the forest to seek tidings from the Weiunwood Alliance and to bear them the news of the downfall of Challerain Keep and of the death of Aurion. There I discovered from one of my kindred that you and Tuck had passed through on the trail of the kinstealers.

"I asked that word be sent to Vidron in Stonehill, and I left Wildwind in the care of my kith, a Lian recovering from a battle wound, and came after you, one 'Darkday behind your track when I started, though

I had nearly overtaken you by the time we came to Arden."

Tuck spoke: "Have you any news of other Warrows? Did any win free? Danner, Patrel, any?"

"I know not, Wee One, for none were with us. The last I saw of any Waerling ere I came to Weiunwood was 'Darkdays past, when we all broke through the sundered north gate." Gildor's eyes glittered in the firelight.

Tuck's heart fell at this news, for he still hoped that others of his kindred had escaped the ruins of Challerain Keep.

Again long moments fled. Finally, Galen returned the red patch to his breast pocket. "You say you spoke with a wounded Lian at the Weiunwood," said Galen. "Many went off to battle with *Spaunen* when last we were there. Did he say aught of the outcome?"

"Nay," answered Gildor, "for he knew it not. Yet that explains the empty campsite I came to on the eastern edge of the 'Wood: they had gone to War and I was a full 'Darkday behind then. I know nought of that battle, for I but followed you."

Little was said after that, and Tuck bedded down and went to sleep. But when his turn at watch came, he spent the time scribing in his journal, recording Gildor's words.

After an uneasy rest, they broke camp and continued southward through Arden Gorge. High stone canyon walls loomed up to either side, at times near, but at other times two or three miles distant, beyond the limits of Galen's vision in the Shadowlight. Tuck again rode upon the packhorse, trailing behind Gildor as the trio wended through the pines along the frozen river.

Some fourteen miles south they went, enwrapped in snowy silence, saying little or nothing, and Tuck's mind fell into a state where he was at one with the woods: moving among the evergreens and watching the trees go by, thinking no thoughts of substance, attuned only to the canyon forest.

Gildor's voice fell unexpectedly upon his ears, breaking into his state of accord: "We are less than a mile from the end of Arden Vale," said the Elf. "Around the bend we will come to the camp of my kindred standing Arden-ward. We shall take a meal with them under the shelter of the Lone Eld Tree."

"Lone Eld Tree?" asked Tuck, trying to remember what he'd heard about these legendary forest giants. "Aren't they the ones said to *gather* the twilight and *hold* it if Elves dwell nearby?" At Gildor's nod, Tuck was surprised: "But I thought that was just a myth."

Gildor laughed. "Then, Wee Waerling, if they are myths, you had better not let this Eld Tree know it, for it might vanish, and so might the entire forest of Darda Galion."

Tuck smiled at Gildor's reply and wondered at his own ignorance as onward they went.

The river curved 'round a bend, and now a distant roar of falling water could be heard as they rode through the pines. Gildor pointed ahead, and there Tuck could see that the gorge squeezed to a narrow cleft that seemed to be filled with a white mist streaming up into the Winternight sky. Gildor pointed again, and Tuck's eyes fell upon an enormous tree, pinelike but with broad leaves and not needles; and even in the Shadowlight, the Warrow could see that the leaves were dusky, as if unaffected by the Dimmendark but shining with a soft twilight of their own.

"Lor, what a giant!" exclaimed Tuck, his tilted eyes wide at the sight of a tree looming hundreds of feet into the air. "Are there other Eld Trees in Arden?"

"No. Just this one. That is why we call it the Lone Eld Tree," answered Gildor. "It was brought here from Darda Galion by my sire when it was but a seedling and planted in the rich soil of Arden Gorge soon after this hidden vale was first discovered by my people."

"Planted by your sire? By Talarin? But this giant must be thousands of years old . . ." Tuck's mind boggled to think of the age of Elves.

Galen spoke: "That tree is the symbol of the Warder of the Northern Regions of Rell, now Lord Talarin. That sigil has been nobly borne into battle many times 'gainst dark forces: green tree 'pon field of grey. Such a flag hangs in the Gathering Hall of Caer Pendwyr, and another at Challerain Keep."

"No more at Challerain Keep, I fear, Galen King," said Gildor, "for Modru's Horde will have rent it down as well as the other flags of the Alliance."

No more was said as they spurred toward the Elven camp under the branches of the Lone Eld Tree.

"Aye, the approach to Crestan Pass is held by the *Rûpt*," said Jandrel, Captain of the Arden-ward, "and the Ghûlka, Modru's Reavers, patrol the Old Rell Way. Somewhere south a Horde marches along the abandoned road. Down out of the Grimwall north of the Pass they came, three 'Darkdays past. Where the *Spaunen* are bound, I cannot say, yet they march apace. Perhaps they strike for Quadran Pass and Drimmendeeve, or Darda Galion beyond."

"We ride for Quadran Pass," said Galen, pouring himself another cup of tea from the pot hanging on the fire irons above the small campblaze. "If we can cross the Grimwall there, we will warn the Lian in the Larkenwald of this Horde as we pass through on our way to Pellar."

"Be wary," said Jandrel, "for not only are there Ghûlka and Rucha and Loka with the Horde, but Vulgs, too. Give them wide berth, for Modru's evil scouts will smell you out should you come near."

"Scouts?" asked Tuck. "Vulgs are scouts?"

"Aye, Master Waerling," answered Jandrel, "scouts. It has ever been so that Vulgs do Modru's bidding, and at times he uses them on vile missions where their speed, stealth, or savagery suits his ends. But for the most part, he uses them to ward the flanks of his Hordes, or to spy out the Lands that he intends to invade."

"Spy out Lands . . . but they were in the Bosky!" cried Tuck, leaping to his feet, the sense of tranquility he had felt under the branches of the Eld Tree completely shattered. "They're going to invade the Bosky! I've got to get back! They must be warned! Merrilee . . ." Tuck took several running steps toward the horses, but then jerked to a stop as if arrow-pierced and slowly turned toward his comrades, falling to his knees in the snow and burying his face in his hands.

In six swift strides Galen knelt by the Warrow. "Tuck, if you must return to the Boskydells, you are free to go, though how you will get there, I cannot say."

"I can't go. I can't go," whispered Tuck. "There are no ponies; even if there were, I'd be too late. And you need my eyes."

Flowing under the ice, the swift-running Tumble River emerged from the last walls of Arden Gorge and fell down a precipice in a wide cataract. Swirling vapors rose up and obscured the view of the cloven vale, and where the mist settled unto the frigid rock, strange, twisting shapes of ice formed.

Behind the roar of water the trio went upon a hidden icy road, the stone clad in thick sheets of frozen mist: here was the secret entrance into the hidden valley—an entrance concealed by the fall of water. At last, they emerged from behind the cataract and twined through crags to come at last to the wolds of Rell.

The horses were spurred to a canter, and south they ran, and Tuck looked back toward Arden Gorge, back at the final cleft where the high, sheer stone walls split out of the earth, but the perpetual white mist veiled all beyond Arden Falls: neither pine forests nor stone walls were visible through the mist—not even the Lone Eld Tree could be seen.

Yet Tuck's bitter thoughts were not on the hidden valley; instead, he fretted over the Vulg scouts spying out the Boskydells, foreshadowing an invasion. And he recalled Galen's words spoken only two 'Darkdays past: *"These are evil days for Mithgar, and evil choices am I given."* Now more than ever, Tuck realized the truth of Rael's words: *"Evil . . . forces us all down dark pathways we otherwise would not have trod."* And Tuck thought, *Even when I would choose to fight a great evil elsewhere, no choice am I given, for if King Galen does not reach Pellar, then a greater evil will fall upon the world . . . Oh, Merrilee, my love . . .*

Tuck turned his face away from the vale, for he could no longer see it.

Less than one mile south the Tumble turned westward while the trio bore on; and just after, they passed over the Crossland Road, the main east-west pike reaching far overland from the distant Ryngar Arm of the Weston Ocean to the nearby Grimwall Mountains. Although this tradeway was extensive, most commerce in this part of Mithgar flowed on the watercourse of the Isleborne River, or came by road from south and west. Beyond the Crossland Road they went, south through the folds of the land, another fifteen miles before they made camp.

Tuck stood at the edge of the thicket, peering to the west, his jewel-eyed vision limited by the Dimmendark. Gildor came and stood beside him.

"West some twenty miles or so lies the Tumble River," said the Elf. "Beyond Arden Ford is the Drearwood, and beyond that the River Caire. Yet I know your thoughts roam far to the west: beyond Rhone and Harth and to your Land of the Thorns, a fortnight away by swift steed.

"Tuck, the Vulgs have roamed your homeland at the Evil One's command, and this I think is the why of it: Once before, all of Mithgar faced this Foe, and he was overthrown at the last. In his defeat it was your Folk who played the key role, and Modru has not forgotten; that is why he sends his minions against your Land. I would that it were not so, for the Boskydell is a gentle Realm of peace, ill fitted for a War against Modru's *Spaunen*.

"Yet hearken: *no* Land is well suited to War. And I have seen your kindred in battle. There is surprising grit to be found in your Folk.

"And though you would be in your beloved Bosky, there are those who will stand in your stead. Trust in them to choose the correct course, just as you have chosen rightly."

Gildor turned and walked back to the small shielded

fire, and Tuck said nought. But soon he came and took supper, and afterward he slept well.

Although Elves pay little heed to hours and days and even weeks, seeming to note only the passing of the seasons, still they know at all times where stand the Sun, Moon, and stars. And even the murk of the Dimmendark changed not this power of theirs. And though at times the dim disk of the Sun vaguely could be seen as it passed through the zenith, still it was Gildor who kept track of time's flow for the trio.

Three more 'Darkdays they bore southward, riding parallel to and ten or so miles west of the Old Rell Way, an abandoned trade route, long fallen into run. The land they passed through was rough, high moor with sparse trees, there being barren thickets or lone giants clutching with empty winter branches at the Dimmendark sky. In the folds of the land grew brush and brambles, and cold winter snow covered all. Yet across the upland they went, bearing ever southward.

Five 'Darkdays past they had left the Elvenholt in the northernmost reaches of Arden Vale, nearly fifty-five leagues behind. Eleven leagues a 'Darkday they rode, more or less, thirty-three miles each leg, for haste was needed in these dire times. Yet though they had pressed long and hard, neither Jet nor Fleetfoot nor the packhorse seemed to be tiring, and Tuck wondered at their endurance.

The sixth 'Darkday they turned at last to the Old Rell Way, for now they had to follow its course through the wide gap in a westward spur of the Grimwall Mountains standing across the way.

Tuck sat astride Jet's withers before Galen, for the

road was fraught with peril and the Waerling's eyes were needed up front to ward the way rather than "in back lolling on a pack animal," as Galen smilingly put it. Yet though Galen had smiled, they were come to a dangerous pass, and if Spawn roamed it, the way would be filled with risk.

Southward they went, through rising hill country, ten miles before coming to the Old Rell Way where it first entered the wide gap. No enemy did they see, though the snow was beaten down in a wide track made by many feet tramping.

"This wake is fresh, perhaps a 'Darkday old, made by an army moving south," said Galen, remounting Jet.

"The Swarm Jandrel spoke of," said Gildor. "Keep a sharp eye, Tuck, for they are before us."

Into the gap they went and beyond, riding another two leagues; and the land began to fall, the close hills spreading out, while the route they followed swung southeastward, rounding the side chain and heading for the Quadran through mounting hill country.

"Well, my Wee One," said Galen, "it appears that the danger is past, for the land opens up and we can leave this abandoned road once more. Though there be a Horde before us, we will travel beside its course, this time to the east, I think." Then he turned to Gildor: "We must go swifter and 'round the Spawn ere we come to Quadran Pass, for we would not want them to get there first." Galen reined Jet to a halt. "Tuck, you may once more ride at your ease upon the cargo."

Smiling, Tuck swung his leg over to leap to the ground. One last time he swept his sapphirine gaze to the limits of his vision, and far to the south . . .

Quickly, he threw his leg back over Jet. "Hola! Galen

King, something afar: down the Old Rell Way in the flats below. Take me closer."

Jet was spurred forward, Gildor following upon Fleetfoot, leading the packhorse. Swiftly they cantered along the abandoned road to bring Tuck's eyes into range. And as they went, Tuck strained his vision to its uttermost limits, and soon he gave a groan, for there before him down in the flats nearly five miles distant, a dark Rūcken Horde boiled southeastward, force-marching down the Old Rell Way. No sound reached up to Tuck's ears from the Swarm, the distance lending the illusion of a vast army moving along in eerie silence.

"Galen King, it is the Horde," gritted Tuck. "We must leave this road and swing around them."

To the east of the Way they slipped aside, riding once more across the open moors. And as they went, the land began to rise, for they were bordering upon the foothills of the Grimwall. An hour they rode, and then another, Tuck's eyes keeping the Swarm just in view as the trio passed behind thickets and hills to the east of the *Spaunen*.

"We have drawn even with them now," said Tuck grimly as Jet at a walk bore him from behind the flank of a hill and his jewel-hued vision saw the foe once more.

"How many are there?" asked Galen, for his own eyes could not see them.

"I know not," answered Tuck, "but they flow as a dark flood perhaps three miles in length. How like a plague of ravenous vermin they seem, swarming forth to ravage the Land."

"It is well that this Realm has been long abandoned, then," said Gildor, riding beside them, "else this blight would have struck down many an innocent victim."

"Are there Vulgs?" Galen's thoughts turned to the dire scouts of Modru.

"Yes," answered Tuck, seeking and finding the sinister dark shapes gliding o'er the land. "They roam the Horde's fringes, but I see none more than a mile from the Swarm."

"Keep your eyes set for them," said Galen, "for if they scent us, they will bring the Ghola."

Once more they spurred up the pace, and Jet and Fleetfoot bore them southeastward and the packhorse cantered behind. An hour they rode at a varying gait, for they must needs husband the strength of the steeds, and at the end of that time Tuck could no longer see the Horde behind.

"On the morrow we must risk the road once more," said Galen, "for our pace will be swifter upon its abandoned bed than through this rough hill country."

"But, Sire, won't the Vulgs smell us out if we run along a course they will soon follow upon?" protested Tuck.

"That is a danger, Wee One," answered Galen, "yet we cannot make haste through this broken land unless we soon take to the Old Rell Way; it begins its long run up to the Quadran, and ravines and bluffs will bar our route if we are not upon the Way. And haste is needed, for not only must we hie for Pellar, we must also try to warn the Larkenwald of the Horde behind us. There is this, too: if we start up to Quadran Pass and find we cannot cross through—because of snow or Spawn—then we will be forced to retrace our steps, coming back down before turning south for Gûnar Slot. And we must not meet up with this Horde on that narrow road down from the heights.

"Aye, Tuck, you are right to think of the Vulgs, and we will not rejoin the Old Rell Way until we are far ahead of here. Perhaps they will not scent a 'Darkday-old trail. But we must at last come again to the Way to gain greater speed, for not to do so poses a greater risk."

Through the hills they wended, bearing southeastward, and the land grew rougher as they went. And as Galen had said, ravines and bluffs began to bar their way. And as if the Fates had conspired perversely, ramparts and fissures slowly began to force the trio south, back toward the Old Rell Way. *Too soon!* thought Tuck. *Too soon! We go where the Vulgs will scent us!* Yet there was nought they could do to change their course as they turned through stone and rounded thickets and rode along the faces of low-walled, sheer bluffs.

"I deem we must now strike for the Way and make a run for it," said Galen grimly, "for where we ride now, the Vulgs will cut our trail." And so they turned and deliberately pressed toward the abandoned road, coming down through the ruptured land.

As they came along a twisting valley, suddenly Gildor kicked Fleetfoot forward and grabbed Jet's bridle, bringing the horses to a halt.

"Hsst!" he said. "Listen!" And the Elf pointed ahead toward a bend.

Both Tuck and Galen strained their hearing, and above the blowing of the steeds they could faintly hear the skirl of steel upon steel, the clash of combat, the clangor of a duel.

At a motion from Galen, Tuck mounted behind the Man just as a pony bearing supplies scaddled around the bend and bolted past them, his eyes rolled white with terror, his hooves beating a frantic tattoo upon the stony ground.

Tuck gripped his bow and pulled an arrow from his quiver: it was the red shaft from Othran's Tomb. Quickly he replaced it and took another, stringing it to his bow.

Galen drew his sword and Gildor had Bale in hand, its blood-red blade-jewel streaming scarlet fire along the weapon's edge, silently shouting, *Evil is near!*

At a nod from Galen, forward they went, the steeds at a walk, nearing the bend. Tuck's heart thudded as he prepared for fight or flight, for they knew not what lay ahead. *Ching! Clang!* came the sounds, louder.

Slowly they rounded the bend, to come upon a scene of great carnage. Rūcks there were, lying dead, slain Hlōks, too, cleft by great gaping wounds. *Chank! Dlang!* Ponies were slaughtered, some still kicking in their death throes. But Tuck's eye was drawn elsewhere, for here and there other warrior Folk lay: *Dwarves!*

Dwarves slain by scimitar and cudgel!

Dwarven axes asplash with black Rūck grume bloodily attested to the deaths of the *Spaunen*, just as red-washed Rūcken blades spoke of the Dwarven dead. *Chank! Shang!*

At last the trio came full 'round the bend; from the roadbed of the Old Rell Way the ring of steel upon steel hammered forth. *Dhank! Chang!* It was a Dwarf! And a Hlōk! And they fought to the death: the last two survivors of a gory slaughter, the last two. And they fought on in a bloody battleground, awash with the ichor of the slain.

Tuck leapt down and drew his arrow to the full, aiming at the Hlōk, waiting for a safe shot.

"No!" shouted the Dwarf, hate-filled eyes never leaving his foe. "He is mine!"

The Hlōk's eyes darted toward the trio, and he snarled in rage and leapt toward the Dwarf. *Clank! Dring!*

Galen's grim voice spoke above the ring of steel: "Hold your arrow, Tuck. He has the right."

It was axe against scimitar, but an axe wielded in a manner that Tuck had never imagined. The Dwarf grasped the oaken helve with a two-handed grip: right hand high near the blade, left hand low near the haft butt. And he used the haft to parry scimitar blows; and stabbed forward with the cruel axe beak, and shifted his grip to strike with fury, lashing out the double-bitted blade in sweeping blows, driven by the power of broad Dwarven shoulders.

Yet the Hlōk was skilled, too, and stood a full head taller than his foe. His reach with the scimitar was considerably longer, and the hack and thrust of his broad, curved blade was swift and deadly. And the edge of his weapon was smeared with a black substance, but whether it was poison, Tuck could not say.

Clang! Chank! cried the tortured steel, as blade met blade, and the Dwarf was pressed back, and Tuck readied his bow. But then with a hoarse shout, the Dwarf vented the ancient battle cry of his Folk, *"Châkka shok! Châkka cor!"* (Dwarven axes! Dwarven might!) and attacked in fury. The Hlōk desperately hacked downward—a mighty blow—but the curved blade chopped into the soft brass strip embedded the length of the axe helve, inlaid there for just that purpose. Swiftly, the Dwarf whipped the helve left, thrusting the edge-caught scimitar aside, then jabbed forward the steel axe-beak, taking the Hlōk in the chest, the iron fang bursting through the Hlōk's scale mail and spearing into his heart. And ere the dead Hlōk could fall unto the ground, the Dwarf whipped the axe back and swung a chopping blow, the bit cleaving through the Hlōk's temple, and bile filled Tuck's throat to see it.

And as the foe fell dead to the snow, the Dwarf stepped back and raised his axe and cried: *"Châkka shok! Châkka cor!"*

Sheathing his sword, Galen dismounted, and so did Gildor, and with Tuck they strode unto the Dwarf, the sole survivor of the nearly two hundred forty combatants slain there that 'Darkday. And he stood among the dead—*as if he owns this bloody battleground,* thought Tuck—and warily watched as the trio came nigh, his gore-splashed axe gripped in gnarled hands.

Dwarf he was, dressed in earth-colored quilted mountain gear; linked rings of black-iron chain mail could be seen under his open jacket. He stood perhaps four and a half feet tall, and brown locks fell to his shoulders from his plain steel helm. His eyes were deep brown, nearly black, and a forked beard reached to his chest. His shoulders were half again as wide as a Man's.

"That's close enough," he growled, wary of the strangers, raising his axe to the ready, "close enough till I know more of you. I was here first, yet still will I give you my name: I am Brega, Bekki's son. What be you hight?"

It was Lord Gildor who answered: "The Waerling is Sir Tuckerby Underbank from the Land of the Thorns, from the Boskydels." Tuck bowed to the Dwarf and received a stiff bow in return, yet wonder shone in Brega's eye.

"I am Gildor, Lian Guardian, seed of Talarin and son of Rael, of old from Darda Galion but now of Arden." Gildor bowed, and Brega returned the courtesy, his axe now resting with its beak down to the ancient pave.

"And this is Galen King, son of slain Aurion King, now High Ruler of all Mithgar."

Brega's face blenched to hear this news. "Aurion Redeye is dead?" he blurted, and at Gildor's nod: "What ill news you bear." And then Brega made a sweeping bow to Galen.

"King Galen," said the Dwarf, "it was in answer to the summons from your sire that I and the comrades I captain marched north." Brega swept his hand in a wide gesture over the battlefield, and then seemed to realize for the first time that he stood alone. Shock registered upon his features, and without another word he stepped to a cloak lying in the snow and fixed it around his shoulders and cast the hood over his head, in deep mourning.

"Galen King," said Tuck, pointing northwestward along the Old Rell Way, "the Horde: they heave into my view."

Back along the abandoned road the dark Spawn boiled southerly, swarming toward the four.

"Horde?" barked Brega, his face enshadowed within his hood.

"Aye," said Galen, "south they come, a dark tide bound toward the Quadran, but whither they go, we cannot say. This band your warriors slew was perhaps the vanguard of the Horde that comes behind."

"How know you this?" Brega's voice was harsh as he peered to the northwest. "I can see no Foul Folk, no Grg, through this cursed blackness."

"The Waerling sees them," said Gildor, "for his jewel-hued eyes pierce further through this myrk than those of other Folk."

Brega stepped close to Tuck and looked into the Warrow's wide, tilted, sapphirine gaze. "Utruni eyes," grunted the Dwarf. "I believe you now, Waeran."

"Then let us mount up and get south," urged Tuck, glancing north.

South came the Horde.

"But my dead kindred," protested Brega. "Are we to leave them lying here upon the open battlefield? Stone or fire, that is the way of the Châkka. If they are not laid to rest in stone, or burned on a fitting pyre, their shades will wander an extra age before a rebirthing can occur."

"We have not the time for a proper burial, Warrior Brega," said Tuck, "for the press of Modru's Spawn will not permit it."

"Aye, you are right, Waeran. It is not the time for mourning or burial." Brega cast back his hood, and retrieved a pack from the snow and shouldered it. Then he looked over the field of carnage. "They were fine comrades, the forty Châkka I strode beside, and mighty were their axes."

"Forty?" Galen's voice was filled with amazement. "Do you say that but forty Dwarven warriors slew all of these foe? There must be two hundred *Spaunen* here. Hai! mighty *were* their axes."

Still the Horde marched onward, drawing closer.

Galen mounted Jet and drew Tuck up before him. Gildor, too, vaulted to the back of Fleetfoot, and held a hand out to Brega: "Mount up behind, Warrior Brega."

Brega looked up at Fleetfoot looming above him, and the Dwarf's face blenched. Quickly he backed away, holding his hands before him, palms out. "No, Gildor Elf, I shall ride a pony, and not upon the back of such a great beast."

Exasperation filled Gildor's voice: "Drimm Brega, you have no choice!" Gildor's gesture swept the field. "All of the ponies are slain or have fled. You must mount my horse. It is not as if you will be commanding Fleetfoot, for I will do that deed. You will sit behind, nothing more, while we fare south."

"But I do have a choice." Brega's voice flared with ire at Gildor's tone, and his eyes smoldered. "I can stand here athwart the road and meet with the Horde. My axe will drink more blood of the Squam ere this 'Darkday is done." Brega unshouldered his weapon and turned to face the north.

Southward swarmed the Horde, their hard stride bearing them toward the four.

"Up behind me, you stubborn fool!" commanded Gildor. "The *Spaunen* have hove into *my* sight now, and we have not the time nor patience to argue with a stiff-necked, horse-fearing Drimm!"

With a snarl, Brega spun around to face Gildor and hefted his axe.

"Wait!" cried Tuck, "let us not fight amongst ourselves. We are allies! Warrior Brega, the maggot-folk will just slay you from afar by black-shafted arrow, and you will have died for nought. Come with us and you will be able to avenge your brethren, as I will be able to avenge mine."

Brega lowered his axe.

Then Galen spoke: "Warrior Brega, I need your strength and skill by my side. Our journey south is fraught with peril and I must reach the Host. With you in our company our chances improve. I ask you in the name of all Mithgar to join us."

The Dwarf looked at the High King, and then to Tuck, and his eyes strayed to his slain kindred. To the shadowed north he looked, where beyond his sight the Horde boiled southward. Last of all he looked at Gildor's outstretched hand, and with a growl Brega slung his axe down his back by its carrying thong and reached up to grasp the Elf's grip, stepping into the stirrup and swinging up onto Fleetfoot's back behind Lord Gildor. And Tuck's sharp ears heard the Dwarf exclaim, *"Durek, varak an!"* (Durek, forgive me!)

And as they spurred forward through the Shadowlight, Tuck looked back at the Horde and gasped, for they were but a league distant, and the Vulgs that loped before them had drawn even closer.

Southeasterly along the Old Rell Way ran Jet, with Fleetfoot alongside, the packhorse in tow. Swiftly, the gap between horses and Horde widened, and soon Tuck could no longer see them. Galen dropped back the pace, and they went single file once more.

"Fear not, Tuck," said Galen in a low voice, "they saw us not, for I did not see them. And though I did not say this before Brega, when the *Spaunen* come to the scene of the battle, they will stop to loot and mutilate and search for survivors, and perhaps make camp. And now our southward track mingles with that made by the Dwarves going north, and so the Vulgs will not single out our passage, confusing our spoor with that of Brega's force.

"We shall ride another ten miles or so and then make our camp. The Swarm will not come that far, for we have covered more than thirty miles to here, and since we did not see sign of where last the Horde camped, it must have been back beyond the gap. Even Rukha and Lōkha will not march forty miles a leg.

"No, I think that they will camp back at the slaughterground and squabble over the loot of the slain." Galen fell silent, and the horses cantered on.

The four made camp in a barren thicket well up and off the road. And as they took travelers' rations, Brega told his tale, and Galen's face became grim, for the news from Pellar was dire:

"There's War, bloody War to the south. The Rovers of Kistan, the Lakh from Hyree, through Vancha and Tugal they came marching, across Hoven and Jugo, and over the Avagon Sea in ships.

"Pellar was unprepared, and was struck to the knees, nearly a killing blow. But Valon rallied, and the outlying muster sounded. Even now the struggle goes on.

"Word was sent north to High King Aurion, yet no messages returned. Then we learned that the Hyranee held Gûnarring Gap and the heralds had been felled.

"Word came, too, from far Riamon that a fearful darkness had fallen upon the Grimwall and now swept south.

"At last a rider from Challerain Keep won through. How? I cannot say, but he bore word of Modru's Horde in the north.

"We could send but a token of the Red Hills Châkka to aid at the north Keep, for the rest stood against the Jihad.

"I was chosen to captain the forty, and by pony we marched north. Up through Valon we went, staying west of the Gûnarring Gap, for it was and perhaps still is held by the foe. North we went instead, some fifty miles up from the Gap, for there lies an ancient secret way across the Gûnarring, known to Châkka as the Walkover.

"By this route we came, crossing into Gûnar, and then north again. Up through Gûnar Slot we went, and when we came to the River Hâth, there we found this foul darkness. Agog we were, but through the blinding snow we pressed, across Hâth Ford and into the Dimmendark beyond: and it was like walking into a deep phosphor cave, this Shadowlight.

"Through the Winternight we marched, along the west flank of the Grimwall: we were making for Rhone Ford, the Stone-arches Bridge, and finally for the Signal Mountains and Challerain Keep at their end.

"A long trip would it have been, for we had already been on the march nearly thirty days and expected to tramp twenty more; but the vanguard of the Horde fell upon us. All were slain but me." Brega fell silent and once more cast his hood over his head.

"Ai, this is foul news indeed," said Gildor, "but it explains much: why our messages did not get through and why no word came from the south, for Gûnarring Gap is held by the foe. It also explains why the Host has not come north, for it wars against the enemy from the south."

"The War, Brega, what news?" asked Galen, his voice grim, his eyes cold.

"Sire, I know not how it fares now," replied Brega, "for a month has fled since last I knew. Pellar reeled under the onslaught, but the horsemen from Valon came and drove them back a ways. The battles seesawed like a teeter-totter, but more enemy came in ships. At the time I marched north, the scales seemed tipped against us, and our prospects seemed dire."

No one spoke for a moment, then Tuck called down

from atop the rock where he sat watch: "You used a word I do not know, Brega: 'Jihad.' What is a Jihad?"

"It is a great Jihad they fight," answered Brega. "A Holy War. *They are convinced that Gyphon will return and cast Adon down.*"

Gildor's face turned ashen. "How can it be?" he gasped. "The Great Evil is banished beyond the Spheres. He cannot return."

Brega merely shrugged his shoulders.

" 'How can it be?' you ask," said Galen, his voice bitter. "Lord Gildor, I shall answer your question with one of my own." He gestured at the Dimmendark. "How can *this* be, I ask, that Adon's Covenant is broken by the Winternight? What dark force, what eater of light, rules the Sun such that it cannot pierce this shadowy clutch? And if this can be—that Adon's Covenant is broken after four thousand years—then perhaps Gyphon can indeed return."

"Ai," cried Gildor, "if that could happen, then the world would be cast down into a pit so cruel that Hèl itself would appear as a paradise in its stead."

No word was said by any for a long while, and dread pounded through Tuck's veins, for although Tuck knew little of Gyphon, the effect upon Gildor had driven terror like a cruel spike into the Warrow's heart.

At last Galen spoke: "We must get some rest, for tomorrow we ride to the foot of Quadran Pass, and the next 'Darkday we attempt to cross over."

"I'll watch," said Tuck from his perch, "for the Horde is behind us and my eyes are needed now. Besides, I don't think I can sleep."

"Nay, Waerling," countered Gildor. "You are weary, I can see it, and during these next few 'Darkdays your vision will be most critical. You rest and I will watch, for my eyes, though not equal to yours in this myrk, are more than a match for the *Rûpt*. And the sleep of Elves is different from that of mortals, for I can rest and watch at one and the same time, though not forever—even Elves need sound sleep on occasion—yet many days can I keep the vigil ere that comes to pass."

And so all bedded down but Gildor, and he sat upon the high stone and kept the watch, resting his mind in gentle memories while his eyes warded them all.

But it was a long time ere Tuck fell asleep, for still his heart pounded with apprehension, and his thoughts had returned to that long-past day that Danner had told of Gyphon's downfall, and had spoken the last words the Great Evil had uttered, and the words echoed through Tuck's mind: *"Even now I have set into motion events you cannot stop. I shall return! I shall conquer! I shall rule!"*

When they broke camp, once more Brega seemed reluctant to mount up behind Gildor on Fleetfoot, and Tuck wondered how such a fierce warrior as the Dwarf could be so *daunted* by the thought of riding a horse. Yet Brega gritted his teeth and bestrode the steed.

With a hand up from Galen, Tuck swung onto Jet's withers, and once more they rode southeastward.

Up through the foothills they went, the land rising around them as they made for the Quadran: four great mountains of the Grimwall: Greytower, Loftcrag, Grimspire, and the mightiest of all, Stormhelm. Beneath these four peaks was delved Drimmen-deeve, ancient Dwarven homeland, now abandoned by them and fallen into dread, for therein dwelled a horror: a Gargon: Modru's Dread: an evil Vûlk: servant of Gron in the Great War of the Ban. And as Vanidor's words had suggested to the trio ere they set out from Arden Vale, the Dimmendark may have set this vile monster free from its exile under the Quadran and loosed it to reave within the Shadowlight. A hideous ally to Modru's Horde would it be, for the Gargon is a fear caster: armies would break and run before its dread power, or the soldiers would be paralyzed with terror, frozen like unto stone itself, and easy prey.

And toward the domain of this horror the four rode, for they thought to cross through the Quadran Pass and warn the Lian in Darda Galion of the Horde marching behind them.

Twenty miles south they rode, up through the rising foothills. Then the abandoned road divided: the Old Rell Way continued south along the western flanks of the Grimwall; the other path turned left and east and climbed up into the mountains, for it was the road over the Quadran Pass.

This left-hand way they followed, going some fifteen miles more before making camp. Thirty-five miles they had ridden that leg, and they were weary.

They supped on wayfarer's rations: tea, mian, and chewy cubes of a salted meat said by Brega to come from cod prepared by the fishermen of Leut and brought to Jugo in trading fleets of Arbalin.

"What is it that you do, Waeran?" asked Brega as Tuck sat near the small shielded fire, drinking tea and making notes.

Tuck looked up from his diary. "I scribe the day's events, Brega." The Warrow held up the booklet. "It is my journal."

Brega cocked his head to one side but said nought, so Tuck read his final sentence aloud: "Tomorrow we try Quadran Pass, up the flank of Stormhelm. Perhaps we will cross if it is free of snow or Rūcks or the Dread said to dwell in Drimmen-deeve."

Brega grunted, and stroked his forked beard. "Stormhelm. Drimmen-deeve. Your tongue is a mixture of Man and Elf, but I do not hear words of the Châkka."

"Châkka?" Now Tuck tilted his head, questioning.

"Châkka: the name Dwarves call themselves," said Galen.

"We name them Drimma," came Gildor's voice from his lookout.

"Then Drimmen-deeve means . . ." Tuck groped.

"Dwarven-delvings," supplied Galen.

"Aye," grumbled Brega, "Drimmen-deeve to Elf, Black Hole to Man, but its true name is Kraggen-cor. Yet no matter what it is called, it is the ancient Châkkaholt delved under the Quadran"—Brega shook his head in regret—"though the Châkka no longer dwell there." Now the Dwarf leapt to his feet and paced in agitation, a dark look upon his face, his eyes smoldering in ire. "Four times have we been bested by a foe beyond our limits: twice by Dragons, once by a Ghath—a Gargon—and the other time I shall not speak of. In Kraggen-cor it was the Ghath.

"Glorious were our days spent in that mighty Realm: mining ores, gems, and precious starsilver—what you call silveron. There, too, were our unmatched forges where were crafted tools and weapons and worthy things. And our homes were filled with happiness and industry. But the old tales say a silveron shaft was driven on a course of little promise; why, I do not know. Some say it was Modru's will that set our way, for our digging set free the evil Ghath, Modru's Dread, from a chamber he had been trapped in since the Great War of the Ban."

"The Lost Prison," said Gildor, then fell silent.

"Prison you name it"—Brega looked up at the Elf and smote a clenched fist into an open palm—"and prison it was, until that fatal day the Ghath burst from his lair and through the end of the shaft wall and slew many Châkka.

"In vain we tried to slay it, but it overmastered my Folk, and in the end we fled: out through the Dusken Door and out through the Daūn Gate, west and east of the Grimwall, for the corridors of Kraggen-cor reach from one side of the Mountains to the other."

Brega slumped down upon a log, and his fierce manner evaporated, replaced by a dark, somber mood. "More than one thousand years have passed since last the Châkka dwelt in Kraggen-cor, and still we yearn for its mighty halls. Yet although many have dreamt of living in those chambers, none have gone back but Braggi's squad, for Braggi led a raid to slay the Ghath: the Doomed Raid of Braggi, for none of that band were ever seen again.

"Some say that Kraggen-cor will be ours once more when Deathbreaker Durek is reborn. Then again will we dwell there: under Uchan, Ghatan, Aggarath, and Rávenor—Mountains you name Greytower, Loftcrag, Grimspire, and Stormhelm. And we will make it into a mighty realm as of old. When, I cannot say, for none knows when Khana Durek will return."

Morose, Brega fell silent, and nought was said for long moments while Tuck scribbled in his journal. "Lord Gildor, what names do the Elves give to the Quadran?" Tuck asked.

"In the Sylva tongue they are named Gralon, Chagor, Aevor, and Coron," answered Gildor, naming them in the same order as did Brega.

Again Tuck scribed, then said, "Brega, something puzzles me: When you spoke of the eld days, you said, '*our* forges, *our* homes, *our* digging, *we* fled.' But those days are a thousand years past. Surely *you* were not there."

"Perhaps I was, Waeran. Perhaps I was," answered Brega. The Dwarf fell silent, and just as Tuck thought he would learn no more, Brega spoke on: "Châkka believe that each spirit is reborn many times. And so, every Châk now alive, or those yet to be born, perhaps at one time walked the chambers of mighty Kraggen-cor."

Again long moments passed without speech, then Gildor broke the silence: "Once in my youth I strode through the halls of Drimmen-deeve, a journey I have long remembered, for the Black Deeves are mighty indeed."

"You have walked in Kgraggen-cor?" Brega was astonished.

Gildor nodded. "It was a trade mission from Lianion to Darda Galion, and the way across the Quadran Pass was blocked by winter snow. Through Drimmen-deeve we were allowed to pass, from Dusk-Door to Dawn-Gate, though we paid a stiff toll to do so, I recall. Yet the toll was less than the cost of faring south through Gûnar and north again through Valon. That was in the days when there was much trade between Trellinath, Harth, Gûnar, Lianion, and Drimmen-deeve."

Brega rocked back and looked long up at Gildor. "Lord Gildor," said the Dwarf at last, "if this Winter War ever comes to and end, you and I must have a long talk. Priceless knowledge of Kraggen-cor has been lost to my people, and you can tell us much."

Little else was said ere they bedded down while Gildor once more kept the watch. But though he was weary, Tuck found it difficult to fall asleep, for names whirled through his mind: *Kraggen-cor, Drimmen-deeve, Black Hole; Châkka, Drimma, Dwarves; Gargon, Modru's Dread, Lost Prison; Dusk-Door, Dawn-Gate, Grimwall; Quadran, Quadran Pass . . .*

It was this last name, Quadran Pass, that surfaced in Tuck's thoughts over and again, for none of the four comrades knew whether Rūcks or snow or the Gargon barred the way, or if they could get through. But on the morrow they would attempt to cross it, and Tuck fell asleep wondering what the morrow would bring.

As they broke camp, Galen set out their strategy: "Tuck, you will ride behind me, for the way before us is narrow and twisting, and so my eyes will serve during most of this passage, though where needed you will peer around me. We shall go first, Gildor with Brega to follow, leading the packhorse. Keep sword, axe, and arrow to hand.

"Should we come to snow blocking the way, we must turn and swiftly come back down, for a Horde force-marches behind us, and we must not become entrapped upon this mountain flank.

"Yet should the way be held by the Yrm, then we will try to slay them—if their force is small. In that case, Tuck, your bow may become all-important in striking down a sentry in silence and from a distance.

"If a larger force holds the way, we may try to burst through and flee down the far side. Yet, too, we may simply turn back without alerting them and come this way once more, again at haste to elude the Horde now at our heels.

"Should the Dread hold the way, we will know it by the terror in our hearts, and turn back ere we come unto him, for he is a foe we cannot face.

"And if we do not cross, then we will make south for Gûnar Slot and hope it is free of the enemy, as it was when Brega came north.

"But if neither snow nor Spawn nor the Gargon block the Quadran Pass, then we will make our way down the Quadran Run to the Pitch below, then east turning south for Darda Galion to warn them of the coming Horde.

"Is there aught that any would add to the plan?" Galen peered into the face of each.

How like his sire is Galen, thought Tuck, his mind returning to the War-council at Challerain Keep.

Brega spoke: "It will be a cold crossing, for not only is it winter, but this evil Winternight clutches the heights above. Were this the Crestan Pass, I think we would not survive; but it is the Quadran Pass, and it does not reach to the same heights. Yet we must be swift, else we'll not move again until a spring thaw." Brega turned and in vain his sight tried to pierce the Dimmendark to see the way upward. "It may be many a year ere a spring comes again unto this Land, for Modru intends to grasp it forever."

"Not if I can help it, Dwarf Brega," said Galen, his grey eyes resolute. "If it be in my power, these mountains shall once more feel the warm kiss of the Sun."

Gildor mounted Fleetfoot with Brega after, and Tuck swung up behind Galen. But just ere they spurred forward, Brega called, "King Galen, I have this moment remembered an eld Châkka tale: there is the story of a secret High Gate somewhere upon Rávenor's flank, a gate that opens into Quadran Pass, a gate that leads down into the halls of Kraggen-cor. It may be a fable, it may be true; but if this legend is so, and if the Ghath or Squam hold it, then they may issue out of it to assail us. Fact or fiction, I know nought else of this High Gate."

Galen paused and then said, "High Gate or no, still we must try," and spurred forward.

Up the slope of Quadran Road they pressed, Jet first, with Fleetfoot and the packhorse following. A league they went, and beyond, the way rising before them, and now Tuck's eyes could see mighty mountain flanks soaring upward into the Dimmendark. To his left was Stormhelm and to the right Grimspire, two of the four peaks of the Quadran. The Road itself was carven along Stormhelm's flank, and buttresses and groins of rust-red granite vaulted in massive tiers up Stormhelm's side, or fell away sheer, dropping down to meet the looming ramparts of dark Grimspire. Sheets of ice glazed the lofty pinnacles, and the Shadowlight glow glittered in the hoarfrost, giving the tall rocks a phosphorescent luminance. And up the twisting walls of the Quadran Road shuddered the echoes of knelling hooves as Man, Dwarf, Elf, and Warrow rode up through the Winternight.

Through defiles they rode, and upon ridges where crests had been carven flat and the shoulders of the road pitched steeply down to either side. Yet always upward the comrades went. In places they dismounted and led the horses to give them respite from bearing riders, but they walked a quickstep, for time was not their ally.

Miles passed—ten, fifteen, and more—and with each mile the air grew thinner and colder, and hoods were drawn over heads and cloaks were wrapped tightly around.

At last the path started down: Tuck could see it falling below them, down Stormhelm's eastern flank.

"Sire, the twisting way before us drops," said Tuck in jubilance. "I do believe that we have crested the brow of Quadran Pass."

Galen's voice came muffled by his cloak: "No guards as yet. But stranger still, no great depth of winter snow, only this shallow fall, and that hardly on the road."

Down they rode, with Tuck in deep thought. At last he spoke: "They say Modru is the Master of the Cold. Perhaps it is he who has kept the deep snow from these ways. But why?"

"You have it!" exclaimed Galen. "Without snow, his Horde can cross this gap to fall upon the Larkenwald. Now more than ever we must warn the Lian."

On they rode, descending along Quadran Run, as the eastern way was called. Beside the road fell a stream—also named the Quadran Run—now frozen in Winternight's icy clutch. They passed along ridges and through defiles and around tall spires as they descended, heading for the unseen Pitch below, a sloping valley hemmed by the four mountains of the Quadran.

Tuck leaned out to see the way, but for the most part stone walls and tall rocks blocked the view. Yet at times he could glimpse through the juts and spires to see the Run below.

It was at one of these places: "Hold, Sire!" Tuck urgently whispered, and slipped off the back of Jet.

The Warrow ran to a slot between two tall rocks and peered intently downward. Galen dismounted and came after.

"Ghûls," said Tuck, his voice bitter. "Twenty or thirty. Perhaps three miles downslope. They come this way riding Hèlsteeds."

"*Rach!*" swore Galen. "See you any place to hide?"

"Nay, Sire," Tuck answered after but a moment. "The way ahead is open ridge."

Galen's voice shook with frustration. "Then we must turn back ere they see us."

"But we've come such a long way!" cried Tuck.

"We have no choice!" spat Galen, then more gently: "Ah, Tuck, we have no choice."

Galen turned to Gildor and Brega astride standing Fleetfoot. "We must turn back: Ghola come this way."

Ire flashed in Brega's eye, and he unslung his axe and raised it on high. "Have we come all this way just to suffer the thwart of Modru's lackeys?"

"How many, Galen King?" asked Gildor.

"A score or more, says Tuck," answered Galen, remounting Jet and hoisting the Warrow up after.

Gildor turned to the Dwarf, saying, "Sling thy axe, Drimm Brega, for even thy vaunted prowess is overmatched by twenty of the corpse-folk."

Brega ground his teeth in rage, yet slung his axe as they started back the way they had come.

As they rode swiftly back up the Run, Tuck asked above the clack of hooves, "Sire, the Ghûls, why come they this way? Where have they been?"

"I know not," answered Galen over his shoulder. "Mayhap they are an advance party that came from the Horde down the far slope, and they return from the margins of the Larkenwald—returning to the Swarm to report what their foray has revealed."

The Horde! Tuck's heart pounded. *I had forgotten! And now we ride toward them!*

Back to the crest of the Pass they ran along the twisting Quadran Run, and they started down the western way, the way they had just toiled up. Tuck's eyes searched ever downard for sign of the Horde, glimpsing the way below as it shuttered by through slots among the rocks, at times getting long looks when they crossed open ridges. Always, too, he scanned for places to slip aside, to hide and let the Ghûls pass; yet there were no crevices nor canyons into which they could ride: the Quadran Road twisted down the flank of Stormhelm with no places to step from its stricture.

Down through the steep-walled defiles they went apace, coming ever lower on the margins of the mountain. Three hours they had ridden, and now the road began to level out as they came toward the flats.

"Sire, the Horde! I see it!" cried Tuck.

Boiling up through the foothills came the dark Swarm, and before it loped black Vulgs. Tuck threw a glance back the way they had come. Just at the limit of his jewel-hued vision along an open ridge rode the Ghûls. *Trapped!* Tuck's mind shouted. *A Swarm before us and Ghûls behind us!*

"When can we leave this road?" Galen's voice cut through Tuck's dismay.

"Wha—what?" Tuck found his tongue.

"When can we leave this road?" Galen repeated, his voice crackling with tension.

Tuck's eyes swept along the way ahead. "A mile or so!" he cried, his heart leaping with hope. "We can leave the way to the left, just where a ridge comes to a defile. We can ride up onto a plateau above. There is no path, yet we can escape the road!"

"I see it," declared Galen, urging Jet to greater speed. The black steed leapt forward and Fleetfoot sprang after, with the packhorse running behind.

Down the way they ran. Before them came the Rūcken Horde; behind them rode the Ghûls. Swiftly the comrades galloped out upon the ridge, thundering across, then bore up and left, off the road, up onto the plateau.

Galen immediately reined to a halt, throwing up a hand, stopping Lord Gildor. "Brega! Your axe!" Galen barked. "Cut bracken! Sweep our tracks from the snow!"

Brega leapt down and cut a winter-dried bush with his axe and ran back down to the rocky road. With great sweeping arcs, he obliterated their tracks, backing as he went. A hundred feet or more he came, nearing the horses, and at Galen's terse call, he dropped the bush and remounted Fleetfoot, and the horses leapt forth. South they bolted, away from the Quadran Road, through a blasted land, rough and boulder-strewn. And as they raced, Tuck looked back over his shoulder to see the Ghûls on Hèlsteeds cantering down one of the ridges toward the Horde force-marching upward.

When they had run two miles from the Quadran Road, Galen reined Jet to a walk, and Gildor slowed Fleetfoot and the packhorse, too, the lathered steeds blowing white from their nostrils, their lungs pumping.

"Ai, but that was close," called Gildor, whose eyes had also seen.

"We've slipped their trap," gloated Brega. But then his voice caught in his throat, and he stabbed a finger forward and rage flashed over his face. *"Kruk!"*

Tuck's head snapped 'round in the direction Brega pointed, and there in the Shadowlight padding out from behind a huge dark boulder trotted a black Vulg, one of the scouts of the Horde. The horses snorted and shied, the pack animal rearing in panic, trying to break free, but Brega held firm to the lead line. The dark Vulg's baleful yellow eyes glared at the four, and writhing jaws snarled. Then this evil outrunner raised his slavering muzzle to the Winternight sky and loosed a yawling cry. Again the black brute voiced a wrawl to the Swarm, a cry answered in kind by bone-chilling howls from other Vulgs, and Ghûls, too.

Tuck leapt down from skitting Jet and set an arrow to his bow and let fly as the Vulg gave vent to another ululating yowl, a cry that was chopped off in mid-howl as the true-sped arrow struck the black beast in the throat and it fell dead. Tuck spun to see Ghûls on Hèlsteeds burst over the ridge and up onto the plateau, snow flying from cloven hooves as they came in answer to the howling summons. Hurtling alongside raced black Vulgs, muzzles to the ground.

Tuck leapt to Jet's flank. "Quick, Sire, they come now on our track: Ghûls and Vulgs. They know we are here."

Galen hauled the Warrow up and spurred Jet forward, with Fleetfoot and the packhorse galloping after. And Tuck despaired, for he knew not how far they could fly, for the hard-running horses already were weary.

South they fled, across a snow-covered, broken land, south along a plateau caught between the looming flank of dark Grimspire to the east and a small mountain to the west: Redguard. And running on their trail behind came Ghûls on Hèlsteeds, and Vulgs with their snouts to the track.

Southward hammered the great black Jet with Fleetfoot's white stockings flashing after. Last of all scaddled the packhorse in tow, fleeing in panic from the chill Vulg howls. How long they had run, Tuck did not know, but slowly they gained ground on their pursuers, twisting through great rocks and spires, running across long, flat stretches.

Five or six miles they galloped, and gradually drew away. But then Tuck's heart plunged in despair, for Galen harshly reined Jet to a skidding halt on the brink of a great cliff falling sheer before them.

"Tuck!" barked Galen as Fleetfoot thundered up. "Use your eyes! Look for a way down!"

Tuck leapt to the snow and flung himself belly-down on the verge of the bluff, looking over the edge and down. He scanned left then right. *There! Just to the right and running past below!* "Sire! A long sloping path down the plumb face! Fifty paces westward!" Tuck started to stand, then groaned as he leapt to his feet. "Sire, ahead two miles or three, I think I see the brink of another drop like this one."

"Mount up, Tuck. We have no choice." Galen extended his hand, hauling Tuck up behind. "We'll plunge down that one when we get there, not before."

They spurred to the sloping path and turned and started down, and as they went below the level of the rim, Tuck's last sight of the upper plateau showed running Vulgs and Hèlsteeds.

The way down before them was narrow and icy, with sheer, frost-clad stone looming on the left and open space plunging perpendicularly to the right. Slowly, Jet picked his way down the treacherous course, and Tuck could hear Fleetfoot and the packhorse stepping behind. Tuck glanced down the fall but once, then kept his eyes firmly fixed upon Galen's back. The Warrow could feel Jet's hooves slip along the ice, and each time the steed lurched, so did Tuck's heart, pounding in fear. The descent seemed to drag on without end as slowly they crept downward. And above, back upon the plateau, loping Vulgs and Ghûls on Hèlsteeds came.

At last Jet reached the bottom of the cliff, coming out upon another plateau, with the other horses right behind, and once more they ran to the south. And as they hammered away, Tuck flung a glance back to see the great stone massif jutting upward; nearby, a great black vertical crack was riven in its face, and west of the cleft, silhouetted against the spectral Shadowlight sky, came Modru's creatures. And when the Ghûls saw the horses fleeing southward below, they set up a wild howling, for now they knew they pursued but four riders. One Ghûl's howl rose above the others, and they turned and made for the icy path, to work their way down after the quarry.

Swiftly south the four rode, the gap widening between hunters and hunted, for the Ghûls were slowed by the descent. Two miles south the horses ran, to come to another sheer drop. This time there was no sloping path.

"Sire! East! There seems to be a canyon that I can see coming out through the face below." Tuck leapt to his feet. "Perhaps it is a way down." Once more Galen pulled him back upon Jet.

East they ran, to come to a canyon at their feet so narrow that Tuck thought a horse could perhaps leap its width. They could not see its bottom, but it did breach the face of the massif that thwarted them.

Back to the north they ran, back toward the Ghûls, the horses racing along the rim of the cleft, seeking to find its entrance.

At last they came to where the narrow split emerged upon the plateau. A path led into the dark cranny.

"In we go!" cried Galen. "Else we are trapped along the rim wall."

"Hold!" Brega called. "I have a lantern. Follow us. I will light the way."

Tuck could see that the Ghûls had just reached the base of the distant cliff, and Vulgs loped across the flats.

Brega fumbled in his pack and drew forth a crystal-and-brass lantern, throwing the shutter wide; and without a flame being kindled at all, a blue-green phosphorescent light leapt forth. "Go!" Brega barked at Gildor, and Fleetfoot sprang forward into the dark slot, with Jet following the packhorse.

Down a narrow, twisting corridor they went, Brega's high-held lantern casting swaying, pendulous shadows among the rocks and boulders, and blue-green light glinted and bounced amid the great icicles hanging down from the ragged, shadowed stone overhead. The sound of blowing horses and the clatter of hooves reverberated along the broken walls and echoed back from dark holes boring away, their ends beyond seeing.

Tuck felt the black walls looming above him, and it seemed as if he could nearly reach out and touch the sides, spanning the width. He looked upward, and high above was a swatch of dim Shadowlight, jagging in a thin line, marking the rim of the narrow crevice they followed.

Downward they went, ever deeper, twisting along a tortuous path, at times scraping against the ice-clad rock, Gildor leading, Galen following, Brega's lantern showing the way.

At last Tuck's eyes saw a great vertical cleft filled with spectral Winternight glow, and he breathed a sigh of relief, for they had come to the end.

Out of the crack they rode, out into a broken hill country. "South we go, bearing west," called Galen as Brega shuttered the lantern and returned it to his pack. "We strike for the Old Rell Way. And if ever we elude the curs at our heels, we'll make for Gûnar Slot."

And on they ran, black Vulgs following the scent, Ghûls on Hèlsteeds after.

Fifteen more miles they went, south verging west, and the mounts were near to spent, for each was bearing double and the chase was long, with little or no respite. And behind them the hills blocked Tuck's view, and he could no longer see the pursuers; hence, he did not know the length of their lead.

"Galen King," called Gildor, "Fleetfoot begins to falter. We must do something to throw the Ghûlka off our track."

Galen signed that he had heard but did not otherwise reply, riding onward instead.

At last they came out of the hills to see the Old Rell Way before them, and they rode along its abandoned bed, finally coming to a fork: to the left was a cloven vale; to the right the road bore on southward. Here Galen reined Jet to a halt, and Gildor stopped Fleetfoot and the packhorse, and the steeds stood lathered and trembling.

"Tuck, Lord Gildor, retrieve your knapsacks from the packhorse," said Galen. "Fill them with provisions. Get grain sacks, too, for Jet and Fleetfoot.

"Brega, again use your axe to chop brush: three large bushes. I have one way we may escape."

While Brega cut the winter-dried brushwood, Galen, Gildor, and Tuck took provisions from the packhorse. Then, while Brega filled his own knapsack, Galen tied the brush close behind the two riding mounts by loops of rope, each horse with a large bush set to drag close upon its heels.

To the packhorse, though, he broke off and fastened a brushy limb above the pack cradle. Then, temporarily shedding his outerwear, he removed his sweat-soaked jerkin and tied it to a long rope so that it would trail along in the snow behind the animal.

"Lord Gildor, take up Jet's reins as well as Fleetfoot's," said Galen. "Hold them firmly; keep them calm. Here I turn the packhorse eastward into the valley. Brega, grasp his reins now. Tuck, your flint and steel: set some touchwood glowing. I am going to set this brushwood on his back afire."

"But, Sire," protested Tuck, "he will burn."

"Nay, Tuck, the cradle will protect him, though he will not think so," answered Galen. "He will bolt east into the vale, spreading my scent after, while we fare south, the brush we drag behind obscuring our tracks. Let us hope the Vulgs are fooled."

Tuck struck steel to flint, setting touchwood glowing, thinking, *Poor beast; yet we have little choice, and perhaps he, too, will escape the Vulgs in the end.* The Warrow handed the small tin of glowing shavings to Galen, who held it to the brush and blew it aflame. As the tinder-dry branch burst into flame, Jet and Fleetfoot pulled back, but Gildor held them firmly by the bit-straps. The packhorse, too, plunged and reared, and as the flame roared up, Brega loosed the reins and stepped aside as Galen cried, "Hai!" and slapped the horse on the rump.

Screaming in fear, the animal fled in panic, running full tilt to escape the flame riding the cradle on its back, and trailing in the snow behind was Galen's sweat-soaked jerkin. *But the horse wheeled and bolted south instead of running east!*

"Rach!" spat Galen.

"Sire, he drags your scent along our course!" cried Tuck, dismayed.

"Stupid horse," growled Brega. "Now it is *we* who are left with the eastern way. Let us ride into the valley and hide until the danger is past."

At the mention of danger, Tuck turned his sapphirine gaze back toward the foothills. "We must go quickly," he said bitterly, "for again I can see the foe coming along our track."

East they bore, into the valley, the brush dragging in the snow behind, obscuring their tracks. The slopes of the vale rose up around them, looming higher the farther east they went, till they rode in a deep-riven valley far below a distant rim. The floor of the vale curved this way and that, and the road they followed ran along the edge of a winding ravine, shallow and rocky and without water or ice, though a dusting of snow covered the dry streambed.

As they rode, Tuck saw Galen glance at the gentle slopes rising to either side, where the vale canted up finally to meet a wall that loomed sheer. Suddenly, Galen smote his forehead with a palm.

"Sire?" called the Warrow above the weary beat of hooves.

"Tuck, don't you see?" called Galen back. "We are

trapped. We should have ridden west out onto the open land and not east into this sheer-walled cleft, for here we cannot get out. And now it is too late to turn back. The packhorse should have bolted this way and not us, and I was distracted when he ran south, a lapse that may cost us our lives." Galen's voice was bitter.

"But, Sire, they will follow the scent of your shirt and not our scrubbed track," responded Tuck, though a shiver ran through him.

"Let us hope, Tuck," answered Galen. "Let us hope."

Tuck looked back along the twisting way, but he could no longer see the entrance to the valley, and he desperately hoped that their trick had deceived the Vulgs and Ghûls, and prayed that their wake was clear of those evil creatures.

On they rode eastward without speaking, and the only sounds made were the ragged thud of overweary hooves, the labored gasps of pumping lungs, and the scraggle of brush hauled behind.

How long they had fled, Tuck was not certain, yet both Jet and Fleetfoot had borne double to the limits of their endurance, and they were near to foundering.

Galen reined to a halt and dismounted, signing for Tuck to do the same. As the Warrow dropped to the snow, Fleetfoot stumbled to a halt behind, and Gildor and Brega leapt down, too.

Galen began walking east leading Jet, the horse trembling with each step, his breathing tortured, his flanks foamed with lather, and Tuck could have cried over the steed's agony. The Warrow looked back at Fleetfoot following, and Gildor's horse, too, had been ridden to his uttermost limits.

Of their pursuers Tuck could see nought, but the

way behind curved beyond seeing, and whether the Ghûls followed false trail or true, he could not say.

Galen looked at the valley around him, a puzzled frown upon his features. "Tuck, there is something strangely familiar about this vale: the road, the ravine to our right, the sheer rim. It is as if I should know it, though I have never been here, but from childhood a haunting memory gnaws, though I know not what it is."

They rounded a curve and stopped, for less than a mile before them was the head of the vale: a high stone cliff jumped up perpendicular from the valley floor; the spur of road they followed cut upward along the face of the bluff, to disappear over its top. Also carved in the stone of the face was a steep stairway leading up beyond the rim, up a pinnacle standing high above the bluff, up to a sentinel stand atop the spire overlooking the valley. And beyond the rampart and dwarfing it, looming out and arching over, was a great massif of Grimspire Mountain rising up into the Dimmendark.

Gildor and Brega came to their side. Brega spoke, his voice hushed: "It is as we suspected: this is Ragad Vale."

"Ai! Of course!" Galen slapped a palm to his forehead. "The Valley of the Door!"

"Valley of the Door?" Tuck asked. "What door?"

"Dusk-Door," answered Gildor. "The western entrance into Drimmen-deeve. Atop that bluff and carven in the wall of the Great Loom of Aevor stands the Dusk-Door: shut now for nearly five hundred years, though it stood open for five hundred before that, left ajar by the Drimma as they fled from the Dread, loosed at last from the Lost Prison and stalking through their domain."

"I must see it now that I am here," said Brega.

Forward they started, following the abandoned road, and while they went, Brega spoke: "There on that pinnacle is the Sentinel Stand, where Châkka warders of old stood watching o'er the vale. Down the bluff, water once fell in a graceful falls—Sentinel Falls—fed by the Duskrill, the stream said to have carven this very valley.

"This road we follow is the Rell Spur, a tradeway of old, abandoned when the Gargon came to rule Kraggen-cor.

"If the tales be true, the Dusken Door itself stands within a great portico against the Loom, on a marble courtyard surrounded by a moat with drawbridge.

"Long have my eyes wanted to see this Land, yet I had hoped it would be when the Châkka came to make of it a mighty Realm as of old, and not as a fugitive fleeing vile foe."

"The Dusk-Door," said Galen, "it is told in the old tales that it opened by word alone. Is that true?"

"Aye," answered Brega, "if the word be spoken by a Châk whose hand presses upon the Door—at least Châkka lore would have it so."

"The Lian say that the Wizard Grevan helped in its crafting," said Gildor.

"With Gatemaster Valki he made it," said Brega.

"Do you know the lore words that cause it to open?" asked Tuck, his great tilted eyes wide with wonder.

"Aye, they are with me," answered Brega, "for my grandsire was a Gatemaster, and he taught them to me. But I followed the trade of my own sire, Bekki, and chose to be a warrior instead. Yet, even though I know the lore, I would not open that Door for all the starsilver in Kraggen-cor, for behind it dwells the Ghath."

Leading the steeds, they came to where the road turned up the face of the bluff, the way free of snow. They stopped long enough to discard the brush they had dragged behind the horses, for it was no longer needed. The comrades then started upward, both horses quivering at each step with the effort of mounting up the slope.

"The steeds are spent," said Galen, his voice filled with regret. "What evil fortune, for until they have rested long—a week or more—feeding upon grain and pure water to restore their strength, we cannot ride."

"But then, how will we fare south?" asked Tuck.

Brega gave a terse answer: "Walk."

"No, I mean our plans to hie to the Host and lead them against Modru will be delayed greatly," protested Tuck, "just as our plans to warn the Lian in Larkenwald of the marching Horde are dashed. How can we recover from this ill fortune that has befallen us?"

"I know not," said Galen, wear in his manner.

Gildor spoke: "Wee One, our plans to warn Darda Galion and to fare swiftly south may be dashed, as you say, yet though we do not know our course, still we must strive and not abandon hope."

All fell silent as they trudge onward.

Up the slope of the road along the bluff they went, at last topping the rise. Above them, hovering over, was the great natural hemidome of the Loomwall, and within its cavernous embrace lay a long, thin black lakelet, no more than three furlongs across, and, from the north end where they stood, Tuck saw that it ran nearly two and a half miles to the south. The lake was made by a dam of great stones wedged in a wall across the ravine atop the Stair Falls. The Rell Spur they followed disappeared into the ebon waters.

"This black tarn should not be here!" cried Brega.

"It is the Dark Mere," said Gildor, "and the Lian tell that something evil dwells within. What, I cannot say, but stay wide of its shore."

"Ai-oi! Here's a riddle!" exclaimed Galen. "Why is not this lake frozen?"

Tuck realized that Galen had indeed pointed out an enigma: except for a narrow rim of thin ice embracing the shoulders here and there, the black waters of the Dark Mere undulated torpidly, *As if pulsing with evil,* thought Tuck.

"Perhaps it is not frozen because it is sheltered by the Loom," said Brega, eyeing the great vault of stone above.

"Perhaps it is not frozen because Modru does not want it to be," responded Gildor. "Just as the Quadran Pass held no snow, this Dark Mere, too, escapes the clutch of deep Winternight. Mayhap it does not suit Modru's purposes to have it otherwise, and he *is* Master of the Cold."

"What purpose could he have to keep this lakelet free of ice?" growled Brega, but none could give him the answer.

"It is so *black,*" said Tuck.

"Even were there sunlight, it would look so," said Gildor. "Some say it is because it lies under the black granite of the Loomwall above; others say it is because the Dark Mere is evil."

Tuck looked up at the Great Loom arching cavern-like hundreds of feet overhead. Then his eyes roamed the distant shoreline. "So ho! Over there against the Loom I see tall white columns holding up a great roof."

"It is the portico of the Dusk-Door," said Brega, his eyes following Tuck's pointing finger. "Lying before it should be a marble courtyard, bounded by the Dusk-Moat fed by the Duskrill. Yet they are flooded by this Dark Mere. But see, there endures the ancient drawbridge, standing open above where the moat should have been. There, too, is the Rell Spur, where it runs along the base of the Loom. But all else is drowned in blackness." Brega's voice was filled with rage over the desecration of the environs by the Dark Mere.

"Perhaps—" Galen started to say, but his words were interrupted by a long, chilling, Vulg howl echoing up Ragad Vale. Jet and Fleetfoot jerked their weary heads up, and their ears stood listening.

"Vulgs!" cried Brega. "In the Vale!"

Tuck's heart pounded, he spun and looked down the valley, but he could see nought 'round its curves. "The Sentinel Stand!" he cried, and ran for the stone steps some two furlongs to the south.

Huffing with effort, up the steps he scrambled to the top of the spire, and he could see past the curves and down the valley before him: Ghûls with torches rode slowly toward the head of the Vale, searching out the crevices and shadows where fugitives might hide, while Vulgs with their snouts to the snow slow-stepped along the faint scent-trail obscured by the dragged brush.

Back down the steps Tuck scuttled, down to the others, now waiting below. "Ghûls! Vulgs, too! They comb the Vale, seeking where we hide. They are spread wide, blocking the width of the valley."

"Yet we cannot burst past them," gritted Galen, "for Jet and Fleetfoot can bear no more."

"If we can get across the old moat," said Brega, "we can hide on the portico."

"But the drawbridge is up!" cried Tuck. "We cannot float through the air!"

"Do not abandon hope until we look," said Gildor, his voice sharp.

"Aye," added Galen, "cross no bridge until it stands before you; burn no bridge if you would go back."

"Let's go, then," chafed Tuck, "though I fear we will have burned all of our bridges behind us when we come to the one before."

North they ran, drawing the horses behind, around the end of the Mere, crossing through a shallow, muck-bottomed seep. Now the stone of the Loom arched above them, and Tuck felt as if he could almost hear the weight of the rock groaning overhead.

South they turned and swiftly they went alongside the dark granite wall, perhaps a half mile before coming to a sundered causeway where the Rell Spur emerged from the black waters of the Dark Mere. The pave of the Spur was riven with age, and they wended through the upheaved rocks south toward the portico, the Loom to their left and the Mere to their right but a few paces away.

Three furlongs more they pressed, coming at last to a great drawbridge made of massive wooden timbers. Out upon the span they strode, their steps ringing hollowly, and the waters of the Dark Mere lapped less than a yard below. But they had to stop short, for the bascule was up, and open water undulated before them.

And from Ragad Vale came the howl of a Vulg.

"When the Châkka fled Kraggen-cor, the span was left down," growled Brega. "Now it is up."

Gildor began stripping his outer garments, handing over Bale sword and Bane long-knife to Tuck. "It was raised by *Rûpt*," said the Elf. "If we survive, I will tell you the tale. But now I will swim to the far side and try to lower the bascule."

"But the ropes are made untrustworthy by age," protested Brega.

"I do not see we have a choice," said Gildor, now clothed only in breeks.

Incongruously, Tuck thought, *He goes without armor!* for no mail nor plate had the Elf taken off, not even a steel helm.

"Take care," said Tuck, sensing danger, though he knew not why.

With a flat dive, Gildor plunged into the frigid dark waters. Swiftly he stroked across the gap, no more than twenty yards wide. But as he clambered up a stone pier and onto the far span, a great swirl twisted in the water at his feet, as if something huge had passed near under the black surface, and Tuck gasped in fear; but the waves and ripples quickly died away, and the undulate surface pulsed slowly again.

Gildor grasped hold of the ancient halyards controlling the bascule, and they were stiff with age. Looking up, he shook them, and dust flew from the pulley blocks atop the anchor posts. Then with a grimace of effort, the Elf hauled against the lines. And with the pulleys squealing in protest and the great bridge axle groaning, slowly the bascule began canting down from vertical.

"Once we're across, we'll pull it back up," said Brega. "Then if the foe finds us, still they wifl not be able to get at us unless they swim." Brega thumbed his axe. "Easy prey."

Slowly, down tilted the protesting span, descending toward the mooring pier. Halfway it had come, and just as Tuck was beginning to breathe easier, with a dull snap, the ancient rope haul broke. Squealing and groaning, the massive bascule rushed down faster and faster to slam to with a thunderous, juddering *BOOM!* that rolled forth from the hemidome of the Great Loom to reverberate down the length of Ragad Vale:

BOOM! Boom! boom! boom . . . oom . . .

As the dinning echoes crashed along the walls of the valley, Galen shouted, " Swift!" and bolted across the span hauling the frightened horses behind, with Brega and Tuck running after.

And from the Vale came shuddering howls of Vulgs and Ghûls, now in full cry.

Over the downed bascule ran the trio, Brega last, for he had paused to scoop up Gildor's pack and clothing.

"Can the haul be repaired?" Galen's question shot forth, directed at Gildor, but the Elf handed the frayed end of the rope to Brega, taking his clothes in return.

The Dwarf looked at the ancient halyard fiber and then up to the pulley blocks chained to the anchor posts. "Nay, King Galen, not in time."

"Sire!" cried Tuck, pointing.

Along the Rell Spur over the lip of the butte loped black Vulgs, their snouts to the ground. The lead Vulg turned, making for the spire of the Sentinel Stand, following the scent of their prey.

"The Ghûls can't be far behind." Tuck's voice trembled and his heart pounded.

Brega hefted his axe. "Shall we defend the bridge or the portico, King Galen?"

"The portico, I think," said Galen, his voice grim but steady. "They cannot bring the Hèlsteeds to bear down upon us between the great stone columns."

Gildor tugged his last boot on and leapt to his feet fully dressed. Tuck handed over the sword, Bale, but as Gildor buckled on the blade, he said to the Waerling, "Keep Bane as your own weapon, Tuck, for the long-knife will be as a sword to you, and in this fight there will come a time when your arrows will be spent, or the quarters will be too close for bow, and then you will need a blade."

"But I know nothing of swordplay, Lord Gildor," protested Tuck, yet the Elf would hear nought of his agument, and the Waerling girted Bane to his waist and drew the long-knife from its sheath. Blue werelight burst forth from Bane's blade-jewel and ran a bright cobalt flame down the sharp edges.

"Bane's light speaks of evil nearby," said Gildor. "Yet the Vulgs are still distant, and the Ghûlka farther yet, and the blade should not glow with this intensity." Gildor drew Bale, and its red light, too, was flame-bright; and the Elf frowned in concentration: "They both whisper that evil is nearer."

At Gildor's words, Tuck's eye was drawn irresistibly to the black waters of the Dark Mere.

"Ar, we can't stand here all day puzzling over the fine points of Elven blades," growled Brega. "Let us to the portico to make our stand, and though we may not survive, this will be a battle the bards will sing of if word of it comes their way."

Tuck and Gildor sheathed the blades and the four comrades ran to the great portico, drawing the horses behind, following along the Loomwall. Through fluted columns they went, to come upon a great semicircular stone slab held within the half ring of pillars around. Above, a great carven edifice was supported. As they discarded their packs, Tuck looked out upon the dark waters covering the sunken courtyard where stood the clawing hulk of an enormous tree, drowned, dead for ages, yet still anchored upright. Black water lapped at the steps rising up from the unseen flooded court.

"They come," said Gildor softly, pointing back toward the far side of the lake.

Torch-bearing Ghûls on Hèlsteeds burst over the rim of the bluff and cast about, questing for the fugitives. The Vulg pack loped north from the Sentinel Stand, still on the scent. The Ghûlen leader howled at the dark brutes, and growls from the beasts answered him.

Along the north bank of the Dark Mere the Vulgs raced, on the wake of the hunted, and the hammer of cloven Hèlsteed hooves shocked along the Loomwall as the Ghûls plunged after.

Around the north end of the lake they came, and the four comrades looked on grimly. Brega grasped his double-bitted axe in the Dwarven two-handed battle-grip, and Gildor drew Red Bale, while Galen held Jarriel's gleaming steel in his right hand and in his left the rune-marked silvery Atalar Blade from the tomb of Othran the Seer. Tuck readied his bow and stepped to a pillar, taking a stand where his arrows would fly unhindered.

Now the Ghûls turned southward, riding along the Loom, plunging straight toward the sundered causeway and, beyond, the bridge and portico.

Yet, of a sudden the Ghûlen leader howled and savagely reined his Hèlsteed to a halt, and behind, the other Hèlsteeds were cruelly checked.

"What's this?" growled Brega, stepping forward for a better look.

The Ghûls had ridden to the causeway but no further, and now they milled in seeming confusion, as if unwilling to ride its length to get at the four. Some called glottal commands at the Vulgs, and the black beasts stopped, too, and turned and slunk back to sit on their haunches, tongues lolling over slavering, fanged jaws, but they came no closer. Ghûls dismounted.

"What's this?" growled Brega again. "Can they be afraid of us? We are but four while they are thirty."

The four comrades looked long at the Ghûls and Vulgs, yet no clue came as to what halted their charge.

"I know not why they stopped," said Gildor, "but as long as they stand there athwart our path, we are trapped here."

"No we are not, Lord Gildor," Tuck spoke up. "We can always go through the Dusk-Door."

"The Dusk-Door!" exclaimed Galen. "I had forgotten! Tuck is right! We *can* escape the Ghola!"

"Out of the crucible and into the forge your plan would lead us!" cried Brega. "Do you forget, King Galen, that the Ghath rules Kraggen-cor?"

"Nay, Brega," answered Galen, "I forget it not, but this I propose: We will enter the Dusk-Door and close it behind, and the Ghola will think we seek to make our way under the Grimwall and out the Dawn-Gate.

Yet we will wait to see if they leave; if so, then back out we go and south to Gûnarring Gap."

"But what if they don't leave?" blurted Tuck. "Then what?"

"Then we are no worse off than we are now," answered Gildor.

"But, I mean, why can't we do as Galen King has suggested?" asked Tuck. "Why *can't* we go under the Grimwall?"

"You know not what you ask, Wee One," answered Gildor. "Better would it be to face a hundred Ghûlka than but one Gargon. Were it just the *Rûpt* that dwell in Drimmen-deeve that we had to win past, then I would counsel that we try it; but it is their master I would not face. Nay, if we use the Door it will be to deceive the Ghûlka, and not to tread through the Black Deeves."

"Well, then, where *is* the Door anyway?" asked Tuck, his eyes searching the blank stone of the Loom. "Though I cannot see it, it must be here somewhere."

"There," said Brega, pointing, yet still Tuck saw nought but frowning rock. "There where the pave is worn leading up to it," Brega continued. "It is closed and cannot be seen, though when the Châkka abandoned Kraggen-cor, we left it ajar."

"*Spaunen* closed it," said Gildor, "five hundred years after the Drimma fled. But that, too, is a long tale to be told later, for now we are concerned with Galen King's plan."

"I like not this plan," growled Brega, "this game of cat and mouse, for it is one where we chance the Ghath; yet I have none better."

"Are we agreed then?" asked Galen, and at each one's nod: "Then let it be done."

Brega slung his axe across his back by its carrying thong and stepped to the Loom and placed his hands firmly upon the blank stone; and he muttered low, guttural words. And springing forth from where his hands pressed, *as if it grew from the Dwarf's very fingers,* there spread outward upon the dark granite a silver tracery that shone brightly in the shadow. And as it grew it took form. *And suddenly there was the Door!*— its outline shimmering on the smooth stone.

Sensing something amiss, Tuck glanced up at Gildor, and the Lian was pale and trembling. Sweat beaded on his brow. Only Tuck seemed to note it, and he asked the Elf, "What is wrong, Lord Gildor?"

"I know not, Tuck," answered the Lian warrior, "but something terribly evil . . . afar . . ."

Brega stepped back and unslung his axe. "Ready your weapons," Brega said, his voice hoarse, and Gildor and Galen gripped their blades while Tuck hastily shouldered his bow and drew the long-knife. Bale's red light blended with Bane's blue, while Galen held gleaming steel and the blade of Atala.

Brega turned back to the Door and placed a hand within the one glowing rune-circle, and he called out the Wizard word of opening: *"Gaard!"*

The glowing Wizard-metal tracery flared up brightly, and then, *as if being drawn back into Brega's hand,* all the lines, sigils, and glyphs began to retract, fading in sparkles as they withdrew, until once again the dark granite was blank and stern. And Brega stepped back away. And slowly the stone seemed to split in twain as two great doors appeared and silently swung outward to come to rest against the Great Loom. A dark opening yawned before them, and they could see the beginnings of the West Hall receding into darkness;

to the right a steep stairwell mounted up into the black shadows.

Tuck's heart was pounding furiously as he stared into the empty silence yawning before them, and his knuckles were white upon blue-flaming Bane's hilt.

And from behind came shattering screams!

The four whirled to see great, slimy tentacles writhing out of the black water, grasping the struggling, screaming horses, drawing them toward the foul waters.

"Kraken!" cried Galen.

"Madûk!" shouted Brega.

"Fleetfoot!" Gildor sprang forward, Bale blazing, but ere he could bring the sword to bear: "*Vanidor!*" he cried, and dropped to his knees as if stunned, his face in his hands, Bale falling from his nerveless fingers, the blade ringing upon the stone. "*Vanidor!*" Again he cried his brother's name in anguish, and a ropy tendril whipped around the stricken Elf and drew him toward the Dark Mere. Galen leapt forward and brought his sword down upon the great arm, but the blade did not cut. Once more Galen hacked down to no avail. Then he chopped the rune-marked Atalar long-knife into the tentacle, and the silvery weapon from Othran's barrow cut a great gash in the Kraken's flesh where the sword blade had been turned back.

Gildor was flung aside unconscious as the wounded tentacle was jerked back into the black waters. The screaming horses, too, were savagely wrenched under the ebon surface, and other arms boiled forth to rage and whip and grasp at the four.

Brega leapt forward to pull stunned Gildor back,

while Tuck scooped up the red-blazing Elven blade and darted for the portal.

"The packs!" cried Galen, catching up one and then another while Brega hauled Gildor through the Dusk-Door.

Tuck dashed back, dodging through whipping arms, and grabbed up the other two packs, but he was slapped down by a glancing blow as he tried again for the portal. Scrambling and scuttling, he scurried toward the Door on all fours, packs, bow, Bane, and Bale in his possession. Galen came behind and boosted the Warrow to his feet, and they stumbled forward through the portal and into the West Hall.

The enraged Monster lashed at them, and pounded at the Door with a great stone, and wrenched at the gates. The great dead tree was rent from the Mere and hammered at the portal, its limbs to shatter in the lashing; and deadly, jagged, flying bolts of wood hurtled into the chamber, to scud across the floor or to smash to shivers upon the stone. And great tentacles twined around the pillars and wrenched back and forth.

"The chain! The chain!" cried Brega, leaping to a great iron chain dangling down from the darkness above. "We must close the gates, else they will be rent from their hinges!"

Tuck and Galen leapt forward, and the three hauled upon the great iron links trying to close the Dusk-Door, but the strength of the raging Kraken opposed them and was too much to overcome. And writhing tentacles whipped and groped within the portal to seek them out.

Into this nest of snakes Brega leapt and slapped his hand against one of the great hinges and cried, *"Gaard!"* leaping back to avoid the Monster's clutch. And slowly, the shuddering doors began to grind shut, responding to the Wizard word, and all the while, the creature hammered at the gates and struggled to rend them open, yet still they slowly groaned toward one another. And as the protesting gates swung to, Brega's last sight through the portal was of the creature wrenching at one of the great columns of the edifice, grinding it away from its base. And then the gates swung to and Brega saw no more.

The Kraken loosed the Door just as it closed—*Boom!*—and the four were shut in the pitch blackness of dark Drimmen-deeve.

"My pack," Brega panted. "Where is my pack?" Tuck heard him fumbling in the darkness. "The lantern. We need light," muttered the Dwarf.

Tuck took his flint and steel from his jerkin and struck a spark. In the flash he saw the other three, frozen by the brief glint.

"Again," said Brega.

Once more Tuck struck steel to flint, and again and again. Each time the spark showed a different frozen scene as Brega made for his knapsack.

The soft blue-green phosphorescent glow bathed the four as Brega unshuttered his lantern. Gildor was now sitting up, his features white and drawn as if he were in pain or grief.

A loud crashing rumble sounded through the Door.

"Wha—?" cried Tuck.

"The edifice," answered Brega. "The Madûk in its fury has torn down the columns. It has collapsed."

Boom! Boom! Boom! A thunderous whelming sounded.

"The Hèlarms hurls stone at the Door in rage now,"

said Gildor, "for you have thwarted him, cheated him of his victims."

"Brega, can you try to open the doors again?" Galen looked grim. *Boom! Boom!*

"Aye, King Galen, *but why*? There is a mad Monster waiting to crush us on the other side." Brega was dumbfounded by Galen's request. *Boom! Boom! Boom!*

"Because we may be trapped, Brega," answered Galen. "And Modru's Dread dwells in our prison."

Brega's face blenched, and grimly he went to the Door. *Boom! Boom!* Once more he put his hand to one of the strange, massive hinges and muttered words, and after a moment he cried, *"Gaard!"* But nought seemed to happen, though Brega held his hand to the portal and said, "It trembles, but whether from trying to open or from the fearful pounding, I cannot say. The hinges now may be broken or the Door may be blocked, but it opens not." *Boom! Boom! Boom!* Once more Brega placed his hand on the hinge. *"Gaard!"* he barked, revoking the command to open.

"Did I not say, 'I do not like this plan'? And now we are trapped. We cannot get out." Brega's voice was bitter. "We cannot get out." *Boom! Boom!*

"Except perhaps through the Dawn-Gate," Galen said grimly.

"But that is on the other side of the Grimwall!" cried Brega. "And I do not know the way."

"Gildor has strode it," said Tuck.

"That was long ago, and but once," answered Gildor, holding a hand to his chest and breathing slowly. But Tuck could sense that the Elf suffered a distress beyond that of punished ribs, and the Warrow wondered at Gildor crying out his twin brother's name, *"Vanidor!"*

Boom!

"Yet we have no other choice," said Galen. "We now must try to pierce the length of the Black Hole and escape through the Dawn-Gate, for the Dusk-Door is closed to us. And we must be out and away ere the Ghola can ride over the Quadran Pass and carry word of us to the Gargon, else that evil Vûlk will seek us out." *Boom! Boom!*

"What you say is true," said Gildor, groaning to his feet and retrieving Bane and Red Bale from under the packs where Tuck had dropped them. Handing the blazing long-knife to the buccan, the Elf sheathed his own scarlet-flaming sword, saying, "We must attempt to go through, and quickly. In this we have no choice." *Boom!*

And so the four shouldered their packs, and, after some thought, Gildor led them up the stairs, Brega at his side holding high the lamp, with Tuck and Galen coming after.

Into Black Drimmen-deeve they strode, into the halls of the Dread, while behind them knelling down the ebon corridors the enraged pounding went on: *Boom! Boom! Boom!*

CHAPTER 3
THE STRUGGLES

Out through the sundered north gate of Challerain Keep fled the pony bearing double, past struggling Men and Ghûls, beyond screaming horses and grunting Hèlsteeds, away from the ring and skirl of steel upon steel and the howls of ravers and the cries of death. And Danner clasped Patrel tightly around the waist as west they galloped under the shadow of the first wall, turning across the foregate flats and bolting up and into the foothills.

On the slopes of a low hill they stopped and watched the battle boil out of the gate, raging in fury. Clots of struggling Men broke free only to be engaged again, and many fell dead unto the snow.

"Have you any arrows?" asked Patrel.

"None," answered Danner. "I spent my last when I slew Snake-Voice."

"Weaponless, we cannot rejoin the combat"—Patrel's voice was grim—"for then we would be a hindrance rather than a help."

They dismounted and looked down upon the seething battle: Patrel squatted before the pony, his gaze intent; Danner stood and glared, clenching and unclenching his fists.

This way and that the fighting raged, a swirling chaotic mêlée of riving swords and thrusting spears along the edge of a ravine. Helms were sundered and mail was pierced, and cries rang out through the air. Men fell dead, and Ghûls, too, and now and then a Warrow. Horses ran free, unchecked by their fallen riders, and at times ponies fled alone.

And Danner stomped back and forth in the snow, his teeth grinding in fury, his smoldering amber eyes never looking away, while Patrel squatted impassively, his viridian gaze glinting.

Suddenly Patrel sprang to his feet. "The King!" he cried, pointing to where combat swirled around gray Wildwind.

Aurion Redeye was surrounded and he smote mightily with his sword. Ghûls fell dead, skulls cloven, beheaded, yet others pressed inward, one to hurl a lance that pierced the King through. Still Aurion hewed and smote, and two more foe fell slain. Into the clot charged the Elf Lord Gildor, his blazing red sword slashing, a flaming blue long-knife fending tulwar strikes. To Aurion's side he rived a path, and the Ghûls quailed back before the werelight of the two Elven blades. For a moment they faced the foe—warrior Elf and spear-pierced King confronting raver Ghûls—and neither side moved; but then Aurion slumped forward upon the back of Wildwind, and the howling Ghûls turned and spurred away.

Danner stood stock still, his face gone cold, his eyes auric ice, while Patrel now paced in fury, green fire in his gaze. And then they both stood without moving as they watched Lord Gildor ride away from the battleground leading Wildwind; when he was clear of the mêlée, the Elf dismounted and lowered Aurion to the ground and after a moment composed the King's hands across his breast and laid his sword beside him.

"Aurion Redeye is dead," said Danner, his voice flat and emotionless, while Patrel turned his face away, his emerald eyes full of tears.

"Hai, look!" called Danner. "Vidron breaks away!"

Patrel turned to see a force of Men burst free at last, led by silver-bearded Vidron: horses running east, Ghûls in hot pursuit. Gildor, too, spurred forth, Wildwind in tow, swinging wide to pass outside the pursuing Ghûls, Fleetfoot's swift strides racing around and beyond the Hèlsteeds' hammering pace.

Rūcks and Hlōks boiled out of the north gate, as well as an Ogru or two, and began looting the bodies of the slain. Ghûls, too, there were, standing athwart the path taken by the fleeing Men.

"They block our way," gritted Danner. "Now we cannot follow without a detour."

"The rendezvous is at the Battle Downs," said Patrel. "We'll circle west and go down the Post Road."

Again they mounted Patrel's pie-faced pony, Danner behind, and made their way into the Shadowlight covering the foothills clutched unto Mont Challerain.

"Did you see aught of other Warrows who broke free?" asked Patrel.

"No," grunted Danner. "Neither afoot nor on pony nor astride horse behind Man."

"Only eight of us made it to the north gate," said Patrel. "And I saw two, no . . . three, fall after that, though I am not sure who they were. Sandy, perhaps, but who else I cannot say."

"Tuck?" Danner's voice nearly choked.

"I don't know, Danner," answered Patrel. "It could have been Tuck, but I just can't say. Listen, Danner, we've got to face the fact that we may be the last of the Company of the King. No one else may have survived."

They rode in silence for a while. "We'll find out at the rendezvous whether or not any other Thornwalkers came through," said Danner at last.

Onward they went, winding through the slopes.

"Look!" cried Patrel, pointing. Ahead in the vale before them stood a white pony, saddled and bridled—one of those ridden by the Warrows.

"Go easy," said Danner, "for he still may be spooked by the battle, or the stench of Hèlsteeds."

Slowly they rode down to the small steed, and Patrel's pie-faced pony whickered, and the white came trotting, as if glad to see another pony, and the Warrows, too.

Danner dismounted and, cooing, took up the reins, inspecting the white for battle wounds. "She's unscathed," said the buccan after a pause, then: "Looks like Teddy's pony, though it could be Sandy's white."

"No more, Danner, no more," responded Patrel. "Whoever had her before, she's now yours to ride."

Danner mounted and on they went, swinging southward now, edging through the hills.

Twenty miles they rode before making camp in a thicket on a rolling slope upon the plains south of Mont Challerain. Crue they had in their saddlebags, but no grain for the steeds. Danner dug under the snow and found quantities of prairie grass, still nourishing to the ponies, for Modru's early winter had preserved it.

At last they rebandaged Patrel's wounded hand, the

left one, cut shallowly by an enemy blade at the battle for the fourth wall. "Let us hope that edge was not poisoned," grunted Danner.

Patrel took the first watch and Danner bedded down in the cold; they had made no fire, for they were yet too near the enemy.

Danner had not slept long when he was awakened by Patrel: "A rider bears south out upon the plains to the west of us."

They stood at the edge of the thicket and watched as the far black steed hammered past through the Shadowlight, a mile or so to the west.

"Hoy!" exclaimed Danner. "I think that's a horse, not a Hèlsteed. And look, mounted before! Is that another rider? A Warrow?"

Danner sprang forth from the thicket. "Hiyo!" he cried, waving his arms, but the distant courser hammered on, and ere he could call out again: "Danner!" barked Patrel. "Hail not! For even if it is a horse, and I think you are right, still we know not what other ears may hear your shout—and we are without weapons."

Reluctantly, Danner held his call, for Patrel was right; and they watched the black steed drive onward into the Dimmendark, to disappear at last in the distant Shadowlight.

South they bore, two more 'Darkdays, heading for the Battle Downs, though neither knew just where they should ride, for as Patrel put it: "The Battle Downs is a wide place, easily fifty miles broad and more than a hundred long. An army could be lost in there. How we'll find the remnants of the force from the Keep, I cannot say, yet they'll need our eyes to guide them if no other Warrows have escaped at their side."

"We'll go on to Stonehill, then," said Danner. "That was the next rendezvous point."

And so southward they rode.

The next 'Darkday, as they broke camp, Patrel said, "If my reckoning is correct, it is the last day of December, Year's End Day. Tomorrow is Twelfth Yule."

"Ar, I don't think we'll be doing any celebrating tonight," responded Danner, "even though the old year dies and the new one begins." Danner looked about. "Never in my wildest dreams did I ever envision spending a Year's End Day like this: weary, hungry, half frozen, and fleeing weaponless from a teeming foe through a dismal murk sent by an evil power living in an iron tower in the Wastes of Gron."

Patrel finished cinching the saddle on his pony and turned to Danner. "Tell me, Danner," said the diminutive buccan, "what are you going to do next year when things *really* get bad?"

Flabbergasted, his mouth agape, Danner stared at Patrel. Then gales of laughter burst forth long and hard, Patrel whooping and shrieking, Danner doubled over holding his sides, his shouting guffaws ringing out across the plains. The ponies turned their heads back toward the whooping Warrows and cocked an eye and an ear, and this set Danner to laughing even harder, and he pointed and fell backwards in the snow, while Patrel looked and dropped to his knees, tears running down his face.

Long they laughed, gales bursting out anew, and Danner walked on his knees through the snow and threw his arms about Patrel and hugged him and laughed. At last, wiping their eyes with the heels of their hands, they both stood and mounted up and headed southward once more. Each rode with a great smile on his face and now and again would explode into a fit of giggles or great belly laughs to be joined by the other; and weary and hungry and half frozen, they fled weaponless from a teeming foe through a dismal murk sent by an evil power in an iron tower in the Wastes of Gron—and they laughed.

They had ridden nearly ten miles along the Post Road, wending along the northern margins of the Battle Downs, when they came upon the ravaged waggon train, and the carnage appalled them.

"This is Laurelin's caravan," grated Danner, his fists clenched knuckle-white as they strode past the victims.

Down one side of the train they went and back up the other, searching for survivors, but there were only the frozen corpses of the slain.

"Oi! Look here," said Patrel, kneeling in the snow. "A wide track beats east, cloven hooves: Hèlsteeds."

"Ghûls!" spat Danner, and then as if to confirm it, they saw the slain body of one of the corpse-people, head cloven in twain by sword. "How old is the track?"

"That I cannot judge," answered Patrel. "At least five 'Darkdays, perhaps seven or more."

"Wait," said Danner, "this train left the Keep on First Yule and this is Eleventh Yule. They couldn't have gotten here before late Fourth Yule even if they raced south, nor would they have dallied to pass here after Seventh Yule."

"That would make it six 'Darkdays old, then," said Patrel, "give or take a day."

On they pressed, back along the train, looking into the wains and at the faces of the slain.

"She's missing," gritted Danner. "Prince Igon, too."

"Either they got away or are hostage," responded Patrel. "If they escaped, they've most likely headed south; if hostage . . ." Patrel pointed east along the Ghûlen wake.

Danner angrily smacked fist into palm. "Ponies can't catch Hèlsteeds." His voice was filled with frustration.

"Even if they could," said Patrel, "the Ghûls have got an insurmountable lead on us, and who knows where they're bound? Besides, we know not whether Laurelin or Igon are hostage. Perhaps they escaped."

Danner stood in brooding thought. Without warning, he shouted out a wordless cry of wrath. "Ar, what evil choices!" he spat, and then visibly tried to gather in his emotions. At last he grated, "You are right, Patrel, they ride Hèlsteeds, not ponies, and a six-day lead could as well be sixty for all we could do to catch them, whether or not the two are captive. Let us press on for Stonehill; when we tell this tale, Vidron or Gildor will lead fleet horses in pursuit of the Ghûls if need be—if there is still a chance, though I think it will have gone aglimmering."

Patrel nodded. "Let us find some arrows, and grain, and perhaps other supplies from this whelmed caravan. Then will we push for Stonehill."

An hour later, west they went following along the Post Road, leaving the butchered waggon train behind.

That night, angled far off the road, they sat trimming arrows by a small shielded campfire, the first one they had made since leaving Challerain Keep, and

Patrel looked up to see tears aglisten in Danner's amber eyes. Danner stared into the fire, unseeing, his voice breaking: "She called me her dancer, you know."

The Post Road swung south again as it rounded the Battle Downs, and down it the ponies went, Patrel on the piebald, Danner on the white, and all about them the Shadowlight streamed.

"This road certainly looks different now than when we first fared north," said Patrel.

Danner merely grunted, and the ponies plodded on as snow began to fall. "Welcome to the new year," growled Danner, looking upward into the Dimmendark at the eddying flakes. Then he looked at Patrel: "Welcome to the new year, Paddy, for it's Last Yule. And remember: this is the year our troubles *really* begin." And they managed wan smiles at one another.

On the night of the sixth 'Darkday since leaving Challerain Keep, they camped on a slope to the east of where the Upland Way met the Post Road.

Danner stood looking down at that junction, and as Patrel brought him a cup of hot tea, the smaller Warrow said, "To think, Danner, it was but four weeks past that we came across Spindle Ford and out of the Bosky and up that road."

"Four weeks?" Danner sipped his tea, his eyes never leaving the road. "Seems like years instead of weeks. At least I feel years older."

Patrel threw a hand onto Danner's shoulder. "Perhaps you *are* years older, Danner; perhaps we all are."

Four 'Darkdays later, they rode onto a causeway over a dike and through gates flung wide in a high guard wall and into the village of Stonehill. Around them a hundred or so stone houses mounted up the slopes of the coomb, a great swale hollowed into the side of the large hill to the north and east. The ponies' hooves rang hollowly upon the cobbles and echoed back from the closed and shuttered houses, and no movement at all could be seen on the empty village streets.

"It looks abandoned," said Patrel, unshouldering his bow and setting arrow to string.

Danner said nought as he, too, readied his weapon, his eyes sweeping the dark doorways and closed-up windows. A thin wind sprang up, gnawing around corners, sending tiny twisting streamers of snow scurrying amongst the pave-stones.

On through the vacant streets they went, coming at last to Stonehill's one hostel, its signpost squeaking in the chill wind.

"If anyone's here, they'll be at the inn," said Danner, squinting up at the sign displaying the likeness of a white unicorn rampant on a field of red, bearing the words: *The White Unicorn, Bockleman Brewster, Prop.*

Stonehill was a village on the western fringes of the sparsely settled Wilderland, a village situated at the junction of the east-west Crossland Road and the Post Road running north and south. It was a trading center for farmers, woods dwellers, and travelers. The White Unicorn, with its many rooms, usually had a wayfarer or two as well as a nearby settler staying overnight. But occasionally there would be some "real" strangers, such as King's-soldiers from the Keep heading south, or a company of traveling Dwarves; in which case the local folk would be sure to drop in to the Unicorn's common room for a pint or two and a look at the strangers and to hear the news from far away, and there'd be much singing and merriment.

But when Danner and Patrel unlatched the door and stepped in, only silence greeted them, for the inn was cold and dark and the hearths were without fire.

Patrel shivered in the empty chill as Danner found the stub of a candle and managed to get it lit.

"I wonder where all the people have got to?" asked Patrel as they moved across the common room, past the long-table and benches and through the small tables and chairs.

"South, I should think," answered Danner, spying a lamp and using the candle to light it.

"Or to Weiunwood," said Patrel, answering his own question. "The fit and hale have gone to Weiunwood to fight the Spawn."

"What now, Paddy?" Danner turned to Patrel, the lamp casting a yellow glow upon both buccen's features. "Where do we wait for Vidron and Gildor and the rest that broke free?"

"Right here, Danner," answered Patrel, his hand sweeping in a wide gesture. "The best inn in town."

Danner looked about into the chill, empty darkness surrounding him and smiled. "And you said that this was going to be a bad year."

Patrel smiled back, his green eyes atwinkle, then said, "Why don't you look for something for us to eat while I get the ponies into the stables and out of sight."

They found another lamp and lit it, and Patrel took it with him to stable the mounts while Danner found the kitchen and rummaged through the pantry.

When Patrel returned, Danner had started a small

fire and had set a small kettle to boil, and a pungent odor was redolent in the room.

"Smells good," said Patrel, rubbing his hands briskly. "What is it?"

"Leeks," answered Danner.

"Leeks? Lor, Danner, I *hate* leeks." Patrel made a sour face.

"Hate 'em or not, Paddy," responded Danner, "that's our meal, unless you prefer crue."

Danner set a pot on for tea while Patrel glowered at the leafy leeks bubbling in the kettle. Slumping down in a chair, Patrel said, "You'd think in an inn as big as this one there'd be something to eat besides leeks."

"It looks like they took everything with them, everything but the leeks," said Danner.

"See, I *told* you they were no good," shot back Patrel, then he burst out laughing. "It *is* the worst of years if I've got to eat boiled leeks."

Danner roared.

"I say, they weren't so bad after all," said Patrel, sopping up the last of the leeks with a piece of crue and popping it into his mouth.

"Maybe you've just not been hungry before," said Danner. "I mean, you had three helpings."

"Perhaps you're right, Danner," answered Patrel, chewing thoughtfully. "Perhaps I've not ever been hungry before. Of course, I've never before eaten crue as a steady diet for days on end. On the other hand, I suppose it wasn't too bad finding the leeks; it could have been worse, you know."

"What do you mean, 'worse'?" asked Danner.

"Well, for one thing," answered Patrel, making a face and shuddering, "it could have been oatmeal."

The rest of the 'Darkday, Danner paced the floor like a caged animal, frequently stepping out onto the porch and scanning for sign of Vidron or Gildor or any other survivor of Challerain Keep.

"Ar, I feel trapped, Paddy," said Danner, returning from one of his excursions outside. "You know, we're not at all certain that anyone else escaped. The Ghûls were in hot pursuit. What if no one else got away?"

"If that's the case," responded Patrel, his eyes grim, "then no one will come."

"Oh, no," said Danner, "someone will come alright: Spawn will come. Remember, there's a great Horde at Challerain Keep, and they'll march right through Stonehill on their way south. And we don't want to be here when they arrive."

"You're right, Danner," answered Patrel. "But, the maggot-folk won't be here very soon. They'll pick over the corpse of Challerain Keep first. But you're right: sooner or later they *will* march through Stonehill."

Patrel fell into brooding thought, not stirring or turning his gaze from the fire when Danner stalked back to the door and outside. When the buccan strode in once more, Patrel looked up. "This is the way I see it, Danner," said the smaller Warrow, "horses are faster than ponies, and the Men should have been here by now unless they were driven far afield."

"Or slain," interrupted Danner.

"Yes—or slain," continued Patrel. "In either case we cannot spend too long waiting, for we do not know when Ghûls, Vulgs, or any of the Spawn will get here. But they *will* come.

"This, too, we know: Warrows see farther through this dismal murk than Men or Elves—who can say, perhaps we see through the Shadowlight better than any other Folk. The Realm needs our eyes, Danner, but you and I are not enough: more Thornwalkers are wanted than just us two.

"Here is what I propose: Let us remain here the rest of this 'Darkday and tomorrow. If neither Vidron nor Gildor nor others come, then the day after, we will leave Stonehill for the Bosky. We will go to Captain Alver and tell him what we know. Then we will form a Thornwalker company to fare south to Pellar, a company to join the Host and see for them: to be their eyes, to be their scouts, to watch the movements of the foe, and to give the edge in battle to the King's Legions."

Patrel gripped Danner's forearm and looked him in the eye. "None other than Warrows can do this thing, Danner. What say you?"

A wide grin split Danner's face. "Hai! I like this plan of yours. Even should Vidron or others come, still one of us must return to the Bosky and gather more Thornwalkers." Then the smile evaporated, replaced by a dark look. "Modru has much to answer for."

They heated water and took baths and washed their clothes, hanging them by the fire for drying. And they slept in beds!

All the next 'Darkday they kept watch for sign of survivors from the Keep, riding up the coomb to the hilltop to watch, but nought did they see of Men from Challerain, though they did note several Warrow burrows high up the swale, but they were vacant like all the other homes in Stonehill.

"Some of Toby Holder's kith, perhaps," said Danner, remembering that Toby frequently made trips to trade with the Stonehillers, and the Holders always did claim they'd come from near the Weiunwood originally.

They cooked more leeks, and Patrel managed to find a small wedge of cheese overlooked by the Brewsters when they'd gone to Weiunwood—"Just enough cheese for a bite apiece," said Patrel—but they savored it as if it were priceless ambrosia, and spent the rest of the 'Darkday recounting the feast on Laurelin's birthday eve.

The next 'Darkday they rode once more to the hilltop and looked long but saw nought of survivors, and so went back to the inn and extinguished the fire and gathered their things.

"If I had a copper penny or two," said Danner, casting a last look around, "I'd leave it for Bockleman Brewster to pay for the bath and the washing of clothes and the loan of the bed I slept in."

"The bath alone was worth a silver," said Patrel.

"Even a gold," replied Danner.

"Come on, Danner, let's get out of here before we owe Bockleman a chest of jewels," Patrel laughed, and out the door they strode, latching it behind.

They went to the stables and put grain in their saddlebags for the ponies, and then rode down the vacant streets and out through the west gate. And as they crossed the causeway out to join the Crossland Road, they did not see or hear Hrosmarshal Vidron at the head of a weary band of grimy horsemen ride forth from the twisting hills and in through the eastern gates of Stonehill, into that now empty town.

South and west went the Crossland Road, swinging below the southern reaches of the Battle Downs, heading for Edgewood and, beyond, the Boskydells. Along this way rode the buccen, camping first along the hills and next within the forest.

On the third 'Darkday, through the winter trees of Edgewood they sighted the great Thornwall, and came unto the thorn tunnel leading into the Bosky. They took up torches and lit one, riding into the barrier, and their eyes brimmed with glittering tears, for they had come home.

At last they emerged from the Thornwall, coming to a wooden span set upon stone piers—the bridge over the River Spindle. Of the four main ways into the Bosky, this was the only bridge, the other three ways being fords; Spindle Ford, Wenden Ford, and Tine Ford. But, as is the manner of Warrows in many things, the bridge was simply called "the bridge."

"Hey," said Danner, perplexed as they came out of the thorn barrier and onto the span, "there are no guards, no Thornwalkers."

Patrel, too, cast looks about, concerned, yet he said nought. Beyond the bridge he could see where again the barrier grew, and once more a black tunnel bored onward: two miles had they come within the thorny way to reach the bridge, and nearly three more miles beyond would they go before escaping the Thornwall. Across the span the ponies trotted, their hooves drumming on the great planks and timbers. Below, the frozen Spindle shone pearl grey in the Shadowlight. Soon they crossed the bridge and once more entered the gloom, their guttering torch casting a writhing light upon the great tangle of razor-sharp spikes clawing outward.

In all, nearly two hours they rode within the barrier, to emerge as the last of their torches burned low. And no Beyonder Guard greeted them as they came into the Bosky, only the cold Shadowlight of the Dimmendark.

"What do you think it means, Danner: the 'Guard gone, the way open, the camp deserted?" Patrel's voice was grim as his viridian eyes swept the countryside for sign of life but found none.

"I think it means something foul is afoot," grated Danner, leaning down and jabbing the torch into the snow, quenching the flame. "Let's go; we've got to get to someone who can tell us what's going on."

West they rode, into the Bosky, following the Crossland Road, faring through rolling farmland, now fallow in Winternight's grip. West they rode for nearly three more hours, covering some nine miles, coming to the village of Greenfields. As they approached the hamlet, they could see no lights, as if the village was deserted.

"Hoy, Danner, look!" barked Patrel. "Some of the homes are burned."

Setting arrows to bows, they spurred forward, swiftly coming in among the houses, into the town. Doors stood ajar, windows were broken, and some buildings were charred ruins. The streets were empty; no life could be seen anywhere.

Eyes alert, to the Commons they rode.

"Paddy, by the fire gong . . ." Danner's voice was

grim, and Patrel looked to see the frozen corpse of a buccan, barbed lance standing forth from his back. "Ghûlen spear!" spat Danner. "Ghûls are in the Bosky!"

Patrel's face blenched to hear such dire news, and he surveyed the grim evidence. "He was ringing the gong when the Spawn got him. Perhaps his warning saved others. Let's search further."

Through the small hamlet they rode, dismounting now and again to search houses. And they found more slain: dammen, buccen, younglings, wee babes, granthers, grandams.

In one house twelve slain were found: eleven children and a young damman. Danner ran out into the street shouting in rage: "Modru! Skut! Swine! Coward! Where are you, you butcher?" And he fell to his knees and dropped his bow and pounded the frozen earth with his fist, and his voice sank into dark gutturals, and no word could be understood though words he spoke.

At last Patrel got Danner to his feet and mounted upon the white pony and led him to the west edge of town where stood the Happy Otter Inn, and they bedded down in the hayloft of the inn stable.

And it was late in the dark Winternight when Patrel started up from a deep, dreamless sleep to hear the pounding of hooves thundering past. He glanced at Danner lying in the hay; and Danner did not awaken, though the buccan tossed restlessly and moaned.

Taking up his bow, Patrel crept down from the loft and out into the Dimmendark. In the distant Shadowlight he saw a force of fifty or sixty riders hammering away to the west along the Crossland Road, but whether they were Men on horses, or Ghûls on Hèlsteeds, he could not say, as the sound of the drumming hooves faded beyond hearing and the riders disappeared into the far Winternight.

The next 'Darkday they continued west along the Crossland Road, riding through Raffin and Tillok and coming to Willowdell, and these hamlets, too, were deserted, buildings burned, Warrows slain. And all 'Darkday Danner said no word, though his lips were pressed into a thin white line, and his knuckles clenched tightly upon the pony reins.

They stopped at the edge of Willowdell, staying in an abandoned barn, for neither buccan could bear to sleep in a house of one of the victims.

"Rood," said Patrel. "We're going to Rood. Thornwalker headquarters are in Rood; perhaps we can find Captain Alver there—or the Chief Constable of the Bosky if Thornwalkers aren't about."

"What if they're all destroyed?" Danner spoke his first words in more than a 'Darkday, and his voice was bleak.

"All destroyed?" Patrel turned to his comrade.

"All the villages, all the towns," said Danner.

Patrel blenched at this dire thought, and Danner began saddling the white pony.

"I'm going to Woody Hollow, Paddy," said Danner. "It's only eleven or twelve miles from here. We'll go to Rood after—if there's a need to—but I can't pass this close without going to the Hollow. Are you coming?"

Patrel nodded, for he knew how he would feel were they but eleven miles from the woods where he had been raised.

Mounting up, once more they went west along the

Crossland Road, riding some six miles before turning northwest up Byroad Lane, the way to Budgens and, beyond, to Woody Hollow.

They had ridden nearly three more miles and were just coming past flanking trees and into Budgens when Danner shouted, "Look! Fires! Woody Hollow is on fire!" and clapped his heels into the white's flanks, crying, "Yah!"

Patrel spurred after him, and as he rode, his green eyes saw flames raging in Woody Hollow, some two miles distant.

Through Budgens galloped the ponies, then westward along Woody Hollow Road, skittering on the ice over Rill Ford across the Southrill. Danner turned north, racing along the East Footway and across the frozen Dingle-rill with Patrel plunging after, flying past the Rillstones and up the north bank and into Woody Hollow proper. They turned west and rode toward the Commons.

Upslope and down, fires raged as homes burned. And the buccen could see dark shapes silhouetted against the flames: Ghûls on Hèlsteeds! *Modru's Reavers were in the Hollow!*

Danner and Patrel hauled their ponies to a halt and leapt down, setting arrows to bowstrings. Flitting among the boles of trees, they moved silently toward the reavers now milling in the Commons. But as the buccen worked their way toward the foe, the Ghûls vented howling cries and spurred Hèlsteeds southward, galloping out and across the bridge and down the Westway Trace, leaving Woody Hollow aflame behind them.

Danner ran shouting a few steps after them, and both he and Patrel sent their arrows winging, but the

Ghûls were beyond their range, and the bolts fell futilely in the distant snow.

And as they watched the reavers ride away, they heard a shrill voice cry " 'Ware!" and the hammer of cloven hooves behind. The buccen spun to see a charging Hèlsteed bearing down upon them, and a grinning Ghûl with a blood-splashed tulwar raised to cleave once, twice more.

Sssthock! An arrow flew from the Shadowlighted trees behind, passing over Patrel's shoulder to pierce the charging Ghûl's breast, and the pale white corpse-foe fell asprawl to the snow, slain, while the Hèlsteed ran on.

"Wha—?" cried Danner, and spun again, to see who his rescuer was.

A small form bearing a bow stepped from behind a tree and came forward, sapphire-blue eyes locked in hatred and loathing and horror upon the slain Ghûl.

Danner looked at the grimy, disheveled young damman before him. "Merrilee!" he cried in disbelief. "Merrilee Holt!"

"Danner! Oh, Danner!" Merrilee ran sobbing to the young buccan and clung to him as if she were lost.

"He's dead, alright," said Patrel, standing up from the slain Ghûl. "But I don't know why. I must've feathered ten to no avail back at the Keep."

"Wood through the heart," said Danner above Merrilee's head as he held her to him. "Merrilee's bolt hit him square in the heart." Danner spoke down to the weeping damman: "Anywhere else, Merrilee, and we'd've been the deaders, and not him."

"Lor, you're right," breathed Patrel, looking at the shaft standing forth from the Ghûl's chest. "Wood through the heart! Stakes and spears I thought of, yes, but not of arrows." Patrel then grinned fiercely and clenched one of his own bolts in a fist and raised it to the sky. "Hai! Now we've got a way to fight them!"

"They killed my dam and sire, Danner." Merrilee's voice was muffled, then she pushed back and turned from the buccan and wiped her eyes and nose in the crook of her sleeve and looked down at the dead Ghûl, hatred in her gaze.

"Bringo and Bessie, dead?" Danner's voice was hushed.

"Tuck's parents, too," said Merrilee, her eyes again brimming with tears, but once more she brushed them aside.

"Tuck's parents, too?" burst out Danner. "How?"

"We came to get the last of the ponies at Dad's stable," answered Merrilee, "to take them up to the Dinglewood, where most folks have got to. Tulip and my dam wanted to get their herbs and medicines, and so they came, too.

"While we were down at the stables, my sire and I, the Ghûls came. Dad shoved me into a feed bin and shut the lid. And they came in . . . and just . . . killed him." Merrilee burst into tears. Danner put an arm around her shoulders, his own eyes glistening. Patrel managed to find a kerchief and gave it to her.

After a moment, she continued: "They set the place on fire when they left. I couldn't get to Dad, and I ran out the back way and up across the Pony Field, crying, and through the woods of Hollow End to warn Mother and the Underbanks. But I was too late.

"The Ghûls had Tulip, dragging her by the hair. Burt came running, and the only thing he had to fight them with was his mason's hammer. But he broke the arm of one of them before they killed him. And they speared Tulip, too, as she tore free and ran to Burt. And then they were both dead."

Merrilee's voice rushed on as she relived the horror of those dire moments: "The Ghûls threw a torch into The Root, setting the burrow aflame. And they rode down and across End Field.

"I ran to our burrow, and Mother was lying dead on the walkway: hacked by blade, savagely murdered.

"I went in and got my bow—the one Tuck gave me—but I could find only one arrow." Merrilee gestured at the shaft standing full from the slain Ghûl's chest.

"I came down to the Commons, to kill at least one of the butchers before they got me. But they rode away, all except that one. Where he was lurking, I do not know. But as he galloped to catch the other murderers, he was going to cut you down, like they did Dad and Mom, and the Underbanks. So I shot him."

"It's a good thing, too, Merrilee, else we'd be dead," said Patrel. "We foolishly loosed our bolts at the Ghûls beyond our range, and we had nothing in hand to stop this one."

" 'The arrow as strays might weller been throwed away,' " said Danner, quoting old Barlo. "One of Tuck's favorite sayings."

At the mention of Tuck's name, Merrilee looked out through the trees, then up at Danner. "Tuck. Where's Tuck?" Anxiety filled her voice.

Danner groped for words, but none came.

"We don't know, Merrilee," said Patrel. "The last we saw of him was at Challerain Keep."

"Challerain Keep? But I thought you were at Ford Spindle!" Merrilee's eyes were wide.

"Didn't the word get back? Didn't Tuck's letter come

to you?" Danner asked, and at the shake of her head: "Skut!" he spat.

"We knew some buccen had gone to the Keep, but not who." Merrilee's voice was low. "Tell me of Tuck."

"The last we saw, he was alive at the sundered north gate of Challerain," said Patrel, "when we broke free of the Horde. But we were separated in the midst of that fight, and we know nought of his fate after that."

Merrilee said nothing for a moment, then: "Did any other Warrows win free?"

Patrel spread his hands palms up. "We just don't know."

"Merrilee," Danner's voice was taut, "my folks, are they alright?"

Now it was Merrilee who knew not: "I cannot say, Danner. In the rush of the evacuation—when we left Woody Hollow—there seemed to be nothing but confusion: people running hither and yon, some heading north, others south, some vowing to stay. But your parents, Danner, I didn't see them; I know not their fate."

Danner's jaw muscles jumped as he gritted his teeth. Then he spun to Patrel. "Look, Paddy, we've got to stop the Ghûls in the Bosky, and Merrilee's shown us the way: wood through the heart. We've got to get up to the Dinglewood and get folks organized; then we can strike back at the Modru's Reavers."

"We need Thornwalkers, present or past," said Patrel, "folk who are good with bow and arrow."

"I'm good with bow and arrow." Merrilee's voice was low.

"Wha—what?" Patrel was nonplussed.

"I said, I am good with bow and arrow," answered Merrilee, speaking up.

"I heard you the first time," said Patrel. "What I meant to say is, you're a damman."

"What does that have to do with anything?" snapped Merrilee, snatching her bow up from the snow.

"Why, everything. I mean, you're a damman." Patrel seemed to be groping for words.

"You said that before; it didn't make any better sense then either," shot back Merrilee, her eyes aflash. "Look, Tuck taught me how to shoot and shoot well. He's not here, and may never come, so I'll stand in his stead, though I cannot take his place. But even were he here, still would I join you, for skill is needed and I have it: my arrows fly true, and for that you should be glad, for the proof lies at your feet: the arrow in that reaver's heart is no accident; it struck exactly where I aimed—nowhere else—otherwise you would be dead." A dark look fell upon Merrilee's features and her voice sank low. "They've slain my sire and my dam, and the Underbanks, and countless others, perhaps Tuck, too. And for that they must pay . . . they must pay."

Danner looked at her soot-streaked, tear-stained face and then up in the direction of the Pony Field and beyond, where he knew that Bringo and Bessie and the Underbanks lay murdered. Then his gaze swung in the direction of his own home, and lastly his eye fell upon the slain Ghûl. "She's right, you know. What has her being a damman got to do with anything?"

Patrel sputtered and fumed and several times started to speak but did not, and at last reluctantly gave a stiff nod of his head, and when Merrilee threw her arms around him and hugged him, over her shoulder he cocked an eye at Danner as if to say, "See! I *told* you she was a damman!"

Merrilee stepped back. "I've seen you before," she said to Patrel, "but I don't know your name."

"Patrel Rushlock, from the narrow treeland east of Midwood," said the diminutive buccan.

"Paddy was our Captain at the Keep," said Danner.

"I remember now: I saw you the day Tuck left. On the Commons. You guided Tuck, Hob, Tarpy, and Danner north." At Patrel's nod, Merrilee said, "I'm Merrilee Holt."

"I know," said Patrel. "Tuck spoke of you often."

"Look, we can't stand here the rest of the Winter War," grumbled Danner. "We've got to get up to the Dinglewood and start fighting back. Let's go."

Up through the Hollow from the Commons the three went, swinging by Danner's stone house, but there was no clue as to the fate of Hanlo and Glory Bramblethorn, Danner's parents. Onward the trio went.

The stables burned furiously.

"Bringo would have been proud to know that his damsel saved two from certain death, Merrilee," said Danner.

Merrilee did not reply, and they went past the blazing barn and into the Pony Field behind. There they rounded up eleven ponies and continued on up the coomb.

Gently, they wrapped the bodies of Burt and Tulip Underbank and Merrilee's dam in soft blankets and tied them over the backs of three ponies. "We'll take them up to the Dinglewood and bury them in a peaceful glade," said Danner, his arms about Merrilee as she wept anew.

"They'll pay," she whispered fiercely. "They'll pay."

Merrilee led them to a camp of Warrows in a wide glen west of where the North Trace entered the Dinglewood. When the trio rode in leading a string of ponies, there was a scattering of cheers that quickly fell into subdued silence as the three bodies were seen draped over three of the steeds.

Buccen were dispatched to dig graves, and Danner and Patrel and Merrilee went to speak with the camp elders. A circle of Warrows formed 'round them to listen to their words.

"We return from Mont Challerain and bear woeful tidings: the Keep has fallen to Modru's Horde, and High King Aurion is slain." The onlookers moaned to hear Patrel speak such news, for they loved their good King Redeye, though none there had ever seen him. Patrel waited for the hubbub to dwindle, then spoke on: "Of the forty-three buccen serving upon the walls at the Battle of the Keep, I know of only two who survived: Danner Bramblethorn and myself." Again there was a stir among the onlookers, and Patrel held his hand up for silence. "Others may have won free, but no more than a handful, for only eight of us lived to fight the last battle, and I saw three more fall there."

"What of the King's Host in the south?" asked an elder. "Did they not come? Do they not take the field against Modru's Hordes?"

"We know not where the Host is," answered Patrel, "but they did not come to Challerain. Why? I cannot say, for no word of them came either. And the Keep fell to Modru's Swarm.

"From that ruin, Danner and I fared south, along the Post Road to Stonehill; and from Stonehill we came west, across the bridge and into the Bosky. And much evil have we seen. In the Bosky alone, Greenfields, Raffin, Tillok, and Willowdell all lie in ruins, and there has been much death at the hands of Modru's Reavers. And now Woody Hollow burns—"

Woody Hollow? Burns? Shouts interrupted Patrel, and some turned to go, to ride to their homes. *"Hold!"* thundered Danner, leaping to his feet. "Stop where you are!" Warrows paused and quiet returned. "There's nought you can do now," Danner said, his voice sharp. "What's burned has burned, and what hasn't still stands. There's no need to go running off willy-nilly into the spears of the Ghûls." Danner sat back down on the log, motioning Patrel to continue.

But ere he could do so: "Captain Patrel, do you bring us no good news?" asked one of the elders, and there was a general murmur among council and spectators alike.

"Yes! I bring the best of news," said Patrel fiercely. "We know how Warrows may slay the Ghûls." Amidst a hubbub Patrel held up an arrow. "Wood through the heart. This wood. Arrow wood. And none is better at casting these quarrels than the Warrow." A general murmur rose up among the Wee Folk, and Patrel held up a hand. "Think it no easy task, for the Ghûl's heart must be struck fair and square, else the bolt will have no effect."

Then he turned to the elders. "This is what I propose: Send riders—messengers—to other camps, to speak with free Warrows everywhere. Tell them how to slay the Ghûls. Have all those who live nearby and who are skilled archers come together at some common place, a place well out of the paths that the Ghûls ride." Patrel looked to Danner for suggestions.

"Whitby's barn east of Budgens," proposed Danner. "It is in a vale nearly hidden by woods, yet it will serve as a large meeting hall all know of."

"So be it," declared Patrel. "Whitby's barn it is. There we shall gather together a company to hurl the Ghûls forth from these Boskydells.

"Let the heralds carry forth this word, too: Warrow eyes see further through this murk than those of Men and even those of Elves. And it may be that our eyes see further than those of the enemy. If so, then we will have another advantage over the foe, for by keeping a sharp watch we will be able to slip aside when they come nigh if needs dictate, or to lay a trap at other times. So send the word to post wards, to cover any tracks so that the reavers may not follow sign of Warrow in the snow, and to use Warrow woods-trickery to foil their designs. And if there is no other choice, and you are cornered when you do not expect it, aim for the heart.

"Now let the messengers ride to spread the word, to call upon Warrows everywhere to form companies of archers to defend their districts, and to summon those in this region who are skilled to meet at Whitby's barn, for on the morrow we begin to *fight back!*"

Patrel fell silent, and for a moment none spoke, then an elder, Mayor Geront Gabben, stood. "Hip, hip, hooray!" he cried, and was joined by the fired-up townsfolk: *Hip, hip, hooray! Hip, hip, hooray! Hip,*

hip, hooray! Thrice the shout rang forth. And then Warrows rushed thither and yon; hasty plans were made as to who would ride where and who would stand guard. Messengers were reminded that some skilled archers would be needed to ward the camps, but that others were to form into companies to fight the Ghûls. And since most skilled archers either were now or had at times been Thornwalkers, the formation of companies would come easily.

In the midst of the bustle, a youngling came to Merrilee to say that the graves were ready. With Danner and Patrel at her side, Merrilee went to the glade where stood three fresh mounds; and as the three slain were laid to rest and Merrilee wept, Patrel's clear voice sang throughout the glen:

"In Winter's glade now cold and bare
Your 'ternal rest begins.
There'll be a day Spring fills the air
In woods and fields and fens.

Then Summer's touch will grace us all
And bring forth Nature's Tide.
The Harvesting will come this Fall
As leaves fall by your side.

And Winter's cold will come again
As Seasons swing full 'round.
Goodbye my loves, till we are laid
In this most hallowed ground."

Merrilee, Danner, and Patrel each crumbled a handful of earth into each grave, and then Bessie Holt, Burt

Underbank and Tulip Underbank were covered to become one with the Land.

There was a buzz of buccen voices in Whitby's great barn when Danner and Patrel and Merrilee stepped inside. And in the yellow lamplight they saw nearly one hundred Warrows, each armed with a bow. Buccen seemed to be everywhere: in the loft and stalls, upon bales of hay and feed bins, standing in the main aisle and on barrels—from every nook and cranny curious Warrow faces peered out.

Danner and Patrel and Merrilee wormed their way through the crowd to barn-center where stood a makeshift platform, and onto this the trio climbed. A hush fell upon the assembly as Patrel held up his hands for silence. It was warm in the barn, so he and Danner and Merrilee shed their outer jackets, and a surprised hum rose up among the buccen, for there before them stood two helmed warriors in armor, and a damman. Neither Danner nor Patrel had thought of the impact such a sight would have upon the assembly, for little did they realize just how splendid they looked: Danner in black armor, Patrel in gold. And just what was a damman doing here anyhow?

Again Patrel held his hands up for silence, and once more a hush fell over the assembly. Danner and Merrilee sat down cross-legged upon the platform, and Patrel spoke, recounting the fall of Challerain Keep, the death of Aurion, the bravery of the Warrows that had been slain, the sights that he and Danner had seen on their journey to Woody Hollow. Groans of dismay and cries of rage greeted his words, and often Patrel had to pause until the hubbub died down.

Then he spoke of the slaying of the Ghûl by Merrilee's bolt, and of the hope this boded for the Warrows. He also spoke of the Warrow's ability to see farther through the Dimmendark than others, and the advantage this could give to the Wee Folk.

"This, then, is what I hope to do: to lure Ghûls into traps of our devising, to slay them with well-placed bolts, to drive Modru's Reavers from the Land." Patrel gestured at Merrilee and Danner. "We three here have sworn to do this thing, and I think you all have come here prepared to join us. What say you?"

There was a great shout that rattled the rafters, for the buccen at last could see a way to combat the corpse-people.

Yet one buccan stood to be recognized: Luth Chuker from Willowdell. "Ar, what you say makes plenty of sense, Captain Patrel. All but one thing, that is."

"What's that, Luth?" asked Patrel.

"Uh, well, no offense, miss, but we can't be expected to have this damman in our company," said Luth. Some in the assembly said, *Hear, hear.*

"And why is that, Luth?" asked Patrel.

"Why, she's a *damman!*" exclaimed Luth. "Don't take me wrong, I mean, my wife and my dammsel are both dammen, but . . ."

"But what, Luth?" Patrel didn't let up, for he had slogged through this same morass and knew that the issue needed to be dealt with in the open, and now.

"We just don't let our dammen fight, that's what," said Luth, and here and there, murmurs of agreement were heard.

"Would you rather that they die without a struggle?" Patrel's words were harsh. "Like those in Greenfields, Raffin, Tillok?"

Luth now squirmed, and some in the assembly argued with their neighbors.

"Listen, each of you!" cried Patrel above the babble. "Of all the archers here, including me, and including Danner, Merrilee is the only one I know of who has actually slain a Ghûl. Can any of you say the same? I cannot."

Again arguments broke out, and once more Patrel called for quiet, but now he was angry, green fire in his eyes. "Merrilee saved my stupid skin once with her skill, and until you earn it, I trust her and Danner above all others here!"

Patrel's statement brought forth an uproar from the assembly, and many shouted in ire. But Merrilee, too, was spluttering angry, for she had listened to the buccen argue about her fate *as if she weren't even present to speak for herself.* And she started to spring to her feet, but Danner put a hand on her shoulder and held her down as he stood. Again the assembly fell quiet, for most knew of Danner's extraordinary skill as an archer.

"Captain Patrel is right," said the black-armored buccan, "none else can boast of slaying a Ghûl. But this, too, I would say: Merrilee hit the Ghûl square in the heart, the only place where an arrow would slay him, *and he was on the back of a Hèlsteed running full tilt!* Think you now: would you bar such an archer from our company? And think deeply, *for the skill she has already mastered is the skill you must match!*" Danner paused. "If there are no more objections"—quiet filled the barn—"then let us get on with the planning of this War." Danner resumed his seat, and Merrilee squeezed his hand, her cobalt eyes shining brightly.

Because most of the buccen there knew each other,

at least by reputation, and since all had been Thornwalkers in their young-buccen days, squads were quickly formed and Lieutenants selected. There was never any question that they would serve under Captain Patrel Rushlock and that Captain Danner Bramblethorn was to be second in command. The damman, Merrilee Holt, was the hard one to fit in, for she had not the Thornwalker training. At the last, it was decided that she would serve on Captain Patrel's staff, till her experience could catch up to the others.

Now all the Lieutenants gathered 'round the table, sitting on barrels for chairs, and Patrel, Danner, and Merrilee stepped down to join them. The other buccen in the barn fell silent and strained their ears to hear what was said by the eight: Captains Patrel and Danner; Lieutenants Orbin Theed, Norv Odger, Dinby Hatch, Alvy Willoby, and Luth Chuker who, in spite of his objections to Merrilee, was eagerly selected as a Lieutenant, for such was his reputation as a Thornwalker; and lastly at the table stood the damman, Merrilee Holt, looking small and meek among the warrior buccen. And as they held council, planning the course of the War, other Warrows continued to arrive at Whitby's barn, coming to answer the summons.

Patrel spoke: "Does any here know of the Ghûlen movements?"

"Aye," said Norv Odger, "at least I think I do. They roam the Bosky roads: the Crossland Road, the Tineway, and Two Fords Road, for certain. And if that pattern holds, then they're on the Southpike, the Wenden Way, West Spur, the Upland Way—all of the Bosky roads, reaving the towns as they go."

"They may be reaving the towns for now," said Merrilee, "but soon they'll begin laying waste to farms, and to homes in the woods and fens. No bothy, no cot, no flet, no burrow will be safe from the Spawn." A murmur of agreement rippled through the barn at the damman's bitter words.

"How did they get into the Bosky?" asked Danner. "How did they penetrate the Thornwall, get past the Beyonder Guard?"

None at the table knew the answer to Danner's question, but one of the newcomers to the barn asked to speak, and Patrel signified so, asking his name.

"I'm Danby Rigg from Dinburg. I was up near Northdune when word came that Ghûls were in the Bosky. It was said that they came in through the Thornwall at the old abandoned Northwood tunnel."

"But that only goes partway through the 'Wall," interrupted Orbin, slapping his hand to the table.

"Aye," said Danby, "but let me finish. They came through that way as far as it went, to come to the headwaters of the Spindle River. Then they rode down that frozen waterway: the ice is thick and easily will bear their weight, for now it is solid all the way to the bottom, I hear. They rode to the Inner-break at the fork ten miles west of Spindle Ford. Up over the granite they went; then they were in the Bosky."

An uproar greeted Danby's words, for this was news to them all. The old Northwood tunnel had been abandoned years past, and Warrow grangers had set about encouraging the Spindlethorn to fill in the southern half, and it had grown shut. But the northern half of the tunnel had been left to grow closed on its own, and, without help from Warrows, Spindlethorn grows notoriously slowly. The old north barricades had been left shut, but they could have been moved with effort by Modru's agents. The Inner-break was a great breech in the Thornwall on the south bank of the Spindle where a massive slope of granite hove up through the soil, the great stone slab reaching nearly five miles into the Bosky. And the Spindle River was frozen this year, an event that had never before happened in living Warrow memory.

Patrel asked for silence, and it quickly came, and Merrilee said, "Hai! Then that's how the Vulgs first came to the Bosky, too: through the northern half of the Northwood tunnel, down the frozen Spindle, then up over the Inner-break." Once more agreement rippled through the buccen at the slight damman's words.

Danner spoke: "Alright, so we know how the Ghûls got in and how the Vulgs first came. But now the problem is how to drive Modru's Reavers out. Where do we start?"

No one spoke for a moment, then Norv Odger said, "Each 'Darkday so far, a squad of Ghûls has patrolled the Crossland Road between Willowdell and Brackenboro. It may have been this bunch that set the torches to those two towns."

"Woody Hollow, too," said Merrilee, her voice low.

"Aye, Woody Hollow, too," continued Norv. "There are perhaps twenty, twenty-five of the reavers. They could be our target, but it's a goodly sized gang."

Danner looked about. "I gauge that there are now nearly one hundred twenty-five of us, what with the latecomers. That seems to be good enough odds to me: five of us for each Ghûl and Hèlsteed."

"Yes, good odds," said Patrel, "but remember, the Ghûls won't be sitting targets; and they'll use tulwar, spear, and Hèlsteed to balance the exchange."

Patrel suspended the planning a moment to form another squad from the newcomers and to select a

Lieutenant to command it: Regin Burk, a farmer from near the Mid Ford.

And during this pause Merrilee sat with her hands steepled before her, deep in thought. Regin joined the council and looked at Merrilee in surprise, but said nought.

"Alright," said Patrel, "if this band of reavers is to be our first target, how shall we go about it?"

No one spoke, and silence drummed loudly upon the ear. At last, Merrilee cleared her throat, and Patrel cocked an eye at her, and she said, "I know little of War, and so know nought of strategy, tactics, or battle. I do know how to use bow and arrow, and I know much about ponies. Yet something you said, Patrel, caused me to think. Your words were, 'the Ghûls won't be sitting targets.' But what if they were? Sitting targets, that is. Our task would be immeasurably eased." A murmur washed over the listening buccen, but quickly stilled as Merrilee continued. "These, then, are my thoughts: Let us lure the Ghûls into a high-walled trap and shut the door behind. Then slay them in their pen." Once more a murmur started to swell, but Merrilee raised her voice sharply, and silence fell again. "*Yet!* I can hear some say, *there is no high-walled trap nearby*. But if you say that, then you are wrong. For there *is* a trap, and it is called Budgens—the hamlet of Budgens. Hear now my plan: A band of Warrows on pony will be seen by the Ghûls. Fleeing in panic, the poor Warrows will gallop up Byroad Lane for the village of Budgens. Yet even though the Warrows have a small lead—perhaps but a mile or so—reavers know that ponies cannot outrun Hèlsteeds, and they give swift chase. Into Budgens run the foolish Warrows, down the central street, now the Ghûls right after. But *lo!* as the Spawn charge through Budgens, the Warrows have vanished; instead, there is a barricade across the road and it bursts into flame. The Ghûls turn, and behind is another waggon-borne flaming barricade, now also shut. And the gaps between the buildings cannot be broached, for they, too, are filled. Then Warrows spring up from rooftop concealment and arrows pierce Spawn hearts, for now it is the hunters who have become the hunted, as the Warrows war upon the reavers."

Merrilee fell silent, and quiet filled the barn—a stillness so deep that the hush drummed heavily upon the ears. Then the silence was shattered by a great, wild cheering that shook the walls of Whitby's barn, and broad grins split faces and Patrel grabbed Merrilee and fiercely hugged her to him, calling in her ear above the shouts and applause, "So you are the one who knows nothing of strategy, tactics, or battle? Would that I were so ignorant." And tears glistened in Merrilee's eyes as Danner smiled and squeezed her hand, saying, "Your vow against the reavers will be kept, Merrilee, for with this plan, they *will* pay."

Much was debated ere all the final details of Merrilee's plan were hammered out, and in this the damman proved to ask canny questions and to point out many particulars of value. And when all was said and done, the last detail decided upon, Luth Chuker looked across the table at Merrilee and said, "Damman, I was wrong. Will you forgive me?" And Merrilee smiled and inclined her head, and Luth grinned in return.

Patrel called for silence, then said, "This 'Darkday is done; our plans are laid. Tomorrow we prepare our trap in Budgens, and the next 'Darkday, if the Ghûls are willing, we spring it shut upon the Spawn. But ere we go to take our rest, I would hear a few words from the chief architect of our design: Merrilee Holt."

Again applause and cheering broke out, and Merrilee was stunned, for although it was one thing to tell others of an idea she had, it is altogether a different thing to give a *speech* to a company of warriors. Danner leaned over and whispered in her ear, "Just say what is in your heart." And then two buccen boosted her up onto the table.

She stood and slowly turned, looking at all of the Warrow faces, all of the Thornwalkers with their bows, eager to take the War to Modru's Reavers, eager to avenge their lost loved ones. And sadness fell upon her heart, but so, too, did fierce pride.

And then she spoke in a clear voice, and all heard her words: "Let the word go forth here and now from this place of liberty that no longer will Warrows flee in fear before Modru's Reavers. The Evil in Gron has chosen the wrong Land to try to crush under his iron tread, for sharp thorn will meet his heel and we will wound him deeply. We did not choose this War, but now that it is visited upon us, not only will we fight to survive, we will fight to *win*. Let it be said now and for all the days hereafter that on this day the struggle began, and Evil met its match."

Amid thunderous cheering, Merrilee stood down from the table, and she saw that some wept openly.

"They're no longer calling it the Winter War, Merrilee," said Danner. "Now they name it after what you said in your speech: the Struggles."

Before Merrilee could reply, Patrel strode into the barn. "Well, the trap in Budgens is set. Tomorrow is the 'Darkday we spring it. And, concealed, we watched the Ghûlen squad ride along the Crossland Road on their patrol. There are twenty-seven of them. The odds are good, maybe now even better. How have things gone here?"

"More Thornwalkers, past and present, have arrived. Our ranks have swelled to double their numbers. There's nearly two hundred fifty now, and more trickle in all the time," said Danner. "Lor! Tomorrow in Budgens the air will be solid with arrows. Why don't we leave some buccen behind?"

"No," objected Merrilee. "It will be important that all share in tomorrow. Victory, we think, but perhaps defeat. Yet win or lose, all should be there."

"Tell me, damman, what could possibly go wrong tomorrow?" Luth looked up from the arrows he fletched.

"If I knew, Luth," answered Merrilee, "then it wouldn't happen."

"Well," said Luth, "nothing will go wrong tomorrow. You've just got a case of battle-eve jitters."

"I hope you're right, Luth," responded Merrilee, "for I'm not sure I could stand it if things go wrong."

Danner laughed and changed the subject: "Ah, Paddy, you should've seen it when some of the newcomers objected to a damman in the company. Luth set 'em down, he did."

Luth smiled penitently, but there was an ireful glare in his eye: "Them skuts! Oh, pardon, Merrilee, but they make me angry still."

Patrel laughed, too. "Luth, there's nothing worse than a reformed malefactor, one who has seen the error of his ways. I know, for I am one, too."

Luth stood and smiled again, and handed Merrilee

the arrows. "Here you are, damman, arrows fletched to fit your draw. Wing them well and true, for on the morrow we snap a trap shut upon a squad of reavers."

And as Luth took to his bed, and so too did Danner and Patrel, Merrilee sat and gazed at the arrows and searched for a flaw in her plan.

Nearly three hundred Warrows had mustered when the company rode west through the Shadowlight to Budgens. Buccen took station upon rooftops and behind barricades. A band of twenty upon ponies was dispatched southward down Byroad Lane; they were the decoy, whose job it was to draw the Ghûls into the trap.

Merrilee and Patrel took station upon the roof of the Blue Bull, Budgens' one inn. Across the street upon the smithery Merrilee could see Danner, and she waved before taking her place of concealment. All Warrows slipped out of sight, though some kept watch upon the south where could be seen the pony squad standing now on Byroad Lane near the Crossland Road.

And the wait began . . .

Minutes seemed like hours, and hours dragged by like days. And still the wait went on and the Ghûls did not come. Merrilee fidgeted and checked her arrows again and again, while Patrel hummed a soft tune under his breath, and others spoke quietly and waited; but the Ghûlen squad came not. Time trudged by on halting feet: plodding, lagging, dragging. And Merrilee knew then what her plan did not take into account: "We know not if the Ghûls will even come," she said to Patrel, "for we control not their ranks, their numbers."

And still the wait went on . . .

And Merrilee thought: *All this work will have gone for nought.*

And time dragged past . . .

"Here they come, Captain," said the lookout. "Oh, Lor!"

At the sentry's exclamation, Merrilee peeped over the edge of the roof, looking south through the Dimmendark toward the junction of the Crossland Road and Byroad Lane. Her eyes immediately saw the pony squad; and beyond, coming into view from behind the hills flanking the Crossland Road, cantered dark Hèlsteeds bearing Ghûls. And Merrilee's heart lurched, *for there were fully one hundred of Modru's Reavers and not a mere squad of twenty-seven.* But it was too late to change the plan, for the buccen on Byroad Lane wheeled their ponies and bolted for Budgens, and howling Ghûls plunged in pursuit.

Down the road they thundered, racing for the village, the Hèlsteeds overhauling the ponies at an alarming rate. Merrilee clenched her fist and beat upon the roof. "Ride, buccen, ride! Ride for your lives!" she whispered fiercely, fervently hoping that she had correctly gauged the speed of pony against Hèlsteed.

Now the spears of the racing Ghûls were lowered, as they made ready to lance the fleeing Warrows verging on the fringe of Budgens.

The lead Ghûl howled a command, and a score raced to the left, riding for the gap between Budgens and the Rillmere, striking to head off any Warrows who might flee that way. *These twenty reavers would be outside the trap!*

Merrilee glanced across the street to see Danner take

two squads of buccen, to disappear beyond her vision as they leapt to the ground in back of the smithery.

And then the ponies bearing Warrows thundered past down the street, and behind raced the Ghûls on Hèlsteeds, howling in victory now, for they were closing upon their quarry.

Through the far barricade the ponies scaddled, and the gap in the wall closed as a brush-bearing waggon rolled into the slot. Flames sprang up as torches fired the wood splashed with lamp oil. The racing Hèlsteeds squealed in pain and skidded to a halt as the Ghûls, sensing a trap, hauled hard upon reins, wheeling 'round to ride back south. But there, too, a barricade rolled to, and flames burst forth.

The trap slammed shut.

But twenty Ghûls were outside.

Patrel stood and set to his lips the Horn of the Reach—the silver bugle given to him by Marshal Vidron on the day they first met—and a silver call split the air, its notes belling wide across the countryside, and everywhere that Warrows heard it, a burst of hope sprang full in their hearts. Below in the streets of Budgens, Ghûls quailed from the sound and Hèlsteeds reared in fear. Warrows stood upon the rooftops and at Patrel's second pure clarion call, a storm of arrows whistled through the air to rain death upon the Ghûls.

Merrilee stood straight as a wand, her bow nocked with arrow, and Tuck's voice spoke softly in her mind: *"Inhale full. Exhale half. Draw to your anchor point. Center your aim. Loose."* Again and again she sped arrows down into the Ghûls, and over and over Tuck whispered in her memory. And where she aimed, arrows flew, piercing Ghûl breast and heart. It did not matter that all about her appeared to be confusion and that the streets were a churning mass below, that Hèlsteeds reared and spears were flung at buccen and cries of death rent the air; all that mattered were Tuck's words: *"Inhale full. Exhale half. Draw to your anchor point. Center your aim. Loose."* And feathered Death sped from her bow.

Yet the Ghûls were savage reavers, and they threw spears to pierce Warrows. Ghûls dismounted, some quilled with arrows, and they clambered up porch posts to reach the rooftops where their tulwars clove ere these reavers were felled by arrows loosed in close quarters, or by buccen-wielded wooden lances made for just this purpose.

Merrilee did not note the Ghûl that came upon her roof, but Patrel felled it by an arrow through the heart.

The Ghûlen number dwindled in the streets below. But there came an uproar from the northern barricade, as the score of Ghûls outside the trap fought to tear it open. And the barricade was breached. Surviving Ghûls in the street spurred for the gap to escape this fanged nest. Warrows upon the rooftops ran leaping from roof to roof, loosing arrows at the fleeing Ghûls below. The two squads commandeered by Danner fell upon the twenty foe outside, and arrows thudded into corpse-flesh. The Ghûls wheeled about, and Hèlsteeds bore down upon the Warrows on foot. Spears slew some while tulwars clove others. Yet the buccen stood their ground and carefully aimed, and arrows burst through Ghûl hearts. Danner's two squads were joined by those who had ridden the decoy ponies, and these buccen slammed the barricade shut again before most of the Ghûls in the street could race free, and only four or five of those trapped had managed to flee through the gap. Then the decoy buccen turned upon the Spawn outside, and Death hissed into the once-proud Ghûlen ranks, and but three won free of these barb-spitting Warrows, and those three fled in fear.

In the trap, none survived.

And when the Warrows saw that the Battle of Budgens had ended, a cheering broke forth and there were calls for Merrilee. But she turned to Patrel and clung to him sobbing, and he looked to the others as if to say: "Well, she's a damman, you know."

Ninety-seven Ghûls had been felled: six by spears upon the rooftops, the rest by arrows through the heart. It was a smashing victory by all accounts, but a victory purchased at a dear price:

Nineteen Warrows had been killed, and thirty others wounded, some by tulwar, some by spear; some of the wounded would never fight again, but most would heal to carry on.

Word of the Battle of Budgens spread across the Seven Dells like wildfire, igniting Warrow spirits, for the first of the Struggles had gone to the Bosky, and the Wee Folk now knew that the Ghûls could be beaten. Word spread, too, about the "Damman Thornwalker," but most thought it just a rumor.

And in the Northwood, Southwood, and the hills around Weevin, Thornwalkers came together to fight for liberty. In the Updunes, the Claydunes, and the Eastwood, traps were laid and Ghûls slain. And in Bigfen, Littlefen, and the Cliffs to the west, Warrows smiled, for they had been fighting all along and knew the Ghûls were vulnerable, though the count of Ghûlen dead at Budgens surprised even them.

Back at Whitby's barn, the council of Lieutenants sat in session with Captain Patrel, Captain Danner, and damman Merrilee. Patrel spoke: "We are all agreed then: though we know not how to do it, we must take the fight now to the Ghûls: we must devastate their strongholt in the ruins of Brackenboro."

Merrilee looked 'round the table, and a chill sense of foreboding shivered up her spine.

CHAPTER 4
MYRKENSTONE

Spittle ran down Modru's hideous iron mask, and his eyes blazed with rage. With a backhanded sweep, his black-gauntleted fist crashed into the side of Laurelin's face, and she was smashed to the floor. *"Khakt!"* Modru's spitting cry brought the mute Rukh scuttling into the room. The Rukh's glance darted thither and yon, and he scurried to the mirror and drew the black cloth over the glass. Then he ran to bob and grovel before Modru.

"Shuul!" hissed Modru, and the mute sprang out the door. The black-cloaked figure turned back to Laurelin. "Perhaps your manners will improve after a rest in your quarters," he said, then sibilant laughter hissed forth: *"Tsss, sss, sss, ssth."*

The mute Rukh came scuttling back, and with him were two Lōkha.

"Shabba Dūl!" spat Modru, and the Lōkha jerked Laurelin to her feet and shoved her from the room.

Along the central hall they took her, till they came to a heavy, studded door. One Lōkh hauled forth a ring of keys and rattled one into the lock, while the other took up a brand and lighted it. The portal creaked open and musty air seeped forth. Through the door they led her, the guttering torch held high, and Laurelin saw that they were in a stairwell with steep steps twisting downward into blackness. Down they went, the Princess hugging leftward against the wall adrip with slime, for there was no bannister to the right. Down they went: one flight, two, more; she lost count of the steps. At last, they came to a landing with a rusted iron door, and even though the steps pitched on downward into the blackness below, the Lōkh with the keys stopped, clattering one into the padlock.

Venting oaths, he struggled to turn the key; then with a grating sound, at last the tumblers gave way. The Lōkh hammered on the lock and the shackle opened. He pried the hasp back and then, jerking, inched open the portal until they could squeeze through.

Beyond was a narrow, tortuous passage canting down. Iron-grilled gates were spaced along this twisting way, but they yielded to the keys, and downward the Lōkha took Laurelin. At last they emerged in a foul chamber, littered with filth and splintered bones, the marrow tongued out. The twisting passage could be seen to continue on, exiting out the far end of the chamber. An iron-barred cell with filthy straw on the floor was to the left. And into this foul cage Laurelin was pushed.

Clang! slammed the door.

Clack! shut the lock.

And then the Lōkha turned and stamped away.

And they took the light with them.

Laurelin could hear their foul voices in slobbering speech and raucous laughter as they went back up the way they had come, and the clash of the iron-grilled gates slamming to behind them, and the rusty screech of the iron door as it was forced shut again. And then she was alone in the blackness.

Her good hand stretched out before her, Laurelin slowly stepped forward until she came up against the bars of the cell. Now she turned right and, occasionally touching the bars for guidance, once more stepped slowly until again she came up against a wall, this one made of stone. Again she turned right and paced in the utter blackness, counting as she went.

Laurelin's cell was fifteen paces wide and ten paces deep. Three walls were slimy stone, one wall iron bars. Rotted straw littered the floor. Along the back wall was a small stone pier that Laurelin sat upon as if it were a bench, her back to the wall, her feet drawn up. And for the first time since her capture, alone and in the pitch dark, she pressed her forehead against her drawn-up knees and quietly wept.

Laurelin awakened to hear the distant screech of protesting iron and the clang of gates being opened, and the glow of a flaming torch grew as someone came down the twisting passage. It was her Lōkh jailor. The torchlight was painful to Laurelin's eyes, and she shadowed her face with an out-held hand, blinking back watery tears. The Lōkh set two buckets upon the floor just outside her cell door, then turned and went back the way he had come, slamming the gates behind, shutting the iron door.

Bright afterimages slashing through her eyes, Laurelin fumbled her way to the cage bars, reaching through until she found a bucket. It contained water, and she drank thirstily using the cup found in the bucket bottom; and though the water tasted of sulphur, to her it was sweet. Still on her knees in the sour straw, she groped about and found the other wooden pail. She reached in and discovered a coarse hunk of stale bread. Cradling the chunk in her broken arm, once more she groped into the bucket and snatched her arm back with a hiss of air sucked in through clenched teeth, for something wet with small claws had scuttled across her hand.

Laurelin sat on the stone pier and ate the coarse bread, listening to a far-off drip of water tinking slowly, the sound echoing through the pitch blackness.

The Princess did not know how long she had slept nor what had awakened her. She sat upon the stone pier and listened intently to the dark. Something had *changed*, yet she knew not what, but her heart raced and fear coursed through her veins. She pressed back against the stone wall behind her and held her breath, trying to sense whatever it was she could not see. And gradually she became convinced that in the blackness a huge creature stood pressed up against her cage and reached long arms through the bars trying to grasp her. She drew up her legs and feet and made herself as small as possible, trying to avoid the clutch, and she thought of the splintered bones littering the floor outside the cell. Her throat was dry and she was athirst, but she did not drink, for the water bucket stood where also stood terror.

When next she heard the jailor coming, Laurelin waited until the nearing light faintly illumed the corridor, showing it empty, and she ran to the bars and stood. Again the torchlight was painful, but she squinted and turned her face aside. The moment the Lōkh set the buckets down, Laurelin snatched the cup from bucket bottom and drank greedily: two cups, three, four. She forced the water down while the Lōkh sneered at her, snorting, *"Schtuga!"* Laurelin snatched up the bread and two turnips from the other pail, leaving the meat behind, cradling the food with her splinted arm as she dipped up another cup of water and went back to the stone pier. The Lōkh took up the first two wooden pails, leaving the latest behind, and, laughing harshly, he stalked away up the twisting passage.

And Laurelin sat with her back pressed against the stone and her feet drawn up, a full cup of water beside her as she ate the turnips and bread. And she thought, *Now, monster of the dark, if you are truly there, my food and drink are here with me and not sitting at your feet.*

Over the next few "days," Laurelin lived along the back wall of the cell, spending much of her time on the stone pier, but frequently pacing to one corner or the other for exercise and other needs. And whenever the jailor came, she would step to the bars as soon as the light coming down the twisting passage showed the corridor clear, waiting to force down water and to snatch up her food ere the Lōkh's torch was gone again.

On many occasions Laurelin sensed the sinister presence before her cell, and then she would stay upon the pier. But at other times the corridor seemed empty, and then would she pace the back wall.

Although she had no certain way of telling time, she believed that the Lōkh visited but once each "day," bringing food and water. She kept count of these "days" by using her thumbnail to scribe a notch in the wood of her splint where a stub stuck out beyond her bandage.

She had marked five such notches when she heard the sounds of the doors rattling open and saw the glow of a torch reflecting down the passage. But it had not yet been a "day" since the jailor had last come to her cage. Yet the light came onward, and from her position next to the bars, Laurelin saw two Lōkh enter the corridor.

With a clack of keys, one Lōkh unlocked her cell, and she was shoved out. Blinking from the light, once more Laurelin trod through the twisting passage, and along the stairwell, this time going upward instead of down.

Up the steps they went, and now Laurelin counted: eight flights they climbed before coming to the door at the top. The Princess was trembling when they reached the central hall, for she had been weakened by her captivity.

Yet the Lōkha turned and led her through an adjacent door, and they climbed more stairs, finally coming to a large, empty stone floor, and more steps spiraled upward into darkness, twisting up inside Modru's Iron Tower. Ascending the dark stairwell, one Lōkh before and the other after, Laurelin once again clung to the wall beside her, for here, too, there was no bannister to keep her from falling.

Up they went, past narrow window-slits looking out into the Dimmendark, up flight after flight, Laurelin's breath coming in harsh gasps. And just as she would have collapsed, the Lōkha stopped to rest, for they, also, were winded. Laurelin slumped to the landing and leaned her head against the cold wall and panted.

Sooner than she was ready, the Lōkha got to their

feet and snarled at her, and once more the tortuous ascent began. Four more flights they took her, at last to come to an ironbound door with a brazen knocker that the lead Lōkh let rise and fall once.

After a moment, the door was opened by a Rukh, this one made mute also. Laurelin was led into the great chamber atop the Iron Tower. Round it was and nearly sixty feet in diameter, and full of dark shadows. Yet along the walls dimly could be seen scroll-cluttered tables littered with prisms, alembics and astrolabes, charts and geometrical figures cast in metal, vials of chemicals, and other strange devices and books of lore.

Here, too, were instruments of torture: a brazier with hot irons, shackles, a rack, and other hideous implements.

But the thing that drew Laurelin's eye stood on a massive pedestal in the center of the room; yet her gaze was baffled by what she saw atop the platform: it looked like a great irregular *blot*; not so much black it was, but rather it seemed to be an *absence* of light that held her gaze. It had the shape and size of a ponderous irregular stone: huge, seven feet long, four high, four wide. And it sat massy and jagged, like a great dark *gape* sucking light into its bottomless black maw.

The Lōkha led Laurelin around this *thing* and to a chain affixed to an iron post, and cuffed her good hand in the iron bracelet. And as they stomped out, Laurelin tore her gaze from the black blotch and looked elsewhere and gasped, for there, wrists shackled to the wall, head slumped forward, was an Elf!

"Lord Gildor!" Laurelin cried.

Slowly the Elf lifted his head and looked at her; his

face was badly battered. Long he gazed, then said at last, "Nay, lady, I am Vanidor, Gildor's twin."

Sibilant laughter hissed forth from the dark shadows: *"Tsss, sss, sss, ssth.* So, it is Lord Vanidor, is it?"

Laurelin spun about to see dark Modru step out of the blackness.

Lord Vanidor, fifth in line to the Lian Crown," said the Evil One. "Perhaps, my dear, he should take your place, for although you stand next to the throne of the High King, he bears the blood of the *Dolh.*" Then Modru paused and spread his hands. "But alas, the noble blood of a royal damosel suits my needs even more so than that of a high Lian, for you are of Mithgar and he is not."

"Royal damosel?" Vanidor looked again at Laurelin.

"Yes!" Modru's voice gloated as he grasped the Princess by her matted hair and twisted her face into the torchlight. "Here is the prize you seek, fool!"

Sunken-cheeked and hollow-eyed, the left side of her face purple with bruise, covered with sour rot from the cell, her clothes and the bandage of her splinted arm unspeakably filthy, Laurelin was displayed to Vanidor, and it was long ere the Elf spoke, and then it was but to say, "I am sorry, my Lady."

"Faugh! Sorry?" hissed Modru, but then his eyes flashed triumph through the iron-snouted visor. "Yes, I see. Sorry. But more than you know. You would have rescued this maiden—if you could have found her, and recognized her, and if you had not been captured. But she would not have been an easy prize to snatch, even had you managed to elude the guards in the courtyard, for she has been keeping company with one of my . . . aides. And *he* would not have spared those who came to steal his . . . pretty. Oh, worry not, my dear, for he has been instructed to be . . . gentle. *Tsss, sss, sss.*"

Modru spun and faced Vanidor, and his voice lashed out harshly: "How many of you came on this fool's errand?"

Vanidor said nought.

"Surely more than three," spat Modru.

"Ask them," said the Elf.

"You know they are dead, fool Vanidor," hissed Modru, "and so I now ask you. And you will tell me also how you breached my walls."

Again Vanidor did not speak.

Modru signed to the mute Rukh: *"Vhuul!"* The Rukh scuttled out the door and away, while Modru walked to the massive pedestal and gloated at the ponderous black maw. "I'll give you but a moment to reflect upon your reticence, oaf, and then if you will not give me the answers I seek, I will extract them from you."

At these words Laurelin's heart plummeted, and she looked into Vanidor's green eyes, and her own grey ones brimmed with tears. But Vanidor said nothing.

"Perhaps I should persuade you to speak by dealing with the Princess while you watch," Modru's cold voice suggested. "But, no, I need her unblemished."

The door opened and in scuttled the Rukh, and stooping through the portal behind came a great cave Troll. Twelve feet tall he was, with glaring red eyes and tusks that protruded through his lips. Greenish was his skin, and *scaled*, like armor plate. Black leather breeks he wore, and nothing else. Into the room he shambled, stooping over, his massive arms hanging down. Steering wide of the *blot* on the pedestal, he came before Modru, his brutish face leering at Laurelin.

Her heart thudded heavily, and she had barely the will to stare back without blenching.

"Dolh schluu gogger!" commanded Modru in the foul Slûk tongue. And the Ogru turned and grasped one of Vanidor's arms while the Rukh unlocked the wrist shackles. Then the Elf was hauled to the rack and his feet and wrists were locked again. The great Ogru-Troll sat hunkered beside the rack, one arm hugging his knees in anticipation, a massive hand upon the turn-wheel, a dull-witted leer upon his face.

At a sign from Modru, the Ogru slowly turned the wheel: *Clack! Clack! Clack! Clack!* the wooden rachet clattered as the wrist cuffs pulled upward. *Clack! Clack! Clack!* Now all of the slack was gone from the ropes and Vanidor's arms and legs were pulled straight. Here the Troll stopped, his mouth gaping wide, his thick tongue running over his yellow teeth.

"How many came with you?" hissed Modru.

Vanidor said nought.

Clack!

"I ask you again, fool: were there more than three of you?" Modru faced Laurelin, and she said nothing, her lips pressed in a grim line.

Clack!

"Tell me this, oaf: what were the names of your slain companions?" Modru faced Vanidor, the Elf's body taut.

"Tell him, Lord Vanidor!" cried Laurelin in anguish. "It cannot hurt, for they are dead!"

"Duorn and Varion," said Vanidor, speaking at last.

"Ahh, the dolt *does* have a tongue," hissed Modru. "Duorn and Varion, eh? And what of other companions: did they, too, have names?"

Again Vanidor clamped his lips shut.

The Troll grinned in glee.

Clack!

"You might as well speak, fool," sissed Modru, "for your silence will not stay my Master's return."

"Your Master?" Vanidor's question jerked out through clenched teeth. Sweat beaded upon the Elf's brow and trickled down his face.

"Gyphon!" Modru's voice lashed out in exultation.

"Gyphon?" gasped Vanidor. "But He is beyond the Spheres."

"At the moment, yes," crowed Modru, "but on the Darkest Day the Myrkenstone will open the way.

"But we dally, fool. Name me manes."

Silence.

Clack!

A groan escaped Vanidor's lips, and Laurelin wept silently.

"Myrkenstone?" Vanidor's breath shuddered in and out.

Modru gloated at him and paused as if debating whether to share a secret. "Why not? You'll not tell this tale to others." The Evil One strode to the *blotch* on the pedestal. "Here, fool, is the great Myrkenstone. Sent on its way by my Master four millennia agone. Long was its journey, but it came at last, five years past. Did not my Master say unto Adon: *'Even now I have set into motion events you cannot stop.'* Did He not say so?"

Modru strode back to Vanidor. "Your companions, dolt, their names."

The Elf bit his lip till blood came, but spoke not.

Clack!

Vanidor was in agony, his shoulders separated from

their sockets, his hips and spine pulled near their limits. His ribs stood stark upon his heaving chest.

"Why, my Lord Vanidor," sneered Modru, "you look puzzled by my tale of the Myrkenstone. Whence came this thing, you ask? From the sky, fool! What you simpletons name the Dragon Star, that was Gyphon's sending: a great flaming comet whose only purpose was to bear the Myrkenstone to me, to plunge to Mithgar in dark, blazing glory, the 'Stone plummeting to fall at my retreat in the Barrens. Why think you I dwelled there *lo* these many years? Out of fear? Nay! Say instead out of anticipation.

"Now yield me the names of your comrades."

Only Laurelin's sobs answered him.

Spittle drooled from the corner of the Troll's mouth.

Clack!

Vanidor's wrists bled, and his ankles were disjoint. Wordless sounds came from his throat.

"Think you that it was an accident of nature?" Modru's viperous voice asked. "Nay, 'twas my Master's doing! And a great weapon it is. How deem you the Dimmendark is made? What's that? You cannot say? Then I shall have to tell you: by the Myrkenstone, fool! It *eats* the cursed sunlight, sending Shadowlight in its stead. And with it I control the reach of Winternight, to the woe of the world. But when my Master comes, I and my minions will be set free from the Sunbane, then nought will stop our rule."

Modru's clenched fist smote the rack, and he loomed darkly over the Elf. "Names, fool, names," spat Modru.

"Oh, my Lord Vanidor, speak!" cried Laurelin. "Please speak!"

Cries were wrested from Vanidor, but he said no name.

The great Ogru's lips smacked wetly.

Clack!

"Ride, Flandrena, ride!" Vanidor's cry was rent from his screaming throat.

Flandrena?" hissed Modru. "Is that one of your companions?"

Vanidor's hoarse shrieks filled the tower, and Laurelin jerked at her chain and wrenched back and forth and cried in great gasping sobs and tried to reach the Elf.

Clack!

"Gildor!" Vanidor's tortured scream shattered through the tower, and then was no more, for the Lian warrior was dead.

Laurelin fell to her knees, her arms clutched across her stomach, and she doubled over, rocking back and forth in torment, great sobs racking her frame. Yet she was driven so deeply into grief and horror that no sounds issued from her throat. And she was but vaguely aware of Lōkha unshackling her from the iron post and leading her back down the twisting stairwell; for the torturous murder of Vanidor Silverbranch had pushed Laurelin beyond her uttermost limits. And as she stumbled blindly down the steps, behind her sissed Modru's sibilant laughter.

She was taken down to a main corridor, but the Lōkha did not force her back to the dark cell. Instead, she was given over to two scuttling Rukha who led her into a richly appointed room.

" 'Unblemished,' he said," croaked one Rukh.

"But, *sss*, the arm, the arm," hissed the other.

"The drink'll heal that, you stupid gob," snarled the first, "after we bind it."

Ungently, the two Rukha stripped the foul clothing from the Princess, hauling her this way and that. And when she was naked, they used iron shears to cut the wrappings holding the splint in place. And all the while they worked, Laurelin sobbed quietly, tears smearing through the grime on her face.

At last the injured arm was bared, and although the bone had already begun to knit—for it had been twenty-three days since it had been broken—still the Rukha set Laurelin's break in a binding made by dipping long, wide strips of cloth in a liquescent paste and wrapping them 'round her arm where they quickly dried. When the two were done, the stiffened wrap went from above her bent elbow to below her wrist.

And they poured the hot burning drink down her throat, the same fiery liquid forced upon her by the Ghola on the long ride to Modru's Iron Tower.

They took her into another room and sat her in a hot bath, and with harsh soaps and rough hands they scrubbed her hair and scoured the filth from her face and elsewhere. And Laurelin paid but little heed to their unfeeling ministrations.

That night she slept in a bed, but her dreams were of the Iron Tower, and she woke up screaming, *"Vanidor!"* And, weeping, she fell back into exhausted sleep.

And in her dreams, a golden-haired Elfess came to her and soothed her.

And then a sad-eyed Elf stood before her. *Are you Vanidor? Are you Gildor?* But he said nought, smiling gently.

Lastly, she had a vision of her Lord Galen, and he stood in a dark place and held her locket at his throat.

When she awakened, she found she was weeping, and her mind kept returning to those unbearable moments in the tower: unspeakably cruel, ruthless moments that endlessly repeated in her thoughts.

The mute Rukh brought her food, yet she touched it not, and sat abed watching the fire in the chimney with unseeing eyes: grieving. All 'Darkday she sat thus, cold horror clutching her heart; for what the slaughter of a waggon train had failed to do, what eighteen 'Darkdays at the hands of the Ghola had failed to do, and what five "days" locked in a filthy, lightless cell had failed to do, being forced to watch helplessly the torture-murder of Vanidor had at last done: it had driven her spirit into a dark realm of no hope.

That night, again Laurelin dreamed of the golden-haired Lady. And this time the Elfess planted a seed in black soil. A green shoot emerged and swiftly blossomed into a beautiful flower. Just as swiftly, the flower withered and died. And a wind blew, carrying the shriveled leaves and petals swirling up and away, but also bearing silken fluffs floating upon the breeze. And the Elfess reached up and caught one of the fluffs and held it for Laurelin to see. And *lo!* it was a seed.

Laurelin awakened, and sat in the flickering firelight and pondered the fair Lady's message, and the Princess at last thought she knew its import: *From Life comes Death, from Death comes Life, a never-ending circle.*

And in that moment, aided by a golden-haired Elfess she had never met, Laurelin's spirit began to heal.

CHAPTER 5

DRIMMEN-DEEVE

Up the long staircase they climbed, Brega and Gildor first with the lantern, Tuck and Galen after. And from below pounded thunder as the maddened Kraken hammered upon the Door: *Boom! Boom!*

At the top of the steps they paused, catching their breath.

"Two hundred treads," said Brega, and turned to Gildor. "It is odd that a trade route would start with such an obstacle as a two-hundred-step rise."

"Nevertheless, Drimm Brega," answered Gildor, "this is the way I came. Mayhap heavy goods are borne by train a different way, perhaps out through a level passage from the chamber below; yet when we trod under the Grimwall through Drimmen-deeve those many years past, this is the way we were led."

Brega merely grunted.

Boom! Boom! Boom!

"Let us move on," said Brega, "else the Madûk may jar loose the hidden linchpins to bring these passages down upon us."

Onward they went, along a high, curving corridor, passages and fissures alike boring blackly off to either side. The floor was level and covered with a fine layer of rock dust, and no tracks could be seen in it except those they left in their wake.

Boom. Boom. Behind, the Kraken raged on, the rolling echoes fading with distance as the four strode forth: *boom . . . boom . . . oom . . .* until finally they could hear the savage hammering no more.

The floor had begun to slope downward, and still corridors and crevices radiated outward, away from the passageway the comrades followed. But Gildor stayed in the main tunnel and did not turn aside.

Down they went, deeper under the dark granite of Grimspire Mountain, and their pace was swift. Four miles, five miles, and more, they marched away from the Door, their hard stride carrying them onward. For as Galen put it: "We must be away from this Black Maze ere the Ghola can bear word to the Gargon that intruders now walk his Realm."

But each one of the four was weary, exhausted by the long pursuit ere they had set foot into Black Drimmen-deeve, and so, when they came into an enormous, long hall, nearly four hundred yards in length, perhaps eighty yards wide, set, according to Brega, some seven miles from the Door, Gildor called a halt.

"We must rest and eat, and let me study the ways before us," said the Lian warrior, waving a hand at the four major portals gaping blackly into the chamber, "for I must choose the proper path out."

Grateful for the chance to rest, Tuck slumped to the floor in the middle of the hall. He fished around in his pack and gave a biscuit of mian to Galen while keeping one for himself. They sat in the shadows in the center of the chamber and watched as Gildor and Brega made the rounds of the exits, peering down each and discussing the paths that they saw. At last the Elf and Dwarf came and sat beside the Man and Warrow and took food for themselves.

Brega wolfed down his ration, yet Gildor but barely touched his food, seeming pensive, troubled.

"Elf Gildor," said Brega, sipping from his canteen, "be there water along this path of ours?"

"Yes, if I step it out true," answered Gildor. "Water aplenty for the drinking, sweet and pure when I came so long ago."

"Elf Gildor," Brega spoke again, "while we rest ere we go on, you said you would speak of some events of long ago, after the Châkka abandoned Kraggen-cor. How came the drawbridge to be up? The Door to be closed? The Black Mere to be made?"

"Ah, yes," said Gildor, "I did promise you that tale. Hear me, then, for this is what I know: When the Dread broke free of the Lost Prison, the Drimma fled Drimmen-deeve, and some Elves fled Darda Galion, for such is the Gargon's horror. Drimma fled east and west, turning north and south; so, too, did the Elves that ran, or they rode the Twilight Ride.

"With the Drimma gone, Rucha and Loka began to gather in the Black Deeves, coming to serve the Gargon in his dread-filled Realm. Many were the skirmishes with the *Spaunen*, and the Lian set watch upon the portals: Dusk-Door, Dawn-Gate.

"The *Rûpt*, too, set wards at these entrances, though why they guarded this place, it is not known; yet guard it the *Spaunen* did. Perhaps they feared the Lian Guardians would enter, yet even the Lian cannot withstand Gargoni: it was but through the power of the Wizards of the Black Mountain of Xian that these dread creatures were held at bay during the Great War of the Ban. And had there been more Gargoni, even the Wizards would have failed.

"Yet the *Spaunen* guarded the Door, though none else would enter, and the Lian watched patiently as the seasons passed into one another and the years flowed by.

"Then came a time five centuries past when two great Trolls came each night and quarried stone, building a dam across the Duskrill. A year they labored, until it was done at last. No longer did the Duskrill tumble down the linn in a graceful waterfall; instead, the water was trapped behind the Troll-dam. And the Black Mere—the Dark Mere—grew swiftly and soon filled all the swale up under the Loomwall.

"Another time passed: one more year, I think. And then in the dark of night a mighty Dragon came winging."

"Dragon!" burst out Tuck.

"Aye, Dragon," answered Gildor, nodding.

"Then the old tales are true," responded Tuck. "Dragons are real and not just fabulous creatures of legend, not just hearthtale fables."

"Aye, Tuck," confirmed Gildor. "Dragons are real: Fire-drakes and Cold-drakes both. Once, all Dragons gushed flame, but those who aided Gyphon in the Great War were bereft of their fire and became Cold-drakes; and they suffer the Ban, for the Sun slays them, though they die not the *Withering Death*: their Dragon-scaled hides spare them that. Even so, Cold-drakes are awesome enemies, and their spew is terrible: though it flames not, still it dissolves rock and base metal—even silver corrodes under that dire drip, and the spume chars flesh without fire."

"Then where are they, the Fire-drakes and Cold-drakes?" asked Tuck. "I mean, if Dragons are real, why don't people see them around?"

"They sleep, Tuck," answered Gildor. "For a thousand years they hide away in lairs in the remote high mountains only to awaken and ravage the Land, bellowing their brazen calls. Five hundred years agone they took to their lairs to sleep; five hundred years hence they will awaken, and they will be hungry, and begin a two-millennia rampage ere they sleep again."

"Evil will be the day when Dragons wake," said Brega grimly, "for they are the bane of all Folk. The Châkka have often suffered from these dire creatures: Dragons would plunder our treasuries and hoard our hard-won wealth." Brega turned to Gildor. "But the Dragon that came through the night to the Dusk-Door, was it a Cold-drake, like Sleeth?"

"Aye, like Sleeth but not Sleeth, for that Orm had already been slain by Elgo," answered Gildor. At the mention of Elgo's name, Brega's eyes flashed with ire, and he seemed about to speak, but Gildor went on: "When the great creature winged south from the Northern Wastes, at first we thought it was mighty Ebonskaith himself, but then we saw that instead it was Skail of the Barrens. And he bore a great burden—a *writhing* burden—something evil and alive, and he dropped it in the Black Mere."

"The Kraken," said Galen.

"The Madûk," echoed Brega.

"Aye," answered Gildor, nodding, "though then we did not know what it was, today, five hundred years later, we four have discovered to our woe it was a Hèlarms."

"Hèlarms?" Again Tuck bore a puzzled look. "Whence came this creature?"

"I deem it most likely that Skail bore it here from the Great Maelstrom off the Seabane Island in the Boreal Sea, for that is a haunt of these creatures, hauling ships down into the great whirlpool, there where the Gronfang Mountains plunge into the brine," answered Gildor. "Yet it could have come from other places as well: It is told that fell monsters from beyond the borders of time inhabit the deeps—not only the great ocean abysses, but also the cold, dark lakes: the Grimmere, Nordlake, and others. And the waters rushing in blackness 'neath the Land—the lightless undermountain torrents, the rivers carving stone, the bottomless black pools—they, too, are said to hold dire creatures, and are better left undisturbed."

Tuck shuddered and gazed about into the shadows mustered near as Gildor spoke on: "Skail dropped the burden into the Black Mere and then winged north, anxious to be safe in his lair ere the Sun arose. And with this Monster now in the waters, when daybreak came, the Lian Guaridans saw that the drawbridge was up and the Dusk-Door closed; the *Rûpt* no longer stood watch at this portal."

"There was no need," said Galen, "for the Krakenward now guarded this entrance."

"Aye," answered Gildor, "and now we know why the Ghûlka attacked us not: they feared the Hèlarms."

Again Tuck shuddered. "What a vile Monster: lurking in black waters, waiting to snatch innocent victims."

No one spoke for a moment, and then Galen quietly said, "I loved Jet."

"And I Fleetfoot," Gildor added.

Again no one spoke for long moments, and tears glimmered in Tuck's eyes. Even Brega seemed stricken by the deaths of the horses who had striven to their uttermost limits only to be cruelly slain by a hideous creature, for Brega said, his voice husky, "No two steeds could have given more."

At last Galen stood, saying, "Be there ought else, Gildor? We must press on."

"Only this, Galen King," said Gildor, rising to his feet also, "the Monster was put here at the behest of Modru, on this you can mark my words, for none else would do such a vile thing. Hearken unto this, too: the power of the Evil in Gron must be vast to cause a Dragon to bear a Hèlarms from the Great Maelstrom to here, and to cause a Hèlarms to suffer being borne."

"Perhaps," said Brega, shouldering his pack, "there is something to the legend that Dragons mate with Madûks."

"*What?*" burst out Tuck. "Dragons mate with Krakens?"

" 'Tis but a legend," answered Brega, "yet it is also true that no female Dragons are known to the Châkka." Brega cocked an eye at Gildor, who merely shrugged and agreed that no female Dragons were known to the Elves either.

Once more they set out upon their journey, striding to reach the Dawn-Gate ere they could be detected. And the deeper they strode into Drimmen-deeve, the more uneasy Tuck became, yet he knew not why.

The corridor that Gildor chose continued to slant downward, and less than a mile from the "Long Hall," as Brega called it, they came to a wide fissure in the floor, nearly eight feet across; the passage continued on the other side. And from the black depths of the crack came a hideous *sucking* sound.

"Ah," said Gildor, "now I know we follow the path

I trod long ago, for this *slurping* crevice I remember well. Yet there was a wooden span when we crossed it."

"What makes the suck?" asked Tuck, peering down into the blackness but seeing nought, then pulling back. "It sounds as if some hideous creature lies below, trying to draw us into its maw." Tuck's thoughts were upon Gildor's words about monsters living in deep, dark places.

Brega listened. "A whirl of water, I think. Had this place a name, Elf Gildor, when you last were here?"

Gildor shook his head, and Tuck said, "Then I name it the Drawing Dark, for it seems to want to pull us down into its lost depths. A slurking whirl of water it may be, but a sucking maw it sounds."

"Think you that you can leap this, Tuck?" asked Galen.

Tuck eyed the distance, the jump a long one for a three-and-a-half-foot-tall Warrow. "Aye," said the Wee One, "though I'd rather have a bridge."

"Here, Waeran," said Brega, setting down the lantern and his pack and uncoiling a rope, "remove your pack and tie this to your waist, then throw the loose end to me; I will anchor you if you fall short."

With three running strides, Brega sprang across. Tuck threw the Dwarf the coil of rope, one end tied to the Warrow's waist. When Brega had looped it over his shoulders and had taken a firm grip, he nodded to the buccan.

Tuck took one last look at the black gap, trying to banish the thought of being sucked down into a monstrous maw, and ran and leapt with all his might. He cleared the gap by a good two feet.

The packs and lantern were tossed across, then Gildor and lastly Galen leapt the fissure, and they strode onward, leaving the hideous suck of the Drawing Dark behind.

Deeper under the dark granite of Grimspire they strode, the path ever pitching downward, corridors and branchings splitting outward from the passage they trod, unexpected cracks yawning in the floor, though none the width of the Drawing Dark. And the farther they went, the more Tuck's heart pounded in vague apprehension.

"It is the Dread, Tuck," said Gildor, noting the perspiration beaded upon the Waerling's lip. "We stride toward him now, and the fear will grow."

Onward they went through the shadowy maze, coming to a great oval chamber—"Eleven miles from the Door," said Brega. This hall, too, was enormous: nearly three hundred yards in extent, two hundred at its widest. Straight across the floor they strode, out the far side.

Still the passage pitched downward, and Tuck was most weary, his steps beginning to lag. Long had this "day" been, for it had begun many hours past with the attempt to cross Quadran Pass.

"When next we come to a chamber, we will rest," said Galen, "for worn-out legs will not bear us swiftly if fleetness ever becomes our need."

But they tramped four more miles through the black tunnels, downward past splits and forks and joinings, before coming to another chamber, this one also huge. Brega held high the lantern and Gildor smiled in relief and pointed. "This, too, I remember, for here is where we stopped to take water."

Tuck peered past Gildor to see a chamber nearly round, two hundred yards across. And by the phosphorescent glow of the Dwarven lantern he could see a low stone bridge crossing above a clear stream that emerged from the wall to the left and rushed through a wide channel cutting across the west end of the chamber to disappear under the wall to the south. Several low stone parapets beringed the room.

"This is called Bottom Chamber," said Brega. "Châkka lore speaks of this bridge o'er the drinking stream. Sweet has been this water in all the Châkka days."

"Sweet, too, was the Duskrill ere the Dark Mere came to be," said Gildor. "But now that water has been spoiled by the Hèlarms, and it is foul to the taste and touch. Let us hope the drinking stream remains safe and pure."

Across the carven arch they went, stopping long enough at the far side to stoop and test and then drink deeply and refill their leather water bottles with the cold, clean, crystalline liquid.

They sat with their backs to one of the stone parapets and took a meal. And as they ate, apprehension coursed through Tuck's veins; the fear had grown, for they had strode four miles nearer to the Dread.

They had but finished their rations when Gildor softly spoke: "Galen King, I bear woeful news. I could not speak of it before; my grief was too great. Yet now I must say this while I can: I fear the mission to rescue the Lady Laurelin has failed, for Vanidor is dead."

"Vanidor . . ." Tuck blurted; then: "How know you this, Lord Gildor?"

"The place where he stood in my heart is now empty." Gildor looked away, silent for a moment, then spoke on, his voice but a whisper: "I felt his final pain. I heard his last cry. Evil slew him."

Gildor rose up and walked into the shadows. And now all the company knew why the Elf had fallen to his knees, whelmed, crying *"Vanidor!"* in that dire instant when the Krakenward had struck.

After a moment Galen, too, arose and went into the shadows, following Gildor's steps. And they stood and spoke softly, but what they said, Tuck did not know as tears slid down his face.

And Brega sat with his hood cast over his head.

Again Gildor stood guard while the others slept; and the sad eyes of the Elf watched the faint ruby flicker running along Bale's edges, the sword whispering of evil afar.

After but six hours' respite, once more they took up the trek.

From the Bottom Chamber they took a southeasterly exit that curved away to the east as they followed the course of the corridor. Now the floor rose upward as they tramped on, and still crevices and tunnels bore away to left and right.

Three miles they marched, and Gildor stopped where a large corridor came in from the south. He stood unsure and spoke with Brega, but the lore of the Dwarf was of little or no help. They stepped southward along this large corridor to enter a great side hall, and Gildor shook his head and led them back out to follow the eastward way instead.

Still the passage sloped upward and curved unto the north, and along this section there were no side tunnels nor crevices cleaving away.

Three more miles they strode, to be confronted by four passages: the left way was wide and straight and sloped downward; the right-hand passage, too, was wide, only it bore on upward; the two middle ways were twisting and narrow, one bearing up, the other down. To the immediate left a stone door stood open.

"Ach! I cannot remember," said Gildor, looking at the four ways before him.

"No matter which of the four you choose," said Brega, "they all lead into Rávenor."

"Stormhelm?" asked Tuck. "But I thought we walked beneath the stone of Grimspire."

"Look, Waeran, and see," pointed Brega. "Here is the black granite of Aggarath, while there is the rudden stone of Rávenor. Yes, here we leave the dark rock of what you call 'Grimspire' to trod the rust red of 'Stormhelm.' "

In spite of the growing feeling of disquiet as they had trod eastward, still Tuck's heart gave a leap of hope. "Isn't the Dawn-Gate upon the flanks of Stormhelm?" At Brega's nod: "Then we have come to the mountain that holds our gateway eastward."

"Ah, but Friend Tuck," said Brega, "though we have come twenty-one miles under the rock of Aggarath, still we must stride twenty-five or thirty miles more beneath the red stone of Rávenor ere we can walk in the open again."

Tuck's heart fell to hear these distances, and plummented even further when Gildor said, "Twenty-five or thirty miles if I can find the way, but much longer if I cannot."

Galen spoke: "Let us rest and take some food while you try to recall the way, Lord Gildor."

At the Elf's nod, Brega led them through the open stone door into a small chamber no more than twenty feet square, with a low ceiling—the first small room they had seen in Drimmen-deeve.

"Oi!" exclaimed Brega, holding up the lantern.

Centered in the room, a great chain dangled down through a narrow, grate-covered square shaft set in the ceiling and passed through a like grate placed in the floor, the huge links appearing out of the constricting blackness above and disappearing into the darkness of the strait shaft below.

Brega examined the iron-barred grille set in the floor. " 'Ware. This grate is loose, though at one time it was anchored firmly in the stone."

Tuck looked at the small chamber in puzzlement, and at the narrow shaft piercing the room, the massive chain, and the grids covering the openings above and below. "What is it for, Brega, the shaft and the chain? And why the iron bars?"

The Dwarf merely shrugged. "I know not its purpose, Friend Tuck. Air shafts, window shafts, shafts to mine ores, well shafts for water, holes to raise and lower things: these I understand. Yet this construction is beyond my knowledge, though other Châkka could, no doubt, explain its purpose. As to the bars, all I can guess is that they are set there to keep something in."

"Or to keep something out," added Gildor.

"Is this the Lost Prison?" Tuck's heart skipped a beat.

"Nay, Tuck," said Gildor, gesturing at the stone door and iron bars. "Such a flimsy construction would not hold even a determined Ruch, much less thwart the power of an evil Vûlk."

Brega bristled. "Elf, this room was crafted by Châkka; you exaggerate when you say it could not hold an Ukh . . . though you speak true of the Ghath."

At the naming of the Dread, Tuck's heart again raced loudly in his ears.

"I stand corrected, Drimm Brega, and I apologize for my errant mouth." Gildor bowed to the Dwarf, and Brega inclined his head in return.

They sat and took a bit of mian and water, and Gildor pondered the question of the four corridors: "This I think: Neither of the two middle corridors should be our path, for I know that long ago I trod not their narrow, twisting ways. But as to the far left or right, I cannot say which one we should follow."

"Does your lore speak aught of this fourfold split, Brega?" asked Galen.

"Nay, King Galen," answered the Dwarf.

"Then, Lord Gildor," said Galen, "you must choose one of the two ways and hope we come to something that you recognize."

Suddenly, a great wash of dread inundated Tuck's heart, and he gasped in terror. Galen, Gildor, and Brega also blenched. Just as suddenly, the fear was gone, leaving racing hearts behind.

"He knows!" cried Gildor, leaping to his feet. "The Dread knows we are in his domain and casts about, questing for the spark of us."

"The Ghola," spat Galen, "they've borne the word to him."

"We must get out!" cried Brega. "We must get out before he finds us!" In haste the Dwarf shouldered his pack and stepped to the door, holding high the lantern as the others scrambled after.

And they stood before the four passages. "Which way, Lord Gildor?" asked Galen. "We cannot delay. You must choose."

"Then let it be the leftmost," answered Gildor, "for the way is widest."

And down the sloping corridor they hastened, matching Tuck's stride, for the Warrow was smallest and so he set the pace.

And Gildor withdrew flickering Red Bale from its scabbard and bore the sword in the open, its werelight to warn the four should *Spaunen* come near.

A half mile they went through the smooth-walled carven tunnel, but *lo!* Gildor's steps began to slow as if he were reluctant to press oward, yet Bale's scarlet blade-jewel glinted but lightly.

Another furlong they paced, and then the Elf stopped, and so, too, did the companions, Brega pattering on but a few more steps. "We must go no further this way," gritted Gildor, his face white.

"But the path is wide and smooth," growled Brega, pointing to the open passage before them.

"We walk toward a foul place," responded Gildor. "It has the stench of a great viper pit, though no vipers in it dwell."

Now Tuck sniffed, and a faint reek of adders hung on the air. "What is it, Lord Gildor? What makes this foetor?"

"I know not for certain, Tuck," answered the Elf, "yet when I strode the battlefields of the War of the Ban, it clung where Gargoni had been."

They retraced their steps to the corridors at the Grate Room, and this time they took the right-hand passage. And as they stepped upon its upward-sloping floor, again the pounding fear swept across them and away, leaving Tuck trembling, his legs weakened.

"He searches." Gildor's voice was tight, and he spoke to faces drawn grim.

Up the passage they strode, Tuck's legs continuing to set the pace as they marched through a delved corridor, the stone arching above them. Swiftly along the carven tunnel they went, but slowly its character changed: the walls became rougher, less worked by Dwarven tools. And then a small crack appeared along the floor and swiftly widened to become a chasm to their left, yawning black and bottomless; the floor they strode along narrowed, becoming a broad shelf lipping the fissure; and then the shelf constricted to a narrow ledge, and they sidled for scores of feet along the wall, the gulf yawning below them. At last they came once more to a wide floor, and Tuck sighed in relief as he stepped onto the broad stone.

At that moment dread fear again shocked through the four as the Gargon tried to sense them, his questing power coursing through the stone halls of Black Drimmen-deeve.

Upward sloped the way, and wide cracks appeared in the floor, and Tuck had to leap over three- and four-foot-wide crevices: long jumps for one who was only three and a half feet tall.

But finally the floor smoothed out, and once more they strode through an arched tunnel, and after three hours of walking, leaping, and sidling—going some six miles in all—they came to a great round chamber, and Tuck asked for a short rest.

Tuck sat and massaged his legs, yet his heart was filled with dire foreboding, for they had come six miles closer to the Dread. To distract his own mind Tuck said, "Well, now I have gone from being a Thornwalker to being a Deevewalker."

"Ai, you have named us, Tuck," said Gildor, "and

if our tale is ever told, they will call us the Walkers of the Deeves."

"Ar!" growled Brega. "Deevewalkers we are. But of us four, only *I* have long dreamed of striding the corridors of Kraggen-cor, and now it is so, yet I would have it otherwise. For I come not marching in triumph, but instead slink through furtively. And if I live to tell of this journey to my kindred, this is what I will say: I have walked in Kraggen-cor, a bygone Realm of might; but its light is gone, and dread now stalks the halls."

Again the pounding fear washed over them, stronger now than before, and all four leapt to their feet as if to fly; then it passed onward, and Tuck unclenched his fists.

They made a circuit of the round chamber, and Gildor spoke with Brega; and the eastward way was chosen, for its path was broad and worn by the travel of many feet. Forward they strode and the floor was smooth and level.

"Is there aught the Gargon fears?" puffed Tuck, stepping along swiftly upon his Warrow legs.

"Nought that I know of," answered Gildor, "else we would use it against him."

"He fears the Sun," said Galen, striding at Tuck's side, "and perhaps he fears the power of Modru, yet neither of these are at our beck to stave off the Horror."

"What about Wizards?" asked Tuck. "Lord Gildor, you spoke of them as fending Gargons in the Ban War."

"The Mages of Xian have not been seen since that time," responded Gildor, "except perhaps by Elyn and Thork in the Quest of Black Mountain: it is said they found the Wizardholt."

Onward they strode, the lantern casting swaying

shadows along the hall, its light revealing passages and arched openings to the side.

"Is there aught that Modru fears?" asked Tuck, still keeping the pace for all.

"The Sun," answered Galen, "and Gyphon."

"Too, it is said that Modru loathes mirrors," added Gildor.

"Mirrors?" grunted Brega, surprised.

"I think he sees something of his true soul cast back from the glass," answered Gildor. "And it is told that he cannot abide his reflection in a pure silver mirror, for then his image is stripped of all disguise and stands revealed before him; yet it is also said that those who have seen Modru's reflection in an argent speculum are driven foaming mad forever."

The passage they followed curved to the northward, and their hard stride bore them along its wide level floor. They had come nearly two miles from the Round Chamber, as Brega had dubbed it, when Gildor held up a hand. *"Hsst!"* he whispered sharply. "I hear iron-shod feet; and look: Bale speaks of evil. Shutter the lamp, Brega."

Quickly, Brega snapped the hood down upon the lantern, and they stood in the dark hall listening. Ahead, they could hear the clatter of scaled armor and the tread of many feet slapping upon the stone. And the light of burning brands could be seen bobbing in the distance, growing brighter as a force of many came toward them. And Tuck's heart hammered in fear.

"The Dread sends Rukha and Lōkha searching these halls for us," said Galen, his voice grim.

Brega raised the hood of the lantern a crack and searched for an exit to bolt through. "This way," he whispered, and they entered a narrow corridor bearing eastward.

The hall they followed was but lightly worked and had the look of a natural cavern. And there were occasional splits and fissures in the floor; most could be stepped over, but at times Tuck would have to spring across, though none of the others did, being taller than the Warrow.

They strode a mile and stopped to listen, and Gildor's sharp senses told them some of the *Spaunen* followed down the corridor behind.

Onward the four continued, and the further east they went, the more finished the passageway became. Gildor kept a sharp eye on Bale's blade-jewel; yet the red glimmer told that the evil was yet distant, though each step they took caused the fear to increase, for still they strode toward the Gargon.

Again, pounding dread swept across them, causing Tuck to gasp. And when it was past, on eastward they went.

At last they came unto a broad hall and cautiously peered in, looking for the flame of Rūcken torches: the hall stood dark and empty. Brega threw the lamp shutter wide, and they saw by its glow that the chamber was enormous: nearly four hundred yards long, two hundred across. The four had come in through the west side.

"Ai!" said Gildor softly. "I remember this place, though then it was that we came in through the far north portal. Yes, and now our path lies there to the east."

"How far, Lord Gildor, how far to the Dawn-Gate?" asked Galen as they strode across the chamber.

"Perhaps fifteen miles, perhaps twenty," answered

Gildor, "I cannot say for certain." Gildor spoke to Brega: "Drimm Brega, how far have we come?"

"Two and thirty miles from the Dusken Door," answered the Dwarf with a certainty that brooked no dispute.

"Then, if I can find the way," responded Gildor, "we are more likely to be fifteen miles than twenty from the distant exit."

Out through an eastern portal they went, and entered a lightly delved corridor: though the floor was smooth, the walls and ceiling were but little worked by Dwarven tools and had a rough look. The floor sloped up and the corridor curved this way and that, once turning in a great long spiral upward. There were many side fissures cleaving off into the darkness, their ends beyond seeing.

"If I am right," said Brega, excitement rising in his voice, "Châkka lore calls this the Upward Way. It is part of the trade road through Kraggen-cor and runs from the Broad Hall to the Great Chamber of the Sixth Rise. That must have been the Broad Hall we just left. And though I know not the way, we indeed stride toward the eastern portal, for the spoken lore tells that the Great Chamber is just under two miles from the Daūn Gate."

Up they went, their hopes rising, but so, too, rose their fear, for they strode ever toward the Dread.

"Hsst!" Again Gildor shushed the others and Brega shuttered the lantern. Red Bale's flame grew, and the clatter of Rūcks came toward them.

They slipped aside into a crevice, hiding deep in its dark recesses. Bale was sheathed so that its ruby light would not give them away, and they waited.

Now they could hear voices, speaking in the foul

Slûk tongue, and louder came the tramp of feet and the rattle of arms. Torchlight grew, and passed the mouth of the crevice. And Tuck's pulse hammered in his ears. *And one of the Rūcks stepped in to search the fissure, his burning brand held aloft!*

Deep in the dark at the back of the crack and as yet unseen by the Rūck, Tuck reached for an arrow, but ere he could string it to bow, the lash of the dire Dread swept across them all, and a wail of fear rose up from the Rūcks, and the one coming along the crevice shrieked and dropped the brand and covered his ears in terror. And then the surging horror was past, and the Rūck snatched up the torch and ran back to join the others, abandoning his search of this fissure.

A snarling Hlōk amongst the Rūcks flailed about with a whip and drove them back to their hunt. But they had moved beyond the crevice hiding the four and so found them not, as onward tramped the foul squad, ferreting out the other fissures as they went, their torchlight fading in the distance.

"The Dread has foiled his own search," whispered Tuck, his hands still trembling. "Yet it surprises me that his power whelms the Rūcks, too."

"To his fear casting none are immune," said Gildor, "perhaps not even Modru himself."

"Let us go ere other Squam come this way," insisted Brega.

Gildor withdrew Bale and the blade-jewel's light faded as they watched, for the Rūcken squad had moved on, passing beyond seeing. Swiftly, back out of the crevice the four stepped and to the east, and soon they came to another huge cavern, and great square-cut stone blocks were scattered across the floor.

Brega pointed at one of the cubes. "I name this the

Rest Chamber, for I think the Waeran's wee legs grow weary, and we can rest among these stone seats, and hide among them should searchers come."

"Good advice, Warrior Brega," said Galen, sitting upon the floor with his back to stone, "for on our next leg I deem we must be prepared for swiftness, and rest is needed."

And so, with Red Bale standing silent sentry, they sat in the Rest Chamber and took mian and water, and their hearts pounded in fear.

According to Brega's measure, they had marched thirty-nine miles since leaving the Dusk-Door, and had taken but six hours' sleep in the Bottom Chamber and no more than an hour's rest at their other stops. Drained, they sat in the Rest Chamber for perhaps another hour, gathering strength for the final dash to the Dawn-Gate, estimated by Lord Gildor to be less than ten miles eastward.

Once more an intense lash of fear brought them to their feet ere it swept on, leaving them standing in grim alarm.

"Aie," moaned Brega, "we must get out."

"Let us go now," said Gildor, taking up Bale, "for to wait invites disaster."

"Tuck?" questioned Galen, and at the buccan's nod, eastward they went upon weary legs.

Upward the passage led, rising gently, curving leftward then right again. Bale's blade-jewel flickered a faint ruby, the glimmer slowly growing, warning of a distant danger coming closer as the four strode on. Quickly they marched between vertical walls and under an arched roof. Along the way, deep-carven runes were etched in the walls, but the Deevewalkers took no time to read the ancient messages. Long they strode, nearly two hours, and no side entrances nor exits did they see; neither were there crevices, only smooth carven walls. And the roadway continued to curve gently upward, turning left once more and again rightward.

At last they came to a huge cavern, its ends lost beyond seeing in black emptiness. Bale now cried that evil lurked near, and their hearts pounded in dread, but no sign of any foe did they see.

"Quick, across the floor and out the passage to the east," said Gildor, "for evil is coming."

They strode great strides upon the stone, and Tuck trotted, setting the pace. Two hundred yards, three hundred, and more they went, and still the blank emptiness stretched out before them.

"This is the Great Chamber of the Sixth Rise," panted Brega. "We are less than two miles from the Daūn Gate."

"Hsst!" shushed Gildor, sheathing Bale. "Look ahead. Lights. Someone comes. Shutter the lantern, Brega."

Tuck could see torchlight reflected from a portal far to the east.

"South, too," hissed Galen, pointing to lights coming up a passage that way also.

"To the north a passage stands dark." Brega's voice was low and urgent.

"North it is!" barked Galen, and they bolted across the stone floor, Brega's lantern hood now but barely cracked, the faint light showing them the way.

No sooner had they entered the north passage than from the east and south, Rūcks and Hlōks beyond count boiled into the Great Chamber.

"It is the Horde," said Galen, his voice weary as he peered out at the distant tide of Spawn flooding into the Great Chamber. "They have come at last across the Quadran Pass and into the Black Hole to join the Gargon."

"Ai, and the Horror will use the Deeves as a black fortress and launch War against Darda Galion, and the *Spaunen* will be his army." Gildor's words fell grim.

"But first the Squam will search for us," snapped Brega, "and if we would escape to warn the Larkenwald, let us fly now."

North they fled, nearly two furlongs ere coming to a broken door upon the right. The corridor stretched on before them, turning to the left in the distance, but they could see torchlight reflected around its curve.

"Quick, in here!" cried Brega, and they bolted through the damaged door.

They came into another great chamber, narrow but lengthy, and with a low ceiling. One hundred paces long it was and only twelve wide, and an exit could be seen at the far eastern end.

But supporting the ceiling mid way was a massive arch, and great runes of power were carven into its stone.

And as they started across the floor for the distant exit, Tuck's eye fell upon signs of an ancient battle: broken weapons, shattered armor, the skulls and bones of long-dead combatants.

And smeared upon the walls in a black ichor now dried were the Dwarven runes: ŦΓV⧅⧅I

Brega looked, too. "Braggi!" he cried. "That is Braggi's rune, written with the blood of Squam. He came to slay the Ghath but was nevermore seen." On they strode without pause, passing now among the remains of the battle-slain. Dwarf armor there was, and the plate of Spawn, as well as shattered axes, broken scimitars, War hammers, and cudgels.

Brega cast his hood over his head as they hurried onward. "Here in the Hall of the Gravenarch, Braggi made his stand. But the signs tell the tale that the Ghath came and slew Braggi and his raiders as they stood frozen."

Tuck shuddered, his gaze darting into the far reaches of the hall, his glance seeking to avoid the mute evidence from that long-ago time when the Gargon stalked down the length of a fear-rooted Dwarven column, the monster slaying as it went—and when the hideous creature had come to the last Dwarf, Braggi and his valiant raiders were no more.

Across the floor swiftly the four strode for the eastern portal, coming to the rune-marked Gravenarch. Just as they passed below it, the surging fear of the Dread pounded through their veins, *yet this time it did not sweep on past them but stayed locked upon their hammering hearts, and terror arrested their steps.*

"He has found us!" gasped Gildor. "He comes, and is near!"

Tuck's lungs were heaving, yet he could not seem to get enough to breathe, and his limbs were nearly beyond his control, for he could but barely move.

Brega clutched his arms across his chest and air hissed in through clenched teeth; his face turned upward and his hood fell back from his head. His eyes widened. "The arch," his voice jerked out. "The keystone . . . like a linchpin . . . cut off pursuit."

Dread pulsed through them as Brega forced himself

to stoop and grasp a broken War hammer. "Lift me up," he gritted. "Lift me . . . when I smite it, drop me . . . run . . . the ceiling will collapse."

"But you may be killed!" Tuck's words seemed muffled in the waves of fear.

Now Brega's rage crested above the numbing dread. "Lift, by Adon, I command it!"

Galen and Gildor hoisted the Dwarf, and he stood upon their shoulders as they braced him, his left hand upon the stone of the arch, the War hammer in his right. Tuck stood behind them, and only the Warrow's eyes were upon the portal where stood the broken door. And it seemed as if he could hear massive steps stalking through the terror, ponderous feet of stone pacing toward the door. And just as something dreadful loomed forth through the shadows: *"Yah!"* cried Brega, and swung the hammer with all the might of his powerful shoulders. *Crack!* The maul shattered through the keystone of the Gravenarch, and with a great rumble the vault above gave way. Gildor, Galen, and Brega tumbled backward, scrambling as stone fell 'round them. And Brega grabbed up Tuck and ran, for only the Warrow had glimpsed the shadow-wrapped Gargon, and the buccan could not cause his legs to move.

East they dashed for the door, just ahead of the ceiling crashing unto the floor behind them, filling the chamber with shattered stone. And as they raced through the portal and down a flight of steps, the roof gave way completely in one great roar, blocking all pursuit.

And waves of numbing dread beat through the stone and whelmed at them, and Tuck thought his heart would burst, yet now the Warrow could move again under his own power, and down a narrow hall they struggled while behind them endless horror ravened.

"Down," gasped Brega, "we've got to get down to the Mustering Chamber of the First Neath—the War Hall—for there is the drawbridge over the Great Dēop. And we must pass over it to come to the Daūn Gate. At least the lore says so."

"Ai, Drimm Brega, we crossed the Great Deep by drawbridge," answered Lord Gildor, his voice thin with fear, "though we came not this way, but instead passed down long steps to come to an enormous chamber: your War Hall."

"We are here upon the Fifth Rise," gritted Brega, his face blenched, for the power of the Dread was now locked onto their hammering hearts. "Six flights we must go down to reach the War Hall."

Passing by a tunnel on the left, east they reeled, curving south, down another flight of steps. "Fourth Rise," Brega grated as southward the narrow passage led. They passed one more tunnel to the left and kept on straight and down another staircase. "Third Rise," said Brega, and still the fear coursed through them and they knew the Gargon pursued by a different route. The tunnel they entered bore east and west, and to the east they fled, their legs seeming nearly too cumbersome to control. Another flight of stairs; "Second Rise," came Brega's trembling voice.

Tuck and his companions were weary beyond measure and the hideous fear sapped at their will, yet onward they fled, for to stop meant certain destruction. North and south the passage now went, and rightward they turned, southward, and once more steep steps pitched downward. "First Rise," Brega counted, and beyond a footway leading west the tunnel curved east.

On they faltered in abject fear, the dread power lashing after, and then came once more to stone steps down; "Gate Level," Brega croaked at the bottom, and still they staggered on.

Again the passage arced to the south, and, as before, they ignored another tunnel on the left, for the ways they chose bore down, south, and east, and all other paths were rejected.

One more long flight of steps they stumbled down, and *lo!* they came into a great dark hall. And they tottered outward into the chamber, and still the terror whelmed their hearts, and they could but barely carry forth.

"Ai, a Dragon Pillar," gasped Brega, pointing to a huge delved column carven to resemble a great Dragon coiling up an enormous fluted shaft. "This is the War Hall of the First Neath. To the east will be the bridge over the Great Dēop."

Leftward they reeled, their legs trembling with fear and barely under their control. Now along the lip of a deep abyss they staggered, to come to a great wooden span springing across the chasm. And *behold!* the bascule was down, the bridge unguarded!

"Great was the Gargon's pride," Galen's voice grated, "for he ne'er thought we would reach this place, else he would have posted a Swarm here to greet us."

They passed among barrels of pitch and oil and past rope-bound bundles of torches used by the maggot-folk to light their way through the black halls of Drimmen-deeve; and they came to the bridge at the edge of the Great Deep, a huge fissure that yawned blackly at their feet, jagging out of the darkness on their left, disappearing beyond the ebon shadows to their right, as much as a hundred feet wide where Tuck could see, pinching down to fifty where stood the bridge. And sheer sides dropped into bottomless depths below.

And as they stepped upon the span: "Hold!" cried Galen. "If we fell this bridge, then pursuit will be cut off."

"How?" Tuck's heart hammered, and every fiber in his being cried out, *Run, fool, run!* yet he knew Galen was right. "How do we fell the bridge?"

"Fire!" Galen's voice was hoarse. "With fire!"

No sooner were the words out of Galen's mouth than Brega, spurred by hope, sprang to a barrel of pitch and rolled it out upon the span, smashing the wooden keg open with his axe. Gildor, too, as well as Galen, rolled great casks out to Brega, and these the Dwarf smashed open as well, the pitch flowing viscidly over the wooden span.

"A torch, Tuck!" cried Galen as he pressed back for another keg.

And the buccan drew blue-flaming Bane and cut the binding on a stack of torches, and he ran across the span while Brega crashed open two more kegs of the oily pitch.

Standing at the eastern end of the bridge, Tuck struck steel to flint and lighted the torch. And now Gildor, Galen, and Brega came, and Tuck gave the burning brand to the Elf, saying, "You led us through, Lord Gildor; now cut off our pursuers."

The Lian Guardian hefted the torch to throw it, and Horror stepped forth out of the shadows at the far end of the span and fixed them with its unendurable gaze.

The Dread had come to slay them.

Tuck fell to his knees, engulfed in unbearable terror, and he was not at all aware that the shrill, piercing screams filling the air were rent from his own throat.

Thdd! Thdd! Onward came the grey, stonelike creature, scaled like a serpent, but walking upright upon two legs, a malevolent, evil parody of a huge reptilian Man.

Gildor stood paralyzed, transfixed in limitless horror, his eyes fastened inextricably upon a vision beyond seeing.

Thdd! Thdd! The ponderous Mandrak stalked forward, eight feet tall, taloned hands and feet, glittering rows of fangs in a lizard-snouted face.

Beads of sweat stood forth upon Galen's brow, and his entire being quivered with an effort beyond all measure. And slowly he raised up the tip of his sword until it was pointed level at the Gargon, but then he froze, unable to do more, for the Dread's gaze flicked upon him and the hideous power bereft him of his will.

Thdd! Thdd! Now the evil Gargon stalked past Tuck, the shrill-screaming Warrow beneath his contempt. And the stench of vipers reeked upon the air.

And as the Gargon passed him, the buccan was no longer under the direct gaze of Modru's Dread, and in that moment Tuck's horror-filled eyes saw Bane's blue light blazing up wildly, the weapon still in his grasp; and shrieking in unending shock, with fear beyond comprehension racking through his very substance,

Tuck desperately lashed out with all the terror-driven force of his being, spastically hewing the Elven long-knife into the sinews of the Gargon's leg—*Thkk!* Keen beyond reckoning, the elden blade of Duellin rived through reptilian scales and chopped deeply into the creature's massive shank, and a blinding blast of cobalt flame burst forth from the blade-jewel.

With a brazen roar of pain, the Gargon began to turn, reaching for Tuck, the massive talons set to rend the shrilling Warrow to shreds.

Yet the Dread's eyes now had left Galen, and the Man plunged Jarriel's sword straight and deep into the Gargon's gut—*Shkk!*—the blade shattering at the hilt as the hideous creature bellowed again and glared directly into Galen's eyes, blasting him with a dread so deep that it would burst a Man's heart. And Galen was hurled back by the horrendous power.

But at that moment came a tumbling glitter as Brega's axe flashed end over end through the air to strike the creature full in the forehead—*Chnk!*—and the roaring monster staggered hindward upon the span.

And Gildor threw the torch upon the pitch-drenched wood, and with a great *Phoom!* flames exploded upward, and Brega snatched Tuck forth from the bridge as the fire blasted outward.

And they dragged stunned Galen away from the whooshing blaze, for the Man had been whelmed by the Gargon's dreadful burst of power.

And upon the bridge the Gargon bellowed brazen roars, engulfed in raging flame, an axe cloven deep in his skull, a shivered sword plunged through his gut.

In the War Hall behind, there came the sounds of running feet as Rūcks and Hlōks poured out of corridors and into the great chamber. They ran among the fourfold rows of Dragon Pillars to come to the far edge of the bottomless Great Deep. And Tuck could hear them crying, *Glâr! Glâr!* (Fire! Fire!)

And then great waves of unbearable dread blasted outward, and *Spaunen* fell groveling upon the floor of the War Hall and shrieked in terror, while Gildor, Brega, and Tuck gasped for air and dropped to their knees, transfixed like unto stone statues.

And the dreadful crests of racking horror seemed to course through them forever.

But then the Gargon collapsed and lay in the whirling flames of the burning span, and of a sudden the harrowing dread was gone.

"Quickly," gasped Gildor, recovering first, "we must bear Galen King beyond arrow flight."

And so, weak with passing fear, they dragged the stunned Man up a flight of steps and to the outbound passage. And while Gildor worked to revive Galen, Tuck and Brega stood guard, one with an Elven long-knife, the other with Gildor's sword, the red-jeweled blade seeming awkward in the Dwarf's gnarled hand—a hand better suited to wield an axe.

"Ai, look at the vastness of the Mustering Chamber, Tuck," said Brega, in awe, as the flames roared upward. "It must be a mile to the far end, and half that wide."

And Tuck looked past the Rūcks and Hlōks running hither and thither, and by the light of the burning bridge he saw the rows of Dragon Pillars marching off into the distance past great fissures in the floor, and he knew that Brega gauged true.

At last Galen regained consciousness, yet he was

weak, shaken, his face pale, drawn, and deep within his eyes lurked a haunted look, for he had been whelmed by a Gargon's fear-blast, a blast that would have destroyed Galen; but he had been saved in the nick of time by Brega's well-thrown axe. Even so, Galen nearly had been slain, and he could not rise to his feet. And thus, they waited on the stone landing above the broad steps leading down toward the shelf of the abyss while strength and will slowly ebbed back into the Dread-hammered King. And long they watched the flames until the burning span collapsed, plummeting into the Great Deep, carrying the charred corpse of the slain Gargon down into the bottomless depths.

And when the drawbridge plunged, the four Deeve-walkers stood and made their way eastward, Galen on faltering feet, supported by sturdy Brega. Along a corridor they went two furlongs, up a gentle slope, up from the First Neath unto the Gate Level. Now they came to the East Hall and crossed its wide floor to pass beyond the broken portals of the Dawn-Gate and out from under the mountain, out into the open at last.

Before them in the Shadowlight of the Dimmendark stood the sloping valley called the Pitch leading down out of the Quadran. And out upon this cambered vale the four went, heading east, soon to bear south, for distant Darda Galion, to bring to the Lian word of the Horde in Drimmen-deeve and to tell them the remarkable news of the Gargon's death.

It had taken all four to slay the Horror, and it was by mere happenstance that they had succeeded. Yet among these four heroes there was one who had struck the first spark, for as Galen King said, his voice strained, halting—for the impact of the Gargon was still upon him—"When . . . when we stood frozen . . . lost beyond all hope, Tuck, yours was the blow that released us . . . yours was the strike that told."

CHAPTER 6

SHADOWS OF DOOM

Tuck's jewel-hued eyes swept to the limits of his vision through the Shadowlight lying across the 'scape of the cambered valley held in the lap of the Quadran, and no enemy was in sight. And down from the Dawn-Gate on weary legs trudged the four Deevewalkers: Tuck and Gildor first, Galen and Brega coming after. Down out of Drimmen-deeve they trod, down onto the old abandoned tradeway that ran south a short way ere swinging easterly to follow the slope of the Pitch as it slowly fell toward the mouth of the Quadran, perhaps twenty-five miles distant.

And as they wearily paced down the steps and onto the ancient pave, Brega gravely said, "All my days were filled with a yearning to come unto Kraggen-cor, yet now I am glad to leave it behind."

Onward they plodded, Galen no longer leaning upon Brega. The four were exhausted beyond telling, yet they had to get well away from the vicinity of the Gate, for as Galen pointed out, "Ghola were not among the Yrm in the Black Hole. I deem they ride this Dimmendark somewhere. But they will return unto Drimmen-deeve, and we must be gone long ere then."

And so they trudged down the old trade road, southward along the shore of the Quadmere, a lakelet less than a mile from the Dawn-Gate. Normally, the clear tarn was fed by the high melt of Stormhelm flowing pure down Quadran Run; but both the Run and 'Mere were now frozen by the Winternight cold. And as the lagging steps of the four carried them alongside the iced-over water, Tuck could hear a far-off low rumble of . . . *what?* . . . but his mind was too weary to grasp an answer.

Along the high-bluffed western shore of the Quadmere they plodded, down past a snow-dusted, runecarven Realmstone marking the ancient boundary where began the Dwarven Kingdom of Drimmen-deeve.

Southeastward down the Pitch they went, now following the course of the Quadrill, a river running down from the Grimwall to come eventually to the Argon River far to the east.

They trudged without speaking ten miles or so, weary unto their very bones, leaving the Dawn-Gate and Drimmen-deeve behind, the mysterious rumble fading as they went, and at last they made camp in the whin and pine along the slopes of the Pitch. And though they were exhausted unto numbness, still they took turns at watch in spite of Gildor's protest that he alone should stand the ward. And each in his turn fought off sleep by walking slow rounds circling the camp. No fire was kindled and the cold was bitter; even so, dressed as they were in quilted down and enwrapped in cloaks, they slept the sleep of the dead.

Twelve hours or so they remained in the pines, all sleeping except for the one on watch; and red-gemmed Bale stood ward with each sentry, the blade-jewel whispering only of distant evil. But at last Gildor, who stood the final watch, awakened the others, for he knew that still they were too near the Deeves to be safe and could remain no longer.

"We must press onward," said the Elf, "for when the Ghûlka return to the caverns, they will be swift on our trail." Gildor gestured to the barren, wind-swept pave-stones of the old trade road below, its course for the most part free of snow. "The *Rûpt* will soon discover that this is the way we follow, for no tracks will they find crossing the land.

"But beyond our immediate danger, Galen King, I sense a doom lying in the days ahead, but what it is I cannot say. Yet I feel we must go forth swiftly, for ever since the Hèlarms struck, I have felt an urgent need to press on, else I think all will fail and Modru will have his way."

At these dire words the four took a quick meal of mian and water. But ere they set out, Brega borrowed the Elven long-knife from Tuck, using Bane to fashion a wooden cudgel of yew as a weapon, while Galen plied the Atalar Blade to cut a quarterstaff of pine for himself to bear. The work was done swiftly, for Bane's edge was keen beyond reckoning, and the blade of Atala hewed sharply, too.

"There," grunted Brega, hefting the wooden club as he gave over the Elven knife to Tuck, "this suits me better than that toothpick of yours, Waeran."

"Oh, not mine," answered Tuck, preparing to un-buckle the worn black leather sheath to return the long-knife to Gildor. "It was just borrowed for the jaunt through Drimmen-deeve."

But Lord Gildor would have none of this return of the blade. "Wee One, keep Bane. You have earned this weapon. Had you not been bearing it, we all would have fallen to the Gargon. It is now yours."

Tuck was astounded, for Bane was a "special" weapon, and like most Warrows he knew little or nothing of swords. "In my hands it is but wasted!" he protested.

"Nay," said Gildor. "In your hands it was used well for the first time since its forging. I deem it was made for you."

Thus it was that when the four strode down from the pines and back to the road, each now was armed: Brega bore a blunt wooden cudgel; Galen carried a quarterstaff and an Atalar long-knife; Gildor wore Bale strapped to his side; and Tuck bore bow and arrows, with Bane, the Elven long-knife, girted at his waist, the blue-jeweled blade a sword to Warrow hands. And they went apace, for Gildor's dire words pushed them forth.

Although each had slept but nine hours or so—standing three hours at watch—still they were rested somewhat, and the pall of fatigue that had smothered them was gone. And now their stride was firm and their eyes clear, except for Galen's, for a faint haggard look still lingered deep within his gaze: the afterclap of the Gargon's blast. Even so, he along with the others searched to the limits of their vision, but Modru's myrk still hid the distant 'scape. Yet in spite of the Dimmendark, Tuck reveled in the *openness* of the land before him, and though the air was icy with Winternight cold, he listened to *distant* sounds instead of close echoes from confining cavern walls. And there was a slow susurration of free-moving air, a silence of open space.

"Brega," asked Tuck, "when we came down the steps of the Dawn-Gate, I could hear a faint rumble off in the distance. Now it is gone. Can you say what it was?"

"Aye," grunted Brega, "the Vorvor. Tucked in a great fold of stone on Ghatan's flank is the Vorvor: a mighty whirlpool of water where a great underground river bursts from the side of Ghatan to thunder around the walls of the canyon and disappear down under the Mountains once more. There it was that the Wars with the Grg began, for jeering Ukhs and japing Hrōks cast Durek—first King of my Folk—into its ravening depths." Anger crossed Brega's features and fire smoldered in his eyes at the thought of the sneering Squam, but with visible effort he mastered his passion and continued the tale: "And First Durek was sucked down under the stone by the rage, yet somehow he survived, and he became the first Châk to stride the undelved halls of Kraggen-cor, for that is where the suck drew him. And it is told that he came out from under the Mountains at the place where Daūn Gate was later delved, yet how he crossed the Great Dēop it is not known, though some say it was the Utruni who helped him."

"Utruni?" Wonder filled Tuck's voice.

"Aye, Utruni," answered Brega, "for it is said the Stone Giants respect the work of the Châkka, for we strengthen the living stone. And the Utruni detest the Grg, for though the Squam live under the Mountains, too, they befoul the very rock itself and destroy the precious works of the ageless Underland."

"But how could the Utruni aid Durek?" asked Tuck. "I mean, the Great Deep is at least fifty feet wide, and who knows where its bottom lies—if it even has a bottom—so how could they help?"

"Utruni have a special power over stone," answered Brega. "They are able to pass through rock that they fissure with their very hands *and then seal shut behind as they move on.*" Tuck gasped, and Gildor nodded, confirming Brega's words. Brega spoke on: "With this gift, they could aid anyone trapped as Durek was."

Tuck pondered upon this tale of Durek as the four strode southeasterly, following alongside the Quadrill as it led down the Pitch toward the unseen exit from the Quadran.

"Brega, when first we met, you said I had Utruni eyes," said Tuck. "How so?"

"I meant only that your eyes perhaps resemble theirs, Waeran," answered Brega. "It is said Utruni eyes are great crystal spheres, or are gems. And they see by a different light than we, for they can look through solid stone itself. And your eyes, Waeran, see by a different light, too, for how else could your vision pierce this myrk?"

Tuck strode along in silence and deep thought.

The Dwarf's statement had echoed what the Elves had said earlier. Yet Tuck had listened to Brega with great interest, for, just as were the Giants, Dwarves, too, are stone dwellers, and somehow that lent credence to Brega's words.

South and east they strode, down the Pitch, called Baralan by the Dwarves, and named Falanith by the Elves; but by any name it was the great tilt of land hemmed in by the four mountains of the Quadran: Stormhelm, Grimspire, Loftcrag, and Greytower. And as they went, Tuck noted a curious thing: "Hoy, Brega, can you see the stone above yon slopes?" Brega shook his head, no, and Tuck spoke on: "It is almost white. We came from the red granite of Stormhelm, past the black of Grimspire. Now I see the granite of another mountain and it is pale grey."

"That is Uchan, what you call Greytower and the Elves named Gralon," answered Brega. "Now the only Mountain of the Quadran you have not seen is Ghatan, and its stone is blue-tinged. Rust, ebon, azure, gris: these are the colors of the four great Mountains, and under each, different ores, different treasures, lie."

Down along the old tradeway they strode, between the Quadrill and Greytower, and their pace was hard. Some twelve hours they tramped in all, and their path swung south around the flank of the mountain as they came at last down off the Pitch and out of the mouth of the Quadran. Finally, they stopped to make camp and rest, again hidden in a grove of low pine. They had marched some twenty-five miles and were too weary to stride on.

When they took up the trek again, their course bore due south as they strode for Darda Galion. Still the frozen Quadrill ran upon their left while to their right rose the steep eastern ramparts of lofty Greytower. And the farther south they trod, the less they saw of the ancient pave they followed, for in places the stones lay half buried, while elsewhere they had sunk beyond seeing into the loam of the land alongside the river-bank.

Some nine hours they strode, faring ever southward. They stopped but once for a meal and a short rest, and then moved on quickly, for Lord Gildor felt a vague sense of foreboding, as if distant pursuit came upon their heels, drawing nearer with every step they took. Yet, as they marched, the scarlet blade-jewel of

Red Bale was examined often, but no glimmer of warning flashed in its depths.

Another hour they walked, and Tuck's eyes searched to their limits, scanning for foe, friend, or aught else, yet nought did he see but sparse trees and sloping land falling southward along the Quadrill.

But then: "Hoy, ahead," said Tuck. "Something looms, barring our way. I cannot say what. Perhaps a mountain."

"There should be no Mountain before us," growled Brega. Gildor nodded in agreement with the Dwarf's words.

"How far?" asked Galen.

"At the bound of my vision," answered Tuck. "Perhaps five miles at most."

Onward they strode, Tuck's gaze seeking to see what stood across their way. Another mile they went. "Ai!" exclaimed the Warrow. "It is a storm. Snow flies."

"Ha!" barked Brega. "I *knew* it was no Mountain."

"The flakes are dark in this Shadowlight," responded Tuck, "and the snow looks like a stone-grey *wall* from here, for it seems neither to advance nor retreat."

Onward they pressed, and the wind began to rise as they came toward the fringes of the stillstorm. Soon they walked in a moan of air, and scattered flakes swirled about them.

"Hsst!" warned Gildor, casting his hood from his head. "Listen!"

Tuck, too, pushed his cloak hood back and strained his ears, yet he heard nought but the sobbing wind.

"I thought . . ." Gildor began; then: *"There!"* And all four heard the drifting howl of distant Vulg.

Once more Gildor drew Red Bale from scabbard,

and the Elf sucked a hiss of air through clenched teeth, for a crimson fire glowed in the blade-gem. "They come," said the Lian warrior grimly.

"Kruk!" spat Brega upon seeing the jewel's gleam, while Tuck stared long and hard to the north, back along the way they had come.

Again there came the shuddering howl of Vulg.

Through the scant wind-borne flakes Tuck's eyes scanned. "I see them now: a great force: Ghûls on Hèlsteeds: fifty or more. Swift they run on our track."

"Wee One," said Gildor, "I see no place to hide. Is there any?"

"Lord Gildor," interjected Galen, "you forget, they have Vulgs with them: Vulgs to follow our scent. E'en were there a place to hide, still Modru's curs would find us. Instead, we must seek a site we can defend." Galen hefted his quarterstaff and turned to the Warrow. "Tuck, look for a stand where neither Vulg nor Hèlsteed nor Ghûl can come at us easily: a narrow lieu or a place up high: close-set rocks or trees, or a tor."

Again Tuck scanned the Dimmendark. "None, Sire. The trees are sparse and the land is nought but a long slope—"

Once more there came the feral howl of Vulg.

Brega hefted his cudgel and set his feet wide. "Then we make our stand here on the bank of the Quadrill," gritted the Dwarf.

"Nay, Warrior Brega," barked Galen, "not here."

"Then where, King Galen?" Brega's voice was sharp with exasperation. "The Waeran said that there is no site to defend, and we cannot hide from Vulgs. This bank, then, is as good a place as any to make our last stand, for they cannot come at our backs if we choose to fight here."

"Debate me not, Warrior Brega; there is no time," snapped Galen. "For there is a way we might lose the *Spaunen*: the storm! If it thickens ahead, if it rages, and if we can come unto its fury ere the Spawn can catch us, the wind and snow will cover our track and hide us. Let us forth—quickly!"

Galen the Fox! cried Tuck's mind as the buccan ran southward.

And behind careered hurtling Vulgs and hammering Hèlsteeds, swiftly closing the gap.

From the fringes and toward the heart of the tempest sped the four—seeking its blast—and the farther south they ran, the greater was the storm's turmoil; yet behind raced the Spawn, their pounding strides drumming over the land at a headlong pace, rapidly gaining upon their distant quarry.

On ran the four, and the wind howl rose and the snow thickened, flying darkly in the Shadowlight. Tuck threw desperate glances over his shoulder through the grey swirl, and his heart lurched to see how swiftly the Spawn came.

Now the Vulgs gave vent to juddering howls, and Ghûls answered them, for although they had not yet seen their prey, the spoor was growing fresher as they rapidly overhauled the hunted.

Tuck's lungs pumped in harsh gasps as he ran on, his legs pounding over the frozen ground. And all about him groaned the dark-laden wind, whistling flakes stinging his face as he plunged deeper into the storm.

Yet the howl of the Vulgs and Ghûls rose above the cry of the wind, for the Spawn at last spotted the fleeing game, and exultation filled their ululating yawls.

Headlong into the thickening snow rushed Tuck, the rising shriek of the driven wind drowning out all noise but his own racking breath, and now he could no longer see his companions in the black swirling blast. He threw a look over his shoulder, only to trip and fall sprawling flat upon his face. And as he struggled up to his hands and knees, a Hèlsteed thundered past, for the spear-bearing Ghûl upon its back did not see the fallen Warrow.

Tuck sprang to his feet and ran on, and he was unable to see more than a pace or two in the shrieking dark howl. Yet vague black shapes hurtled by, and the buccan knew that it was but a matter of time ere he would be spotted. Even so, onward he ran.

Now the fury of the driving storm about him somehow altered: still the raging blast screamed and blinding snow hurtled through the air, yet the blizzard was *brighter*: less black, more grey. Did the storm weaken, the snow diminish? Nay, for yet he could see no farther than a pace or two and did not know where either friend or foe went in the blinding clutch, as on he plunged.

Once again he fell, and as he rose up, the wind around him seemed to pause, and a dark shape loomed out of the blast twenty yards behind and stalked toward him: a leering Ghûl upon Hèlsteed. And the corpse-foe lowered his barbed spear and charged as Tuck fumbled for his bow and arrow. The buccan stood no chance, for the Hèlsteed was too swift. Death came on cloven hooves.

The spear dipped to pierce the Warrow, and Tuck sprang aside, rolling in the snow; the Hèlsteed hammered past, and *lo!* Tuck was unscathed, for inexplicably the Ghûl had not shifted his aim to strike the dodging Warrow; yet something was amiss with the corpse-foe, for the Hèlsteed ran on another twenty yards and then *collapsed*, and the foe did not rise up from the snow.

Tuck drew blue-flaming Bane and ran to the downed enemy, the Warrow girding himself to strike off the Ghûl's head; yet, as he came near, the corpse-foe twitched convulsively, fingers scrabbling, face grimacing, and then the Ghûl began to *wither, shriveling* even as Tuck looked on, the snow blowing whitely, the wind shrieking. And as Tuck's horror-stricken eyes watched, the reaver's body began to *buckle* and *fold in upon itself*, and collapse into ashen ruin to be whipped at by the howling blast. Shuddering in revulsion, the young buccan pressed on into the blinding whiteness.

The shriek rose until Tuck could but barely think, yet he stumbled onward. Forward he struggled, within a ravening white wall, but at last he passed through the worst of it and the sound began to diminish, the wind still ripping at him, but its force lessening as he struggled on.

And then he seemed to stumble out of a wall of white and into the arms of his comrades.

And overhead the Sun shone brightly.

And Tuck then knew that they were no longer in the Dimmendark, and the Warrow burst into tears.

South they went, another ten miles or so, away from the shrieking wind and blinding snow that raged along the flank of the hideous Black Wall; and they left the dread 'Dark behind. And all the while they walked,

Tuck reveled in the sensations of vision: bright daylight, high blue sky, distant winter forests and mountains. And his heart was filled near to bursting with gladness, for there was the *Sun!* And Tuck marveled at how his own shadow matched him stride for stride and grew longer as the Sun rode toward the evening. And he was amazed that the day seemed so bright.

And his talk was full of wonder: "Is the Sun a flame eternal?" he asked. "Will it one day die? The sky is so blue; whence comes its color?"

To most of his questions his comrades could but shake their heads and smile and answer, "Only Adon knows."

Even though the Sun was still in the sky, they made camp on a small tor overlooking the Quadrill, a tor easily defended, for although they had passed beyond the Black Wall, night would still fall and Spawn could rove. Yet the comrades were weary beyond measure, for they had walked long since their last camp and could not press any further.

Exhausted, Tuck sat in the waning sunlight, his back to a rock as he took a meal with the others. The buccan's wayworn gaze strayed back along the direction whence they had come; and he still could see the distant Black Wall standing across the valley and reaching up into the Grimwall Mountains like some great, dark, stationary monster poised to strike. With a shudder the Warrow wrenched his eyes away, only to catch the gaze of the Lian Elf.

"Lord Gildor," asked Tuck, "though we now stand in the light of day—and I would not have it otherwise—still I wonder, why has the Dimmendark stopped? I mean, why does it stand there just to the north, halted, not moving?"

"Bear in mind, Tuck," replied Gildor, "the myrk stood for days, weeks, in the Argent Hills north of Challerain Keep even while the Dimmendark marched down the Grimwall to engulf Arden Vale and rush on toward the Lands to the south. And as you know, later Modru caused the Winternight to sweep from the Argent Hills down through Rian to swallow Mont Challerain, and the Weiunwood, and beyond. Hence, the Evil One can cause the myrk to stand still in places while elsewhere he presses it forth to smother the land."

Gildor paused, his own eyes following the towering flank of the Wall, then he spoke on: "As to your question: I know not why the Black Wall has stopped where it has. Perhaps it stands at the limit of Modru's power, though I doubt it, for I think he intends to use the Horde in Drimmen-deeve to attack Darda Galion, and he will need the myrk to do so. Hence, I deem he but pauses, biding his time till all is set, and then once more the Wall will sweep forth at his bidding. Yet I cannot say for certain that my thoughts are true, for I know not the mind of the Evil One."

Brega bit off a chew of mian and growled, "Mayhap he leaves this Land undarkened for the Lakh of Hyree to invade, or the Kistanee Rovers."

"Perhaps," responded Gildor, "and perhaps not. Yet no matter the which of it, whether Lakh, Rovers, or Horde, whether Modru bides his time or is at the limit of his power, here the Wall lurks while we must not. We *must* press on, yet we cannot do so without rest. Let us bed down and permit the eventide to renew our spent energies."

Tuck finished his meal in silence and watched as

the Sun slipped down between the crags of the Grimwall; and though he tried to scribe in his diary, he was too exhausted to do so and fell asleep ere dusk.

Sometime in the night Tuck startled awake, and the blackness was so deep that his heart lurched, for he thought that he was somehow back in the Dimmendark. But then he saw the Bright Veil spangled across the heavens, and the silvery stars overhead, and the fingernail-thin crescent of a last-quarter Moon that rode wan in the sky; and Tuck sighed in contentment and slipped back into slumber. And none of his companions awakened him for a turn at watch, for the Warrow had tramped more than thirty-five miles that day alone—a grueling journey for one so small.

As the four took breakfast the next morning, Tuck watched with tears in his eyes as the Sun rose through the dawn. And again he marveled at how bright was the day and how dark had been the night, so different from the foul Shadowlight of Winternight. Sun, Moon, stars, sky: what wonders to behold! And Tuck was not the only one entranced by the sight of the Sun, for Galen, Gildor, and Brega stood as if spellbound and watched the golden orb rise over the rim of Mithgar to shine down upon the Land.

South they strode, down the wending valley of the Quadrill, the land about them richly filled with the subtle shades of winter—drab to any but those who had just come from the long 'Darkdays of Shadowlight.

Tuck's eyes swept out across this wondrous 'scape: Up the slopes to the west reared the Grimwall Mountains, marching out of the north and onward to the south, their mighty peaks capped in snow. Beyond the valley slopes to the east, and hence unseen by the four, a rolling upland wold fell toward the distant Rothro River and beyond to the Argon. At their backs, to the north, loomed the now distant vile Black Wall of the Dimmendark. And as they rounded a bend, ahead far to the south Tuck saw . . .

"Hola! Lord Gildor, to the fore," said the Warrow. "What is that? I cannot make it out."

"Hai!" answered the Lian warrior. "Here in the day of Adon's Sun, once again Elven eyes prove to see farther than those of all other Folk. It is the margin of Darda Galion, Tuck, the Land of the Silverlarks. Your Waerling eyes look upon the beginnings of the great forest of Eld Trees—the Realm you call the Larkenwald."

Larkenwald, thought Tuck, his mind envisioning the maps of the War-council. Larkenwald: an Elven Land running from the Grimwall on the west to the Argon River in the east, and from the wold to the north to the Great Escarpment along the south where began the Land of Valon. Larkenwald, also called Darda Galion: a Land of trees, a Land of rivers—the Rothro, the Quadrill, the Cellener, and the Nith, and all of their tributaries, their sparkling waters to course through the forest to flow at last into the broad rush of the mighty Argon.

South they tramped toward the distant forest, and as they went, Tuck heard the sound of running water, and he looked to see dark, gurgling pools in the ice of the Quadrill where the grip of the cold had been broken and water tumbled past. And unbidden, the Warrow's thoughts slipped back to the night at Ford Spindle when the Kingsherald's horse had crashed through a stream such as this, and the Man and Tarpy had drowned.

Wrenching his mind from this dark path, Tuck studied the Eld Trees as the four comrades neared the forest: mighty were these great-girthed sylvan giants, soaring into the sky, their leaves a dusky green, for Elven Folk lived among the mammoth boles and so the trees *gathered* the twilight.

"Lor," breathed Tuck. "The trees . . . how tall are they?"

Gildor smiled. "It is said that if their heights could be stepped out, one hundred fifty Lian strides it would take for each; yet I know of one old fellow deep in the woods at least two hundred paces tall."

Tuck looked at the Elf's stride—a yard or so when stepping out a measure—and the Warrow gasped.

"Ah, Wee One, but these are not as great as the ones in Adonar, whence these trees came as seedlings long ago, borne hence by my ancestors, and planted in this Land of many rivers."

A forest from Adonar! Borne here as seedlings! Yet now they are giants! Tuck's mind boggled at the scale of the work undertaken by the Elves to plant an entire forest of Eld Trees here in the Middle Plane: the span of time needed was staggering.

At last they came among the massive trunks towering upward, the dusky leaves interlaced overhead, the land below fallen into a soft twilight though the Sun stood on high.

"Kest!" barked a voice, the speaker hidden.

"Stop," said Gildor, and the comrades halted. *"Vio Gildor!"* (I am Goldbranch!) called the Lian.

Tuck gasped, for of a sudden they were surrounded

by a company of grey-clad Elven warriors seeming to take shape from the very twilight shadows of the Eld-wood itself. Some bore bows, others gleaming swords, but striding to the fore came a Lian bearing a black spear.

"Tuon," said Gildor, recognizing the flaxen-haired spear wielder.

Tuon smiled at Gildor, yet he did not ground the butt of his spear to the earth; instead, he held the ebon weapon at guard, his wary gaze scanning Lord Gildor's companions, his eyes showing surprise as he looked upon the Waerling. "Ah, Tuon," said Gildor, raising his voice so that all could hear, "set aside Black Galgor, for these are trusted companions."

Tuon's grip shifted upon the weapon and the black spear swung aside. "These are chary times, Alor Gildor, for the Enemy in Gron reaches forth with his mailed fist to grasp the Land. Yet though I would not gainsay thy words, still I would know thy comrades' names."

"Nay, Tuon," answered Gildor, "though I intend no slight, I will hold fast their names, for such are the deeds of these warriors that Coron Eiron should be the first to hear their names and listen to the tale of their valor. Yet this I will tell: Drimm, Waerling, Man, Lian: these past days we four have strode through the halls of Drimmen-deeve! We have pierced its lightless maze from the Dusk-Door to the Dawn-Gate! *Hai!* We are the Walkers of the Deeves!"

Cries of amazement rose up from the Elves of Tuon's company, and eyes flew wide in wonderment; the Elf Captain stepped back a pace, startled, and his mouth groped for words, yet Gildor held up a hand. "Nay, Tuon, it is to the Coron I would first speak my words, for the marvel of our news must be borne to Eiron's ears before all. Yet if you must name these three, call them Axe-thrower, Bane-wielder, and Shatter-sword." Gildor gestured in turn to Brega, Tuck, and Galen. "And you may name me Torchflinger.

"But other news—dire news—I bear, and you of the March-ward need know it first: A mighty Horde of *Spaunen* now camp in Black Drimmen-deeve—ten thousand or more *Rûpt*, I deem. Yet I do not think they will strike south for many days or weeks to come, for their ranks are presently in disarray, and the Black Wall as yet stands still and moves no closer to Darda Galion. Yet you must be ever vigilant, for the *Spaunen* writhe in Drimmen-deeve like maggots in a carcass." Gildor fell silent, and a murmur of consternation swept through the Elven ranks.

"Ai, Alor Gildor, that *is* news of dire import!" cried Tuon. "That a mighty swarm of *Spaunen* teems in the Quadran means we must stand on high alert along the margins of the Eld Trees, for Drimmen-deeve lies at our very doorstep. Even so, should the *Rûpt* march, many Lian will be needed to hurl them back; yet most are in the north, as you will learn from Coron Eiron. He himself is but recently returned from Riamon, and you are fortunate to find him here." Tuon then gazed upon the comrades, and questions battered at his lips, yet he did not speak them, but instead inclined his head toward Gildor, accepting the Elf Lord's will to tell the Deevewalker tale first to Eiron, Coron of all the Lian in Mithgar. Yet Tuon was canny, and this he said: "Though you tell of the Horde, Alor, you say nought of the Horror, and I deem your silence speaks loudly to those who can hear its voice. Yet we will abide by your wishes and probe not for names and deeds; forsooth, your story must be mighty if you have strode through the Black Deeves.

"But come, we will share a meal. And there are horses to bear you to a cache of boats along the Quadrill, where the ice reaches not and the river flows free, though it sits low along the banks, for the cold locks much of the water to the north." With soundless hand signals Tuon gestured to the Lian of the March-ward troop; and as the Bearer of the Black Spear spun on his heel and led the comrades toward his campsite, the remainder of his company faded noiselessly into the lofty silence of the Eld Tree forest.

Once more Gildor and Galen rode horses, and Brega was mounted behind the Elf while Tuck sat in back of the Man. And they swiftly cantered among the mighty Eld Trees along the south bank of the Quadrill. Before them rode Theril, Lian warrior assigned by Tuon to lead them to the boats.

Through the soft twilight of the great trees wended their trail, the hoofbeats of the horses muffled by the moss underfoot, and what little sound they made was lost in the dim galleries under the dusky interlace high overhead.

Tuck marveled at the massive trees, and he saw that Gildor had spoken truly, for the giants towered hundreds of feet into the air; and the girth of each bole was many paces around. Tuck knew, too, that the wood of the Eld Tree was precious—prized above all others—for none of these giants had ever been felled by any of the Free Folk, though some had been hacked down in malice by *Rûpt*; and Elves still spoke bitterly of the Felling of the Nine. But the Elven vengeance had been swift and utterly without mercy, and chilling examples were made of the axe wielders, and their remains were displayed to *Spaunen* in their mountain haunts in Mithgar; and never again was an Eld Tree hewn in Darda Galion. Yet at times a harvest of sorts was made in the forest, for occasionally lightning or a great wind sweeping o'er the wide plains of Valon would cause branches to fall; and these would be collected by the Lian storm-gleaners and the wood cherished, each branch studied long ere the carver's tools would touch the grain. And gentle Elven hands made treasures dear of this precious wood.

And through this soaring timber cantered three swift horses, two bearing double following a third. Several hours they rode thus, coming at last to the curve of a high bank along the Quadrill where the long moss hung down to the water. Here Theril reined to a halt and dismounted, as did the comrades. And eve was falling upon the twilight Land.

"Here you will make camp, Alor Gildor," said Theril, "and on the morrow ride a boat down the Quadrill to where it is joined by the River Cellener. Just past, upon the south bank, you will find another March-ward camp, where there will be horses to bear you to Woods'-heart, to Coron Eiron."

"Boat?" grunted Brega. "I see none. Must we weave one from moss?"

"Hai, Axe-thrower!" laughed Theril. "Weave one? Nay! Yet from the moss you *will* draw one forth!" And the Lian guide leapt down the bank of the Quadrill and drew aside the dangling bry, and *lo!* concealed under a broad stone overhang a dozen Elven boats rode silently at tether, each slender craft nearly six paces in length, with tapered bow and stern; and spruce ribs curved from wale to wale, giving each craft a rounded bottom.

Brega's laugh barked above the sound of the river, and he looked upon the boats with appreciation, for Brega was a rarity among the Dwarven Folk: he could both swim *and* ply small wherries such as these, even though these shells were paddled, not rowed.

On the other hand, Tuck, although he swam well, knew little or nothing of boats, and he looked askance at the round-bottomed craft and wondered why they did not just roll over and sink.

After camp was made, and a meal taken, once more Theril mounted his steed and caught up the reins of the other two horses. "Alor, I go now to rejoin the March-ward. Is there word you would have me bear?"

Gildor looked to the others, and Galen spoke: "Just this, Theril: The Lady Rael of Arden said that aid unbidden would come along the way of our destiny. Tell Tuon and your comrades that Rael's words were indeed true: first we came upon the Axe-thrower, and then upon your company. Say, too, that the High King ever will have an open hand to the March-ward of the Larkenwald."

Galen fell silent and Theril looked keenly at the Man. "You must be close, indeed, to the High King to know his mind that well, Shatter-sword. There is a tale here that I am eager to hear. Yet I will bear your message to my company, and should any of us ever meet the High King face to face, we will say this: 'I have met with Shatter-sword, a Man of noble bearing, and though at the time I knew not his name, rank, or deeds, I am proud to have helped him and his comrades: Axe-thrower, Bane-wielder, and Torch-flinger.' "

Theril saluted each in turn and, crying *"Hai!"* wheeled his horse and thundered off into the twilit forest, the other two mounts in tow. And Tuck cried after the fleeing steeds, "Fare you well, Lian Theril, and all your comrades, too!"

The next morning found the four in an Elven boat upon the swift-flowing Quadrill. Brega knelt in the stern, his powerful shoulders driving a hand-held paddle while Gildor in the bow stroked, too. Tuck sat on a mid-thwart, aft of the Elf, with Galen behind the Warrow. Galen also plied an oar, and only Tuck was without one; yet the Warrow knew that for him to try to row would merely hinder the others. And so he sat and watched the mossy banks swiftly pass by in the twilight woods, and he marveled at the difference between the soft shadows of this dimly lit land and the harsh blackness of the Dimmendark.

All day they traveled thus, occasionally shooting through rapids where the water foamed white and tumbled loudly among rocks, and here Brega, Galen, and Gildor would stroke swift and strong while Tuck held on tightly. At other times the water flowed placidly between low, ferny banks or high stone walls, and the hush of the soaring Eldwood stole over Tuck and he nodded in doze and lost track of the hours in the timeless twilight.

Easterly they traveled throughout the day, stopping but a time or two, and as evening fell once more, they came to the inflow of the Cellener. And just past the mouth of this river they espied the light of a Marchward campfire set back in the woods on the south bank of the Quadrill.

The next daybreak found them bearing southeastward, once more riding double on borrowed horses. This time they had no guide, for Gildor knew the way to Wood's-heart, some twenty miles distant.

Swift were the steeds, and in midmorn the four comrades were passed through a picket of Lian warders and came at last to dwellings nestled among the giant Eld Trees: they were come to Wood's-heart, the Elvenholt central to the great forest of Darda Galion.

Gildor led them toward a large, low building in the midst of the others; and as the four approached, Elves stopped to watch this strange assortment of Man, Drimm, Waerling, and Lian ride by. At last the comrades came to the Coron-hall, and warders asked their names while other attendants took their steeds.

"Vio Gildor," replied Lord Gildor. *"Vio ivon Arden."* (I am come from Arden.) "My companions I will name to Coron Eiron, and to his consort Faeon."

At mention of the Elfess Faeon, troubled looks passed across the faces of the warders. "Alor Gildor," said the Captain of the Door-ward, "you may pass and speak to the Coron; yet you will find his spirits low, but it is for him to tell you why. I can only hope that you bear news that will lift him from his doldrums."

"Hai!" cried Gildor. "That I can guarantee, for we bear the best of tidings! Delay us no longer; let us pass!"

And into the great hall they strode, yet it was glum and but barely lighted. And at the far end of the long floor, sitting upon a throne among the shadows, was a weary Elf: Eiron, the High Coron of all the Lian in Mithgar.

Across the floor strode the comrades, to come to the steps at the foot of the dais. Eiron lifted his hand from his brow and gazed at the four, his eyes widening in surprise at sight of Man, Drimm, and Waerling. "Alor Gildor," he said at last, turning to the Elf, his quiet voice filled with sadness.

"Coron Eiron," spake Gildor, bowing slightly, "these are my comrades: Drimm Brega of the Red Hills, mighty warrior, *Rûpt* killer, arch breaker, axe thrower; Waerling Tuckerby Underbank, Thornwalker of the Boskydells, arrow caster, *Spaunen* slayer, Bane wielder." Gildor paused, and both Tuck and Brega bowed to the Elven King, who inclined his head in return. Then Gildor spoke on: "And Coron, though I present him last, this Man, too, is a warrior without peer: Horde harrier, Ghûlk slayer, sword shatterer, son of Aurion King now dead . . . Coron Eiron, this is Galen King, now High King of Mithgar."

These last words brought Eiron to his feet, and he bowed low to Galen, who bowed in turn to the Elven Coron.

"Ah, but this is woeful news you bring me, for Aurion and I had nought but goodwill toward one another and I am saddened to learn of his death," said Eiron. "Let us all sit and talk and break bread together, and tell me your tale, for I glean among Alor Gildor's words that you bear tidings of import, yet I hope that some of your news is good, for I am grieved in my heart and would cherish fair word."

Gildor's face broke out in a great smile, and he flashed Red Bale from its scabbard and thrust it toward the sky and cried, *"Coron Eiron, va Draedan sa nond!"* (King Eiron, the Gargon is dead!)

Coron Eiron staggered backward, the hind of his knees striking the throne, and he abruptly dropped to the seat. *"Nond? Va Draedan sa nond?"* Eiron could not believe his ears.

"Ai! It is so!" crowed Gildor, slamming Bale home in its scabbard. "We four slew it five days past in the dark halls of Drimmen-deeve: Tuck slashed it with Bane, thus breaking its dread gaze; Galen King shattered a sword deep within its gut, freeing Drimm Brega; Brega hurled the axe that clove into its skull, setting me loose; and I cast the torch that engulfed it in an inferno; and the flames at last slew it. And it was dead ere the pyre in the end collapsed and fell into the Great Deep of Drimmen-deeve, carrying the charred corpse of the Gargon unto the bottomless depths."

Eiron's face flushed with gladness, and the Elven King leapt to his feet and called a page unto him. "Light the lamps! Kindle the fires! Prepare for a feast! And send me Havor!" And no sooner had the attendant scurried from them than a Lian warrior—Havor, Captain of the Door-ward—strode to the summons of his Coron. And Eiron commanded, "Let the word go forth unto all corners of Darda Galion and to the Lands beyond: to the Greatwood and Darda Erynian, to Riamon and Valon, to the Lian now in the north, and to the Host in the south: *Va Draedan sa nond!* Slain by these four: Drimm Brega of the Red Hills; Tuckerby Underbank, Waerling of the Land of the Thorns; Alor Gildor, Lian of Arden; and Galen King, High King of Mithgar!"

Havor's eyes flew wide, for the Horror in Drimmen-deeve had long ruled the Quadran, and fear of its dread power had caused Dwarf and Man and even Elf to flee from these regions. Yet though many Elves took flight to Adonar, others of the Lian remained behind in Darda Galion, vowing to stay in Mithgar and continue their guardianship. Even so, the faint pulse of the Fear to the north ran like a thread through their lives; and only the Sun held the Horror at bay, for at night it stalked the sloping valley known to the Elves as Falanith and to Man as the Pitch; but at dawn the Gargon would return to the Black Deeves, for Adon's Ban ruled its kind. And none but Braggi and his raiders had e'er challenged the Dread, and they had not succeeded: for never had a Gargon been slain without the aid of a Wizard, and these mages were gone from the sight of all, though where they went none knew. Yet here were four who had killed with their own hands one of the terrible Gargoni—perhaps the last of its kind. The Dread of Drimmen-deeve was dead! Havor raised a clenched fist and cried, *"Hál, valagalana!"* (Hail, valiant warriors!) and the Captain rushed from the hall to start the remarkable news to spreading, while Eiron led his guests to warm hearths and baths and restful quarters where he could hear their tale in full.

Great joy spread throughout the Elvenholt, and heralds on swift horses raced forth across the Land. And everywhere the word went, celebrating began, for long had the yoke of dread fettered their hearts; and when they heard the glad tidings, all knew the tale to be true, for they listened to their inner beings, and the exhalation of fear no longer whispered forth from Black Drimmen-deeve: the Horror was dead.

And in the guest quarters the four heroes rested and spoke quietly with Eiron. Yet not only did they tell him their tale, they learned much from the Coron in return.

"Ay, Galen King," said Eiron, "there is seesaw strife to the south, for the Lakh of Hyree and the Rovers of Kistan muster in endless numbers, and all the Hosts of Hoven and Jugo, and of Pellar and Valon are hard pressed. The Drimma of the Red Hills join the strife, yet the Alliance is woefully outnumbered."

"What of the Lian?" asked Galen. "What of the Men of Riamon?"

"We fight in the north," answered Eiron. "The Evil in Gron sends his Hordes through Jallor Pass and the Crestan, and they come down from secret doors hidden high in the flanks of the Grimwall. My Lian join with the Dylvana—Elves of Darda Erynian and the Greatwood—as well as with the Drimma of Mineholt North, the Men of Riamon, and the Baeron Men. We fight in the fastness above Delon and in the Rimmen Mountains and in the Land of Aven. Yet we have battled as far south as Eryn Ford and the ruins of Caer Lindor. And everywhere we are hard pressed, for Modru's Swarms are mighty and they assail in great strength.

"Hearken, Galen King: I do not wish to cast doubt upon your mission, but surely you now see that your plan to gather the Host and march north to battle *Rûpt* must be abandoned; you cannot come unto the north with your Legions and leave the south undefended, for the Evil One's clutch is everywhere.

"Aye. North, south, east, west—all around—like the coils of a great serpent, Modru's minions seek to crush us. And now you bring me news of a Horde teeming in the Quadran. Yet the force of Lian Guardians presently husbanded in Darda Galion is but a remnant which I had come to gather to lead back to join their brethren in the northern battles. But now I will not do so, for I would not leave this Land undefended in the face of the threat of the Swarm in Drimmen-deeve, even though alone the remaining March-ward could not press back the foe should the Dimmendark sweep south and the *Spaunen* come.

"I curse the day that the Evil in Gron became master of this foul darkness that blots the land, for with it he defies Adon's Ban and looses holocaust down upon us.

"Yet even where the darkness falls not, still Modru works his evil, for the Hyrania and Kistania assail the south, believing that this War is but a prelude to Gyphon's coming. Yet, that cannot be, for the *Vani-lērihha* have not yet returned and the Dawn Sword remains lost."

"*Vani-lērihha*? Dawn Sword?" Tuck's Warrowish curiosity was piqued. "What do you mean, Coron Eiron?"

"The *Vani-lērihha* are the Silverlarks, Tuck," answered the Elven King. "Ere the Sundering, these argent songbirds dwelled in Darda Galion high among the Eld Trees, and their melodies of the twilight caroled beauty throughout the Land. Yet after the Sundering, the *Vani-lērihha* disappeared, and we knew not where they went. A thousand years passed, and the forest stood empty of their song and was the poorer for it. And we had come to believe that they were gone forever; but then the Lady Rael in Arden divined a sooth of baleful portent:

'Bright Silverlarks and Silver Sword,
Borne hence upon the Dawn,

Return to earth; Elves girt thyselves
To struggle for the One.

Death's wind shall blow, and crushing Woe
Will hammer down the Land.
Not grief, not tears, not High Adon
Shall stay Great Evil's hand.'

The Silverlarks of her words we know, and we think that the Silver Sword of the rede is the Dawn Sword—the great weapon said to have the power to slay the High Vûlk, Gyphon Himself. But the Dawn Sword disappeared in the region of Dalgor March during the Great War, and until Rael's portent we thought that it was lost or that Gyphon had contrived to take it, for He fears it. Yet now we think it to be in Adonar, for how else could it be 'borne hence upon the Dawn'? For the same reason, we think the *Vani-lērihha* to be in Adonar, too, though we still are not certain. And both Silverlarks and Silver Sword will return to Mithgar some direful dawn yet to come, to the woe of the world." Eiron fell silent.

After a moment Brega grunted. "The Châkka, too, have baleful sooths as yet unfulfilled, and we dread the day their words fall true. Yet, come, think you not that this prophecy of yours is being fulfilled even now? For we *struggle; Death's wind blows. Woe hammers the Land.* Many of the portents fit."

"Nay, Drimm Brega," answered Eiron. "This prophecy looks yet to come, for there are no Silverlarks in the Land, and the Dawn Sword—the token of power—has not returned to fulfill its destiny."

" 'Token of power'?" asked Tuck. "Just what is a

'token of power,' and what do you mean, 'fulfill its destiny'?"

Again Eiron turned to the Waerling. "As to what is a token of power, they are at times hard to recognize, while at other times known to all. And they can be for Good or Ill: Whelmram is a token of power for Evil—a feartoken—for it has crashed through many a gate for the *Spaunen*. So, too, was Gelvin's Doom, an evil device in the end. Those for Good are sometimes known: one was the Kammerling; too, there is Bale, and Bane, and perhaps Black Galgor: these would appear to fit the mold. Others are unknown until they fulfill their destiny, and beforehand seem to hold no power at all: jewels, poniards, rings, a trinket. Not all are as blatant as Galen King's rune-marked Atalar Blade that hewed the Hèlarms as foretold."

"Foretold?" burst out Tuck in surprise.

"Aye, foretold," answered Eiron, "for it was I who long ago translated the writing on Othran's tomb:

'Loose not the Red Quarrel
Ere appointed dark time.
Blade shall brave vile Warder
From the deep, black slime.'

I knew not what the words meant when I deciphered them, yet it seems certain that the blade Galen King bears is a token of power meant to strike the Warder from the deep, black slime, for that was its foretold destiny. Just as Bane, Jarriel's sword, and Brega's axe, along with a Ruchen torch, were meant to combine to slay the *Draedan*."

"But what if we had not succeeded?" asked Tuck. "What then of the destiny?"

Eiron signed for Alor Gildor to answer the Waerling.

"Tokens of power seem to have ways of fulfilling their own destiny," answered Gildor. "Had we been felled ere reaching Drimmen-deeve, still would the Atalar Blade have sought out the Hèlarms; still would Bane have come against the Gargon: but it would have been by other hands, not ours. Some tokens would seem to have more than one destiny: Gelvin's Doom; the Green Stone of Xian. Perhaps Bane or the Atalar Blade are not yet done with their ordained work; heed me, it may be that their greatest deeds lie ahead, as I think Red Bale's work is yet to be done.

"Aye, Tuck, tokens of power are mysterious things, perhaps guided by Adon from afar. Yet none can say for certain which things are tokens, and we can only guess at best: if a thing was made in Xian, or forged in Lost Duellin, then it would seem to have a better chance of bearing a destiny; yet many have come from elsewhere, and none can say which are the tokens until their destinies come to pass."

At this moment a page came to Eiron, and the Coron announced that the feast was ready.

And as they strode to the Coron-hall, Tuck was lost in deep thought: *If the Lian are right, then it would seem that we all are driven to fulfill the destinies of these "tokens of power." What then does it matter that we strive to reach our own ends? For whether or no we wish it, we are compelled by hidden sway . . . Or is it that the paths of the tokens and their bearers happen to be going in the same direction? Perhaps I choose the token for it suits my aims, and the token chooses me for the selfsame reason.*

They came into the Coron-hall, and it was full of brightness, for Elven lamps glowed fulgently, and fires were in the hearths, and bright Lian filled the hall. And Eiron led them to the throne dais and they mounted up the steps: Brega clad in black-iron mail, Tuck in silveron, Galen in scarlet, and Gildor without any armor at all. Eiron raised his voice so that all could hear: *"Ealle hál va Deevestrīdena, slēanra a va Draedan!"* (All hail the Deevewalkers, slayers of the Gargon!)

And thrice a great, glad shout burst forth from the gathered Lian: *Hál! . . . Hál! . . . Hál!*

And then the guests were led to a full board, and the feast of thanksgiving began. Yet Gildor's eyes swept the assembly, as if seeking a face not there. At last he turned to Eiron. "Coron Eiron, I see not my sister Faeon, bright Mistress of Darda Galion."

Now anguish filled Eiron's features. "Faeon has ridden the Twilight Ride," said the Coron. "Seven days past."

Gildor fell back stricken, disbelief upon his face. "But the Sundering! None has made the Dawn Ride since."

"Alor Gildor, just as you did, Faeon, too, felt Vanidor's death cry, and she was distraught. She has ridden the Twilight Ride to Adonar, to ask the High One Himself to intercede and stop the Evil in Gron." Eiron's hands were trembling in distress.

"But Adon has said—nay, pledged—that He will not directly act in Mithgar." Gildor's voice was filled with woe. "Yet still she went to plead with Him? Did Faeon not consider that the way back is closed: sundered?"

"She knew it all too well, Gildor . . . all too well," answered Eiron. "She knew that not until the time of the Silverlarks and the Silver Sword will the Dawn Ride be made again, and then perhaps but by His messenger. Yet she thought perhaps this once . . ." Eiron drew a long, shuddering breath. "Vanidor's death drove her thus."

Gildor rose and walked to a fireplace and stood long gazing into the flames. Eiron, too, left the table, and his footsteps carried him to a window where he looked out into the Eld Trees and spoke to no one.

"Now we know what grieves Eiron," said Galen after a moment. "His consort Faeon is gone from Mithgar, never to return."

"I do not understand, Galen King," said Tuck. "Where has she gone? And why can she not return?"

"She has ridden the Twilight Ride to Adonar, Wee One," answered Galen, and at the buccan's puzzled look, Galen spoke on: "Tuck, this is the way it was told to me long ago. In the First Days, when the Spheres were made, among the three Planes were divided the worlds: the Hōhgarda, the Mittegarda, and the Untargarda. And days without number passed. And it came to pass that Adon and others of the High Ones began to dwell in Adonar in the Upper Plane, but whence came the High Ones, it is not told. Again days beyond reckoning fled by, but then, in the Lower Plane, in the bleak underland of Neddra, Yrm sprang forth from the sere land—some say by Gyphon's hand. And then only the Mittegarda lay fallow, empty of Folk. But at last, Man, Dwarf, Warrow, and others moved across the face of the world, but how we, the youngest, came to be—by whose hand—it is not known, though some say Adon set us here, while others claim it was His daughter, Elwydd, and yet others say that each of the Folk was made by a different hand. Regardless, now the three Planes each held dwellers.

"In those ancient days, the ways between the Planes

were open, and those who knew how could pass from one Plane to the other.

"And in that dim time, Gyphon—the High Vûlk—ruled in the Untargarda; but His rule was by the sufferance of Adon, and Gyphon was greatly galled, for He coveted power over all things.

"And Gyphon thought to rule the whole of creation, and so He sent His emissaries to Mithgar to sway those living here away from Adon and unto Him; for if Gyphon could gain control of the Middle Plane, the fulcrum, then like the balance of a great teeter-totter, the Forces of Power would shift to Him, and Adon would be cast down.

"And many of the Middle Plane came to believe in Gyphon's vile promises, and thus followed His ways. But others had clearer sight and saw him as the Great Deceiver, and rejected His rule.

"And Gyphon ranted, and sent Hordes of his Spawn from Neddra into Mithgar, for if He could not persuade those who dwelt here to follow Him, He would use force.

"Adon was enraged, and He sundered the way between the Untargarda and the Mittegarda, so that no more *Spaunen* could pass through. And Adon called Gyphon to task, and humbled Him. And Gyphon groveled before the High One and foreswore His ambitions.

"Hence there was at that time no War, but myriads of the Foul Folk now dwelt in Mithgar, and much grievous harm has come of that.

"Yet although Gyphon had sworn loyalty to Adon, still He harbored a lust for power in His black heart. And He yet ruled the Untargarda; could He gain control in but one other Plane—the Hōhgarda or the Mittegarda—then He would rule all.

"His lust seethed long Eras, and at last He set a plan in motion, for in Mithgar He had a mighty servant: Modru! Gyphon launched an attack upon Adonar, and at the same time, Modru struck at all of Mithgar; thus, the Great War of the Ban began.

"But Gyphon's true plan was to thrust across the High World and come unto the Middle Plane Himself, to conquer the lesser beings at struggle here, for none here could withstand the power of the High Vûlk. But ere He could do so, Adon sundered the High and Middle Planes one from the other, just as He had sundered the ways to the Low Plane Eras before. By cutting Adonar off from Mithgar, Adon barred Gyphon from coming to conquer.

"Still, the War was fought upon all three Planes, but the crucial outcome was to be in the Middle Plane, where the struggle here in Mithgar raged between the Grand Alliance and Modru and his minions. And as you know, Modru lost. Hence, the Great Evil did not conquer here. But had the way not been sundered by Adon, the outcome would have been different.

"Yet even in the Sundering, Adon was merciful: for though none can now come from Adonar to Mithgar, still the opposite way—the way from Mithgar to Adonar—remains open.

"You see, for Eras the Elven Folk of Adonar had been passing back and forth between the Hōhgarda and the Mittegarda, for though they love Mithgar well, Elves are a Folk of the High Plane: Starsholm in Adonar is their true home. Yet many would dwell here, for in the Mittegarda they find their skills are much needed. But the Hōhgarda—the High Worlds—call at them, too, for there they can rest and be at peace and develop new skills. And though I do not know it for certain, still I think that only in Adonar can they have children, for legend says that no Elven child has ever been born on Mithgar, yet in past Eras striplings were known to come to the Mittegarda with other Elves on the Dawn Ride. But though they dwell here, still they are of the High Plane, and Adon would have His Elves come home; thus, they can yet take the Twilight Ride."

"Twilight Ride . . . Dawn Ride," interrupted Tuck. "These things I know nought of. What are they?"

"They were the ways between Adonar and Mithgar, Tuck, but only Elves could follow the paths, and not Man, Warrow, Dwarf, or for that matter any other Folk." Galen took a drink of wela, a heady Elven mead, and then continued. "Somehow, at twilight, the way between the Planes is open, and an Elf astride a horse can ride from here to Adonar. And, ere the Sundering, the way from Adonar to Mithgar could be ridden at dawn: *'Go upon the twilight, return upon the dawn'*: it is an ancient Elven benediction. But now only the Twilight Ride can be made, and then only by the Elven Folk."

Brega, who had been listening as intently as Tuck, made a rumbling sound deep in his throat. "Eerie is this Twilight Ride, for in my youth I saw it from afar: Elf astride a horse, riding in the woods below, the steed walking through the forest as if guided in a pattern. My ears may have played me tricks, yet I think I heard singing, or perhaps it was chanting; I cannot say. Dusk seemed to gather around them as they flickered among the trees, Elf and horse going from one to another. They passed behind an oak, and did not come out the other side. I rubbed my eyes, but it was no trick of vision. Quickly I ran down the slope, for darkness was falling swiftly. I found the steed's tracks there by the tree, and they faded away as if the horse and Elf had turned into smoke. I cast about for other sign, but night fell, and starlight is too dim to track by. I hurried on my way and said nought to any, for I would not have had others sneer at me behind my back." Brega quaffed his wela. "This is the first I've told of it."

Tuck was silent for a long moment, lost in Galen's and Brega's words. At last he said, "Well, then, if I understand it correctly, the Twilight Ride is a one-way ride, and Elves who go to Adonar can never come back, for the path from there to here has been sundered and none have ridden the Dawn Ride since." At Galen's nod Tuck looked with sad eyes upon Eiron and Gildor, for Eiron's consort, Gildor's sister, Faeon, had ridden the Twilight Ride to plead with Adon for succor. Yet Adon had never directly intervened in Mithgar in all the Eras past, and He had pledged never to do so. Even so, Rael's rede about the Silverlarks and the Silver Sword *"Borne hence upon the Dawn"* would seem to say that the way would be opened again; but when . . . no one could say. And Tuck's mind conjured up a vision of an Elven warrior astride a horse appearing like a wraith from the early morning mist and bearing a silver sword to be given to another to wield against the Great Evil. The Warrow shook his head to clear it of this image.

"Perhaps that's why the Silverlarks are gone," mused Tuck; and at Galen's and Brega's puzzled looks, the buccan elaborated: "If the Silverlarks could fly the Twilight Path, then they've gotten to Adonar and can't get back." Both Brega and Galen nodded in surprise at the Warrow's canny remark and wondered why they had not thought of it that way.

Soon Lord Gildor and then Eiron returned to the feast board, but the conversation at the table of honor all but dwindled to nought. And even though they sat at a great banquet of thanksgiving, and smiled when toasted by the gay revelers, the hearts of the Deeve-walkers were heavy, for a pall of sadness weighted them down.

Tuck yawned deeply, his eyes owlish, for he was weary. Even so, he paid close heed to what was being said, for he and Galen and Brega now sat in council with Eiron. In the distance, strains of music sounded as the feast continued, but the comrades had retired to discuss the ways before them, and Eiron had joined them to yield up his advice.

Long had they talked, and now Galen set forth their choices: "These, then, are the two courses deemed best: To bear south on horseback across the plains of Valon toward Pellar; and along that path in the Land of Valon is the city of Vanar, some eighty to ninety leagues hence, and it would be our first goal, for there would we find Vanadurin to lead us to the Legions; but if the Host fights in Pellar, then we needs must ride ninety leagues beyond Vanar just to come to the crossing into that southern Land.

"Our other choice is to continue by boat, going down the River Nith to the Argon, and thence southward to Pellar; this way is more uncertain, and perhaps more dangerous, for we may not come unto those who will aid us until we reach the Argon Ferry along the Pendwyr Road, and then it may not be aid we find, for that crossing perhaps is held by the enemy. But even if it is in friendly hands, still it lies some three hundred leagues distant by the great eastward arc of the river route."

Galen paused in long thought, then said: "We will go by river, for although it is longer and more uncertain, still it is swifter, for the Nith and the Argon need no rest and run their courses day and night. And if we eat and sleep in the boat, stopping only as needs dictate, then we can reach the Argon Ferry in a sevenday or less; whereas by horseback across Valon, unless we press the steeds unmercifully, we cannot arrive at the Ferry in less than a tenday—more likely it will take a fortnight if we rest the mounts. Nay, the river is best for those who must fly south in haste."

And so it was decided: by Elven boat to Argon Ferry would the comrades go, for horses tire, but the river does not.

The next morning a great retinue set out from Woodsheart bearing south: Coron Eiron and an escort of Lian Guardians accompanied Galen, Gildor, Brega, and Tuck as they headed for a cache of boats upon the River Nith.

Once more Tuck was mounted behind Galen astride a cantering horse, and the buccan gazed with weary eyes at the passing Eld Tree forest. The Warrow had not slept out all the sleep that was in him, for the discussion as to how to proceed had lasted long into the night, and they had risen early to be on their way. And among the great boles they went swiftly, for a feeling of dire urgency pressed upon them all, especially upon Lord Gildor, who still sensed a *doom* lying in the days ahead, but what it was he could not say.

At the fleet pace they rode, in an hour or so they came to a glade upon the banks of the River Nith, and the purl of its swift-flowing waters murmured through the twilit wood.

The horses were reined to a halt, and all the company dismounted. One Elf leapt down the bank and drew forth an Elven boat from another hidden cache.

Eiron looked upon the craft, then said: "This boat will bear you to the turn above Vanil Falls. On the south shore beneath the Leaning Stone you will secrete it. Down the Great Escarpment by the Long Stair you will come to the Cauldron, and in the willow roots you will find another craft. Stay along the south shore until you pass mighty Bellon and are upon the Argon proper."

The four nodded at Eiron's words, for he but repeated what he had said the night before as they had planned the journey south.

Their replenished knapsacks were laded in the craft, and now the comrades prepared to embark. Yet ere the four stepped into the Elven boat, Eiron bade them stay but a moment more, and he summoned a Lian unto him. And the warrior came bearing a long tray, and it was covered by a golden cloth. The Coron turned to the Deevewalkers, and though his voice was soft, all in the glade could hear him: "*Va Draedan sa nond,* slain by you four heroes. It was a deed beyond our wildest hopes, for the Horror was an evil Vûlk whose dread power drove even the bravest mad with fear. Yet in the end you prevailed where none else had succeeded. But, although Modru's Dread has been felled, the vast power of the Evil in Gron still assails the Land, and so your mission must go forth, and on the waters of the Nith you will leave us; for though we would have you stay, we know that now is not the time for you to rest from your labors. Yet we would not have you depart without being fully armed. Drimm Brega, you lost your axe, and Galen King, your sword: the one clove into the skull of the Dread, the other shivered asunder in his gut; both now lie in the unplumbed depths of the Great Deep. But from the armories of Darda Galion, by mine own hand I have chosen these blades for you to bear as your own." Eiron folded back the golden cloth, and there upon the tray were two gleaming weapons: an Elven sword of silvery brightness and a black-helved axe of steel. Runes of power were etched in each blade, their messages wrought in ebon glyphs. Eiron gave the sword over to Galen, and the axe to Brega.

The Dwarf examined the weapon with a keen eye as if appraising its workmanship. And then with a cry—*"Hai!"*—he leapt out into the open glade and clove the air with the double-bitted blade; and driven by his broad Dwarven shoulders, the weapon *whooshed,* and glittered in the twilight. Then, laughing, he threw it up flashing, and caught it again by its black helve. And the assembled Elves *oohed* and *ahhed* to see the Drimm's power and skill. *"Hai!"* cried Brega again; then: "Squam beware, for this axe fits my hand as if made for it!"

Galen, too, hefted his gleaming blade, feeling the balance of the weapon and noting the trueness of its edge. "I have shattered two swords in the War: one at the gates of Challerain Keep, the other at the bridge in Drimmen-deeve. Yet I deem this blade I now hold shall never be broken in combat."

Eiron smiled, then said: "They were forged long ago in Lost Duellin. The runes speak in ancient tongue and whisper deeply to the metal, telling of the keenness of edge, of the strength of blade, of the firmness of grip of hilt and haft, and of the power to smite. And each weapon is named by its runes: your axe, Drimm Brega, in the Sylva Tongue is called Eborane, which means Dark Reaver; and your blade, Galen King, is named Talarn, which means Steel-heart."

Brega held up his axe. "Elves may call this axe Eborane, and Man, Dark Reaver, but its true name—its Châkka name—is Drakkalan!" (Dark Shedder!)

Eiron turned back to the tray and took up a black scabbard and belt, each scribed with scarlet-and-gold tracery, and he gave them over to King Galen. And Galen slid Steel-heart into the sheath and girted the weapon to his waist. Then he stepped to the boat and untied his old scabbard from his pack, giving the empty sheath over to the Coron, saying, "Perhaps, Eiron, you can find a suitable weapon for this sword holder; it has served Mithgar well, for it bore the blade that shattered deep within the bowels of the Gargon."

With honor the Lian Coron received the scabbard and carefully laid it on the tray. Then he took up four Elven-wrought cloak clasps: gold they were, and sunburst-shaped, and set with a jet stone. And one by one he fastened the jeweled clasps to the collars of the four. "By these tokens all will come to know you as the Four Who Strode the Deeves—the Dread Slayers—and they will welcome you to their hearths and sing of your deeds 'round the fires."

Now the Coron stepped back from the four and bowed deeply, and so, too, did all the Elven warriors of the retinue. And the Deevewalkers bowed in return, and Galen spoke for the four of them: "Coron, in haste we came and in haste we go, for our mission is urgent. Yet a day will come when we can linger awhile, and then would I stride long in the twilight vaults of the

Larkenwald. But now we fare south to find mine Host; yet what else we shall discover, it is not known, though this I say: When Modru is at last cast down—his foul darkness to yield to the light—long will it be remembered that Elf, Dwarf, Waerling, and Man joined axes and swords, arrows and spears, and hands, to throw down Evil. And long will the bond between our Folk endure." Galen flashed Steel-heart unto the air. *"Hál ūre allience! Hál ūre bōnd!"* (Hail our alliance! Hail our bond!)

A great shout rose up from the Lian warriors, and they brandished gleaming swords and spears as the four comrades stepped into the boat and cast away from shore. And as Brega, Galen, and Gildor took up the paddles to prepare for swift journey, the retinue of Elven Guardians mounted their steeds and lined the bank. And as with one voice they cried, *Hál, valagalana!* and wheeled as a company and rode swiftly away to the north to disappear among the great boles of the soaring Eld Trees.

And the Elven boat was plied to midstream, where the fleet current of the River Nith rapidly bore the four comrades easterly, toward the distant waters of the mighty Argon, along the road of their destiny.

Hastily the River Nith hurried apace toward its ending, and the boat rushed down its course. Still, it was some ninety miles whence they had embarked down to Vanil Falls, and the Sun would set ere the four could come to their landing. Hence, they would make camp at sunset, for to approach the high cataract in the dark of a new Moon was too dangerous a thing to do; this last fact Tuck recorded in his diary, along with the statement that Gildor greatly begrudged the delay, for the unknown pressing doom felt by the Elf had grown stronger with each passing day. Yet, delay or not, still they would make camp when the light failed, else they chanced being carried over the falls if they missed their landing at the Leaning Stone.

And so all day the nimble craft coursed through the leaping water, and in turn Brega, Gildor, and Galen sat in the stern and guided the boat, while Tuck sat gazing at the shoreline and into the great woods marching off into dusky dimness, or watching the clear water churn. At times the Warrow would scribe in his diary, and at other times he would doze—such was the case when they made their final landing, for the grounding of the bow jarred the napping buccan awake.

Stiffly, they stumped along the shoreline, Brega gathering scrub for a campblaze, Tuck setting a fire-ring of stone, Gildor and Galen beaching the boat. Soon the fire was kindled by Tuck's flint and steel, and they took a short meal. Little was said ere they bedded down, for they were made weary by the long boat ride. And as Tuck took his turn at watch, he wondered how they would fare when they reached the Argon, for then they would stay in the boat—except for brief stops—until they reached the Argon Ferry at Pendwyr Road, making no camps for nearly a week; the thought of the confinement made the Warrow's legs ache.

Tuck was awakened just ere dawn by Lord Gildor, who paced restlessly, anxious to set forth. "If we leave now, we'll reach the Leaning Stone just after day-break," said the Lian. And so they took a quick break-fast as they broke camp, and embarked downriver just as the eastern sky began to pale.

Now the Elven boat sliced swiftly through the plashy tumble as the River Nith drew narrower and ran more quickly down toward the eastern dawnlight. Two miles they went, then two more, and the river swung northeasterly; and through the dusky Eld Tree leaves where the dawn could be seen, Tuck watched the sky change from grey to pearl to pink to blue; and low through the massive boles now and then the Warrow could glimpse the flaming orange rim of the Sun as it brightly limned the horizon. In the distance Tuck could hear growing the faintest of rumbles grumbling above the splash of rushing water.

"Yon is the Leaning Stone!" cried Gildor, pointing. "Strike for the south shore!" And Galen stroked strongly, following Gildor's lead; but at the stern it was Brega whose massive shoulders swiftly impelled the craft into a safe eddy, bringing the boat into the shadow of a great rock shaped like a huge monolithic column that stood atilt in the water, leaning against the high stone bank. At Gildor's instruction Brega guided the boat into the cavity between the huge stone and the high bank. And in the dimness their craft slid to berth alongside one other slender Elven wherry at tether. Disembarking and tying up their own craft, the four girted their weapons and shouldered their packs and followed a rocky path up out of the shadow and onto the high bank.

A mile or so eastward they marched, alongside the river, to come at last to the Great Escarpment, a sheer thousand-foot-high cliff over which the River Nith leapt wildly at Vanil Falls to plunge without hindrance straight down into a vast churn of water named the Cauldron.

Tuck stood in awe upon the edge of the sheer drop.

Far could his eyes see, far across the land below, and in the morning light his vision followed this massive flank; and some seven miles to the east he descried another cataract, an enormous cascade plunging down the face of the Great Escarpment to thunder into the Cauldron: it was mighty Bellon, the falls marking where the great Argon River plummeted down the vast wall. Eastward, beyond the Cauldron, the Argon continued, flowing at the foot of the Escarpment marching off beyond the horizon.

"Lor!" breathed Tuck. "When the Ghûls chased us south from Quadran Pass, I thought the cliff we came down *then* was a great drop, yet this wall makes that seem but a short step by comparison. How high is this cliff, and how far does it stretch? Do you know?"

"Aye, Tuck," answered Lord Gildor. "In places it is two hundred fathoms from top to bottom, though far to the east it dwindles down to meet the riverbank. Here at your feet it drops one thousand feet sheer. As to its length: eastward it comes twisting behind us, some two hundred miles from the Grimwall to the Argon there before us; on eastward beyond the Argon, another two hundred miles it reaches, curving at last southeasterly alongside part of the Greatwood. On this side of the Argon the escarpment marks the boundary between Darda Galion and Valon: up here to the north it is the Land of the Lian; down there to the south, the Realm of the Harlingar."

"How do we get down?" asked Tuck.

"By the Long Stair . . . there," answered Gildor, pointing.

Tuck could see a narrow, steep path with many switchbacks pitching down the face of the cliff alongside the silvery cascade of Vanil Falls.

By this way the four descended in single file: Gildor first, Brega last, and Tuck before Galen. Long was the descent, and they made frequent stops to rest, for they found that climbing down a long, steep slope was nearly as difficult as climbing up. And all the way down Tuck pressed against the cliff, for the drop was sheer and frightening. And as they came down, the roar of the water of the Nith plunging into the Cauldron became louder and louder, and they had to shout into one another's ears to be heard; but finally all converse became impossible as they neared the bottom, a half mile south of where Vanil Falls thundered into the churn. And rainbows played in the great swirls of mist.

At last they reached the banks of the Cauldron, and in the roar Gildor led them to a grove of willows and pointed out a hidden Elven craft. Quickly they embarked, and by hand signals Gildor directed them along the southern shoreline of the churning water, their powerful strokes driving the boat through the swirling eddies and across the tugging backwash.

A mile or so they went, and again they could hear loud speech as the roar of the Vanil cascade receded behind them. But ahead Tuck could now hear the rumble of Bellon Falls, though it was still some six miles distant.

Swiftly they paddled, all but Tuck, and the banks of the Cauldron sped by. A mile, then two they swept, hugging the south shore, and the water became choppy and full of swirls, and once again they could not hear to speak. Another mile passed, and then one more, and the endless yell of Bellon hammered at Tuck and shook his small frame. Here the Cauldron began twisting the boat this way and that, but the skill of the three paddlers kept the craft on course. Another mile they went, and now they were at their closest approach to mighty Bellon, thundering some three miles to the north across the Cauldron; yet the towering curve of the sheer stone of the Great Escarpment hurled the shout of the mighty cataract out upon them, and its whelming roar rattled Tuck's every bone and jarred his teeth, and his very thoughts were lost in the thunderous blast. Now it was all that the three could do to keep the craft driving straight, for here the chop and churn was great; yet on they pressed, past Bellon.

And as they went by, Tuck squinted and blinked with watery eyes at the great cascade: more than a mile wide, it was, and a thousand feet high; yet where Vanil had fallen silvery, Bellon was tinged pale jade.

East they went, slowly passing beyond the great falls; but it was long ere the roar began to diminish, and still they fought the Cauldron's churn. On they pressed, and the shout lessened, and the chop quelled; and at last the boat passed out of the swirls and eddies, for now they came to where the Argon gathered itself up once more to flow toward the distant Avagon Sea. And as the craft slipped out of the Cauldron and into the laminar flow, Tuck knew that now began their long trip down the Argon to the ferry.

Behind them, Bellon roared on, but by raising their voices, again the comrades could talk.

"In the Châkka speech we call that great cataract Ctor," called Brega. "In the Common Tongue that means Shouter. But though it is called Ctor, never did I dream that its voice was so great."

"Bellon shouts louder still to the Argon merchants," spoke up Galen, "for these River Drummers come even closer to its yell. They portage their trade goods up the Over Stair—there upon the Great Escarpment—

coming within a mile of the bellow. They are said to stuff beeswax in their ears to keep from going deaf."

Tuck looked to where Galen pointed, and winding up the face of the escarpment just to the east of Bellon was another path, a portage—the Over Stair—a trade road considerably broader than the narrow path they had descended back at Vanil Falls. But even though the Over Stair was wider than the Long Stair, still Tuck would not have traded routes, for he could not imagine being closer to Bellon than they had been; and he could fancy his mother saying, *"Why, it just might rattle a body apart!"*

Now began the journey down the Great Argon River. East they went, alongside the Great Escarpment, rearing a thousand feet upward on their left; to their right lay the grassy plains of the North Reach of Valon, and before them was the wide, swift-flowing Argon, the great river of Mithgar. The way ahead would curve over hundreds of miles from east to south and then back southwesterly; their far goal was Pendwyr Road at the Argon Ferry, some seven hundred fifty miles away as the river flowed. And there they hoped to find the crossing in friendly hands, and steeds and guides to lead them to the Host.

All day they rode the river, stopping but once, briefly, on the south shore at sunset. But as soon as their needs were taken care of, again they launched their craft and pulled out into the swift current in mid-river, Tuck now helping, for earlier Brega had used Bane to trim down a paddle to fit the Warrow and had shown the young buccan how to ply it in the straight bow stroke.

Dusk deepened into dark night and stars glittered

brightly in the black firmament, while the shadowy orb of an old Moon clasped in the silvery arms of a thin crescent of a new Moon sank low to the west. And Brega seemed spellbound by the spangled heavens, and pointed to one of the brightest glints standing high in the east.

"Have you the name for that one, Lord Gildor?" The Dwarf's voice was filled with a reverence for the celestial beacons.

"The Lian call it Cianin Andele: Shining Nomad," answered Gildor, "for it is one of the five wandering stars; but at times it pauses, and then steps backward, only to pause again and continue forth upon its cyclical journey. Why, I cannot say, though hearthtales speak of a lost shoe."

Brega grunted, then said, "Châkka lore tells that there are many wanderers, some too faint to see. Five are known, including that one, and it is brightest. We name it Jarak: Courser."

"Is it the brightest star of all?" asked Tuck, looking at the blaze.

"Aye," answered Brega.

"Nay," said Gildor at nearly the same time.

Tuck looked from one to the other in the dark, but nought could he read in their shadowed features. "Which is it," he asked, "the aye or the nay?"

"Both answers are right," responded Gildor, "for although Cianin Andele is usually brightest, at times others grow brighter; in elden days, for a brief time the blaze of the Ban Star surpassed all, though it is now gone."

"Ban Star?" Tuck's voice was filled with curiosity.

"Aye, Wee One," answered Gildor, "when Adon set His Ban upon the *Rûpt*, the blaze of a new star lighted the heavens, a star where none had been before, growing so bright that it nearly rivaled the Sun: not only did the star o'erwhelm the late night sky; it could be seen in the early morning, too. So dazzling it grew that it was hard to look at, nearly blinding, for it hurt the eye. Many long nights did it shine—the Ban Star—growing brighter, but fading at last until it was gone, and once more that place in the night sky stood black and empty. And by this token Adon set His Ban upon those who had aided Gyphon in the Great War."

"Lor! A bright new star," breathed Tuck. "And one that disappeared, too. It must have been quite a sight, perhaps as wondrous as the Dragon Star."

At mention of the Dragon Star, an unseen look of puzzlement came over Gildor's features, as if he were searching for an elusive memory.

Brega pointed to the silvery crescent of the setting Moon. "I deem the most wondrous thing is when the Moon eats the Sun, biting into one side only to spit it out the other."

Again Lord Gildor seemed to cast back in his mind for a lost thought.

"When will that be?" asked Tuck.

Brega shrugged. "Elf Gildor knows, perhaps."

Tuck turned to the Lian. "Know you, Lord Gildor? Know you when the Moon will next eat the Sun?"

Gildor thought but a moment, and then answered, and none questioned his knowledge, for the Elven Folk know of the movements of the Sun, Moon, and stars. "*Aro*! Why, in but twenty-eight days will it happen, Tuck. Yet here the Moon will not swallow all of the Sun; but north, in Rian and Gron and upon the Steppes of Jord, the Moon will completely consume the Sun, taking it in whole and keeping it for many long minutes ere yielding it up again."

"Lor!" exclaimed Tuck once more. "When that happens, there in the Dimmendark, there in the Wastes of Gron, it will be the darkest day ever."

"Aye, Tuck, the darkest . . ." Suddenly Lord Gildor fell silent, for at last his mind grasped the elusive memory—a hidden memory buried deep within the grief and shock of Vanidor's death—and he drew in a long, shuddering breath; then his voice came quiet: "Galen King, we must fare to the Host with all the haste we can muster, for an unknown doom is set to fall. What it is, I cannot say, but still it comes. For when Vanidor reached out with his death cry, he called my name; and in that fearful moment, a dire rede was thrust upon me:

'The Darkest Day,
The Greatest Evil . . .'

Vanidor died giving warning, but I judge his message incomplete, for I sense there was something more—about the Dragon Star, and the Dimmendark—but what it was, I know not, for my brother's flame was quenched by Death."

Gildor fell silent, and nought was said for long moments, and though Tuck could not see the Lian's face, he knew the Elf was weeping, and the buccan's own tears ran freely.

Then Gildor's soft voice spoke once more: "Now I think Vanidor's rede speaks to the day when the Moon will eat the Sun, for Tuck's words ring true: in Gron it *will be* the Darkest Day; and then will come the Greatest Evil."

Again Gildor fell silent, and none else spoke for a span of time. And the Elven craft was borne along the Argon River; the low bordering banks crouched blackly nearly a mile to either side. And to the north the Great Escarpment reared high and shone darkly in the glittering starlight.

At last Galen spoke: "And you say that the Sun Death is but two fortnights hence?"

At Galen's words Tuck shuddered, for to his mind came the image of Modru's standard: a burning ring, scarlet on black: the Sun Death. And the Warrow's memory returned to that 'Darkday upon the field before the north gate of Challerain Keep when the Sun-Death sigil of Modru stood above the broken scarlet-and-gold standard of Aurion.

Gildor's answer broke into Tuck's thoughts. "Aye, Galen King. In four weeks, when the Sun stands at the zenith, then will its light be eclipsed, then will it be the Darkest Day."

"Then will the Greatest Evil come," rumbled Brega. "Perhaps the Hyranee and Kistanee have the right of it: mayhap Vanidor's warning was of the Great Evil, of Gyphon, returning to cast Adon down."

Tuck's heart plummeted to hear Brega's words, and Gildor's breath hissed in through clenched teeth, for what the Dwarf said had the knell of truth.

"Warrior Brega, you may be right," said Galen. "In any case we will follow Lord Gildor's advice and fare to the Host as swiftly as we can, though how we can thwart Modru on the Darkest Day, I cannot now say, for we know in truth not what Vanidor's rede means. But if we are to go swiftly, we must add our own speed to that of the river; we will take turns: two paddle while two rest—four hours and four—till we come to our goal."

"Tuck and I will take the first turn," Brega volunteered.

Tuck was surprised at Brega's choice to pair up with him, for the buccan knew that he lacked the skill and strength to match that of his comrades, especially that of Brega. But Tuck also realized Brega's power alone was nearly the equal of Galen's and Gildor's combined, and so the team of Dwarf and Warrow should match that of Man and Elf.

"Take the bow, Tuck," called Brega. "I will take the stern. King Galen, Elf Gildor, we will awaken you in four hours."

And so it was that while Galen and Gildor bedded down, Brega and Tuck began plying oars to the waters of the mighty Argon, and the Elven boat sprang forth swiftly upon the current. And the race for the Argon Ferry began.

Long, grueling hours of punishing toil followed one upon the other as Dwarf and Warrow, then Lian and Man, plied the Elven boat down the long course of the mighty Argon. Four hours of wearying labor were followed by four hours of restless slumber; and each time it seemed to Tuck that no sooner had he gotten to sleep than it was time to paddle again—and the exhausting grind seemed endless. They would waken from sleep and take a meal of mian and then begin anew their arduous toil; and the Warrow wondered if their food would last, for the Elven waybread was being consumed avidly to keep up their flagging strength.

And they tried every trick they knew to ease their

labor: they sought the swiftest channels, and quartered the craft slightly in the current to gain greater aid from the flow of the river, but the banks passed by at what seemed to Tuck to be a maddeningly slow rate; they rubbed oil from the boat-kit onto their hands to ease the chafing, yet still the paddles caused painful blisters; they rested ten minutes of every hour to renew their waning energy, but slowly it ebbed from them anyway; they stopped perhaps a half an hour of a morning and evening to stretch and take care of other needs, yet muscles became sore and stiff and knotted from the confinement. But, weary and sore, cramped and blistered, down the Argon they struck for their goal.

Mid of night the first eventide found them passing an unnamed isle in the river. Beyond the trees of the river-border forest the Great Escarpment hove up in the northeast, while west and south past the island and over the river and on the far side of the fringing trees lay the wide Realm of Valon. Now Galen and Gildor were awakened to take their turn while Brega and Tuck cast themselves into the bottom of the craft to clutch at sleep. Yet it seemed no sooner had he lain down than Tuck had to groan awake to take his turn again, and still the stars shone forth.

And as Tuck and Brega plied down the river, dawn came, and they could see through the bordering trees that the Great Escarpment had begun to dwindle, the cliff tapering down as the land fell to the south and east. And the sky slowly changed, heralding the arrival of the Sun. The golden orb at last rose up over the Greatwood to the east; this mighty forest reached from the River Rissanin in the far northwest to the Glave

Hills in the remote southeast—a forest stretching some six or seven hundred miles in all. And the trees stood grey and barren in their winter dress.

They grounded the craft on the western shore and took their morning break standing on the soil of Valon.

Once more they took up the journey, and Tuck and Brega slept while Galen and Gildor pressed downstream, and the Sun stood at the zenith when Tuck's turn came again.

That evening, ere sunset, they stopped once more for a shore break, and the Warrow jotted brief notes in his diary. Then it came time to drive on, and Tuck wondered if they would have the energy to reach the Argon Ferry.

And as they embarked, Gildor said, "The coming weather looks foul. We may be in for winter rain or snow."

Tuck looked all around, but the late afternoon skies seemed clear, though some thin clouds laddered the high blue.

Brega watched the Warrow cast about, then grunted, "Look to the west for the coming skies and to the east for those that have gone."

Here the river-border trees were sparse, and Tuck looked out over the plains of Valon, and low upon the horizon stood a dark bank of clouds that the Sun had fallen partly behind.

That night a cold rain drizzled across the land, and Tuck was miserable as he and Brega paddled, but he was even more miserable when he tried to sleep.

The rain stopped just as they landed for their morning break on the north spit of an island in mid-river, and instead of continuing to bail, they beached the boat and turned it upside down, draining the last of the rainwater from the shell. As Galen and Brega uprighted the boat again, Tuck's vision scanned to the horizons: As far as the eye could see, the sky stood bleak and leaden. To the east stood the Glave Hills, marking the end of the Greatwood and the beginning of Pellar. Still to the west lay Valon; yet they had come many miles around its borders: they had started some four hundred fifty miles upriver, traveling east along the North Reach of Valon; slowly the Argon swung in a great arc, from east to southeast to south, and the North Reach became the East Reach; ahead the Argon would continue to curve, to flow southwest between the margins of the South Reach of Valon and the Kingdom of Pellar, where, some three hundred fifty miles ahead, lay the Argon Ferry; since leaving the Cauldron, they had come more than halfway to their goal, yet it was still far downriver.

Once more they embarked upon the Argon, and a cold westerly wind sprang up, quartering across their bow. And Brega cursed, for the thin gust would slow their progress.

At the eleven o'clock of night, the wind started to fall, and the stars began to come out, bright and cold, as the skies slowly cleared.

The morning break of their fourth day upon the Argon found the travelers weak of shank, for the long hours of confinement in the craft had taken their toll. Yet they did not spend overlong upon the Pellarian shore of the river, for as Galen said, "Were we to have many more days of this ceaseless travel, then would we spend a day on shore, resting. But this should be our final Sun in the narrow craft: we should reach the Argon Ferry this eve."

Brega grunted, and patted the outwale of the boat. "This is the finest craft I have ever mastered, yet I will be glad to leave her behind—else the stretch will ne'er return to my legs."

Though Brega seemed casual to think they would soon leave the boat, Tuck's heart thudded to hear Galen's words, for they did not know what awaited them at the Argon Ferry: would they be met by friend or foe?

Once more they set out upon the river, now flowing wider and more slowly, wending between long, gentle curves. South and west lay Pellar; north and east was the South Reach of Valon. Overhead, the vault was blue, and the Sun rose to warm the morning sky. The air was calm, though the headway of the boat caused Tuck's hair to riffle. And the dip, pull, and return of Galen's and Gildor's paddle strokes soon lulled the weary Warrow into exhausted slumber.

At the end of the rest period of the late afternoon grounding, ere they launched the boat, Galen said, "Now will we all stay awake, for the ferry lies but two or three hours ahead. We must approach it with caution—all eyes alert—for it controls the Pendwyr Road crossing, and hence has value to friend and foe alike. There we may find our allies, or the Host; yet there, too, could be the Hyrania or Kistania: Modru's minions."

Again they embarked, and now all four paddled: Gildor in the bow, with Tuck then Galen aft, and Brega in the stern, where power and skill would be most demanded to turn and dart should the need arise.

One hour passed, then another, and the Sun set and darkness fell, and the banks of the Argon slid blackly past. One more hour went by, and—*hsst!*—lights could be seen ahead: on either shore, and in mid-river: it was the ferry!

"King Galen, Tuck, quietly ship aboard your paddles," whispered Brega. "Elf Gildor, make all return strokes under water; we need no drip or splash to give us away."

Cautiously, Galen and Tuck brought their paddles inboard, but kept them at hand should they be needed. Tuck also took up his bow and set arrow to string, knowing that he would be more effective defending them than paddling should they have to flee.

Now they could hear the distant shouts of Men and the jingle of armor echoing o'er the water, for a great crossing was under way; but whether the words spoken were in the Common Tongue, or in the speech of the Southerlings, they could not tell.

Along the shadow of the western shore slipped the Elven craft, Brega and Gildor plying their paddles such that they did not withdraw them on the return stroke, instead reaching forward with the blade cutting edgeways underwater before turning square for the thrusting stroke; neither drip nor splash betrayed them.

Yet the first-quarter Moon was still in the sky, and through a gap in the bordering trees its silvery rays shone down aslant upon them; and just as Tuck wished they were back in the deep shadows of the banks ahead: *"Hold!"* barked a voice from upon high. *"Who be down there in that boat, friends of the King, or scum of Modru?"*

Tuck whirled, and upon the bank above them sat a row of flaxen-haired, mail-clad, horse-mounted warriors, their steel helms adorned with raven's wings and horsehair gauds; and they held bent bows in their firm grips, the poised arrows drawn, set to hurl death down upon the four.

"Hál, Vanadurin!" cried Galen. "We are friends!"

Tuck slumped back against a boat thwart, the arrow of his own bow slipping from his fingers. Relief flooded throughout his being, for the Harlingar—the Riders of Valon—had discovered them. They were in friendly hands.

Yet the bows of the horsemen relaxed not, and again the voice barked, "If you be friends of the King, ground that boat and disembark!"

Brega and Gildor swiftly stroked to a landing, and the four beached the craft and scrambled up the bank to stand beringed by the Riders of the Valanreach.

" 'Ware!" said the Captain of the riders. "Come no closer, for two of you are squatty—the belikes of Rutcha—though howso you come to be here far from the 'Dark, I cannot say."

Brega brought his axe Drakkalan to hand, and ere any other could speak: "Squatty? Rutch?" he flared, anger in his voice. "I am no Ukh! And if you would be separated from your head, say so again."

"A Dwarf," growled the Captain. "I should have known. But what of the other? No Dwarf is he. Do you bring a child into this War-torn Land?"

Before Tuck could say aught, Galen stepped forward and said, to the wonderment of the Harlingar, "Captain, I am Galen, son of King Aurion, and these are my comrades: Warrior Brega, Dwarf of the Red Hills; Elf Lord Gildor, Lian Guardian of Arden Vale; Waerling Tuckerby Underbank, Thornwalker of the Boskydells."

The Captain of the Reach Riders signaled his Men, and bows were relaxed and arrows lowered, for now they could see in the moonlight that it was not foe they faced; on the contrary, if the words spoken were true, then not only was it a Man, Elf, and Dwarf that stood before them, but also one of the legendary *Waldfolc*.

"Captain," said Galen, "any could make the claim to be the son of Aurion as I have, yet take me to your commander and I will prove my words. And I bear news of import."

And so it was that on command two of the Harlingar sprang down and took to the boat, giving over their steeds to Galen and Gildor. And the Man and the Elf vaulted to the backs of the coursers, and Tuck and Brega mounted up behind. And they rode at a gallop unto the camp of the Vanadurin on the west bank of the Argon.

"You have shown me the scarlet eye-patch and bespoken your tale, and I am prone to believe you, if for nought else than you have an Elf and a Waldan at your side." Brega *hmpphed*! at the Valonian Marshal's words. "And of course, a Dwarf, too," smiled the Man, continuing. "Yet I would not be the commander I am if I did not verify words spoken to me when the means were at hand. And one crosses the ferry even now who can support you: he is Reggian, Steward of Pendwyr when the court is away at Challerain Keep."

The speaker was Marshal Ubrik of Valon. He was a Man in his middle years, yet he was hale of limb and bright of eye. Dressed in a corselet of chain mail was he, with a fleece-clad torso. Dark breeks and soft leathern boots he wore. His hair was the color of dark honey, streaked with silver. His face was clean-shaven, and his eyes were blue.

The four sat in the tent of the Valonian Marshal, where they'd been led, while outside, the crossing of an army in retreat from the east bank to the west went on. And time passed in silence as they waited for Kingssteward Reggian.

At last came the steps of an escort, and into the tent strode a silver-haired warrior, his face lined with worry.

"Reggian," said Galen softly.

The elder warrior turned to Galen and exclaimed, "My Prince!" and knelt upon one knee, his helm under one arm.

"Nay, Reggian, I am a Prince no longer," replied Galen. "My sire is dead."

"King Aurion, dead?" Reggian's eyes went wide. "Aie! What dire news!" Then the warrior knelt on both knees, and now Ubrik, too, went to one knee. "King Galen," said Reggian, "my sword is yours to command, though as Steward you may want to replace me, for Caer Pendwyr has fallen to Modru, and his minions now march across Pellar."

Long into the night spoke Galen and his comrades to Reggian and Ubrik. And the news of the War in the south was as dire as that in the north. The Rovers of Kistan had sailed into Hile Bay and landed a great force of Hyrania upon the isle of Caer Pendwyr. Long had that fortress withstood the assault, yet at last it had fallen. The Caer Host had withdrawn up Pendwyr Road, going northwest to the Fian Dunes. Again long battles ensued with the Lakh of Hyree, but the numbers of the foe were too great, and now the Pellarians withdrew across the Argon.

To the west, Hoven had fallen into the enemy's hands, but the foe had been stopped in the Brin Downs, the border between Hoven and Jugo.

To the northwest, Gûnarring Gap was held by an army of the Hyrani who had marched covertly and swiftly at the War's start to capture it ere any knew of Modru's plan. But even now the Vanadurin fought to break the hold on that vital passage.

"What of the Châkka?" asked Brega. "Where do the Folk of the Red Hills fight?"

"In the Brin Downs," answered Ubrik. "Without them, Jugo by now would have fallen, too."

"What of the fleet of Arbalin?" asked Galen.

"They lie up in Thell Cove in secret and make ready to strike at the Rovers," answered Reggian. "If they can pin them in at Hile Bay—even though the Arbalina are outnumbered—they can prevent the Kistani Fleet from being used again. But the Arbalina need perhaps three weeks, perhaps four, to be ready to strike."

"Pah!" cried Brega. "In four weeks—nay, less—the Darkest Day will have come. And then, mayhap, it will be too late."

Ubrik and Reggian shook their heads, for they had been told of Vanidor's Death Rede, and it was dire.

"Modru's grasp squeezes us tightly," said Reggian. "Like that of a—"

"Snake!" cried Brega, leaping to his feet. "That is what Eiron of the Larkenwald said. And list, for this I say: Modru is but Gyphon's servant, and perhaps the Great Evil does prepare to return upon the Darkest Day. And to that end the coils of Modru's minions draw tighter and tighter around us, like those of a great serpent crushing his victim. But this, too, I know: cut the head from a snake and the body dies—thrashing to be sure, and it can cause great damage, yet still it dies." Brega brandished his axe Drakkalan. "Let us go after Modru! Let us strike the head from this serpent!" Drakkalan chopped down through the air, thunking into a fire log, and chips flew.

"But, Dwarf Brega!" cried Reggian. "Gron and the Iron Tower are far to the north, some thirteen or fourteen hundred miles as the horse runs. We can't get an army there ere the coming of the next new Moon!"

"The Harlingar could be there ere then," said Ubrik after a moment. "The horses would be well-nigh spent, yet we could come unto that far land—unto Modru's fortress—ere the Darkest Day."

"You can make it only if you can get through Gûnarring Gap," said Gildor. "And that is held by the enemy."

"Perhaps; perhaps not," answered Ubrik. "Even now the Vanadurin wage War to free it."

"What about the Walkover?" asked Tuck. "The way known but to the Dwarves. Can we go through it and bypass the Gap?"

"Nay, Tuck," answered Brega. "For along that secret way lies a long, low tunnel fit only for Dwarves and ponies. Even a Man would have to stoop. A horse would never get through. Nay, it is Gûnarring Gap or nought."

"But can we fight Modru himself?" asked Tuck.

It was Gildor who answered: "Nay, Tuck, we cannot. But have we any other choice?"

And so after much debate it was decided that Ubrik, Galen, Gildor, Brega, and Tuck would ride for Gûnarring Gap. Extra horses would be taken, and mounts switched off to spare the steeds on the long dash. New horses would be obtained from the garrison at the north end of the Red Hills, and the race for the Gap would go on. If the Gap was free, then the Vanadurin there would be mustered to ride to Gron—to ride to the Iron Tower. And, although they did not think they could defeat Modru, still, if they could storm his strongholt and upset his plans—perhaps even preventing the return of Gyphon, if that was indeed his scheme—then their bold strike would have been worth it, although they all might die.

Reggian would continue to command the allies in the south, for the Steward had fought with cunning and boldness even though at the moment he was in retreat; for as King Galen had said over the Steward's protests: "The War is not over until the last battle. Hark back to the legends of the Great War of the Ban: the Allies, then too, were hard pressed, yet in the end they won. Reggian, none could have done more than you, and many less. You are Steward . . . now be Steward."

And the silver-haired warrior stood tall and struck a clenched fist to his heart.

At dawn, Galen, Gildor, Tuck, Brega, and Ubrik prepared to set out for Gûnarring Gap. Ten horses had they: five were to be ridden while the other five would trail behind on long tethers—remounts to share the task of bearing the riders north. The stirrups on two of the coursers had been shortened for Dwarf and Warrow, and the two were hoisted up astraddle their own steeds; yet neither Tuck nor Brega commanded their mounts—instead, they grasped the high fore-cantle and held on tightly while Galen and Gildor led them forth. And Brega's knuckles were white with the strength of his grip, for once again he was mounted upon a *horse*!

Without a word Galen saluted Reggian, and so did they all, and then the sprint for Gûnarring Gap began.

Northwest along Pendwyr Road ran the horses, five bearing weight, five running unburdened; their gait was at the varied pace of a Valanreach long-ride, and the miles hammered away beneath their hooves. All day they ran thus: the riders switching mounts every two hours, pausing now and again to stretch their legs and feed the horses some grain or to take water from the streams flowing down from the distant Red Hills.

Long they rode into the late night, and when they stopped at last, it was nearly mid of night. And they had covered some one hundred twenty miles. Yet ere the riders cast themselves to the ground to sleep the horses were rubbed down and given grain and drink.

At dawn the next day, once more they set forth upon Pendwyr Road. Tuck was weary nearly beyond measure, and he wondered whether the horses could hold the pace; yet the steeds bore up well, for even though they ran swift and far, still half of the time they carried no burden. It was the riders who felt the brunt of the journey, for four of them had spent days confined in a boat, and the fifth was weary from hard-fought battles.

Yet on they strove, northwest along Pendwyr Road. Now they ran alongside the lower slopes of the Red Hills, homeland of Brega: Tall they were, standing to the left, mountains rather than hills; they sprang up near the Argon and reached some two hundred miles northwest ere dwindling back into the prairie. Valon stood on one flank, Jugo on the other. And the stone of the chain was a rudden shade, like the red stone of Stormhelm. Fir and pine mounted up the slopes, and high, stark massifs sprang up frowning. Occasionally, Tuck could see what might be a dark gape opening into the mountains, into the Dwarven shafts and halls below; here dwelled many of Brega's kith, and here was made the finest steel in all the Realms.

Just after night had fallen, they came unto the Harlingar garrison at the north end of the hills. In spite of the fact that the post was nearly deserted—for the soldiers had ridden to War—in less than an hour the comrades were on their way again, riding five new horses for the Gap, with five more running behind.

Dawn of the next day found them once more coursing north, and Tuck was so sore he thought he would cry out at every thud of hoof; yet he did not, and on they ran.

Now they raced across the open plains between Jugo and Valon, the West Reach to their right, the North of Jugo to their left. Miles of flat grassland rolled away as far as the eye could see: this was the treasure of Valon, yellowed in winter dress; but come green spring, no sweeter grazing could be found for the fiery steeds of Mithgar.

Across this prairie all day they rode and far into the night. And when they stopped to camp, a spur of the Gûnarring stood to their left.

As the Sun rose, once more the five set off for their goal, now but fifty miles northward. And as they rode,

Tuck could see the southeast rim of the Gûnarring, a great loop of mountains encircling the abandoned Kingdom of Gûnar, the ring a part of the Grimwall. Three well-known ways led into Gûnar: the Gap between Valon and Gûnar; Ralo Pass climbing over the Grimwall from South Trellinath into the Land; and Gûnar Slot, cleaving deeply through the Grimwall, from Lianion into Gûnar. Finally, there was the secret Dwarven way—the Walkover—a narrow pass across the Gûnarring, up from Vaon and down into the empty Realm.

And toward the Gap the five rode at the ground-devouring pace of a Valanreach long-ride.

An hour passed and then another, and the mountains of the Gûnarring stood stark upon the left and marched away in a long line stretching out before the riders. Another hour passed, and they stopped long enough to change the saddles over to the remounts, then struck to the north once more.

Now the mountains began to dwindle, sinking toward the Gap. Far ahead, Tuck could see a great column of black smoke rising into the morning sky, but he could not see what caused it, for it lay yet some twenty miles to the north.

Onward they rode, and the Sun mounted up through the sky. At last they could see a great movement of horses and Men on the plains before them, and they came to a mounted squad of Harlingar standing watch athwart Pendwyr Road. The five reined to a halt before the readied spears, and Ubrik paced his steed forward.

"Reachmarshal Ubrik!" cried one of the mounted warriors.

"Hál, Borel!" hailed Ubrik. "What news?"

"The best!" answered Borel. "Victory! The Hyrania are whelmed! The Gap is ours!"

"Hai!" shouted Brega, and the comrades looked one to the other, fierce grins upon their countenances, for the Gap now was in the hands of the Allies, and their plan to assail Modru's fortress perhaps could go forth.

"And King Aranor: how fares he?" Ubrik's voice was tense, for well he loved his warrior King.

"Hai roi! He fought like a daemon, and took a cut or two; yet he is well, though his arm will be in a sling for some days to come." Borel couched his spear in a stirrup cup and so did his squadmates.

"Your tidings are sweet to my ears," said Ubrik, "and I would like nothing more than to hear the tale from your lips, yet we cannot stay. We would pass your ward, Borel, for we have urgent business with King Aranor."

In response to Ubrik's words Borel signaled his squad and reined to one side. And the five were permitted to ride onward. And as they passed, Tuck heard some exclaim in wonder, for never before had any seen a Dwarf astride a horse, and they now saw that Tuck was a pointed-eared, jewel-eyed Waldan! *And* lo! *an Elf rides among them, too! Strange companions portend uncommon events.*

Forth rode the five, and less than four miles before them stood the Gûnarring Gap. Now they came among the carnage of a great battle: broken armor and cloven helms, shattered weapons, slain horses and Men: some were blond-haired Harlingar, more were swarthy Hyrania; yet whether the skin was dark or light, still they were dead: pierced by spear and arrow, slashed by saber and tulwar, broken by hammer and mace. Tuck tried not to look at the slaughtered Men, yet they were everywhere.

They passed by several squads of captured Hyrania, guarded by Vanadurin, and the prisoners moved among the slain and gathered them for burial or burning: the slain of Valon were laid to rest in great mounds covered by grassy turves, while the Hyrania were burned on a vast pyre of logs from which the great column of black smoke rose skyward.

"Why do they honor the dead of Hyree and not the slain of Valon?" growled Brega to Tuck. "Fire lifts up the spirits of valiant warriors slain, just as clean stone purifies them. But root-tangled sod traps their shades, and they are a long time escaping the dark, worm-laden soil."

"Perhaps they think as my Folk do, Brega," answered Tuck. "The earth sustains us while we are alive, and we return to it after death. But fire, stone, soil, or even the sea, it matters not, for it is the way of our living that is testament to our spirits, and perhaps the way that we die; and the way of our burial means little, for what we have been is gone, though our spirits may live on in the hearts of others . . . for a little while, at least."

Brega listened to Tuck's words, then shook his head but said no more.

At last they came to the encampment of the Vanadurin and rode to the pavilion in the center. And the green-and-white colors of Valon flew above the tent, for here was quartered King Aranor.

A guard took them into the King's presence, and Aranor, white-haired but hale, stood cursing as a healer changed a bloody bandage on the King's sword arm.

"Rach, Dagnall, take care with that poultice; I would have this arm next year, too!" King Aranor looked up as the five entered, and his eyes widened. "Hola, Ubrik, I thought you south." Now Aranor's sight took in Ubrik's traveling companions. "Hoy! Man, Elf, Dwarf, and—by the very bones of Sleeth—a Waldan! There is a tale here for the telling. And do my eyes deceive me, or is it truly you, Prince Galen?"

Quiet fell in the tent—Galen's voice at last silent, his tale told—and Aranor again wiped an eye with the sleeve of his left arm.

"Your news saddens me, King Galen," said Aranor. "Aurion and I trained at arms together, and hunted far afield in our youth. He was as close to me as a brother.

"And the rest of your tale bears good news, and bad. The fall of Challerain Keep whelms me, yet I am buoyed by the fighters of Weiunwood. The Dread of the Black Hole is slain, and for that my heart sings, yet this cursed Dimmendark I do not like. And the north is beset by Modru's Hordes.

"But here in the south we, too, reel under the blows of servants of the Enemy in Gron. They seem without number, and ultimately we must fall back before them.

"Yet Vanidor's warning bears dire portent, and you propose to storm the Iron Tower itself. I think your plan cannot succeed, yet this I say unto you: Galen, you are High King of all Mithgar, and my heart and soul are pledged to serve you. You ask for Warriors of the Reach to go with you unto the frozen wastes of Gron, for none else can reach the holt of the Kinstealer ere the fall of the Darkest Day.

"Galen King, here at Gûnarring Gap there are perhaps but five thousand Vanadurin who are War-ready and hale; the others are wounded, such as I, and would merely slow you. Five thousand are but a pittance to take against the Iron Tower, yet they are yours to command as you would.

"This, only, I ask of you: do not cast their lives in vain." Aranor fell silent, and there were tears in both his and Galen's eyes.

Long moments passed, for Galen did not trust his voice to speak without breaking, but at last he said, "We ride on the morrow's dawn."

Horns sounded and the muster went forth. Captains were called and plans were made. King Galen would command, and Ubrik would ride in the stead of King Aranor, for the King's wounds kept him in Valon. On the morrow would they begin the long-ride: some nine hundred miles away lay their goal, and they would have but twenty or so days to reach it. Such a ride had never before been made in the long history of the Harlingar, yet they were confident that it could be done.

And as Tuck scribed in his diary that night, he wondered at their fate. And as he ungirted Bane from his waist to lie down to sleep, he wondered, too, whether any among them bore a token of power for Good: *Bane? Bale? Steel-heart? Dark Reaver? Are any of these weapons tokens whose destinies are rushing toward fulfillment? Or is some other unknown token being borne unsuspectingly toward Gron? And if so, will it stand up to the feartokens of the Enemy?* Tuck fell asleep, his questions unanswered.

Dawn found the Riders of Valon drawn up in ranks as King Galen, King Aranor, and Reachmarshal Ubrik rode forth to pass by them. Somewhere Aranor had found a flag of Pellar, and two standard-bearers followed the Kings: one bearing the colors of Valon: white horse rearing on a field of green; the other bearing the standard of Pellar: golden griffin rampant upon a scarlet field. And the Vanadurin sat in rows on their mounts as the High King of Mithgar passed before them, his armor glinting crimson in the rising Sun.

Now at last the review was done, and King Aranor, his arm in a sling, sat ahorse and looked stern, for he and Galen, had said their farewells earlier. And Galen turned to give the order to begin the long-ride, but ere he could do so, a Valonian black-oxen horn sounded from afar, and a stir went through the ranks.

Ubrik turned to Galen, and Tuck's heart thudded at the Valanreach Marshal's words: "King Galen, hold your command, for we may yet need to fight another battle for the Gûnarring Gap. An army approaches from the northwest—down the Ralo Road. Yet whether they be friend or foe, I cannot say."

Ubrik barked a command in Valur, the ancient War tongue of Valon, and horns sounded, and the files of the Vanadurin wheeled and formed to face into Gûnar, lances and sabers at the ready.

And Tuck turned his eyes to the road through the Gap; in the distance he saw a churning dark mass of hundreds upon hundreds of hard-running steeds, their pounding hooves hammering to strike the land as they bore an unknown force thundering down upon the Gap.

"They attack!" cried Ubrik. "Hál Vanadurin! Draw the sabers! Lower the lances! Sound the horns! Ride to War!" And with the black-oxen horns of Valon blowing wildly, the Vanadurin spurred forward and gathered speed and hurtled toward the oncoming mass of charging warriors.

Here ends the second part of the tale The Iron Tower. *The third part,* The Darkest Day, *tells of the last desperate gamble of the Alliance to thwart Modru's evil plan.*

About the Author

Dennis L. McKiernan was born April 4, 1932, in Moberly, Missouri, where he lived until age eighteen, when he joined the U.S. Air Force, serving four years during the Korean War. He received a B.S. in Electrical Engineering from the University of Missouri in 1958 and, similarly, an M.S. from Duke University in 1964. Employed by a leading research and development laboratory, he resides with his family in Westerville, Ohio. Though he has free-lanced articles for magazines, *The Iron Tower* marks his debut as a novelist.

Suo sibi gladio hunc jugulo.

I will cut this man's throat with his own sword.

—Terence, *The Brothers*, V, viii, 35

In this war there are no rules, there is no referee. I am the ally, and I am the enemy. And only I will decide the weapons and the arena.

—Mack Bolan, THE EXECUTIONER

THE EXECUTIONER:

Jersey Guns

by
Don Pendleton

PINNACLE BOOKS • NEW YORK CITY

THE EXECUTIONER: JERSEY GUNS

An original Pinnacle Books edition, published for the first time anywhere.

ISBN: 0-523-00328-5

First printing, January 1974

Printed in the United States of America

PINNACLE BOOKS, INC.
275 Madison Avenue
New York, N.Y. 10016

Dedicated with pride and congratulations to the edge-of-hell guys of Vietnam—both those who returned and those who never will—of whom it is now being said, "Your war is over." For now, sure, let's hope so. Bolan's is not. Nor, in the deeper truth, will yours ever be.

PROLOGUE

Mack Bolan's most persistent nightmare usually found him waist-deep in a flowing river of blood, sticky undercurrents swirling between his legs and trying to pull him down into the flow which also bore faceless mangled bodies with great gaping wounds. The river groaned as it flowed, alive with the muted symphony of violent dying by the legion who had tasted Bolan's simple applications of criminal justice.

It was a narrow river.

On the one bank were amassed the forces of law and order, grim and silent men who stood in disciplined ranks and fired volleys at his head to the cadenced commands of none other than the President of the United States.

On the opposite bank was a yowling mob of enraged *mafiosi*. These were scampering about their side of the river in a disorganized and sometimes hysterical fashion, dashing this way and that in a cacophony of gunfire and obscene shoutings, throwing at him everything within their reach, including stones and bones, in addition to the whistling spray of bullets. Now and then a triumphantly screaming band of these would rush down from the high ground overlooking the river, bearing above their heads something almost human, which they gleefully lofted at him from the bank; Bolan inevitably caught the grisly object in outflung arms . . . and it was always the same *sort* of thing—a "turkey"—a thing which had once been a sentient human form but was now reduced to a blob of mindless flesh—mutilated and shredded by a fiendish method of torture that ensured the victim a slow and agonizing death.

Bolan always awakened at this point. Not even in the subconscious realm could he confront "turkey meat" without a mind-wrenching reaction.

And, of course, in the deeper sense, Bolan's recurring dream was not a nightmare at all. A nightmare usually portrays some dreaded but unlikely situation—a frightening experience from which the dreamer may awaken to a much more comfortable reality.

There was no comfortable reality to which Bolan may awaken.

The "nightmare" was merely a replay in symbology of the man's normal, workaday world.

Mack Bolan was the "Executioner."

He'd been accorded the chilling tag while serving as a soldier in his country's service . . . during another nightmare called Vietnam. As a member of the most modern army in the world, Bolan had been finely trained in the oldest of the arts of warfare—*killing*—and he had become most proficient in his assigned specialty.

He was perhaps the only American soldier in the Southeast Asian theater to carry an enemy price tag on his head. As leader of an elite penetration team, Bolan had ranged throughout enemy-held territories on "kill missions" directed against specific targets. The "Executioner" tag accorded him was meant as a tribute to his effectiveness—a tribute by a grateful government and by his peers in the field.

When the Executioner returned to home soil to

wage the same brand of unrelenting warfare against a different enemy, however, he knew that he could expect no plaudits from either his government or his society. A declared War Against the Mafia, on Bolan's terms, could bring nothing but official denunciation and forceful reaction.

> The law can't stop the mob . . . can't even touch them. Someone has to. I guess what is needed here is a war against the cannibals. The same kind of war we fought in 'Nam. Sure, it's going to be a lonely battle. But so were all the others. And this one I *know* I can't win. So who said you have to win 'em all? Sometimes the most important thing is to simply *fight* them all. This is one I have to fight.

So saying, Bolan began his one-man response to the menace of syndicated crime, the illegal combine which had been characterized by official spokesmen as "the nation's invisible second government."

Bolan *knew* . . . the Mafia *did* exist—it was the most insistent and insidious threat ever faced by men of noble intentions anywhere, and he felt most strongly the obligation to oppose this spreading cancer which was threatening to destroy the institutions of American life.

The story that follows is the seventeenth installment of Bolan's war chronicle. Still alive and fighting his way along the "last bloody mile" of his hell on earth, the Executioner has just left behind him a monumental slaughter in Sicily, the home and training ground of the Mafia.

Wounded and soul-weary, Bolan is on his way back to the U.S. San Diego and Philadelphia are still repairing the damage of Bolan's most recent hits. Never before had the Mafia been hit with such quick devastation.

A short rest in Algiers hadn't really been enough to prepare Bolan for any immediate action. He knew that they'd be looking for him at every gateway city in the U.S. He also knew that they'd expect him to hit where the action was—wherever the law seemed to be overwhelmed by the underworld.

Boston and Washington were fairly quiet; the local Mafia chapters were still licking their wounds and attempting to put themselves back together.

Things were pretty lively in the Seattle area, though, surprisingly so. And Detroit showed signs of needing some attention. Maybe later . . .

But it was Bolan's thought to follow-up on his Philly job . . . and trace some of the missing links to the Manhattan strongholds. And between Philly and New York stood the Garden State of New Jersey.

A scattering of bedroom communities in Jersey served the Philly-New York axis, and within twenty miles of Times Square, there were at least sixty homes of top *Mafiosi*—quiet, well-manicured ranch-styles and split-levels. The big action and the bloody deals were kept out of these tree-lined communities. Everything should be nice and peaceful in the neighborhood, right? Gotta maintain the respectable image. No crab-grass, no hippies . . . and no fuzz, either.

So, though much of suburban Jersey was quiet and practically devoid of crime statistics, the land was virtually crawling with *Mafiosi*. Mack Bolan thought it might be interesting to visit the boys at home, to see what the big Jersey guns are up to, and how their garden grows . . .

1 DEATH STALK

It was easier getting back into Jersey than it was getting out. That mad flight out of Teterboro was only a month ago, though it seemed like a year. Some itinerary—Jersey to Sicily, Sicily to Algiers, Algiers to Jersey. Who'd believe it?

Someone did, evidently, someone who knew it wasn't going to be Seattle or Detroit. And now Death was tailgating him across that moonwashed Jersey countryside—Death with a capital *D* but spelled *Taliferi*—and it was crowding the rearview mirror of his Mustang with blinding headlights and awaiting only the most efficient place to happen.

Bolan had identified the big crew wagon the moment it swung in behind him; he knew who they were and how they would try it. The *Taliferi* knew the death game quite well. It was their profession, their calling, their primary function in life.

The Talifero brothers, Pat and Mike, were the lord high enforcers of the national combine. They took orders from only *la Commissione,* and their hit crews constituted a standing army of elite storm troopers such as had not been seen this side of Hitler's Germany. No "button men," these—no bumbling hit men or muscle specialists—these guys were Gestapo and, yeah, they knew their business.

Mack Bolan, thankfully, also knew his.

His business was to stay alive, to carry the war back to the Bloody Brotherhood, and to walk up their backs every chance he could find.

Forever the realist, however, Bolan knew that his business, at this moment, was at the verge of bankruptcy.

He was carrying an agonizing souvenir of his Sicilian encounter his in his ribs and in a painful and stubbornly seeping flesh wound of the lower leg. He was bruised and scratched and hurting like hell from head to toe . . . and he was weary enough to simply let go and die.

State troopers were swarming the New Jersey Turnpike and busily sealing every exit along that hundred-mile corridor between Philly and New York. Through some inexplicable extension of the combat sense—or of survival instincts—Bolan had sniffed out that maneuver and made his escape from the toll road at almost the last possible moment.

And now here he was, cruising a lonely back road across central New Jersey with a Talifero head party at his rear bumper.

The sanest thing for a guy in this situation would be to simply let go and let it happen. It would be so easy, so quick, so final.

He'd been a dead man since this damn war began, anyway.

Yeah.

Make it official, Bolan. Stop and die for the men.

He had been cruising at an inconspicuous sixty miles an hour since leaving the turnpike, and when the Talifero meat wagon slid up behind him, he'd watched them nuzzle up and look him over, then drop back again for a pacing into a likely shooting gallery.

The road was narrow and curvy, picking its way through the jumble of factories, farms, and small towns to the east of Trenton. At this hour of the night, only death was stirring along its winding route.

Just the same, the death crew would be looking for optimum conditions; these boys hardly ever left anything to chance; they were not gamblers, they were sure-thingers.

Bolan sighed as he casually checked the clip in the AutoMag. Three rounds of .44-caliber massive death were all that remained for the big silver pistol. The Beretta was totally defanged, empty, useless.

Sure. Time to stop and die, Bolan.

He angled a faint smile into the rearview mirror and quietly declared, "The hell you say."

His foot came down hard on the accelerator, and the rented Mustang leaped forward in instant response, leaving a puff of exhaust gases to mark the spot where the "death stalk" became a two-sided game.

The big Cadillac surged forward also, under expert command and grimly hanging into the tail slot. The Mustang, though, had been designed for games of this nature. The early advantage was clearly hers. The sleek sportsters swept over the abrupt ridges and power-screamed through the sharp curves as though all the laws of motion had been written into her design specifications—and slowly but surely a gap began forming between the speeding vehicles.

Bolan was playing only for numbers, though, not miles—counting the seconds of lead he managed to hold into each turn, calculating the increase with each successive maneuver and pitching his combat mind forward into that moment of confrontation which lay inevitably somewhere on the road ahead.

He knew that one crew wagon on his tail also inexorably meant that others were streaking into the chase—from several directions, no doubt. The fact that they had picked up on him so quickly was no matter of chance or accident. These boys were radio-equipped and -dispatched. They were as good as the cops in an exercise like this one; and in this particular case they had an advantage over the cops—they knew the car Bolan was driving.

Damn right, these guys knew their business. They had to. It was their only excuse for living. And Bolan had been making monkeys of them for much too long. They meant to get him this time, obviously, and that meat patrol that was now about ten seconds off his rear bumper represented but one statement in that determination.

So, sure . . . it had to be a game of numbers. He could not simply outrun them. He had to stop them cold, and he had to do it before the others had time to join the chase.

And so it was when the Mustang screamed into a darkened crossroads with the Taliferi less than fifteen seconds behind. Bolan caught a brief glimpse of a road sign just as he powered into the intersection; one way led to the town of Roosevelt, the other to Perrineville. Neither meant a thing to Bolan. He was seeking *terrain,* not towns—a place with combat stretch—and his instincts swung him eastward, toward Perrineville.

And he found his combat stretch several minutes and twenty numbers later, at a point where the road topped a gentle rise to descend abruptly into a double switch back and over a narrow brook.

He nearly missed the bridge, himself, the Mustang toeing in at the last possible instant to flash across, a hair width removed from the concrete abutment. Then it took him another ten or twelve precious numbers to halt that forward plunge and to bring the Mustang around in a whining return. He killed the lights and swung her broadside across the narrow bridge, then hobbled up the hillside—sternly commanding his injured leg to behave itself.

The glow of swiftly advancing headlights was peeking over the hill as he took up his position. Then the chase car was into the switchback, burning rubber in the sudden slow-down, rocking with the momentum of the double curve at high speed, and struggling for a path onto the bridge.

He could see them clearly as they groaned past his position, could feel the alarm and consternation as eight sets of shoulders hunched forward into the do-or-die curve.

The windows were down. Bolan could hear the cry of warning that erupted from the rear seat as the headlights swept onto that abandoned vehicle at bridge-center.

His own leg kicked in reflex as another panicky leg straightened on the brake pedal and that big limousine with eight headhunters aboard went into its death slide.

The Caddy was out of control even as it reached

the bridge, hunching down onto locked wheels and crabbing into the narrow passageway.

The rear end struck the approach abutment a glancing blow, slamming the heavy vehicle into a full fishtail and a broadside plunge along the bridge —twenty-one feet of Detroit steel grindingly attempting to fit itself within a fifteen-foot cement straitjacket.

The crew wagon was a disaster of disintegrating metal even before it reached the Mustang. It blew on, taking the smaller car with it to the other side. Bolan's vehicle fell away there and spun off onto the embankment, flipped, and came to rest on its top in the brook. The other car took an end-over-end tumble off the roadway and rolled on for another thirty feet or so before shuddering to a final halt on its side.

Bolan began his approach in a complete and deathly silence. A moment later came the weak cries and ghastly mouthings that assured him that he was not getting off all that easy—a mop-up operation was clearly in order.

One of the hardmen had been ejected from the vehicle during that wild plunge across the bridge. The remains were obviously beyond mop-up and even beyond identification; it looked as though he'd been caught in that meat grinder between rending metal and abrasive cement.

Bolan stepped around the soggy pile of hamburger and went on across the bridge, moving slowly to favor the protesting leg and warily approaching the pile of junk which had seconds earlier been a proud testament to man's engineering excellence.

He encountered another grisly bag of pulverized

flesh on the roadway at the point where the crew wagon had taken off on its cross-country roll. From that point he had only to follow the trail of broken bodies, counting three more between the road and the shattered vehicle.

That would leave three still to be accounted for; and from the sounds of the night, they would soon be beyond mop-up also.

The vehicle was lying in the shadows of high bushes, but with enough illumination from the bright moonlight for Bolan to see the two men who were folded into that steel trap.

And, yeah, they were in bad shape.

Both were conscious, though, and carrying on a groaning conversation.

"Can't feel my legs. Think my back's broke."

"How 'bout Carlo? Where's Carlo?"

"Fuck Carlo. Where's that fuckin' *guy?* Where's *he?"*

"Dunno. Who cares now? We're gonna die here, Bill."

"Maybe *you* are."

"We both are."

Bolan joined the conversation then, his voice low-pitched and coated with ice.

"Yeah, you both are," he announced solemnly.

A hand moved into the wreckage to pluck a revolver from numbed fingers. Another hand came in and clamped itself over a bloodied mouth and nose.

"How many in there?" asked the ice man.

The one who had been addressed as Bill replied, "That you, Bolan?"

"It's me."

"I knew we'd meet someday."

"Congratulations, you were right."

Bill groaned and gargled deep in his throat as he asked, "What're you doing?"

"Mopping up."

"Leave us be."

"Can't."

The guy moaned and tried unsuccessfully to move his head for a better look at the big cold bastard outside. "What're you doing to Campy?"

"Helping him die."

"Bastard!"

"Don't feel left out," the cold voice suggested, and the hand moved to the other face.

"Wait! Goddamn it, wait a minute!"

"Too long already."

The guy was mumbling angrily into Bolan's fingers. "Look, don't! Lemme die my own way!"

Bolan slid the hand aside. "Okay," he said quietly. "If you want to die talking."

"About what?"

"How many crews are after me?"

The guy snickered, choked, coughed painfully, then told the big man outside, "Enough. You're dead already, bud."

"So give me something to worry about."

"You'll never get out of this fuckin' state alive."

"How many crews, Matthew?"

The guy coughed again, and sticky warmth flowed onto Bolan's fingers. He turned the head to keep the guy from choking on his own blood, and again asked, "How many?"

"Fuck ya. Die wondering."

Bolan replied, "Okay," and went away from there.

The piercing odor of gasoline vapors was strong in his senses as he stepped around the rear of the wreckage; and then a movement in the bushes a few yards away sent him in a sprawling dive toward the shadows.

He had a flashing perception of a large bulk of a man with a pistol outstretched and spitting flame at him; in that same instant the entire area was brilliantly illuminated by flames as the gasoline vapors ignited with a whooshing explosion.

He felt the bullet from that fateful firing sing past him. By the time he had completed his roll and was coming up to return the fire, his target was a staggering fireball, the brightest thing of the night, spinning in confusion and seeking an escape from the inescapable.

The guy must have been lying in gasoline, soaked in it.

Bolan's appropriated revolver instinctively jerked into the firing lineup and pumped three quick mercy rounds into that tortured hell on earth . . . and he walked quickly away without looking back.

Afoot now, bleeding anew from the old wounds, and with a thousand Jersey guns awaiting him somewhere out there, Bolan nevertheless sent out a quiet "thanks" to the universe at large.

For the moment, at least, he was leaving death behind him.

2 THE FARM

He dreamed interminably of the infinite river and eternal warfare, and he awoke somewhere within that eternity with bright sunlight upon his face.

He was lying in straw, and he was naked. The sunlight was coming through an overhead window, a sort of skylight set into a high ceiling. He was warm, woozy, completely without pain.

A large man in blue jeans and a striped shirt sat on a bench beside him, watching him with attentive eyes.

Someone else was at his other side. He was too comfortable to make the effort of turning his head to see who was there.

From somewhere off in that direction came a gasp and an excited female voice. "Bruno! He's awake!"

Okay. That other someone was a woman, obviously. The big dude in blue jeans must be Bruno. So what?

Bruno looked okay. Balding, a bit overweight, pleasant face, worried eyes.

Bolan tried to ask, "Bruno *who?*" but his tongue clung to the roof of his mouth, and somehow he couldn't get it loose.

Then the woman leaned over him; and she wasn't

a woman, at all. A girl, a mere slip of a girl, dressed also in blue jeans and a shirt made from the same material as Bruno's.

Bruno's daughter?

The eyes were huge pools of dark compassion, framed in smooth flesh of almost dusky hue, but alive and glistening. Long, shiny hair fell in smooth cascades across the shoulders—jet-black, silken.

A kid, and here lay Bolan mother naked.

He made the effort and got a hand in motion, sending it to a flopping and heavy rest somewhere about the thighs. A towel was draped across him down there—or something with a terrycloth feeling.

Okay. Okay, kid, nothing to worry about, don't look so scared.

She was asking him, in a concerned but musical voice, "How do you feel?"

He tried the tongue again and gave it up, settling for a crooked smile that somehow felt all contorted and clownish.

What the hell was wrong with him?

As though reading his thoughts, the girl told him, "Bruno found you in the brook. We've stopped your bleeding, and we've given you something to ease the pain. Can you tell me how you feel?"

Reality crashed in on him, then. Somehow he got an elbow under him and tried to push himself upright. The girl pressed him back down, gently but firmly, and she told him. "You must lie still."

The tongue came unstuck, but his voice sounded like quacking as he mumbled, "No, you don't know. Danger, dangerous for you here."

She was trying to calm him, and the guy came over to place a heavy hand on his head.

He was trying to tell them that their lives were not worth a piece of the straw he was lying upon—not as long as he lay there—but he felt that he was speaking into a well, a deep well which began enlarging and closing in around him; and it was the last lucid moment he had that day.

When next he found an edge of reality he could hang on to, he was lying between soft sheets, and he felt as though he'd been dropped from a high-flying aircraft without a parachute.

The girl was seated at a window just across the room, bright sunlight streaming in on her, writing something on a large tablet which she held on her knees.

She was beautiful.

He watched her for a long moment; then her eyes raised to his with a start, and he was again impressed with the dimensions of those deep pools.

The well, maybe, into which he had become absorbed the last time around?

Bolan did not know, offhand, what else to say, so he asked her, "How long have I been here?"

"This is the second day," she replied in a voice with very little air pushing it.

"Where is it?"

"What?"

"Where am I?"

"This is . . . my bedroom. Our farm, my brother and I. Chicken ranch. Near Manalapan."

"What is Manalapan?"

"A town. On Route Thirty-three, mid-state."

"Now close to Perrineville?"

"Not far. Less than ten miles. We're just about halfway between Philadelphia and New York City."

Bolan groaned at that and raised himself to a sitting position. "Then you must have a special angel," he told the girl. "That's not nearly far enough." He swung one foot to the floor and felt himself toppling off-balance toward the headboard of the bed.

He wasn't even aware that she'd left her chair, but the girl was there instantly, arms about his shoulders, guiding him down to the proper spot on the pillows.

"Don't try that again," she commanded almost angrily. "You're not *that* tough, Mr. Bolan."

His eyes must have asked the question. She perched there beside him and answered it in a no-nonsense tone. "Yes, we know all about you. There's been nothing else on radio and television for the past two days. Bruno took the bullet out of your side, and we did what we could for your other hurts. The rest is up to you, though. You must lie still, or you'll bust loose and start bleeding again. How about some food? Think you could handle some?"

He muttered, "I'll eat a cow if it'll get me out of here."

"That's thanks for you," she said in a solemn little voice.

"The thanks you have coming, kid, will be a bullet up the nose if they find me here. You just can't know—"

"If you mean those hoods, they've already been here twice. We had you hidden in the brooder house all through last night."

"They'll be back," he argued. "Those guys don't know the meaning of quit. Now, you go get my clothes while I get the cobwebs out of my brain."

The girl ran from the room, and he heard her outside a moment later, calling for her brother.

Bolan made another try for the floor, and reached it, then sat there on the edge of the bed and examined himself.

The guy had done a good job with the chest wound. Very little soreness, obviously no infection. Nylon thread for stitches. He grinned wryly and pulled the injured leg up for a look-see.

Inflamed, yeah, swollen . . . and hurting like hell. The ten-mile stroll through that creek bed had not helped it at all. Some sort of evil-smelling poultice was taped over the wound. Bolan removed it and bent down for a closer look. He just hoped that Bruno had cleaned it out thoroughly before he sewed it up. He was still inspecting the mess when Bruno himself came huffing into the house.

The guy was not as old as he looked, Bolan was betting.

Looked fifty.

If he was the kid's brother, though, then he was probably somewhere under forty—certainly no more than that.

He was standing there in the doorway and filling it, a real ox of a man, giving Bolan the concerned gaze.

Bolan showed the guy a scowl and told him, "You're a good medic, Bruno. Thanks. Will you get me my pants?"

"You don't recognize me, do you?" Bruno asked quietly.

Bolan looked him over more closely, then replied, "Should I?"

"I guess not," the guy said. "We met only once, and you were in quite a hurry that time, too."

Bolan was giving him a quizzical smile.

"Dien Huc," the guy explained. "The field hospital. I was on duty there the time you brought that column of kids in. You know, those kids from—"

"Small world, Bruno," Bolan said tautly. "That was Doc Brantzen's headquarters."

"Right. I was one of his medics, surgical assistant."

"And now you're raising chickens."

"Right, now I'm raising chickens."

"Brantzen's dead. I got 'im killed. I'll get you killed, too, Bruno. You and that beautiful kid, both of you. Now, get me my pants and point me toward the coast."

"No way," the guy told him. "You'd never make it. Not on that leg. You could lose it yet."

"Just how bad is it?"

"Bad enough. No vital tissues lost. Everything will rebuild if you'll give it a decent chance. And if you don't lose it to infection. I've got you on antibiotics." The big guy grinned. "Same stuff I give my chickens. If you don't start crowing, I guess you'll survive it."

Bolan said, "The leg. What about it?"

"Use it too soon, and you'll lose it. Give it a couple days, anyway."

"You know I can't," Bolan growled. "The headhunters, Bruno. You know what those guys are. They won't stop with mine. They'll take yours and the kid's, just to keep in practice."

The girl stepped through the doorway and said,

"Stop calling me 'the kid.' The name is Sara, no *h*. And I'm no kid."

"That's right, she's not," Bruno told Bolan in a matter-of-fact tone. "She lost her man in 'Nam. She's a widow already."

Bolan was reminded that hot wars make many young widows, but this was ridiculous. He'd pegged her age at about sixteen.

She caught his look, and repeated, "I am *no* kid. And we didn't pull you out of the brook to make an amputee out of you. So get back in that bed and stop acting silly."

Bolan glared at her for a moment; then his gaze flicked to the man. "How long," he solemnly asked him, "do you think it will take the headhunters to put together a make on two ex-GI's—one wounded and needing medical attention, the other a surgical nurse who just happens to live in the search zone?"

"I figure it may take them another couple of days," the guy replied soberly. He spread his hands and added, "Look, man. What choice do you have?"

What choice? Bolan already knew the answer to that. It was coming from his head, in spinning circles of dizziness, and from that swollen leg, on cresting waves of pain and nausea.

"Okay," he replied weakly.

He lay back down and closed his eyes, returning very quickly to flowing rivers and eternal warfare, and to a new twist in skin-crawling nightmares—a chicken ranch overnight becoming a "turkey" farm.

Yeah. It was the grand-slammer, Doc Brantzen special. Brantzen had been the first turkey on Mack Bolan's soul. But a hell of a long way from the last one.

3 THE HEALING

They were nice people, both Sara and her brother; but during the next forty-eight hours of around-the-clock nursing, feeding, and constant attention, Bolan got to know quite a bit more about his tenders than they of him—or so he thought.

Both of these people had, in effect, already retired from the problems of life—in so many ways.

Sara, as it turned out, had just a few weeks earlier quietly marked her twenty-second birthday. She still looked sixteen to Bolan, but that was just surface stuff. Down in there where she really lived, Sara Henderson was a resigned old lady in a rocking chair, quietly filling in her days the best she could until death overcame her.

She had married David Henderson, her college sweetheart, at the age of nineteen. Two weeks later David kissed her good-bye and went to war. He did not survive. And neither did Sara. She came home—to the chicken ranch—and watched her father die of cancer. The mother had been dead for some time.

Mother and Father Tassily had emigrated from Romania just in time to get in on America's big Depression. Bruno and Sara were their only offspring—their only living kin in America—and now Bruno and Sara were all that was.

Sara ran the farm on her own until big brother Bruno came home from Vietnam; and he returned a maimed man, but not in body.

Bruno had helped the field surgeons hack off too many shattered arms and legs from despairing young men. He had seen too many savageries, too much inhumanity, and far too much senseless death and suffering. He had gone to Vietnam as a conscientious objector on medical assignment. He returned a confirmed athiest in need of considerable medical attention himself.

These were the people who were laying their lives on Bolan's line. Somehow, without actually saying so, they conveyed the idea that they did not regard the event as any sort of sacrifice, but as some weird atonement for nameless sins.

Bolan appreciated what they were doing, of course. But he was appalled by the unspoken implications that he had come along merely to collect their tithes of atonement.

During one of those quiet moments with Bruno, he had told the big Romanian, "The master clock of life doesn't beat just to the *ticks,* you know. It needs the *tocks,* as well."

And he'd told Sara, in the still hours of one of those endless nights, "When I sleep, I dream. And when I dream, I think I'm more awake than at any other time. Life is like that, Sara. Paradoxical. Every hurt carries the seed of some great joy. And every great moment has but one place to go from there, and that's back down to the valley of despair. But we *live* in neither place, you know. We live in the *middle,* and we visit the other places from time to time. Try living in the extremes—either one, Sara—and you're resigning from life."

Bolan was no preacher man. He didn't even know whether or not the things he felt made sense to anyone else, but he did feel them very strongly, and he quietly got in his points with Sara and Bruno whenever he could.

To an outside observer, it may have seemed as though Mack Bolan had been "sent" to the Tassilys. As he mended, so too did they—in so many subtle ways.

By the third day, Bruno had become much more talkative, less solemn and brooding, even humorous and playful at times.

Sara had definitely become aware of Bolan as a man. She'd taken to doing things with her hair, wearing a hint of makeup, and she'd even abandoned the blue jeans in favor of a couple of bright little fashions which she'd whipped out on her sewing machine while Bolan slept.

On that third day, also, Bruno took his chicken truck off to Manhattan on an urgent errand for his star boarder. He left at daybreak, promising to return by nightfall—otherwise, "ring the bells and say a prayer for the rummy Romanian."

Bolan was not overly worried about the safety of the mission. Bruno frequently took his own birds to market. This trip into the city would appear to be routine, in case anyone was keeping watch over the comings and goings at that farm. And he was sending the guy to a trusted friend.

They had moved Bolan back to a loft in the brooder house, which now was alive with thousands of cheeping baby chicks—the move being made at Bolan's insistence. He also took along the remainders of his war armaments—the empty Beretta, the nearly empty AutoMag, and the Talifero revolver with three live chambers.

Bruno had built him a hideaway bunk in the loft above the chicks and padded it down with clean straw covered with a couple of heavy quilts. It was very comfortable. His medications were out there, as was a variety of high-protein "nibblings"—cheeses, boiled eggs, and so on. In addition to that, Sara came out every couple of hours and poked a ration of hot food into him.

On the morning which saw Bruno off to Manhattan, Sara came to the loft at eight o'clock with tape measure, pad, and pencil in hand.

"What's that for?" Bolan had growled at her.

"To see where you're at, with what," she'd replied, twinkling, and took his measurements at every conceivable point and angle.

A couple of times during that operation their eyes locked for overlong periods, and it seemed that things were getting a bit out of hand.

She'd gone out of there without another word, though, and at ten o'clock she was back, with a very close copy of his favored combat outfit—a black, skin-tight two-piecer with all the handy pockets in the right places.

Bolan was deeply impressed.

"How'd you do that?" he marveled.

"Just a little something I whipped up," the girl replied, trying to conceal her pride in the production. "It wasn't all that hard."

She handed him a folded sheet of heavy paper.

He recognized it immediately as coming from the large writing tablet which he'd seen in her possession so often. Obviously the tablet was an artist's sketch-pad, and she had very artistically sketched Bolan, probably as he lay sleeping in her presence, but as she'd imagined him to look in full combat regalia. All of it was there—the weapons, the utility belts, the gadgets—and she'd captured a catlike poise in that rangy body as well as a savagely snarling face which somehow still had a somewhat saintly cast to it.

Very quietly he asked her, "Is that the way I look to you?"

"Yes," she replied, just as quietly.

"How'd you get the combat rig?" he asked.

She shrugged daintily. "Lifted it. I guess you've been sketched by every police artist in the country. I've seen it many times, in the papers."

He said, "I see."

"Try it on. The suit."

"Later," he told her, sighing.

"I've seen your pinky toes before, plenty of times."

"Later, just the same," he murmured.

"Mack Bolan, I believe you're a hopeless prude," she told him. She leaned across the bunk and pulled the sheet away from him, all the way, fastidiously folding it at his feet.

This, Bolan was thinking, was where he'd come in.

Except that now there was not even a towel to protect his sense of modesty.

This was, however, very obviously no time for modesty.

Sara was removing her dress, carefully folding it with the same studied movements with which she'd handled the bedsheet. She laid the dress atop the packing crate that Bolan was using as a night stand, then went to the window for a quick peek outside.

"Am I ready for this?" he asked her, feeling silly with the words even as they left his mouth.

"I don't know about you," she replied, turning to him with a solemn smile. "But I sure am."

"Well, hell . . ."

Sara was removing her bra as she retraced the path to Bolan's bunk. It was odd, he was thinking, how clothing made some girls look so underdeveloped when in fact they were not . . . like this one. She was beautifully put together. The breasts were on the delicate side, but perfectly formed, stiffish, and tightly packed—incredibly glossy.

She put the bra with the dress, then hooked both thumbs into the waistband of her panties and just stood there gazing at him with those limpid eyes.

She seemed frozen there, suddenly, the panties ever so slightly lowered, a statue in glowing flesh tones.

Bolan noticed, then, that those hands were trembling. He took one in his and told her, "Be sure you know what you're doing. This is very probably your last chance to back out."

"You're not helping a bit," she protested faintly in a wobbly voice. "I rehearsed and rehearsed. Had it all figured out—what I'd say, what you'd say—and you're not *doing* it."

He said, "No rehearsals needed, Sara. Not if this is what you truly want."

She cried, "Oh, God, I *do!*" And with that she

broke down completely, hiding her face in her hands and bawling her heart out.

He pulled her on down with him, and gently made room for her, and consoled her with loving touches and reassuring words, and she very quickly became fully a woman in his arms as each to their own need they found that special healing which somehow seems to justify the pains of the world.

And, some time later, Bolan admiringly told her, "You were right, Sara. You're sure no kid."

They lay in slack embrace and talked of various things for quite a while—serious things, silly things, man-woman things—and after they'd run out of words they simply clung to each other in a silent communion outside of time.

Later he donned the black suit for her pleased inspection, then left it on as they snuggled into another quiet mood.

Somewhere along toward early afternoon, Bolan fell into a deep sleep. It was probably his most peaceful rest in weeks, and he did not know when Sarah left.

He awoke with a start, alone, with the sun low in the sky and perfectly framed in his window—and with some animal comprehension of danger.

There had been an outcry from down by the house—a human cry or shout or something—coming in right at the edge of his consciousness, but weakly commanding attention.

He carried the AutoMag to the window and gazed down upon the familiar scene, normally so tranquil.

This time, though, the view sent combat hormones leaping into his bloodstream and coursing immediately to every reach of his system.

A strange vehicle was parked in the drive, near the house. Two guys in fancy silk threads were down there in open view, standing beside the car. One of them was holding a door open, and the other was trying to force a grimly struggling Sara Henderson into the vehicle.

It was one of those sudden-confrontation situations that allow for no combat brief, no tactical planning, no exercise of the intellect whatsoever. And it was sheer conditioned reflex of the combat sense that sent the AutoMag crashing through that flimsy pane of glass, that lined up those doomsday sights, that squeezed the fist that closed the switch that sent 240 grains of screaming death sizzling across that forty-yard range to the target.

The big magnum bullet tore past within inches of that lovely face he'd kissed so tenderly such a short while ago and thwacked home between two startled eyes with what Sara would later describe as "a horrible sucking sound."

Even as that first round was impacting target, the big silver hogleg was roaring another angry bellow, and missile number two was annihilating another firetrack; the dude at the car door found himself with an inexplicably exploding throat, and the two of them died hardly a gasp apart.

Sara had collapsed onto her knees. She was kneeling there in the gore surrounding her, hands clasped in her lap, looking up at him and screaming something unintelligible.

She had quieted down somewhat by the time he reached her, but she was still kneeling there between those two citations of sudden death, and her first anguished words for the Executioner were: "No, Mack, God, no, you shouldn't have! Now they've found you!"

He plucked her out of there and steered her toward the house as he replied to that.

"They have," he said icily. "The hard way."

4 THE MESSAGE

He gave her brandy and scrubbed the blood spatterings from that beloved flesh as she chatteringly related the happening for his interested ears.

The two *mafiosi* had barged in and searched the house, for the third time that week. They'd even checked the dirty laundry, counted toothbrushes in the bathroom, and pawed through the garbage cans.

The younger one had been ordered to search the outbuildings, but according to Sara, he'd done no more than stroll nervously about the grounds and peer warily through partially open doorways.

Then the big one had started pushing Sara about and trying to scare her with broad hints about the penalty "for harboring fugitives."

They'd tried to pass themselves off as "detectives."

It proved to be Sara's undoing.

She unloaded a pile of outrage upon them and finished off by denouncing them as "two-bit hoods."

Apparently it had seemed to the boys that she protested too much.

They decided to "take her downtown" for

"further questioning," and that was where Bolan entered the scene.

He was damned glad he had.

There was seldom any return from those "trips downtown" with the Taliferi.

He asked Sara, "The big guy seemed to be in charge?"

She replied, "Uh-huh."

"Was his name ever mentioned? What was he called?"

"Hugger. Yes, he called him Hugger."

Bolan showed her a thin smile and said, "Great. Now, let's get the voice. Where was it pitched? Here? Here?"

He was giving her a scale of probabilities, and she stopped him at about middle C.

"Good girl. This could be important, so let's make sure we get it right. How about tonal quality? Did he talk like this?" He'd offered her an example of a nasal sound; then he tried her with a grating foghorn: "Or more like this?"

Sara was shaking her head and watching him with growing interest, thoroughly captivated by the virtuoso performance. He finally satisfied her on the basics, then went into accent and diction.

He was speaking with both lips stiffened and the chin nearly frozen when she nodded and whispered, "Yes, yes, that's him!"

Holding that same voice, he suggested, "But not exactly, right? Right, chick? There's no personality in this voice, is there? I mean—"

"Whine a little," she excitedly suggested. "Not overmuch, but sort of . . . sort of frustrated and mad at the same time, but you're trying to keep it under control."

"Right. Right, dolly. Whatta I got to do, honey, kick the hell right outta you? Is that what you want?"

Sara shivered. Her eyes dropped, and she told him, "That's just too real for comfort."

Bolan was guessing that it was no more than an approximation—but that was all most people heard, anyway. Something notable, something to hang an imperfect perception onto—it was that natural human frailty which made Bolan's masquerades possible.

She was asking him, "But what . . . why do you need . . . ?"

He told her, "Come and see."

They returned to the outside, and Sara stood stiffly in the drive, pointedly ignoring the crumpled bodies at her feet, as Bolan leaned into the vehicle and came out holding a microphone.

He smiled at her as he depressed the mike button, pulled on his "Hugger" face, and started his act. "Hey! Wake up!" he snarled.

A voice responded immediately from somewhere beneath the dashboard. "Who's that?"

"It's Little Red Riding Hood," Bolan replied nastily. "Skipping merrily through the goddamn countryside. Who the hell you think it is?"

"What you got, Hugger?"

Bolan tossed the girl a salute as he replied, "What does it sound like I got?"

"Okay, it's the same everywhere. Boss says go on to the next place. Waitaminnit! Hold it!"

Bolan told Sara in his own voice, "Maybe I blew it."

The other voice returned a moment later. "Okay, Hugger. Just got a report on th'other net. That farmer's on his way back, just came off the turnpike at Hightstown. We want you to stay there and check 'im out."

"What for?" Bolan/Hugger snarled back. "Smuggling chickenshit back into Jersey?"

"Boss says we check 'im coming and going, Hugger."

Bolan grimly smiled at Sara and replied, "Okay, but I think I'll meet 'im on the way. Gettin' dark soon. I don't wanta be out here in the dark with a daylight crew."

"Sure. Whatever makes you feel safe, Hugger."

It was a sarcastic sign-off.

Bolan was smiling coldly when he returned the microphone to its clip. He took the keys from the ignition and went around to open the trunk.

The girl followed him, questions in her eyes. "What was that all about?" she wanted to know.

"It's called covering tracks," he informed her. "When these boys come down missing in action, we don't want their buddies beginning the search here, do we?"

She soundlessly framed the reply "No" and moved out of his way as Bolan began the unpleasant task of stowing limp bodies and cleaning up gory evidence from the driveway. That job completed, he banged the lid on his cooling cargo, got into the car, and moved it to a place of concealment behind one of the sheds.

As he strode back to the house, he felt the spring

returning to his step, and he knew that his combat quickness was settling in on him again.

He was healed and ready for battle.

Almost ready.

Sara was waiting in the precise spot where he'd left her.

In a small voice she asked him, "What now, Mr. Bolan?"

"Now, love," he replied quietly, "we wait for the farmer. And his precious cargo from Manhattan."

The sun was disappearing into a red veil of smaze along the western horizon when Bruno Tassily wheeled his live-produce transporter with its empty cages into the farmyard.

The girl fled to her brother's arms and allowed herself a few luxurious tears as she greeted him; then she backed away, gave Bolan a somewhat embarrassed gaze, and ran into the house to quit that man's world for a while.

The men shook hands, and Bolan asked the big fellow, "How'd it go?"

"Directly on your numbers, Sarge," Bruno reported with a tired grin. "The stuff is in the tool well."

"Get it all?"

"Yeah. Uh, that Meyer boy . . . you didn't tell me. He's a double amputee. But, hell, he—"

"Yeah, he does all right, doesn't he?" Bolan said quietly.

"Like gangbusters, that's all. Uh, he gave me a message for you. Says business is booming all of a sudden, the past few days. Selling to guys he never heard of before. Says the word's out all over town.

They're recruiting guys right off the damn street corners. And he's having a run on guns like he never had before."

Bolan was smiling, but only with his lips. "Guns for Jersey, eh?"

"That's the impression Meyer has. He thinks they're fielding an army over here. And listen. I contacted that other friend of yours, too. He says . . . well, wait till we get inside. I have it written down."

They had moved on to the rear of the truck. Bruno was unlocking the tool compartment and ogling Bolan's black suit, apparently having just taken note of it. "Where'd you get that?" he asked.

"Sara made it," Bolan told him. "Quite a gal."

"You'll never know," Bruno said admiringly. "Sara has talents she hasn't even discovered yet."

Bolan could have told the big Romanian that his sister had discovered one or two that very day. Instead he said, "We had an incident, Bruno. Pretty unnerving for Sara. I had to shoot a couple of guys off her back. They're over behind your equipment shed, with their car. I'll be moving it away from here when it gets dark."

The big guy merely blinked his eyes at Bolan and began removing tools from the compartment. Then he got down to the part that counted, and Bolan began taking delivery of his new arsenal, checking it piece by piece as it came forth, grunting now and then with satisfaction over a particular item.

It required ten minutes to transfer the stuff to the shed. When they finally got into the house, Sara had coffee waiting, and the three of them sat at a small table near a window that provided an excellent view onto the roadway out front.

Bolan reminded his host about the "other message," and Bruno hastily whipped out a small notebook and began flipping the pages while the man in black quietly loaded clips with big ugly rounds of .44 magnum ammunition.

"Yeah, here it is," Bruno announced. "You'd never make it out. I better read it for you."

The message was from Leo Turrin, Bolan's secret comrade since almost the beginning of this war on the Mafia. Turrin was an underboss in a Massachusetts arm of the mob. He also was an undercover federal agent. Bolan scratched Leo's back, and he scratched Bolan's—in every way possible, and always at fantastic jeopardy to the man with the double life. It seemed as though it had been just days ago that the two of them had collaborated on Bolan's hazardous assignment in Philly. And then Leo had come in when Bolan needed his cooperation to accomplish the job in Sicily.

Stumbling as he deciphered his own notes, Bruno reported his conversation with Leo Turrin thus:

"He says you should lie low, don't move, don't even breathe hard. Federal marshals and state troopers are watching every highway and all public transportation facilities. Uh, and, yeah, he says to avoid all urban areas like the plague, especially, uh, the Jersey City and Newark areas. Cruise, uh . . . oh, he must have said *crews* . . . crews are coming down from all around the Northeast to plug Jersey solidly. They smell your blood. Know you're wounded and grounded somewhere. They're moving in for the kill. Says if you have to move, then move toward the sea. Long Beach, Asbury Park, that area. But even there you should count every grain of sand before you trust your foot to it. Uh . . . Marinello? Is that . . . ? Marinello is personally running the show. He takes it very personal what you did in Philly, as well as Sicily."

The big guy raised quizzical eyes to Bolan. "Who is Marinello?"

"Boss of all the bosses," Bolan said quietly.

Bruno shivered and took a quick sip of coffee before resuming the reading.

"He's got rolling command posts all over the area. Radio-equipped, with the smartest enforcers in his outfit personally directing the operations. Mike, uh, Talifero? . . . is also out somewhere in Jersey with a, uh, posse of headhunters, swearing to get you, or else he's not ever coming back."

Bolan chuckled at that, a chilling sound which momentarily clouded Sara's eyes.

"He says to give yourself a 'well done' for Philadelphia. The whole Angeletti family has fallen apart, or else at each other's throats, or else running clear out of the state. But he says to stay clear of Philly for now. The feds are looking for you to fall back in that direction, and they're primed and waiting for you to show."

Bolan lit a cigarette and blew the smoke into his hands.

"Also he said be sure to give you this report on Frank the Kid. Who's Frank the Kid, Sarge?"

"The heir to old man Angeletti's throne," Bolan explained.

"Well, not anymore. Here's what your guy said. Tell the Sarge that Frank the Kid was executed less than one hour after his arrival in New York. He got there with the wrong head."

The wondering eyes came up again to lock onto Bolan's expressionless gaze. "What does that mean? The wrong head?"

"He thought he had mine," Bolan said.

"Oh."

Sara quietly excused herself and hurried out of the room.

Bruno nervously shuffled the pages of his notebook and said, "That's it."

"Thanks," Bolan said. "Bruno, you're a hell of a guy."

"Forget Bruno," the Romanian replied in a very subdued voice. "What are *you?* How can you sit there all calm like that? Don't you know what I've just been telling you?"

"I know."

"You haven't a chance. Not a chance in a million."

"Guess I'll have to make one, Bruno."

"I . . . I know you can if anyone can, but . . ."

Bolan sighed, squeezed the big man's shoulder, and went to find Sara.

She was on the porch, arms folded across her bosom, staring morosely at the spot in the drive where she had been a close bystander to sudden and violent death.

He came up behind her and put his arms about her. "Don't let it bug you," he said, speaking softly with his lips at her ear.

"Why not?" she replied with a strangled little sigh. "That was no message. It was a sentence of death."

"I've had them before," he pointed out. "And I'm still here."

"Just barely." She sniffed.

His voice had a lilt to it as he reminded her, "That's not what you told me this afternoon."

She was very quietly and very unemotionally weeping. "Don't die, Mack," she said in a tiny voice. "Please, please don't die. Go back to the loft. We can keep you safe."

"No you can't. Each hour I spend here now is another fifty guns I'll have to face sooner or later."

"You don't *have* to—"

"Yes I do. You said something about a sentence of death. That sentence was pronounced a long time ago, Sara. The only way I avoid it is by shoving it back through their teeth. The minute I start trying to duck it, then I'm a dead man for sure. Besides . . ."

"Yes," she said in a tightening voice. "Finish it. Besides *what?* You *love* it, don't you? You're just *aching* to get back out there and . . . and—how did you say it?—shove it back in their teeth."

"Wish me well, Sara," he requested humbly.

"Oh . . . *God!"* she cried, twisting about and throwing her arms around him.

Yes, Him too, he thought bleakly.

Whatever and wherever You are, God, wish me well.

And suffer the young widows their solace.

5 COUNTERPOISE

He was in full combat rig.

The black suit that Sara had designed and built was a better fit than any he'd worn. It was made of an expanding, tough material that moved with him like his own skin; even the pockets hugged close until they were filled with something.

The Beretta Belle occupied her usual position of honor—shoulder-slung beneath the left arm. The AutoMag, fully armed and backed up, now rode heavy military web at his right hip.

A compact, folding-stock autopistol dangled free from a strap about his neck to ride loosely across his belly.

A miscellany of carefully selected munitions dangled from utility belts or lay snugly in the elastic pockets of the skinsuit. These included small fragmentation grenades, percussion pods, incendiaries, chemical smoke compressors, even a couple of small transistorized explosives.

Spare clips for the guns, a stiletto, and several small tools completed the ensemble.

Bruno looked the warrior over and commented, "You must be carrying a hundred pounds over your own weight."

"About that," Bolan agreed.

"Does the leg know it yet?"

"A little. But it'll get used to the idea."

"Just watch it," the worried Romanian cautioned in a curiously flattened voice. "Damnit, don't let them . . ." His voice broke. He spun about and marched stiffly toward the house.

Bolan stopped him with a quiet call, but the big guy did not turn all the way around.

"Bruno. You're a hell of a guy."

"Thanks. You too. Watch those *tocks*, eh."

"Name of the game," Bolan replied, chuckling.

Bruno went on, then, and Bolan stepped over to the vehicle.

He had carefully stowed the rest of his arsenal in the back-seat area and covered it with some empty feed sacks.

The two corpses remained in the trunk compartment.

A lovely young lady occupied a small portion of the front seat.

In a tinkly voice she asked him, "Are we ready to go?"

Gruffly he replied, "*We*, hell."

"I can run as fast as you."

"I'm not running, love," he quietly informed her.

"Well . . ."

Bruno burst back upon the scene at that moment, trotting from the rear of the house and waving a heavy money belt above his head.

"You forgot the war chest, Sarge!"

Bolan accepted the fat belt, stared at it for a moment, then shoved it back into Bruno's hands. "Hang on to it for me," he requested.

"You crazy? There's nearly a hundred thousand—"

"I took what I'll be needing for now. And if I don't make it through . . . well, can't take it with you, Bruno."

"Hey, Sarge, I can't—"

"Sure you can," the Executioner replied brusquely. He pulled the girl out of the car, slapped her lightly on the bottom, and told her, "All ashore."

She gasped, "Mack, I—"

He stopped her with a kiss, holding her deliciously close despite the intefering hardware.

When they came out of it, Bruno had disappeared.

Their eyes locked together, and a very special message quietly had its say there.

Then the girl's eyes fled that moment, and she told Bolan, "I-I'll always remember."

"Remember, too, what I told you this morning."

"I will," she whispered.

He slid into the car and closed the door.

"How did your husband die, Sara?" he gently asked her, through the window.

"I . . . they just said 'killed in action.' "

"Then he died living," the man in black told her. "I intend to do the same thing. But—damnit, Sara—you are a very special item. Promise me you won't live dying."

"Promise," she whispered. She wiped the moisture from her cheeks then, and told him, "The, uh, clothing you wore in here. It's all patched and pressed and hanging in the back window."

"Thanks, I noticed," he said, and then he kicked

the war wagon to life and quickly put that paradise behind him . . . and he did not look back.

The girl ran down the drive and stood there —a pathetic figure with slumped shoulders and dulled eyes—until the glow of his headlamps disappeared finally into the night.

She was walking dispiritedly toward the house when Bruno's truck lumbered around from the rear and gunned along the drive beside her.

She cried out, "Bruno! What are you . . . ?"

The truck rumbled on past and turned onto the road in Mack Bolan's wake.

Sara's hands went to her face, and she held that pose while tormenting thoughts and pictures spilled across her reeling consciousness.

Die living. Live dying. Kill, be killed. Fight, struggle, die, die, die, a million times die—what sort of world . . . ?

Remember what I told you this morning!

Yes, Sara, remember always.

"The universe must love you very much, Sara. Because you're a woman. And the female of every species is the universe in miniature, the living plasma of creation. She's the positive, uplifting force, the collector, the preserver, the nest-builder. You're the bridge of the generations, Sara. It's up to you to preserve what we men would destroy . . . without you."

Okay, sure, she could understand that kind of talk. Even from a relentless war machine like Mack Bolan. And he was more than that, of course. Much more. Yes. He was some kind of man.

She straightened her shoulders and turned back toward the house.

Okay, Mother Sara, preserver of the races and wife of the universe. Get in there and start nesting.

She went inside, turned on all the lights, put the Tijuana Brass on the hi-fi, found her sketchpad, and began designing herself a new summer wardrobe.

6 DRAW PLAY

"What you got, Hugger?"

"A suspicious. Just off Thirty-three by the fairgrounds. I don't wanta go down in there with just me 'n' the kid. Some guy's camping down there, fire and everything."

"Where'd you say that is?"

"A box canyon on this little road just east of the fairgrounds, by that new interstate."

"Our sectionals don't show no box canyon around there, Hugger."

"Well, damnit, you better look again! I'm telling you . . . Whuup! Change that, it's no *suspicious!* It's him, it's the guy! You get me some help here damn quick!"

"Boss says damnit you sit tight! Don't try nothing on your own. We're on the way!"

"I'm sittin'! But you shag ass!"

Bolan smiled a smile that was not a smile and thumbed off the microphone. All he had to do now was to wait. And he'd learned, long ago, to wait.

He had traveled not east from the Tassily farm, but west—clear to the approaches of Trenton; and he'd found his battle site near a place called Mercerville, not far from the state fairgrounds.

The terrain here was not the most ideal, but he had desired to get as far west as feasible, hoping to draw the hounds away from the trails he planned to travel later that evening.

And he'd found a pretty decent site for a fire trap—more or less remote, a bit of woods, some open area with a bit of high ground overlooking it . . . and an escape path to the rear.

He had covered the area thoroughly in a walking recon, in the dark; then he'd built a small campfire at dead center, dumped his cargo of cold meat and carefully laid it out just so, then moved the vehicle to the elevated land overlooking the scene.

The target range would be about fifty yards. It would be a hellish lay for those foolish enough to be caught down there.

Before summoning the foolish ones, he carefully investigated the back way out, found it passable in the vehicle, then returned immediately to the fire trap and began setting up.

He positioned infrared floods and took rangefinder readings from three different locations on the ridge, then set up a couple of LAWs (light antitank weapons) and made them ready, put some heavy grenades out, checked his personal weapons . . . and went to the radio to spread some blood for the shark pack.

At this range the LAW would do about anything a bazooka could do, and Bolan had a couple of special missions in mind for those deadly dudes.

He also had a honey of a new nighttime sniper piece which had come from the William Meyer & Company "munitions-at-a-price" supermarket in Manhattan—and at a very dear price.

Meyer was more than an illicit arms dealer. He was also a physically shattered survivor of Vietnam, a skilled armorer like Bolan, and a genius at modifying old arms to newfangled kill specifications.

A lifetime victim of warfare, Meyer had found a way to make the human proclivity for destruction pay off in a particularly ironic and profitable fashion . . . or so he'd told Bolan at the height of the nightmare in New York. Meyer had discovered that munitions makers do not take sides in small wars; they merely build destruction to specification for whatever damn fools want to come along and set it loose upon the world.

Hinting, of course that Bolan was one of the damn fools.

Bolan had never argued with the man. Damn fool or not, he had a job that needed doing, and there seemed to be no one else around who was ready, able, or willing to take it on. It just happened that Bolan had all three of those qualifications; and here he was—damn fool, maybe—but here nevertheless, on a Jersey hillside in the dead of night, waiting his chance to let loose quite a ration of destruction upon the world of damn fools.

And the foolish ones came, recklessly, straining at the bit like so many excited bloodhounds with scent strong in their nostrils, tearing along that lonely road down there like the hounds of hell had done since the beginning of life.

Two vehicles, then a third, and finally a streamlined van sort of thing—one of those houses on wheels which gentler people used to get back to nature without really suffering. And now Bolan knew what the boys were utilizing for their "rolling command posts."

The mob, too, liked their comforts. Even on kill missions.

He let them come, and watched the two lead vehicles jounce into that clearing and tear off on opposing circular paths toward the far end. The third car was a standard crew wagon. It came on through the slot and halted just inside; doors popped open; energetic men found their feet and their weapons in a quick debarkation and an even quicker fanning out across that clearing.

Then the camper came down, halting right in the slot and squatting there with lights ablaze.

Pretty damned confident, Bolan was thinking.

Still, damned effective. He'd had a hard time counting heads and keeping track of the maneuvers as well.

He had actually seen twelve heads. There were probably at least twenty, not counting whoever was in that command van.

All four vehicles had left their headlamps on high beams, and they were taking up positions to flood that entire clearing with light.

Bolan grinned and leaned into the first LAW.

He lined up the pop sights onto the steering wheel of that glass-fronted van just as an excited shout from down by the campfire advised everyone present, *"Here they are, both dead!"*

"So where's their car?" This, an amplified voice of authority from a loudspeaker mounted somewhere on the van. The man was in there, some man with rank.

And the dismal reply from the campfire: "Forget it, the guy's gone. I guess he's got their car now."

"Correction," Bolan sighed as he squeezed the little missile out of the tube. "The guy has not gone."

The AP rocket whizzed along its beeline of destruction and impacted precisely where Bolan had sent her, and she came in with a happy hurrah and a mushroom of flames as glass, metal, and all else in that immediate vicinity stood aside, and departed, and gave over the night to this ill-behaved and uninvited guest.

Bolan abandoned the throwaway tube and took up his next firedrop as panic erupted down there, and screams, shouts, and startled commands rushed in to fill the void.

He hit them with a heavy grenade, dead center in the campfire, following immediately with another directly on the front bumper of the crew wagon; and now the pandemonium was in full sway.

"Turn off them goddamn lights!"

"Oh, shit, shit . . . help me!"

"Boss! Boss! Al is blowed all to hell and I . . ."

"Up there! The bastard's up . . ."

Bolan was into the nighttime sniper, jaw tightened and twitching as he bent to the infrared nightscope, and the big piece began jolting his shoulder as scurrying men stumbled into his cross hairs and catapulted out of them.

There were no blazing headlamps down there now—just blazes period as here and there scattered firebrands from the campfire plus small fires in the two rearward vehicles lent ghastly relief to the ever-growing carnage of the night.

Bolan's sniper was cracking methodically in evenly spaced retorts to the chattering of automatic weapons off there in the darkness. The invisible infrared floods were doing their bit for the moment, painting the scene ghoulish as viewed through the sniperscope. Bullets sprayed the trees behind him, chewed turf and chipped rock all below him; still the big piece continued its chilling toll of the night, while men screamed, and wondered aloud how he was spotting them, and pleaded for assistance from gods who knew not their names, and simply yelled foul imprecations upon their fate.

And, after a while, Bolan switched off his infrareds, stowed his gear, and made his withdrawal in an eerie silence.

He stopped briefly at a service station on Route Thirty-three, stepped onto the service ramp in full combat regalia, and suggested to two pop-eyed attendants that someone call the police.

He swung immediately northward from there, found the little state road that connects Mercerville to Edinburg, and made fast tracks toward the sea.

So, okay. It had been hellish . . . but not entirely damn-foolish. Maybe he would succeed in drawing some of the opposing guns this way.

So call it eight hundred Jersey guns waiting for him now.

He smiled faintly into the enshrouding night.

The odds were coming down.

7 THE GAME NAMED

He had been running the back roads, carefully avoiding major routes and intersections, and his instincts had drawn him past the toll road at Cranbury and on south of Prospect Plains, from where he hoped to angle on eastward to Freehold, thence on to the coast via Neptune.

This would set him down roughly midway between New York and Atlantic City, with an endless selection of small coastal towns from which to work another angle of escape.

Twice he had narrowly avoided a confrontation with police authority, and twice he had sent up a shaky thanks to whatever powers controlled chance and circumstance.

Running head-on into elements of the outfit was one thing; into the cops, quite another. Mack Bolan did not fight cops. They were "soldiers of the same side." His only defense from that quarter lay in studious avoidance.

And now he was thinking that it would be wise to give the enemy—and the police—some reaction time *vis-à-vis* the hit near Mercerville. Already, it seemed, he was encountering cross-currents or pursuit in that direction. A wise warrior knew when to strike, when to retreat, and when to simply lie low.

Thus it was that the Executioner elected to seek a snug harbor for a brief period of détente. It was a matter of pure coincidence that he found that harbor just a few miles to the north of the Tassily farm, near a sleeping village called Tennent.

It was a trailer camp with a weathered sign announcing a rather unemotional welcome for "Campers and Overnighters—All Hookups Available."

The place was all but deserted; apparently its season had not yet arrived.

It boasted a public rest room and shower, an all-night laundromat, a couple of picnic tables just off the roadway, several rows of unoccupied trailer spaces, and a small office building with a single dull bulb over the door with instructions to "Ring for Service."

All Bolan desired was a secluded place to park awhile—but not too secluded—and he felt no need to "ring" for anything. He angled the vehicle in the rear of the public buildings, appropriately positioned for a quick out, and spent ten minutes or so studying the detailed maps that had come with the car. One of these was singularly revealing, seeming to pinpoint "patrol zones" and specific rendezvous areas.

He tucked the intelligence away for possible future consideration, loath now to abandon the plan he already had cooking.

Then he spotted the public phone booth in the shadows of the laundromat, briefly debated a call to New York . . . and lost the debate.

He pulled the car closer to the phone booth and

a few minutes later was speaking into a connection to a fashionable hotel in midtown Manhattan.

"This is Al La Mancha," he told the familiar voice at the far end. "I gotta talk to Mr. Turrin; it's very important."

"This is Turrin," came the cautious reply. "Who'd you say that is?"

"Al La Mancha. Listen, this is pretty hot stuff."

"Uh . . . look, Al. I was just going out. Why don't you try me in a little while, at, uh . . ."

It was a familiar routine. These contacts with the most wanted dude in the country were potentially disastrous for "the man from Mass" who rode two steeds through the jungle called life. To preclude any deadly compromise of his cover, as well as to shield him from possible official embarrassment at the other side, the friendship with Mack Bolan was necessarily a furtive thing. Early in the wars, therefore, they had worked out the contact routine.

Bolan knew that Turrin was at this moment digging for the number of a nearby public telephone, which he quickly found and relayed to "La Mancha" —a sort of comic-relief code name for Mack Bolan.

Early in his wars, some segments of the press had taken to referring to Bolan as "a latter-day Don Quixote"—the fabled windmill-slayer of another grim era of man's misadventures. Therefore, "the man from La Mancha."

Precisely five minutes following that hang-up, Bolan had another quick connection.

"That you, La Mancha?" asked the voice of the truest friend the Executioner had ever known.

"It's me. Where are you, Leo?"

"Downstairs, basement lobby. It's okay. What's your situation?"

"About normal," Bolan replied, trying to keep the voice light. Leo Turrin was a worrier.

"Then you haven't been hearing the words I've been getting," came the taut response. "I'm not going to ask you where you are, and I don't want you to tell me. Just tell me this: are you anywhere near Mercerville?"

Bolan chuckled as he replied, "The word's out, then."

"Yeah, and so is everything else," was the wry rejoinder. "You really know how to stir the pot, Sarge. I hope you hit and ran like hell."

"I did."

Turrin sighed heavily, and Bolan heard the snap of a cigarette lighter close to the mouthpiece. "It came as quite a shock. The heads all thought you were down and just awaiting the final count. Tell the truth, I'd started wondering along those lines myself until your friend contacted me today. By the way—"

"He's okay, Leo. But I hope you covered your end."

"Oh, sure. I caught the coded flicker and knew right away he was a stand-in. Don't worry, he never knew who he was talking to. Anyway, what I was about to say . . . a guy by the name of Tassily walked into a state police substation tonight and . . . Is this the same guy, Sarge?"

Very quietly Bolan said, "Same guy, Leo."

"Well, don't sound so . . . Hear me out. The guy claims he's been a prisoner of the Executioner these past few days—he and his sister—on a chicken farm or something they have down mid-state. The Jersey fuzz don't know whether to buy his story or not. They're out at that farm right now, sifting the place down for some back-up. Anyway, Tassily says you're springing southward. Claims you've been studying maps of lower Jersey, particularly that area down below Wharton State Forest. Says he thinks your ultimate goal is Delaware Bay, where he hints you've got a boat stashed."

Bolan was chuckling now. "Some kind of guy," was all he said.

"Yeah, well, that's privately the way Hal and I look at it. We guessed the guy is trying to lead the chase down a dead end."

"You're in present contact with Hal Brognola?"

"Yeah. He's pushing the federal troops, from here in New York for the moment."

"Give him my best. And tell him not to crowd me too much for now. I have plenty to occupy my time as it is."

The undercover fed was chuckling. "You know how Hal feels about you. But there are plenty of mixed emotions there, buddy. He's got about a dozen top-level bureaucrats just laying all over him. If they ever get the notion that he's dogging it, even a little . . . well, you know."

"Yeah, I know. I respect the guy for doing his job, Leo. Well . . . I better—"

"Wait, don't be so touchy. Listen, now, nobody is offering you a license or anything like that, but . . . well, Hal is advising the local officials to buy Tassily's story. It's as good a lead as any they've had. Also, Hal threw in that bit of past history where you seem to favor escapes by sea. He cited the escape at Los Angeles, the one at Miami, in France, the recent one down in Washington where you had a boat stashed on the Potomac. . . ."

Bolan sighed and agreed. "I guess it fits."

"Sure it does. Simple police logic. And the hit at Mercerville fits like a hand in the glove. The Jersey troopers are considering rushing everything they can spare into a coverage along U. S. 206 South. That's the fast route to Wharton. They're spread pretty thin already. So . . . But I guess they'll buy Tassily. Need I say more?"

"There's one very large fly," Bolan quietly decided.

"And what is that?"

"The *boys* won't buy Tassily. They've been laying over that farm like a mother hen all this week. They've seen the guy going and coming freely, and they were in there several times on a shakedown. His story won't hold water in their bag, that's sure. You'd better get the guy and his sister out of there, Leo. Protective custody or whatever it takes to keep them covered until this thing blows over."

"Yes, I see your point. Okay. I'll get on that as soon as I hang up."

"Tell me something, Leo. With cops crossing tracks all over this damn state, how is the mob operating so openly? They're running regular armed convoys around here."

Turrin released a hissing sigh, and Bolan knew that he was in for a classroom discussion. "You've never spent much time in Jersey," the undercover man pointed out. "You couldn't know . . . well, it's a most unusual state, let's put it that way. The [illegible]sent administration is going through all manner of nightmares trying to correct the . . . well, it's just a horrendous mess. The problem is as much geography as anything. The whole place lies in the shadow of New York and Pennsylvania—almost completely overshadowed. The greater population is massed along those borders, with Philly and New York City providing more of a swing to the state than anything Jersey can get together within her own borders. That urban mass up around Newark and Jersey City is actually feudal states within their own right—and that's just an accentuation of the general problem everywhere in the state. The corruption is just . . . well, don't let me start on that. Just get this understanding, buddy. You are in the heartland, the mob's green acres, and if they want to chase you around in armed convoys, don't think for a minute there's anyone to really oppose them."

"Okay. That fits my reading."

"Sarge, there's not even a national television outlet into that state. The people of Jersey get their contact with the outer world via Philly, Bethlehem, and New York City. They don't even have a newspaper with statewide circulation."

"Yeah, I get that. A state without a state. You say the present governor is—"

"He's trying," Turrin replied, sighing. "But then, there's all that cloud from beyond the borders, and the very real political power of the city-states."

"Well. Maybe I'll look around some while I'm here."

"Good Christ! I was afraid you were starting to lean that way! Perish the very thought, Sarge."

"I hear that Augie Marinello is leading the charge this time."

"He is. From here, though, on his fat ass."

"I guess he's a bit unhappy over Philly."

"In spades. By the way, you can forget the *gradigghia,* for now anyway. Augie got your message from Sicily. He put out an edict yesterday. No more imported guns. He was simply appalled by the slaughter in the Old Country."

"I see. What you are telling me—"

"I'm telling you that you did a good job in Sicily. Next time why don't you just take a quiet ocean cruise."

"Okay," Bolan replied, sighing. He lit a cigarette and listened to Leo Turrin's tight breathing for a charged moment; then he said, "I'd rather go into an operation with a bit more visibility . . . but . . . I guess I'm here, aren't I?"

"Aw, no, Sarge. No. Come back if you want, and I'll help you set up some solid intel. But not now. There's just too much working against you. Get out and take some R and R."

"It just tears my guts, Leo. To think of these guys running around like savages, lord of the domain, doing whatever they damn please."

"I know how you feel. Hell. But you've survived this far on cool, Mack. Go on surviving, damnit. We need you. This whole dog-eat-dog world needs you. Hey. I can talk to you like that, can't I?"

Bolan chuckled. "Sure. What's happening up north?"

"Newark-Jersey City? About two hundred guns are happening, I'd say. Manning the ramparts into New York. Don't try it."

"I get the feeling you're nudging me somewhere, Leo."

"Try Atlantic City, Sarge."

"Why?"

"Because there's a boat headed that way. It's the *Lotta Linda.* Off the boardwalk, north. Steel Pier. Anytime after midnight."

Bolan chuckled again. "You're so damn cute. Well, I'll give it a look. Thanks, Leo. Uh, don't forget the chicken ranch."

"I'll get right on it. Stay hard, man."

"Name of the game," Bolan said quietly, and hung up.

He signaled the operator and settled his overtime charges, then returned to his vehicle, deep in thought.

The name of the game, he thought, wryly, was *beat it!*

But . . . he was just a few miles north of the farm.

If there was the slightest chance of . . .

After all his pains to cover his tracks around that place . . . Well, Bruno couldn't be expected to know. It was all Bolan's doing, anyway. He'd leaked in there and talked the guy out of passive living, and if the guy was in a mess now, then it was Bolan's mess, not Bruno's. Certainly not Sara's.

Some nightmares had an uncomfortable propensity for coming true.

And Bolan just could not shake from his head that latest twist in skin-crawling dreams—that one wherein a chicken ranch becomes a horror-farm of screaming turkeys.

Leo was right, too, of course. He simply was not ready for a Jersey operation.

As sure as God made lush green valleys, though,

the Executioner would be returning to Jersey one day . . . prepared!

He fired up the war wagon and kicked her southward.

For now, he could run past the Tassily farm, reassure his mind, then angle on down to Atlantic City. It was the only route of sanity.

Or so he thought.

New routes, beyond Bolan's immediate power of manipulation, were at that very moment being plowed by the Jersey guns.

8 FROM THE TREETOP

He cruised by the Tassily farm in a slow pass, taking a reading of the situation there.

A police car was in the drive, beacon flashing; another was pulled more toward the rear of the place, out by the sheds, no lights showing except an interior lamp, the driver's door standing open.

The house was lit up all over, as were the outbuildings. The yard floodlights were on.

But he had seen not one thing moving back there, no signs of life whatever.

The scene struck him as unnatural.

He seesawed across the road and went back, pulling into the drive with headlamps extinguished and motor idling.

Then he saw it, the thing in the driveway beside the police cruiser—a crumpled human form.

He descended into that place with all his senses flaring into the alert.

There was not a sound about, except for the faint whirr-click of the cruiser's beacon and a muffled squawking from its radio.

The uniformed trooper was lying face-down in the drive. He had been shot in the back of the head. He was dead.

The vehicle in back was a sheriff's car. He found the two deputies by the brooder house. Also shot dead.

Bolan came upon the live one inside the house. A state trooper, young, twenty-five maybe, with a bullet in the gut and suffering like hell.

He knelt over the guy and asked him, "You okay?"

The cop's eyes flared into that confrontation with the man in black, and he groaned, "I *was*."

"Then you still are," the Executioner assured him.

He broke out a battle compress, sprinkled it with antibiotic powder, and applied it to the wound.

"Hold it down tight," he suggested. "You'll make it if you can stand the pain. What happened here?"

"Gunmen," the cop replied through gritted teeth. "Surprised us . . . took Tassily and . . . his sister."

"How long?" Bolan asked, in a voice pitched from hell.

"Not . . . long. Few minutes at most."

"What were they driving?"

The young officer's look was an even mixture of pain and self-disgust. "That's the . . . dumb part. Big camper. You know . . . these . . . Land Rover things. Who would've thought . . . ?"

Bolan said, "Okay, don't push it. I'll get you some help. Did you see which way they went out of here?"

"Sounded like . . . up the road."

Bolan was rising to take departure when the cop's hand flopped over to pull weakly at his arm. "Those guys . . . they're . . . worst kind. Camper wasn't all. Two limousines came in . . . after. They wanted those people . . . worst way."

"So do I," the Executioner grimly assured the cop; then he pulled away and hurried out of there.

He paused briefly at the cruiser out front and got on the police radio. "Officer in trouble," he reported. "Tassily farm, you know where. Send an ambulance, and scream it!"

The police dispatcher wasted no time over technicalities. He obviously "knew where" very well.

Bolan ignored the terse requests for further information and put that place quickly behind him.

And, yes, the hounds from hell had barked up a very mean tree this time.

Mack Bolan was deadly enough in his most passive moments.

And now that black-clad doomsday guy was seething with anger, trembling with determination, the usually expressionless face twisted into a torment of anxiety and utter resolution.

The hounds were to discover very quickly that they had tried to tree a dragon.

Bolan knew this jungle well, and he knew how to read the signs left there. He found the fresh impressions left by the heavy van as it cornered too tightly onto the back road to Trenton, and he found other signs beyond there which told of a gleeful and reckless joyride toward the headshed of local power.

Once he thought he'd actually caught a glimpse of their lights on a curve far ahead, but the terrain was working against him this time.

He swung away from the track a few miles east of the next junction and gambled on a cross-country plunge along a narrow dirt trail which, he hoped, would put him somewhere out front of the turkeyland express.

It did, and he was, and he met them at that backcountry crossroads in the moonless night with perhaps fifteen seconds of advance preparation.

He was lined and targeted into the crossroads itself, and he met them there as they flew through in convoy procession, the two crew wagons leading.

The first car through the target zone took a LAW hit on the forward door post, exploded immediately into flames, and went into a cartwheel down that narrow road.

Car number two was already into the wreckage of the first casualty and pulling like hell for freedom when the next rocket slammed into her rear quarter. She went to ground on an expansive cushion of flame, then blew straight up with raining droplets of fiery gasoline and settled in a screeching heap directly in the path of the oncoming van.

The van jockey was already pulling brakes with everything he had, and now he overreacted with a lunging turn on locked brakes and blew through the flaming wreckage in a broadside skid that ended abruptly and disastrously with the rear section wrapped around a steel light standard.

A secondary exposion rocked the remains of the first car and flung shards of heavy glass and metal all about that disaster zone at the same moment that the camper came to rest.

Bolan, however, was like a homing missile with but one objective in mind. Totally ignoring the crew wagons and what was left of their passengers, he walked through that raining chaos with the big silver AutoMag thrust forward at chest level, headed unerringly for the turkey wagon, and the first man to come stumbling out of there was met in the doorway with 240 grains of exploding fire power right in the center of the forehead.

Another was trying to eject a revolver through a twisted porthole; the AutoMag again roared massive anger, and a mutilated hand was quickly jerked back inside.

He did not wait for the debarkation, but went in after them. The driver was bent over the steering wheel in his luxuriously padded seat, hands clasped to a bleeding face. Bolan jerked the head back, thrust the snout of the silver pistol through clenched teeth, and blew that fucking head off.

Another guy was seated at a small table just down the aisle, except that now the table was riding the guy's chest and pinning him to the wall. The butt of a pistol was showing from one of the guy's pockets, but he was too stunned even to go for it.

Bolan left him with a grotesque third eye that made the three as one as he passed on into the interior.

He found the "boss"—a guy he vaguely recognized as one of the top torpedoes out of Marinello's Manhattan head shop—emerging from a curtained-off area at about midships.

The guy was dragging Sara Henderson along in front of him—a thoroughly terrified and bug-eyed Sara—and he was bleeding all down the front of her from the shattered hand that pinned her to him.

The other hand held a pistol at her head, and the guy was yelling, "Okay, now! Watch it, Bolan!"

Bolan watched it.

He watched a 240 grain extension of cold fury

plow right past Sara's pink little ear to splatter that ugly face behind it, leaving not even a dying reflex to tickle that trigger at her head.

For the second time that day, Bolan had shot a monster off that girl's back, and he felt utterly miserable about the whole thing.

She was undoubtedly feeling rather miserable, herself. The dress was torn half away from her. Ugly splotchy bruises marred that lovely skin in every place that showed, and her eyes were absolutely wild.

She collapsed into his arms and nestled her head on his shoulder as he carried her out of that hellbox.

"Where's Bruno?" he asked as soon as they reached open air.

"Gone," she moaned. "They took him."

"He wasn't with you?"

"Not now."

He gazed toward the fiery limousines and told her in a choked voice, "In this game, it's all or nothing, Sara. I had to go for the numbers."

Bad off as she was, she noted the anguish in him and hastened to tell him, "No! Not there! They took him away, some other cars."

Well . . . that was good, and it was bad.

Good because there was still a chance for Bruno. But a mighty slim one.

Bad because sudden death in an exploding vehicle just beat the shivers out of the slow but certain lingering reality of a turkey-style interrogation.

"Don't faint, Sara! Suck in your gut and chuck it up if you have to. Scream, cuss, call me names, whatever ticks you. But damnit, don't faint! You've got to help me find Bruno!"

"Don't worry about me, Mack Bolan." The voice was tiny but firm. "I understand you now, your war. I truly understand."

Yes, Sara had been through some hell, herself.

But she was fighting back. God love her, she was fighting back.

9 THE UNDERSTANDING

There was more pain for Sara than problem—pain and a rather jarring loss of feminine composure.

The boys had not been too rough on her—a bit of pinching in sensitive places and slapping around, routine terrorizing.

They'd fondled her where no man had a right to without permission, and indulged in some low street-corner humor and wisecracks.

The really rough stuff would have come later.

Bolan took her to his vehicle, where he gave her a canteen of water and some gauze with which to swab away the blood and other washable marks she'd collected from the dead torpedo. Not much could be done about the welts and bruises she'd picked up before that; only time.

He left her there in privacy and went back for a quick shakedown of the command van.

A surface search of the vehicle and its crew left him with very little of useful intelligence. A couple of maps, some identities, a few odds and ends that might come together later.

When Bolan returned to his own vehicle, Sara was cleanly composed and ready to travel. He took one last look at the site where God or something had intervened in that girl's fate; then he burned rubber away from that place, leaving flaming wreckage and cooking bodies behind.

Most people, he knew, would find it difficult to believe the depth of horror that had been awaiting Sara Henderson on that bleak Jersey night. Sara herself would not have believed.

Everyday people simply had no mental concept of the deeper depravities that stalked this tired old earth.

Memories of places like Buchenwald and other infamies faded all too quickly from the human experience.

Bolan knew. His "memories" had been kept up to date.

It would not have mattered that Sara had already told the turkey-makers everything she knew, which she had. She'd seen no reason to conceal the truth. She had thought Bolan well clear of the area. And she told them all of it, a couple of times.

No matter if they had been convinced that she'd told all—even that would not have saved her.

The "talk-turkey" theory differed from brain washing and other gentler techniques in that it featured a greatly accelerated and heightened approach—not brain *washing,* but brain *busting.*

The technique was based on the idea that human perception and recall is a tricky and often deceptive thing. It followed (quite by accident) the same psychological reasoning as the more socially acceptable "encounter-group" techniques of emotional release. Bits of intelligence could be hidden in the subconscious as involuntarily as could bits of destructive emotions and psychic trauma. The art of turkey-making, however, was far older than the quasi-science of human psychology, and much more effective.

The "encounter-group" technique of psychotherapy amounted to a voluntary submission to emotional shock and nonphysical torture.

Turkey-talk "therapy" was aimed toward the same result, but with a much more straightforward approach, and a much quicker result.

Though the various steps of the technique had never been formulated into a precise discipline, the practice of the art went somewhat along these lines:

Begin with fear and terror, threats, promises of severe physical suffering.

Then induce actual physical pain, gradually. Get the victim to screaming and pleading for mercy.

A lot of stuff would come flinging out of the mind right there, at that point, a lot of stuff the victim never even knew was there.

So, induce more pain. A hell of a lot more. Get the entire physical stystem involved in it, until the victim is flopping about all over the place and yelling his head off.

So, keep it up. More, more, and then a hell of a lot more . . . until the poor bastard has reached the absolute limit of human endurance. Watch the whole damn nervous system collapse, and listen to what pops out of that.

But keep him conscious and aware. Let off for a little while, give the strength a chance to build back. Then do it again, all the way; get him back up there, and keep prodding until something new splits loose.

Let off again. Be nice. Smile at the suffering shit.

But watch how he shrinks back each time you make a gesture in his direction; listen to how he screams if you so much as touch him with a finger. Now you're getting into the guy; you're almost there.

So, hit him now with massive shock. Confound the very soul, fragment it, send it screaming through hell. If the turkey is a guy, cut off his cock. If a broad, slice off a tit or shove a busted Coke bottle up her snatch.

And listen to all the shit pouring out now.

And the time has arrived when you can become *really* creative.

Hit them in their hottest spot. If the guy happens to be a surgeon or a piano player, for example, off with his goddamn fingers . . . one by one. Show them to him, play catch with them, shove 'em up his ass. But keep him alive. Get a blowtorch or something and cauterize those stumps.

It could go on and on like that, taking the guy apart in pieces, for as long as he could be kept aware and screaming and alive.

All kinds of shit would pour out, maybe even how he screwed Maryjane in the sandbox at kindergarten. These slobs got so goddamn anxious to tell you everything they knew, everything they could conceivably know and not know, they even started inventing stuff, making it up, trying to find something to satisfy you so you'd stop.

But you didn't stop.

You never stopped until the guy stopped.

You kept right on busting through that brain, shredding that soul, dissolving that personality into scattered bits and pieces; and you kept that poor shit talking turkey until he talked himself dead.

That was the technique.

And if you were a real artisan, a really masterful turkey-maker, you could probably keep something like that going around the clock. Some guys in Chicago had once kept it going for more than three days. Of course, in all fairness to the other masters, they'd had a three-hundred-pound turkey to work with.

Sara, by the grace of God, had been spared that.

Bruno could still be facing it.

But not if there was anything beneath God's heaven which Bolan could do to prevent it.

Mack Bolan was a mighty tough guy—*genuinely* tough, in the spirit, where it counted.

He could steel himself to almost anything. But he could not steel himself into an acceptance of turkey meat.

He would have killed his own mother, quickly and without regret, before he would allow her to fall into a turkey-maker's hands.

And he would quickly do the same for Bruno Tassily, if that was the last resort.

He had not thought it necessary to explain such things to Sara. He had not told her *why* he so quickly, and with such seeming recklessness, had twice that day placed her under the fire of his own guns.

But, in some vague fashion, Sara understood; he knew that. She had received only the merest hint of what could have lain in store for her that night, but it was hint enough and she had made a point to let him know quickly that she understood.

Bolan could only hope that Sara's understanding would never become complete.

Not every *mafioso* was a turkey-maker, of course. Even the meanest of the button men sometimes turned green if someone even mentioned turkey to them. It took a genuine sadist, a really sick mind, to pull that kind of duty, even as an assistant.

So, there were the specialists.

Mike Talifero, it had been said, had a full assortment of such "specialists," and Bolan would bet a million bucks that each of those command vans cruising the Jersey hellgrounds that night was carrying a Talifero specialist.

These guys were out here to collect the Executioner's head, and they meant to have it.

They would stop at nothing . . . and nobody.

And how they would love to get Mack Bolan's brain to bust, his soul to shred. Just for fun.

That idea did not particulary bother the man in black. He would live until he died; and if he died screaming, well, okay. Bolan did not contemplate his own death.

He contemplated the death of others. Those who roamed and ranged and plundered the human estate, those who degraded life itself and sucked out dignity and meaning and hope.

Yes. He contemplated their deaths even in his sleep.

He would contemplate their deaths even while he himself was dying.

And if Sara understood *that,* then she'd done a bit of brain busting on her own—but in a much, much gentler fashion.

10 THE SITUATION

Bolan's modus operandi was slipping badly.

He was a hellfire guy, hit and git, disappear quickly, pop up again at some far-removed spot to hit and fade again. It was guerrilla warfare, and it had kept his hide intact through fifteen major encounters with this enemy.

But now, here in Jersey, the whole game had changed in a most disheartening manner.

He was running around in tight circles, highly visible, with very little design and no plan whatever.

Certainly he was not on a battleground of his own choosing.

Jersey had been on his hit list, sure. But not for this particular point in time. Mainly because it was much too close to one of his most recent theaters of operation.

At first Jersey had been an escape route, not—to his mind—a field for combat. He liked to pick them a bit more carefully than that.

But also he was not prepared for a war with the Jersey mob. In the first place, there was no Jersey mob, *per se*. The guys up around Newark and Jersey City were hardly more than an arm of the New York group, especially since their ranking member on La Commissione had started getting his tail salted by the feds.

A couple other New York outfits had the Port of New York under contest, including the Jersey side of it.

Trenton, the capital city, had its own special problems, not a few of which were caused by old Stefano Angeletti, the fading boss of Philly, plus varied and sundry oddfellows from just about every Mafia interest in the Northeast United States.

New Jersey was not only a state without a state; it was also a mob without a mob.

The entire area was a refuse bin for everything the states of New York and Pennsylvania wished to toss over—including their underworld garbage.

Leo Turrin had not been exaggerating when he described the problem as a "horrendous mess."

It was easily that.

Bolan was beyond being amazed at the capacity for American citizens to accept the clearly unacceptable.

But he had always felt a bit numbed with every glance at the state of New Jersey.

The situation here was more than horrendous. It was appalling.

So . . . no. Bolan was not prepared to tackle New Jersey. If the Mafia was an octopus, then Jersey was an octopus whose tentacles were detached and wriggling about the entire landscape on independent and all-encompassing feedings.

Bolan would need a very close-cadence group of numbers to tackle an enemy like that. And that meant painstaking intelligence, planning, logistics, a very precise battle strategy.

At the moment, Bolan was no more than another piece of garbage flung onto the Jersey soil.

His only desire had been to get the hell out of there.

Bruno Tassily and his sister had made it possible for him to achieve that objective. And, sure, he could have done so, without too much sweat, by simply playing his game his way.

Following the diversion hit at Mercerville, he could have scooted free and clear to the coast, and probably, at this very moment, be floating down the Atlantic to freedom and better battlefields.

Very probably he could still do so.

But it would be a "freedom" totally without meaning.

Bolan was not a glory guy. And he was not fighting merely to remain alive. The thing went much deeper than that, into an area of the human dimension which Bolan could not put words to.

Nothing in life could be measured in precise terms of right and wrong, good and bad, black and white. He knew that. And he knew how corny it sounded to talk about "good versus evil," and the like.

Bolan had discovered, though, that things usually become "corny" only because they are so universally applicable—the "true" does have an annoying way of becoming commonplace, mainly because it has such durability.

But he also understood that "evil" was self-propelling, and much stronger than passive "good." That latter condition needed a bit of propellant itself if it was going to remain in the race with the other.

Maybe Edmund Burke was simply being "corny"

when he declared, "The only thing necessary for the triumph of evil is for good men to do nothing."

But Mack Bolan agreed with that statement, corny or not.

Bolan *lived* that philosophy, cornball or not.

He did not respect meaningless freedom.

He did not cherish "life at any price."

He did, though, very strongly wish to spring a friend from the shadows of hell.

And he would, by God, do so, if there was any way under the sun.

That was the entire damned "situation" of the moment.

11 THROUGH THE MAZE

"There were three cars," Sara explained. "I remembered the importance of . . . I pretended I had a pad and that I was sketching it all. Tried to burn it into my mind as vividly as possible. There was a sports car, some foreign make. I never could tell one from the other, except this was an expensive type. Then there were two big cars, Cadillacs I guess, the kind with the folding jump seats, gleaming black.

"The men all looked very hard, brutal. Except the one. He got out of the sports car, with another man. He was . . . well, handsome in a way. A little older than you, Mack. About the same general physique, except an inch or so shorter than you. Very expensively dressed, very sharp. A blue doubleknit suit with flared legs, wide lapels. Most beautiful shirt I've ever seen . . . I couldn't even guess at the material."

"Anyway . . ." Bolan prompted.

"Oh. He had blond hair, blue eyes. Easy, relaxed, laughed quite a bit, but with . . . well, I guess with dignity, or reserve. Nothing at all like the other men. But he was in charge; that much was clear. His name was never mentioned. They all addressed him as 'sir.' They sirred everything they said to him.

He was . . . I would say . . . cultured. And obviously well educated, very self-assured."

"Talked something like this," Bolan suggested, affecting a refined New England accent. "Harvard College, you know, class of Fifty-nine."

"That's him," she agreed quickly. "Sort of like the Kennedys. You know who he is, then?"

Bolan growled, "One of the Talifero brothers. Probably Mike. Has an identical twin. A pair of rattlers, I'll tell you that."

"Yes, I . . . felt that about him. Even though he treated me very nice. Respectful."

"What else?"

"They talked for several minutes, inside the camper, but I couldn't catch much of it. Except that I was to be taken into Trenton. For some . . . I don't know for what. But they kept looking at me and grinning. Made my skin crawl. And they'd decided that the blond man would take Bruno with him, wherever he was going. I don't know why, but I . . . assumed that it would be to somewhere nearby. Don't know how I got that impression, but . . ."

"Think about it," Bolan suggested. "It could be important."

She replied, "Okay. But it's just ahead now. On the left. That service station."

They were arriving at a crossroad.

This was the place where the kidnap convoy from the Tassily farm had rendezvoused with Mike Talifero and his head party.

The spot being indicated by Sara was a small combination grocery and service station. It was closed.

Bolan pulled in to there and immediately consulted

the sectional map that had come with the vehicle.

That spot was marked on the map—circled.

Something else was marked, also, something which he had briefly wondered about and then dismissed as having no consequence that other time he'd studied that same map.

Someone had penciled in a dotted line from this junction to the one where Bolan had paused so briefly about twenty dead men ago—that empty trailer park from where he had telephoned Leo Turrin.

Of course!

So why hadn't he. . . ?

He asked the girl, in a very flat voice, "Which way did they go from here?"

"Straight ahead, the way we just came in."

He hit that road with the transmission screaming into an over-demand response, catching Sara entirely off-guard and causing her to lunge about in the seat and clutch at him for support.

"Wow, you come to quick decisions," she commented when they'd leveled out. "What hit you?"

"A trailer park," he replied tightly.

"That's it!" she cried.

"That's what?"

"It's where I got my . . . The blond man said they would be *at the camp!*"

It was odd, Bolan was thinking, how things had a way of coming together.

It was such a small damn world, and he had to wonder if—via some dimension which the sense perceptions of man had not yet pierced—it was not far smaller than anyone could imagine.

It seemed remarkable to his mind that Bruno

Tassily had known Mack Bolan in Vietnam—however briefly. That, moreover, Bruno had worked for nearly a year at the elbow of Dr. Jim Brantzen; that Brantzen himself had been the first sacrificial victim to the Executioner home-front crusades; and that . . . Hell, there was so much of "coincidence" in the lives of men, sometimes a guy simply had to wonder how much of it was *truly* coincidence.

Bruno had gone to Vietnam to save lives, Bolan to take them.

Bruno's war had never started; Bolan's had never ended.

Bruno had come home from Vietnam to die, Bolan to "live" more vigorously than ever before—Bruno as a man philosophically bankrupt, Bolan just now coming into an understanding of himself and his world.

And then, from Bolan's near-death arose Bruno's new awareness of some of the values of life.

The guy had pulled him out of a half-filled creek, sodden, bleeding to death, with a wound one shade lighter than gangrenous. Bruno the conscientious objector had, in effect, resurrected the Executioner, whose only justification for living lay in killing.

Yeah. Paradoxical. And small, a very small and intricately mazed dimension of being, this place called life.

Smaller yet. The resurrected Bolan had been beating it along the withdrawal trail, seeking a neutral zone, almost home free when he decided to pull in to a deserted trailer park to let the trail ahead cool awhile. And it was from there that the Executioner's withdrawal game had changed, because of a telephone call which he hadn't really wanted to make, and because of a fear which had been born in his dreams.

Very small world, yes.

Because the Executioner was at this very moment hotting it back to that very same trailer park, one which had been deserted such a short while earlier, but one that would accommodate a hell of a lot of big camping vans . . . *when they were not out rolling the highways searching for heads.*

An electric little sensation popped from that compartment of mind where men store their most elemental and vestigial thought processes, and it sent an involuntary shiver along Bolan's spine.

He was wondering where this paradoxical circle of cause and effect would find its natural end. The thing that had wrecked Bruno in Vietnam had been his exposure to countless maimed young bodies.

How would Bruno "take" the deliberate maiming of his own body?

Bolan experienced another tremor, and the girl beside him caught it.

"You're very worried about Bruno, aren't you?" she asked in a tiny voice.

No sense denying it. He said, "Sure."

"Me too. Bruno is so . . . sensitive. He has a very low threshold of pain. I have seen him go to bed sick over a stubbed toe."

Bolan's stomach lurched, and his foot found the floor beneath the accelerator.

Perhaps Bruno had dreams, also.

Maybe it was the dreams that had defeated him at 'Nam.

Maybe he'd had premonitions of his own fate.

TRUE

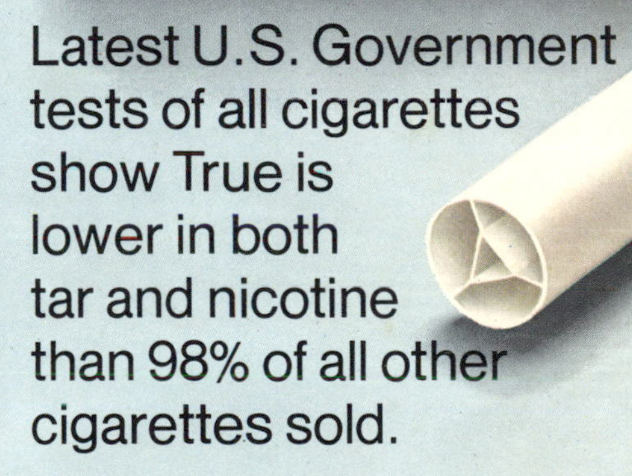

12 MOMENT OF TRUTH

He parked the car in a cluster of trees about a hundred yards downrange and told his charge, "I'm going to have to leave you alone for a short time, Sara. You follow my instructions to the letter. Get out of this vehicle and go into the middle of that field out there. Lie down. Don't show your head, and don't make a sound, whatever you may see or hear. Don't let anyone approach you, not anyone."

He gave her two small grenades.

"Even if you knew how to use a pistol, which I'm sure you don't, you're better off with these. No big deal here. You just depress the little gadget here and throw it like a baseball. For you, throw it to the ground, right in front of your target. But not too close to your own position. If I'm not back in five minutes, take off. But not in this vehicle. On foot. Stick to the fields, away from the roads. Get to a telephone and call the cops, then stay put. If I do get back—"

"If?" she gasped.

"If I do get back, I'll let you know it's me. I'll call you in a way that only I could. Got that?"

Sara nodded and forced a weak "Yes" through

a very dry throat. She took her grenades, carrying them very delicately, and left.

Bolan watched her fade into the darkness; then he began his own move.

He circled in from the rear, pausing every twenty yards or so to sample the atmosphere for sounds, odors, presences; and when he reached the perimeter of the property, he settled there for a full minute, frozen, reading the place, getting its feel, its vibrations; then he moved on in.

The arrival was somewhat anticlimactic. He had somehow expected to find a congregation there. Instead, he found a lone command van and a single crew wagon parked beside it.

There were no sentries.

The curtains were pulled across the van's windows; dull light seeped through.

It was worse than anticlimactic.

The sports car—and therefore Mike Talifero—was not at *this* "camp."

And what of Bruno?

There was but one way to know for sure.

Bolan sprang the Beretta Belle from her sideleather and affixed the silencer, then followed the shadows to that camper door. He tried it, found it locked, rattled the catch, and rapped lightly with the Beretta, calling out as he did so in a convincing New England accent, "Come on, what is this, you all tucked in for the night?"

A drapery moved at the big window, and a blunt face appeared there, squinting out through the darkness.

Bolan stayed with the shadows as he delivered a Talifero laugh and again called, "Going to keep me waiting out here all night, boys? In this no-man's-land?"

The drapery fell back into place, and he heard a hasty rustling inside; then the door cracked open and a guy inside was apologizing, "Sorry, sir, we just—"

Bolan never did learn what "we just" were doing. He exploded through that doorway at that instant, and the guy fell away from there with nine-millimeter whistler up his nose.

Another guy who had been hastily mopping spilled beer from a table just inside hastily released the whole can and nearly turned himself inside-out trying to find a path to his hardware. Another whispering *phu-ut* from the Belle opened an inside-out pathway right between his eyebrows—and there was something a bit messier than beer to mar that gleaming table now.

No one was left in sight or sound.

But then he heard a guy cough from someplace down the aisle, and a testy voice called out, "What the hell're you guys doing out there? Stop the grab-assing around!"

Bolan stepped down to there and snapped open a folding door.

It was the john, and a guy was seated there, pants at half-mast, reading a funny book.

"Hey, what . . . Jesus!" The reaction to the intrusion began as an angry snarl and finished in fading resignation.

The Belle's silencer was making a warm impression on the guy's forehead.

He followed Bolan's eyes up and out of there,

pussyfooting along, with his pants and drawers hobbling him.

Bolan had never met this guy, but he'd seen his mug shots here and there. He was Jack "Scales" Scalisi, up-and-coming muscleman from the Jersey City docks, suspected of complicity in several "unsolved" murders during the current intrigue up there; three arrests, no indictments.

It was rumored, in the tighter circles, that Scalisi was actually a Taliferi, a gestapo super-goon doing a bit of secret-policing for the New York headshed.

Bolan needed no rumors. He knew that Scalisi was one of Mike Talifero's interrogation specialists.

He removed a pistol from the guy's shoulder harness and showed him where to sit. "Get your cock in hand, Scales, and tell it good-bye," he suggested in that graveyard voice.

This was language which a turkey-maker could understand better than anybody. Scalisi's face turned gray. His eyes fled the cold fury confronting him there, to dwell briefly on the two bloodied corpses now decorating his living room. The mouth wobbled, and the voice was dry and cracked when he finally found it. "Jesus, mister, I . . . What can I do? I don't want this. Do you?"

Under more relaxed circumstances, Bolan would have thought that very funny.

The voiced was pitched straight from hell, though, as he replied, "What the hell would I do with it, Scales?"

"No, I don't . . . I didn't . . . I mean, look, sir, I don't even know you. I got no beef with you."

Just a poor sweet guy, fallen in with the wrong friends, no doubt. Bolan asked him, "So what are you doing out here running around the hell grounds?"

Scalisi spread his hands and bunched up his shoulders to indicate his status as a poor victim of harsh circumstances. "Well, I . . . hell, a guy makes a living. Right, sir?"

"Wrong, sir," said the voice from hell. "What you're doing, Scales, a guy makes a dying."

"Well, shit, let's talk it over!" Scalisi squawked. "Let's figure something out!"

"*You* figure something out, Scales."

The guy still had the comic book in his hand.

He stared at it for a moment with glazed eyes, then told the big cold bastard who was standing over him, "I don't blame you for being sore. I'd be sore too. All these guys all over your ass."

It was easy to see that the turkey-maker was bleeding for the Executioner.

Bolan made it official.

He shot him in the knee.

The kneecap just blew away. Whiteness showed there for an instant; then welling redness bubbled and flowed.

The impact jerked the guy halfway around. He flopped back with shock and disbelief mingling with the beginning awareness of massive pain, both hands instinctively applying pressure to shut off the bleeding.

And he was already beginning to bleat, with only one small installment paid.

This turkey-maker had little stomach for the shit, when it was coming *his* way.

"No more silly bullshit," the iceman told him.

"You start talking turkey right now, maybe I'll let you die quick."

The fear of Talifero and of the consequences of broken *omertà* was stronger, at that point, than the fear of death or pain.

Scalisi's mouth clamped shut, and he gave Bolan a pained go-to-hell look.

Bolan gave him, in return, another disappearing kneecap; and the guy fell apart then and there, at the second installment of his tab.

"Leave me alone!" he screamed. "What are you doing? Whattaya want with me?"

"I want Mike Talifero," Bolan calmly told him. "And a guy named Tassily. I want them both, right now."

Those eyes went wild. Scalisi cried, "Mike is . . ." Then he choked and dropped his eyes and watched his life flowing away from him in spurts and rivulets.

"You get to call the next shot, turkey-maker. Balls? Or elbows? You call it."

"They took the guy to the camp!"

"What camp?"

"Down the road! The hunt club!"

"Make me believe it."

"Jesus, leave me alone! I came down and bought this joint out for the week! Mike didn't like it! He took one look and laughed like hell! Went right down and took over that fuckin' hunt club! They run foxes, I think, down there, but not right now! Down the road there, three or four miles! We're just using this joint as a substation! God's truth, that's it! Now, let's get together, let's—"

The Beretta Belle bought "God's truth"—with a softly whispering mercy round straight between the eyes, and the turkey-maker's mouth was still moving as he died.

His suffering had been minuscule, as viewed through the shredded souls of those who had tasted his own applications of shrieking death.

But the muscles in Bolan's cheek were jerking of their own accord as he trotted back to his vehicle.

This was not his style.

He had always tried to kill clean, as any self-respecting "executioner" should.

Only the unrelenting awareness of Bruno Tassily's plight could have moved Mack Bolan into even this microscopic emulation of the turkey men.

And, of course, Jack "Scales" Scalisi had possessed undoubtedly a much higher threshold to pain than the gentle medic, who would find no mercy, no mercy whatever, not even with God's hallowed truth pouring through his lips.

13 ONE FOR BRUNO

He gathered Sara and related, in a half-dozen well-chosen words, the result of his "probe" into the trailer park. Then, following an impulse of the combat sense, he returned to the park, went inside the van, and found the keys to the crew wagon that was parked beside it.

He checked the gas gauge, then hastily transferred Sara and all his effects to the limousine.

As they swung onto the road aboard their new steed, Sara's eyes were asking him the questions her lips would not, or could not.

He told her, "Bruno could still be okay. I think I know where they have him. Guy said a hunt club, three or four miles down the road."

"Oh!" she cried. "Boots and Bugle!"

His eyes flashed as he snapped back, "You know the place?"

"Well, sure, it's only . . . I used to go there when I was in high school. To parties. I never could . . . those adorable little foxes . . . but they rent the place out for local dos. I've been there many times."

"Could you give me the layout?"

"Well, it's been . . . I guess it's the same. Sure. Let's see, it's—"

"Pencil and paper in the map case," Bolan interrupted. "Lay it all out. The property lines, buildings, interiors—I need approximate dimensions, distances, functions, anything and everything you can recall. And damn quick."

Sara's hands were already busy. As she worked her memory, she worked also her mouth—probably, Bolan guessed, as a release of unrelenting tensions. "You think they're doing . . . something . . . terrible . . . to Bruno. Don't you?"

Brutal truth was often far easier to handle than gentle half-truths. He replied, "Yes, Sara. I'd call it a dead cinch. Unless I can beat them to it. And they've already had. . ."

She took a moment away from artful fingers to dispatch escaped moisture from those deep-pool eyes.

Stolen gazes met in the light from the open map case, and she told the man, "I loved the way you called to me, back there."

He had summonded her from her security drop in the field with an impromptu identification signal. "Let's go, Little Mother. Time to build a universe!"

And she'd come running.

Now he told her, "It's past time to *re*build, Sara. Way past time."

He was referring to her own very personal universe, and she whispered the reply, "Yes, I think I understand."

He wanted to leave her alone, to give her memory cells and her artist's fingers full sway, but she plaintively told him, "Talk to me, Mack. Hold me together. I can't . . . I can't believe that all this is actually happening. I mean, right here. This is home.

It's where I grew up, where Mama and Daddy . . . How could this be happening here?"

She was working as she spoke. He assumed that she could work and listen as well. And maybe she needed some anchor to hang on to.

So he let his own stream of thoughts flow into the open, giving utterance to ideas long held but seldom voiced.

"It's an imperfect world, Sara. Nobody with sane mind ever said any different. I'm a soldier, and not much else, but I . . ."

"Oh, you're much more than that," she said. "Go on, tell me, talk to me."

"One psychopath with a hunting knife, you know, can cow and dominate a hundred gentle people. Indirectly, he can enslave millions. It's been done. Many times. Past, present, and . . . I guess, future. It's that kind of world, Sara. It's our heritage. We have to understand that."

The girl was actually sketching the joint to scale —in that moving vehicle in bad light—even shading in terrain features. And with only about one-half of her mind. The other half asked him, "Are you saying that these . . . men . . . are all psychopaths? I mean, these hoods?"

He said, "Sure they're psychopaths. The hard-core bunch, certainly. The ones who dominate. It takes a psychopath to rule brutal men."

Faintly the girl commented, "Oh."

"How's it going?"

"Fine. Please keep talking."

He sighed and checked the odometer. Another mile or two to go. He slowed, to give Sara more time. If he was heading into what he thought, then he would need—and Bruno would need—everything possible going for him.

"It's why the world is always in such turmoil," he went on, aware now that his voice was a sort of beacon for this girl's floundering sense of reality. "Maybe it takes a soldier to realize it. I think . . . there is a 'conqueror' instinct in the human animal. Guys who seek power over other men often are operating from this instinct. All kinds of guys. All kinds of legitimate pursuits. The stronger *it* is, the more dangerous *they* are. If the guy is a psychopath, then look out. If he also is a guy who has no legitimate avenue to power, then the whole world had better look out."

In a murmuring voice, Sara asked, "How do you know a psychopath when you run into one?"

Bolan replied, "It shows, in many ways. This guy answers to only one idea of morality, that idea which tells him that anything *for* him is good, anything *not* for him has just got to be evil. And he can rationalize all the world's great values to fit that framework of what is *good* for *him."*

She said, "Selfishness, to a fault."

He said, "To a sickness."

A moment later, Sara told him, "It's almost done."

"It sure is," he replied, sighing.

"No, I . . . meant the layout."

"I know what you meant," he muttered.

"Are you going to leave me alone again?"

"Have to," he said regretfully.

She finished the sketch with a flourish of shading strokes and placed it in his lap. "What if I go crazy and start screaming my head off?" she asked.

"You won't do that."

"No, I . . . suppose I won't."

"You're tougher than that."

"Darned right."

"Women are tougher than men."

"They are?"

"Yes, in many ways. Where it counts."

"Mack. I'm going to tell you this, but I don't want you to think . . . I mean, not to make you feel . . . Mack, I love you. I mean, *love* love. Know what I mean?"

Very quietly he replied, "Yes. Thank you, Sara."

"Thank you," she said in a small voice.

He stopped the car, leaned across her, opened the door, dropped a grenade into each of those cupped little hands, and sent *love* love into an open field in the dead of night without even another's voice for a beacon, and in the shadow of their enemies.

It was a hell of a world.

But the only one they had.

Sara had done her work on a large sheet of tracing paper, the kind used for map overlays. It was a highly skillful piece of work, especially considering the circumstances and the time element involved.

According to Sara's sketch, a narrow lane led from the main road directly into the hunt club. She had indicated chain-link fencing surrounding the entire property, and she'd written "infinity" for the distance to the rear border—meaning, probably, a very deep tract of land.

The road frontage she had estimated as "about two football fields"—about two hundred yards, then.

The access lane went off at dead center, ran to a recessed gateway "about four car lengths" off the road—eighty feet or so—then proceeded on a slightly curving path to the "clubroom," a single-story structure which was "twice as wide as my house and three times as long."

Bolan grinned, despite the tensions of the moment.

Some kind of a gal.

It sat upon a rise of land, this indicated only by shading strokes of the pencil. It could be five feet up, or fifty. Bolan bought it as a small knoll, considering the general topography of this particular area.

The interior of that main building was depicted in exquisite detail. Sara must have remembered it fondly. She'd shown a foyer and a large dining-room/lounge dominating the front, smaller rooms at the rear, marked "Bugle Bar," "LR Gals," "LR Boys," "Powder Room," "Office" respectively, left to right. Bolan read "LR" as "locker room."

Other buildings fanned out from the main structure. The stables, leather shop, various other odds and ends. Fox pens and corrals were also depicted. Trails, running into the interior of the property. A meadow, woods, several streams.

That girl had a photographic mind.

And the mental photograph that she had recreated for the Executioner could become a damned nightmare—for a hard hit.

If the place was actually a "camp," then it would damn sure be a nightmare. There could be . . . possibly a hundred, maybe more, hardmen inside that fence.

What was that message from "William Meyer & Company"?

Street-corner recruiting? A run on weapons?

Yeah. Easily a hundred, if this was a field-headquarters site.

And the joint was eminently defensible—chiefly because an invader would have a tough time pinpointing power pockets. They could have fire teams set up all around that property, patrols along the fences, patrols on *horseback*—why not?—and sentries, sentries everywhere.

It was the way the Taliferi operated. Massive power, scorched-earth capabilities. Sure, even in a field exercise. The guys did not gamble. They highrolled.

But it would mean—unless they'd pulled all of their first-line troops in from all around that region of the country—it had to mean that they were going with a recruited *militia*. Green troops—*street-corner* soldiers who even had to go out and buy their weapons before they could join the party.

And all that "sirring" of Mike Talifero, as reported by Sara.

Sure, it fits. And it gave Bolan his "directions to the front."

This would be no hard hit.

This one would be soft, very soft.

For the big softhearted guy.

A soft probe for Bruno.

14 PURSUIT OF THE FOX

He removed his combat rig and placed it in the luggage compartment with the rest of his arsenal, retaining only the Beretta in shoulder suspension.

Then he donned, over the black suit, the same clothing he'd worn from Philly—Johnny Cavaretta's fancy threads, just the slacks and jacket.

The silk scarf, which he had used earlier to bandage the leg wound, was again dazzling white and glossy—and he had to wonder how Sara had managed that. He draped it around his neck and let it fall casually just inside the lapels of the jacket. With that decorative effect, maybe the blouse of the skinsuit would look like a turtleneck sport shirt.

Cavaretta's clothing did not fit Bolan all that well. Too much in the waist, not enough in the legs. He had to compensate for that by wearing the slacks down around his hips, and it came out about right then.

Cavaretta had been one of the VIP hit men, a Taliferi of high rank. Everyone knew, of course, that he was now gone forever. His head had been borne to Augie Marinello as a stand-in for Bolan's, delivered by the gleeful son of Philly boss Stefano Angeletti—and *that* had taken some engineering—

while Bolan himself prowled around the Angeletti headshed posing as Cavaretta.

Frank the Kid's glee had been short lived, of course, woefully deflated—as reported to Bolan by Leo Turrin.

All of this simply illustrated the interesting fact that few living *mafiosi* possessed a really clear idea of what the Executioner really looked like.

Bolan left few survivors in his wake who could provide any sort of coherent description of the man. Since the face job by Doc Brantzen, early in the wars, there were no official photographs of the blitzing warrior. From an occasional and brief eyeball encounter with the law, here and there, various police artists had rendered composite sketches which bore a resemblance—but only a resemblance—to the man in black.

Of course, as Bolan had learned long ago—as far back as that other war, in 'Nam—most people "see" with a clarity and precision which is nowhere in the class with photographic film.

A truly "photographic mind" was a human rarity.

The human mind, Bolan had discovered, was a paradox of itself—a living dimension of space-time, which also, odd as it may sound, *created* space-time.

More than two thousand years before Einstein, a Greek dude of the old world had observed that, "The world is composed of nothing but atoms and voids. All else is illusion."

And the observation was true, even in this modern age of scientific brilliance. It was, in fact, truer than ever. The deeper the scientists probed into the heart of "matter," the more stark became the reality that the world is indeed composed of little more than "atoms and voids"—with the accent on *voids*, or nothingness—sheer energy, arrested here and there in submicroscopically frozen bits that the brilliant minds labeled "matter."

Put a couple hundred billion of those arrested bits together in a losely packed mass, and maybe you've got an atom. Keep putting billions upon billions of atoms together and maybe you'll come up with something which the human mind can perceive—something to "see" or "touch" or "smell" or "hear."

Sure. Bolan was no science-theoritician, but he could understand such things.

The "mind" becomes aware of what the sense perceptions allow inside; and, conversely, the sense perceptions allow inside—to a large extent—only what the "mind" has already been programmed to recognize. Few men living would even claim to understand what the "mind" actually is.

And who had ever actually "seen" a spring breeze?

You felt a movement of something across your skin, sure. Maybe you saw a motion within the branches of trees or in the blades of grass at your feet, and maybe you picked up an odor perception of blooming things which was carried along in that "breeze."

But all you *saw* were *effects*. You never *saw* that rustling movement of molecules in transit.

And few people ever *saw* Mack Bolan—not enemy people, anyway.

They experienced his *effect*.

They usually *saw* no more than something dark and deadly, moving swiftly like a breeze through the limbs of trees and shaking things up and moving them around and scattering them in its path.

And this, of course, was what they "recognized": the effect, the motion—the frightening, mind-numbing, terrifying vision of death in motion.

During those other moments when Bolan chose to walk among them, he was a careful blending of other familiar perceptions. He was "one of the boys" or "just a delivery guy" or "the telephone guy" or something equally innocuous. Sometimes he was a "boss" image, fearful in its own right, benumbing to some minds, perception-scattering through its imputed power over life and fortunes.

And the mob's own modus operandi contributed to Bolan's success with such masquerades. An organization which is based on fear, secrecy, deception, and brutality has a price to pay for the use of those lower attributes. Bolan collected that payment whenever the time seemed right.

And that time seemed right, once again, at this moment in the shrouding Jersey night.

A crew wagon with only one guy inside pulled casually into the little lane and rolled to a quiet halt a few yards short of the chain suspended across the gateway to the place called Boots and Bugle.

Three men stood there, one on either side and the other at dead center. There was a tension in the air there, an alertness mingled with nervousness.

The middle guy stepped down to stand beside the door on the driver's side of the Cadillac, eyes roving the interior of that vehicle.

The window slid down under silent electric power, and the man in there asked the gate boss,

"Do you have a light? Four cigarette lighters in this bomb, you would think that one of them would work."

That voice was collegiate New England, calm, relaxed. The guy was wearing sharp threads, a damned scarf, really, lightly tinted sunglasses—at night, yet.

The gate boss hastily dug into a shirt pocket and handed over a Zippo lighter. Helpfully he said, "Maybe it's a fuse, sir. You want me to check it?"

The "big-time torpedo" lit his cigarette and passed the Zippo back. "No, that's all right," he said, blowing smoke toward the guy in the response. "I'll have one of the boys inside look at it. Is Mike here?"

"He . . . Yes, sir, he came in a little while ago."

"Well, I don't believe it. I have been chasing that guy all over central Jersey."

"You've caught him now, sir," the gate boss assured the Executioner. He chuckled as he passed the sign to the gate crew.

The chain came down.

And the Executioner went in.

So, okay. So far.

He rolled casually along the drive, just Cadillacking along, senses flaring into the lie of that place.

Sentries, yeah.

Here and there he caught the glow of a cigarette out there in that darkness, a cough, a muttered word borne along on the evening breeze.

The encampment, yeah. Field headquarters. Division point.

This was it. This was where the Jersey guns were stacked, awaiting directions to the front.

He passed a dignified, lighted signboard emplaced on golf-green lawn, depicting a young lady on horseback, wearing boots and riding breeches and a bright red jacket, jumping a rock wall; in the foreground, the head of a fox with a malicious smile.

So *who* was the fox?

The whole thing could be a cute game engineered by Mike Talifero, a draw, an invitation which the Executioner could not refuse. The guy might be sitting up there in that clubhouse right now, waiting, a malicious smile on his psychopath face.

Bolan sighed and cruised on.

It was no fox hunt, he reminded himself.

It was a turkey chase.

Even if he wound up, himself, the turkey.

15 INSIDE BOLAN

Mack Bolan had not always been a hellfire guy.

Friends and acquaintances of his earlier years were, without exception, shocked over his identification with murder and violence, the unyielding and unrelenting dedication to war everlasting.

His seventh-grade teacher remembered the clear-eyed youngster vividly, and with fondness. "He was a quiet boy. Very smart, a natural scholar. Never rowdy. Very athletic, though. 'Curious,' I guess, is the best single word to describe him. He was the most curious child I ever had. Everything interested him."

A high-school friend, one of the few who was ever very close to young Bolan, remembered, "Mack was a funny guy. You respected him. And you liked him. He was always out front, leading . . . you know, just a natural leader, never a pusher. But sometimes . . . well, you just felt like he wasn't really there. I don't mean nutty. I mean . . . his body was there, but his mind was somewhere else. Mack was a loner."

Another friend, a girl, told a reporter, "Mack was a boy I always felt secure with. I could say things, and he wouldn't make fun of me about it.

He talked to me sometimes, too, I mean seriously. He told me once that he felt like an observer of life more than a participant."

The essence of these candid portraits of the man was more or less accurate. Bolan was indeed a "loner," though not the hermit type who retreats from the world behind a protective shell of cynicism and distrust.

An "observer," yes, certainly. He had never become overly subjective about this thing called life. Even as a very small child, young Mack was more aware of his environment than of himself. He was an observer, very objectively so, and he generally approved of what he saw. He always had the feeling, during the developing years, that he was standing just apart from the rest of creation, never actually immersed in it but still enjoying it, appreciating it. And yet he could feel so strongly about the problems that he noted there, could sympathize so deeply with those who suffered.

He was not, as the psychologists would say, "ego-motivated." He would undertake independent actions, yes, but seldom out of any desire for personal gratification or reward. He was not "materially ambitious." Positive actions usually came about as a result of some outside stimulus—he was "impulse-activated."

The rest of the personality seemed to close around that potentially destructive fact, providing him with a high sense of personal ethics and an underlying dedication toward positive acts of human excellence.

He had never been what one would term a "religious" person. His army personnel file listed him, in this respect, as "No Preference." But Bolan did have a deep religious sense. Undefined, and only vaguely understood perhaps, but he did possess a somewhat formulated concept of a "universal ethic."

The army psychologist who okayed Bolan for the volunteer penetration-team duty in Vietnam had notated the record thus: "Subject subscribes to universalist concepts, appears to be motivated by transcendent ideals (over and above everyday morality). Subject will command himself."

Bolan had been invited to apply for the army's officer-candidate program. He declined, three times by the record, although he was a career soldier. It appeared that he was one of those persons who shied from official authority; but he was recognized by officers and men alike as a natural leader. Others followed out of genuine respect, not because of the stripes on his sleeve.

He had, from the age of about fourteen, kept a daily journal, in which he recorded passing thoughts, particularly impressing events, rambling ideas. Even the most cursory inspection of those journals would convey to the reader a lasting impression that they had been written by a singularly unique individual.

An entry at the age of seventeen: "I stand at the edge of creation and watch the parade go by from my grandstand seat. So powerful, so beautiful, and so *important*. But where am I? Why do I not march in the parade also?"

When he was twenty, and in the army: "Some people were built to march. Others to watch, and wonder why the others are marching, and to where."

A few hours after his first "kill," in a legitimate war: "He was looking into the sun, and suddenly

I was down there with him, looking into his eyes. I saw the entire universe in there. Then I was back where I belonged, my eye to the scope where it had actually been all the while, and I gave him back to the universe. May his soul forgive mine."

Sergeant Bolan had returned many men "to the universe" while engaged in acts of war and in the service of his country. And, in the midst of that other war, his very personal "homefront war" erupted. His father, his mother, his kid sister lay dead in the home where Mack Bolan was born. He was sent home to bury them and to arrange care for an orphaned minor brother.

And the world had never again been the same—the grandstand seat gone forever, Mack Bolan marching, marching, marching . . . all the way through hell.

The hell-fire guy sent the Cadillac beneath the portico and to a gentle halt just uprange from a gleaming Mercedes.

The building was brightly lighted, but quiet.

Paired-off sentry teams strolled at the edge of light, in all directions about that knoll.

The door captain was looking his way and acting like he wanted to call something over as Bolan stepped from the vehicle, but something else was distracting the guy, from the inside.

He lunged about suddenly and grabbed the glass door, jerked it open, poising on his toes as though about to leap.

Mike Talifero swept out of the building, waving his arms and muttering to himself, a big guy hurrying along behind him.

Bolan leaned back into the Cadillac to avoid any direct encounter; they had met eyeball-to-eyeball on a couple of occasions, and he did not wish to push his luck this time—not with so much riding on it.

He heard the big bodyguard yelling to someone to "Get us an escort!" as the powerful engine of the Mercedes roared to life.

The Talifero vehicle went past him on screeching tires and ignored the driveway circle to swing out across the grass for a direct route to the gate.

There was a scramble of bodies at the far side of the building. Car doors slammed, engines cranked. Then two crew wagons sprang away in the wake of the Mercedes.

Something, evidently, was up.

Mike Talifero seldom lost his cool—or so the story went.

Bolan went on to the door and indignantly told the captain, "Well, that was a hell of a thing. The guy just hops in his chariot and drives away without even a wave. After asking me to meet him here at . . ."

The guy on the door was nervous, edgy. He was giving Bolan a respectful once-over as he replied, "I'm sorry, sir, I guess he got some bad news a few minutes ago. And he has this meeting with someone big."

Bolan gave the guy a "who-the-hell-do-you-think-you're-talking-to?" look and told him, "Well, yes, but he runs out and drives away the second I arrive."

The captain became flustered and said, "Well, no . . . I don't think . . . I mean, he had to meet someone down at the airstrip. I'm sure he's coming right back. Why don't you just go in, sir? The bar's open, you can help yourself, make yourself comfortable. I guess he won't be gone more'n about ten minutes."

The guy was holding the door open for him.

Bolan was still being indignant. "I don't know. I believe I'll just go on back."

"Only about ten minutes, sir, maybe less. Wait, let me get . . ."

The guy would not have asked Bolan who he was if he'd been busting to know. It simply wasn't done. Not in *this* outfit. You either knew, or you acted like you did. He was now halfway through the doorway and trying to catch the eye of another guy inside.

"Will you c'mere!" he called angrily to the inside, then turned back to Bolan with, "Jess will show you the bar, sir. Just make yourself comfortable."

Bolan was allowing himself to be talked into staying. He was grumbling as he stepped through the doorway, "Well, I don't like to be treated this way. You can tell him that for me. My time is important, too. I have a territory to watch, myself."

"Yes, sir, yes, sir, I know, these things happen, don't they? I bet he didn't even see you. He had this bad news, and he was late to meet the plane. You know how these things go sometimes."

A big ugly kid in shirt sleeves with an oversized .38 clipped to his belt was standing there taking it all in. This was Jess. He must have thought he was Jesse James, the way he was wearing that hardware. Maybe it was where he got his name; it worked that way in the mob.

Bolan growled, "Hi, Jess. How are things on Third Avenue?"

The kid was torn between a smile and a frown.

Bolan said, "Haven't I seen you around there?"

The door captain was awkwardly off-balance, trying to hold the heavy glass door open and keep a foot inside at the same time. Again he implored the visitor, "Just make yourself comfortable, sir." Then he fled to the more comforting environment outside, leaving the hot potato for Jess to handle.

That one was scratching the back of his neck and thinking about Third Avenue. He told the big-shot visitor, "I operate mostly around the Bronx, sir. But I guess you could have seen me . . ." He was obviously hoping that Bolan *had* seen him, highly flattered by the notice. "I get around quite a bit."

They were walking toward the bar.

Bolan asked him, "What's going on here, Jess? Why did Mike go flying out of here that way?"

"Oh, something went sour."

"I hope not what I'm thinking," Bolan said ominously.

"Hell, I don't know, sir. Are you here about the . . . ?" His head jerked toward the direction of the locker rooms.

Bolan snapped, "I sure am."

"Well . . . I dunno, sir. They weren't in there very long with the guy. I only heard him yell once, and then it didn't sound like . . . well, it sounded like Bible stuff. Something about putting a goat out in th' woods, I don't know. Then just a couple minutes ago Mr. Talifero came busting out yelling that they'd hit the guy too hard, too fast. I don't know—"

Bolan snarled, "You go fix me something cold and strong, Jess, while I see about this. Which door?"

The guy's eyelids were fluttering. "The men's locker room, sir. Second door down."

"Stay clear!" the VIP who'd noticed Jess around Third Avenue commanded, and the kid nodded and strode on to the bar.

The Beretta was in Bolan's right hand and the silencer was threading itself aboard when he hit that door at full stride.

Everything Mack Bolan had ever been and ever wanted to be was concentrated on that terrible point in Jersey, that awful moment at the end of the turkey chase—at the very doorway to hell.

16 INTERDICTED

The room was long, narrow. Lockers and benches lined both sides, leaving a narrow aisleway through the middle. It T-ed off at the rear, becoming much wider. Latrines and showers back there—showers left, the others right.

Three, at least, of Mike Talifero's people were in there.

One was in shirt sleeves, shoulder-rigged, leaning with his back to the wall, near the entrance, his attention riveted to the activities in the rear.

The other two were in the wide area, wearing white rain slickers and rubber boots—white originally, but now splotched and splattered with something else.

In that initial glimpse, only one of these was in clear view. He was standing back at about the middle of the area, hands on slickered hips, watching whatever the other guy was doing.

The other one was only now and then visible, moving in and out of sight as he busied himself with something back there in the hidden zone.

A human arm, complete from elbow to fingertips, lay on the floor between the two.

A scene straight off hell's front porch, sure, with

all the usual trimmings of odors and electric tension which moved the small hairs on observing flesh; but something very vital to this scene was missing—a loss that only accentuated the bizarre and unreal and terribly inhuman quality of the moment. *Sound* was missing, as though it had fled before something too terrible to be contemplated through human ears.

Yeah, and it was somehow worse, in this silence.

A human being was being taken apart back there, without benefit of anesthesia—quite the contrary, with every technique at human disposal geared to the positive lack of such relief, and without a murmur from the victim.

The guy at the door straightened quickly at Bolan's entrance but gave him only partial attention as he growled, "Ay, this's no damn sideshow. You ain't allowed in here."

The Beretta was at Bolan's side, partially concealed behind his leg. "Mike sent me," he told the guy. "What's the problem?"

"Shit, you tell me," the doorman replied in hushed tones. "It's spooky. The goddamn guy just sits there smiling at them, no matter what they do. Sal is about ready to walk on the ceiling back there, and I don't blame 'im."

Bolan quickly and quietly put the Beretta away. Something was off-key. But what the hell . . . ?

"That's why, then," he said.

"Why what?"

"Why Mike said to scrub it. And I didn't get it. You know."

The doorman shivered and said, "Yeah. I know."

"Go back and tell Sal I said to clean the guy up. I have to take him out of here."

The guard gave Bolan a guardedly piercing look and said, "Now *I* don't get it."

Bolan shrugged. "Ours is not to reason why, ours is but to . . ." He showed the guy a twisted grin and again shrugged his shoulders. "Go get him."

"Not me, I'm not going back there. I just ate."

"Okay. Go out and tell Jess to move my car down in front of the door."

"What are you doing? I mean, what . . . ?"

"I got the bad straw. I get to dump the guy on Bolan's doorstep."

The hardman smiled sympathetically and commented, "Wherever that is, eh?"

Bolan's insides were yelling at the guy to *move it, move it,* but he held onto the grin and quietly urged him along. "We know about where. But we better have this guy out of here before Mike gets back."

The doorman nodded, gave Bolan a final pitying look, and hurried out of there.

The apprentice turkey-maker had become aware of Bolan's presence. He watched the door guard hurry outside before he took a couple of steps up the aisleway toward Bolan to call up, "God, sir, he's still . . ." The guy did a double-take then, and quickly recovered. "Oh, I'm sorry. I thought you was—"

"He sent me," Bolan said, as he walked down there.

The guy was apologizing. "I never saw nothing like this before. This is the damnedest . . . I've worked with Sal before, sir. This ain't his fault. I'm telling you, there's something queer about this turkey."

The pot calling the kettle . . .

Two large suitcases were opened along that back wall.

Turkey kits.

A miscellany of clever tools, gadgets, devices—the sort of stuff you could pick up at any respectable hardware store. Hacksaws, a blowtorch, several different sizes of cutting pliers, other odds and ends of cutting and drilling tools.

A couple of heavy meat cleavers. Power tools, even. A sander and grinder. A jigsaw . . . for trimming nails? Several small electrical devices, even something that looked like a miniature dentist's drill.

A cattle prod.

Medical stuff. A stethoscope. Hypodermic syringes, complete with carefully racked supplies. Rubber tourniquets, many, of varied sizes.

Some kind of black goop in a gallon can, tarry-looking.

They had brought in a swivel chair from somewhere and backed it into the shower area. A heavy-duty extension socket was strung from a wall outlet and a floodlight suspended from a shower head, to give the ghouls their necessary visibility.

A tape recorder sat upon an appropriated bench, the mike suspended from overhead with the extension light.

And, yeah, this place was hell's front stoop.

Bolan could not see the man in the chair.

The other one—Sal, no doubt—was an elephant of a guy. He was standing on the blood-slicked shower-room floor in a white rubber slicker and probably sweating like hell inside it while another man's blood sweated like hell all over the outside of it.

Sal was grunting and breathing hard as he labored over the thing in the chair . . . and, yes, something was definitely out of focus here.

Bolan steeled himself to stoop down and pick the severed arm from the floor. It was cold already. He handed it to the apprentice and told him, "Wrap it up; we're taking it with us."

The guy's eyes goggled and he said, "What?" But he accepted the grisly object and grabbed for a towel.

Loudly Bolan called, "Sal! Come here!"

The fat man turned around to send a hard stare out of there; then he sighed and waddled forward.

Bolan still could not see the thing in the chair.

The fat man declared, "If I'm not left alone, how am I ever to complete my task?"

He spoke from educated years, and Bolan had to wonder, but very briefly, what had brought the man to this place, this time, this circumstance.

But only very briefly.

"You're not completing it," he coldly advised the turkey man. "Mike says we scrub it. We have other ideas now. Patch 'im up, clean 'im up, we're taking him out of here."

The guy seemed prepared to argue his case. "That isn't fair. There are all manner of ways to get around these things. It's just a question of time. I feel that I must protest—"

"Okay, Doc," Bolan interrupted, guessing at antecedents and probably scoring, "you take your protest to the college of surgeons, eh. But right now you make that guy ready to travel. And don't give me any more shit about it."

The turkey man sighed and turned toward his tool kits.

And then Bolan saw Bruno.

And he shivered and ground his jaws and bit his tongue to keep himself cool.

Bruno was nude and strapped into the swivel chair with a broad leather belt encircling the torso.

Ankles were adhesive-taped to the base of the chair, one wrist likewise to the chair arm. The other wrist, Bolan had just handed over to Sal's apprentice. Near the stump of the remainder, a heavy rubber tourniquet was biting deeply into the flesh, and black goop was caked over the raw opening, which, even so, continued seeping red

Horrible, twisting things had been done to the thigh-hip area, great discolored patches of broken flesh attesting to that. Other atrocities had been committed upon the torso and smeared with the black goop.

The eyes were brimming with fresh thin blood, brought there probably by the fact that all the hair just above and about the eyes had been viciously uprooted, probably with blunt-nosed pliers.

Blood was oozing from both corners of Bruno's mouth, and his chin looked as though it had been singed.

But, yeah, the big softhearted guy who'd lost it all in the surgical tents of Vietnam was sitting there with a beatific smile shining through it all.

A-maze-ing, yeah.

Bolan growled, "Hurry it up! I have to get this guy

out of here before Mike gets back. And you both better hope I do."

And he was not kidding about either statement.

Sal was grunting and sighing and pulling things from the medical bag.

"It ain't our fault!" the apprentice whined. "He started right off like that. Well, almost. For about ten minutes he sat there and groaned and gritted his teeth. Then with the first big hit he just flipped out. Started yelling Bible stuff at us. Ever since, he's been just like that. We didn't hardly get started, even."

"He was quoting from Leviticus," the fat man informed Bolan, looking around at him with a resigned smile. "I trust that you will find it in the sixteenth chapter, unless my memory has fogged completely. 'But the goat, on which the lot fell to be the *scapegoat*, shall be presented *alive* before the Lord, to make an atonement with him, and to let him go for a scapegoat into the wilderness.' So you see . . ." Sal spread his arms and shrugged, then waddled over to the "scapegoat."

Bolan muttered, "Yeah, I guess I do."

He sure did.

He saw that something or someone with more authority than the turkey-makers and Bolan combined had interdicted that planned fragmentation of a soul.

"It's a form of autohypnosis," the fat man was explaining. "Imposes what amounts to neural blocks across the sensation centers of the central nervous system. There are ways to overcome this, if I had been given the time. It is quite simply autohypnosis, despite the superstitious shivering of my young friend here."

Yeah, okay, Doc, Bolan was thinking. Call it whatever you like. But the simple truth was that Bruno had snockered them all. Maybe the guy had known what he was about all the while, from the moment he dragged a half-dead hell-fire guy out of blood creek.

One thing was fairly obvious. Whatever Bruno had lost at Vietnam, he'd evidently made a shortcut back through the maze and found it again in this most unlikely outpost of hell.

The turkey-maker was telling him, "All right, my grim friend, your man is as ready to travel as he'll ever be."

"Carry him out to the car," Bolan commanded. "It's parked at the front door."

The turkey man gave Bolan a go-to-hell look, but they took Bruno out, and Bolan followed, carrying the severed arm wrapped in a towel.

Jess was standing in the dining room with a tall frosted glass in his hand, looking as dumb as he was.

Bolan said, "Watch your swinger, Jess," and went on past.

The guy who had been guarding the door to the turkey chamber was now walking quickly ahead of the little procession, hurrying to let them out.

He called outside to the door captain, "Open, mister . . . his door, Tank. The back door. We're bringing the meat out."

Bolan told the guy as he swept past, "Stay hard, man."

"Thanks, I will. You too."

The turkey man and his helper put Bruno on the rear deck of the crew wagon and apparently intended to leave him there, draped across the hump there. "Put 'im in the seat, damnit!" Bolan yelled.

They did so; then Bolan shoved the fat man away and growled, "Beat it!"

"I am blameless," he said, as he huffed away.

"The hell you are, guy," Bolan told that retreating back.

He produced a small manila envelope from an inside pocket and handed it to the door captain. "Give this to Mike the instant he gets back," he instructed. "Tell him I have everything in hand."

"Yes, sir, okay, I'll sure tell 'im, sir."

Most of them seemed to be relieved over the departure of both the VIP and the "meat."

Bolan had to reflect again that many of these men probably hated the turkey-makers almost as much as did Bolan himself. So why did they . . . ? What price some men were willing to pay for . . . for what? Was *this* . . . life?

He got behind the wheel and shook the dust of that place from his feet.

The chain was down and awaiting his exit when he reached the gate. He went on through with a curt wave, and powered on out to the roadway, ran quick and silent for a thousand or so yards, then pulled off the road and leaned over the seat.

"Bruno! Can you hear me? It's Bolan. Are you there?"

Very slowly that abused head turned, and the blood-rimmed eyes stared at him without seeing. Seeing *something*, yeah, but nothing of *this* world.

The smile was still there.

He gave a rattling sigh, the eyes went glazed, and Bruno very quietly departed.

Bolan knew it, without even touching the guy or chasing a pulse.

He resettled himself behind the wheel, shook away the emotions that were clutching at him and threatening to overcome, and he went on to pick up Sara.

She responded immediately to his signal, and when she came running up, he quickly told her, "Get in and don't look behind you, Sara. Look at me, *at me.*"

But she was already getting in, and already her gaze had been drawn magnetically to what was in the rear, so visible in the illumination automatically provided by the interior lights; and she came unglued halfway into the vehicle, that tender jaw dropping in a grotesque scream-without-sound, horrified eyes locked onto that which was there.

Bolan grabbed her and pulled her on in, and held her close against him as he put vital numbers between them and that insane hardsite back there, and she shivered and groaned against him, choking on her own spittle as she fought the very strong need to scream her head off.

Some miles and some roads farther on, Bolan pulled over and stopped the car and took her in his arms to soothe her, and he told her, "That thing back there is not your brother, Sara. It is an illusion left behind by something that doesn't need it any longer. Don't worry. Bruno is okay. He died living . . . in heaven."

Yes.

But some other dudes were *not* okay, and Bolan

meant to see that they died living in hell, where they belonged.

The manila packet he'd left for Mike Talifero contained nothing but a marksman's medal.

Mike would know what it meant.

The Executioner would be returning to Boots and Bugle.

17 FREE AND CLEAR

The night had become time-worn. Bolan and the girl had found another, final, opportunity for the trading of words, ideas, and mutual comforts—a poor substitute, Bolan averred, for life itself—and now they had arrived at a specially arranged rendezvous with a private ambulance from Trenton.

He parked the crew wagon across the rear door of the ambulance. Two white-jacketed attendants hurried out—well cued on their mission, what to expect, how to handle it.

Bolan stepped from the Cadillac and pulled the girl out on his side.

An attendant gazed at him for a second over the hood of the vehicle and remarked, "So you're the guy."

"Just one of them", Bolan replied.

"Sure. I meant . . . I never expected to see you. Not living and breathing, that is."

Bolan smiled tightly and assured the guy, "I'm doing both. Take good care of my friend, eh?"

"You know it. Uh, good luck. You know."

"I know," Bolan replied quietly. He pulled Sara aside and told her, "We keep saying good-bye. Let's say hello for a change."

"Mack, I . . . I'm not trying to stake a claim but . . . if you're ever hurt and bleeding again . . . well, you know the place."

He said, "Sure." Then: "Sara. The hundred thousand I left with Bruno. I'm sure he stashed it somewhere inside the house. It's free money, Sara. Belongs to nobody, and all the blood has been purged from it. I don't need it. I pick it up as I do. Use it. Hear? Use it."

She dropped her eyes and replied, "I . . . I don't . . ."

"Think of it as insurance money if you'd like, or as a reparation of war. It was the mob's money. I can't think of a better—"

All in a rush she protested, "Mack, there are so many important things to talk about, let's not talk about that."

He said, "Yes, but I've brought nothing but hell into your life, Sara. I'd like—"

"You've brought *life,* where before there wasn't any. Bruno would agree with that. I know he would. He'd been a . . . a zombie ever since . . ."

He smiled solemnly and said, "Okay. Let's leave it there."

The guys had Bruno on a stretcher, and covered, and were carrying him to the ambulance. Even these hardened pros were wearing sick faces.

Bolan told the girl, "It's time."

The guy called over, "You ride up front with us, miss."

She replied, "Thank you. But I think I . . . I'd rather have the time to say good-bye to my brother."

Bolan gently suggested, "Instead, tell him hello, Sara."

"Yes, I . . . guess that would be more appropriate, wouldn't it."

He said, "I guess so."

The guy was holding the rear door for her.

She climbed inside, then turned back for a final look. "Good-bye, Mr. Bolan," she said in a trembly voice. "Stay hard, you hear?"

He smiled, solemnly, regretfully, and he replied, "Thanks, little mother. You too."

The door closed, and a moment later another precious segment of Mack Bolan's life was pulling away from him.

Bruno Tassily and his sister, Sara, were now, however—each in their own way—in the very best of hands.

Those two white-jacketed "attendants" were actually United States federal marshals, on volunteer "quiet duty."

They would see that Sara had nothing further to worry about from the fiends of Jersey.

And now Bolan was free.

Free of responsibility, of obligation to anyone but himself, in this still very deadly jungle called Jersey.

Not, however, free to run.

Mack Bolan had run his last yard across Jersey soil.

One more brief appointment, a few miles along this road, with one Leo Turrin. And then, yes, Mack Bolan was going to show the Jersey guns what one free man could do, when he really wanted to.

He was going to show them with a smash right up their middle.

The Executioner was now free to make war.

And let the universe tremble where it would.

"It's a mistake, Sarge."

"Is it?"

"You know it. You stand to lose everything. While gaining nothing."

"It's not a game of gain and lose, Leo."

"Call it what you want, but it's nutty. Mike Talifero has gone completely crazy. With his own hand he shot four boys right between the eyes for letting you waltz in there and take over that way."

"So we're both crazy. That defines the game, doesn't it?"

"There's nothing I can say to change your mind, is there?"

"Not a thing, Leo."

"Damnit, he already had a hundred guns on that place. Now he's calling them all in, from all over Jersey."

"Fine. I like them in bunches. They get in each other's way. Is Augie still there?"

"So far as I can determine, yes. That's one reason Mike had such a violent reaction. You made an ass of him in the presence of his lord and master."

"Did you come down in Augie's plane?"

"Hell no. I came under my other hat. Augie was already here when you called."

"So that was him."

"Who, what?"

"Mike had gone to an airstrip to meet 'someone big' while I was there."

"Okay, yeah. That would be the little private field three miles south of the hardsite."

"Who owns that joint, Leo? The hardsite, Boots and Bugle."

"Some local. No connection. But he knows the

color of the money he's getting. He has rented to them before."

"Okay. Just stay clear, Leo. Go back the other way."

"Sure. I'll be in Trenton. Hal, too."

"You give me two hours, damnit. Two hours!"

"I'd rather not give you two minutes. You know that. And if Hal—"

"Okay, let's lay it flat. I'm collecting a debt. Tell him I said that. I'm collecting from him."

Turrin shifted about in obvious discomfort. "He knows that, Mack."

"Okay. I don't like it this way either, Leo. Nothing asked, nothing expected, that's the best way. But this time it's special. No writs or clouted courts for those guys, not this time. I've got to flatten that joint."

Turrin sighed. "For the sake of a dead man."

"For the sake of men not yet dead," Bolan icily corrected him.

"Sure, I get you."

"And for my own sake."

"I get that, too." Turrin was smiling his solemn smile. "So give 'em one for me, Sarge."

They each smiled that special smile of two men who thoroughly know each other, and they shook hands, and then Mack Bolan returned to the wars, free and clear, with all goals clearly defined.

18 TALIFERI

All of the crew bosses were assembled in the dining room at Boots and Bugle.

Each of these was a full-time officer in the Taliferi. Every man in the Taliferi was an officer, a rank-holder. These were the elite of the outfit, of all the outfits. There were no "button men" or "street soldiers" in the national police force of the mob.

Their allegiance was claimed by no one Mafia family, though they came, in their origins, from all of them. Now they served the *idea,* the *thing* itself, La Cosa Nostra, that bodiless yet terribly effective alliance for larceny which held all the Mafia families together *as one.* And which, in turn, held together *as one* all the organized-crime outfits on the American continent.

The Taliferi were, to the dark world, what the FBI represented to the fifty United States. But that is a poor comparison. Put the FBI under the total control of a despotic President and his cabinet, answering to none other, and the comparison would be more realistic.

The identical-twin brothers, Pat and Mike Talifero, between themselves technically constituted the entire Taliferi. They were the Commissione's men, and the Commissione comprised the ruling heads of the individual Mafia families. Pat and Mike served this body, as their hard arm, their "voice of authority."

Pat or Mike could hit a *capo*, it was said, on their own authority, for specified high crimes against *the thing*, only. But it was said that the two were empowered to act in such matters without prior approval of the ruling council (each of whom was a *capo*) if it could later be shown (to the satisfaction of the surviving *capi*) that their action was justified.

This is a terrible power to be placed in the hands of any human being, especially when it was being placed there by the persons who would be most directly affected by the use of that power.

The story was probably true, nevertheless. The Taliferi had done that very thing on two separate occasions during the Bolan wars; that is, executed one of their own bosses, on their own say-so.

And this is perhaps the best illustration of the incredible machinations of the world of the Mafia. A world peopled by violent and greedy men, living an ethic which Bolan characterized as "psychopathic," so fearful and distrustful of one another that they authorized and erected a personal "doomsday device" to ensure fealty to one another.

This is tantamount to the U.S. Supreme Court hiring itself an executioner to assassinate on the spot any of its members suspected of misconduct.

It was not a world of reasonable men, this world of the Mafia.

Therefore, the Talifero brothers were, it seemed,

a necessary ingredient of any practical "alliance" of competitive families.

And they did compete. The primary purpose of the alliance was to arbitrate the inevitable disputes arising from the division of criminal spoils and, of course, to put forth a united front to guard against encroachment by other ambitious organizations. La Commissione was at once a Board of Trade, a House of Representatives, a Supreme Court, a Department of State, a Labor Department, and a Department of Defense.

And the Taliferi were their teeth.

Long ago the brothers had begun delegating their authority to sharp up-and-coming youngsters in the various families. Like any government function, the bureaucratic spread grew as the job grew, and the job grew as the bureaucracy flourished and sought new tasks to justify its existence.

For some time now the Taliferi had been a national gestapo, replacing the old Murder, Inc. headshed of the early years, wielding a power like no "family" had ever dreamed of.

But it was, in essence, a family in its own right.

It was a family of "elite" cutthroats, many of them fairly well educated and polished, but cutthroats nevertheless.

And the family of the elite was in session at the Boots and Bugle on this fated night in New Jersey.

Their co-*capo,* Mike Talifero, was presiding.

Brother Pat was still recuperating from grevious and near-fatal wounds received in the Executioner's Vegas rumble.

Greatfather Augie Marinello, reputed "boss of all the bosses"—which simply meant that he was the most influential and feared member of La Commissione—was also present, though almost in a *capo emeritus* status.

Little actual information is recorded on the Talifero brothers. That they were brothers was obvious—they were identical twins—but even the name itself was suspect. Perhaps it is significant that it is a blending of two Italian words: *tale* meaning "such" and *ferro,* "iron."

Mike was thought to be about forty years old, certainly no more than that. He was of Sicilian origin, and rumors had him a tenth-generation *mafioso.* He had originally come into the outfit, it appears, under the sponsorship of Marinello—at that time an underboss in the New York family which he now ruled.

There had been a time when the Talifero brothers rarely smiled. Since Miami, though, and that terribly dismal first encounter with Mack Bolan's mind-blowing brand of blitzing warfare, the brothers had been given to smiling and laughing it up quite a bit. Those closest to them knew, too well, that Pat and Mike were in their most deadly moods when they were smiling and laughing it up.

Tonight Mike was smiling a lot and treating the boys to quite a few laughs as he briefed them on the plan for the night.

Twelve tried-and-true men were in his congregation, the elite of all the elite, and they had been brought to Jersey specifically to collect Mack Bolan's hated head.

Each of those present was, at the moment, bossing a crew of ten to fifteen "free-lance" guns—small-time hoods scooped from the streets of Manhattan and north Jersey and pressed into this emergency service. These "soldiers" were not members of the brotherhood. Some were blacks, some were white Anglos, some were Puerto Rican and Irish Catholic and Jewish and whatever else could be bought by the week for the business end of a gun.

There is no national origin to crime.

It comes in every form and guise. The 99.9 percent of good people in the Italian-American community cannot be held to blame if some of their number seem to have a genius for organization and if some of those found a way to make crime pay.

But this *was* a Mafia party, let none wonder about it; the Mafia *does* exist, and it appeared to be alive and well in New Jersey on that night of nights at the makeshift hardsite at Boots and Bugle.

It was a council of war.

And the Taliferi were ready and waiting for a certain son-of-a-bitch to show his tail around that place once more, just once more on that hellish night of all nights in the life of smiling Mike Talifero.

19 APOLOGIA

He made a soft run to the rear of the property, circling in across adjacent farmlands on a cross-country approach, running dark and quiet until finally reaching a stand of trees which marked the property lines.

It was shortly past midnight.

Incredibly, twenty-four short hours earlier he had lain sleeping in the loft of the Tassily brooder house, recuperating in a forced détente. He had lived, it seemed, several lifetimes since then.

Already in Jersey he had killed more men than even a dedicated executioner cared to contemplate. But Mack Bolan did not count the dead, not the *enemy* dead. Body counts had meaning only as applied to the living ones.

And that was the purpose of this initial mission. He had to go in there and count them, locate them, classify them, assess their strong and weak points, establish an angle of attack, determine objectives . . . and figure out a way to get out of there once the battle was ended to his satisfaction.

Mack Bolan was not a wild-ass warrior.

Hell-fire and thunderation were his trademark,

yes, but his blitzers were usually undertaken with cool military preparedness.

He was not anxious to die; willing, perhaps, if that was the way the numbers fell. But he would work those numbers to every possible personal advantage. Victory, for Mack Bolan, was measured not in points of time or as triumphant events; victory in war for the Executioner meant remaining alive to wage war.

He left the crew wagon in the trees and stripped himself to the black suit, forsaking all weapons except stiletto and garrote.

Then he gooped his hands and face and moved out, a fleeting shadow of the darkness, a silent sigh of the night, a mere "observer" at the edge of creation.

Moments later he was inside the enemy compound, moving catlike through the tall grass at the fence line.

When he moved, it was swiftly; when he paused, it was almost cataleptic in its abrupt cessation of all sound and movement.

On a soft penetration, Bolan became to all effects a part of the landscape, *one* with the universe enveloping him, in complete harmony with the nonlife elements.

As the wind rustled through the grasses, so did Bolan.

As shadows leaped with scudding clouds or moving branches, so did Bolan.

And when the universe held still for a moment, so too did Bolan.

The asphalt and concrete boys of the urban jungles were clearly disadvantaged in this game with this child of the universe. Bolan was "at home" here; it was his sort of jungle, and the night was his bosom companion.

So it is no discredit to the street soldiers from Manhattan and Newark, Jersey City, and Brooklyn that the man from thunder moved undetected through their midst, studying their movements and divining their defenses, reading their fears and anxieties, exposing their weaknesses and contemplating their strengths.

He "sectored" them, and made "grid overlays" in the retentive web of his combat consciousness.

He "psyched" them, and made mental combat notes on how best to capitalize on the natural inclinations of this motley army of mercenary ragtags.

Actions under the stress of combat are more often than not purely reactive things, a flexing of the survival instincts along a pathway of strongly conditioned (trained) responses.

The actions before a battle are usually the foretelling of the tale.

Combat—in the organized sense—is a uniquely human pastime, despite the outraged cries from humanitarians down through the ages that combat is bestial, inhuman. It is, literally, intensely human.

The art of combat was perhaps the first art ever devised by the human mind, and the high development of this "art" made man supreme over the other beasts. It is uniquely his accomplishment, even if also his damnation.

The first tools ever developed by the hands of men were very probably tools of combat, and to this day the greatest excellence of technology is usually directed into or produced by this same class of tool-making.

The very intellect of man was fashioned both by and for the grim necessity to do battle, to survive through combat, and many of the most stirring moments of human history were productions of the combat intellect.

To dismiss "soldiers," then, as something less in the human order than artisans and philosophers and prophets is to degrade the very foundations of humanity.

Without the soldiers, the "combat intellectuals," there would be no artisans and philosophers and prophets; nor would the mind of man have ever descended from the trees to survive the brutalities of life on the jungle floor, and on the plains and plateaus of a natural world which knows no natural peace.

There *is* an intellectual excellence inherent in any victory of man over the elements; and man himself, of course, is an "element" of the natural world. Let the "intellectuals" boo and hiss at the military mind as they may, and do—there *is* a human excellence and an intellectual brilliance present in the finely tuned *organized combat sense*. Each boo and hiss sent up from the others has been paid for, made possible by, this older and more refined and superbly excellent exercise of the human intellect . . . and paid in blood.

This does not, of course, mean that combat is necessarily good. At its best, it usually represents the lesser of two evils. But it is, always has been, and—so long as man *is* man—will probably remain necessarily *necessary*.

In any human necessity, we usually find instances of human excellence, high achievement, sincere dedication, genius.

Bolan the warrior was a personification of these very human attributes.

There are those, of course, who follow an innate combative instinct, a raw and untempered yearning for unearned riches and for arrogant power over their fellow humans.

For the gentle folk of the world, then, it is fortunate that men of high human ethics and excellence have applied their energies and intellects to the problems of survival in a brutal world. It is this circumstance, and this alone, which has saved the finer minds from the savages among us.

As Mack Bolan pointed out to Sara Henderson, a lone psychopath with a knife can dominate a hundred gentle people.

By that same token, one finely tuned intellect with a disciplined combat sense can overcome a hundred untrained savages.

Mack Bolan was living proof of that.

It seems a pity, a very human pity, that so many fine minds do shrink from the responsibilities, the everyday dirty and mucky responsibilities of maintaining the world in the face of constant savagery.

And this little detour through the back roads of the World of Bolan is not intended as an apology for the man or his methods.

It is an apology for those who boo and hiss.

20 THE SET

In every sense of the word, the joint was a hardsite. Its defenses had been thoughtfully devised and painstakingly erected, and they were being carefully maintained.

The obvious defense perimeter was an oblong encirclement of the small knoll upon which sat the clubhouse and its outbuildings, the line running about one hundred yards from front and rear, extending one hundred and fifty or so yards to each side.

This was a fire line, with "set" teams of two men each emplaced at intervals of ten yards. These guys were simply chunked out there, entirely visible and with no physical protection whatever, sitting or lying or standing around, talking freely from set to set, trying to while away a long wait in a longer night.

Pistols, mostly. Here and there a shotgun.

This was the dumb line. Bolan had seen them before. So much live meat staked in the jungle to attract the lion. And the poor bastards didn't even know it.

On the rooftops and concealed within the outbuildings were the primary defenses, the "trap sets."

There were marksmen with rifles on those roofs.

Automatic-weapons experts with choppers large and small prowled the shadows of the main building and lurked in the recesses of other buildings.

Undoubtedly, more troops would be found in and around the parking area at the side of the clubhouse, where many vehicles of various types reposed in the quiet wait.

The outer defenses were no more than an early-warning attempt—a combination of solitary set-men scattered widely in no clear pattern and roving patrols of two men each.

Miniature radios and shotguns.

Bolan had counted one hundred and eighteen enemy heads, and he was satisfied that this took care of most of the numbers. There would be others inside the clubhouse, certainly, a "palace-guard" last ditch for the ranking big shots.

Sara's "photographic-mind" sketch of the property had omitted one more or less insignificant detail. Perhaps it was one of those repressions of the psyche which so troubled intelligence-seekers. She had "forgotten" the kennels yard, the place where the hounds were kept, the hounds that chase "adorable little foxes."

It was one of those chain-link affairs with a wire-mesh top, featuring a private run and individual shelter for each dog.

And the dogs were present, about twenty by Bolan's long-distance count—nervous, and pacing, with some primeval sensing of the portents in that night.

If there were horses in the stables, he could find no such evidence. Bolan had thought that clubs such as these probably boarded members' horses, but the question seemed to have no relevance to the night, and he dismissed it.

He knew that it was impossible to account for every conceivable defense that an enemy may have "up the sleeve."

But he was satisfied that he had collected their prime numbers, and this had been the objective of the probe. He knew enough about them now to give himself, at the least, a practical angle of attack, a numbered approach which more than likely could bring him into the destruct zone with most of his firepower intact.

The primary question remaining was: the destruction of whom and which?

That, of course, was one of the variables of warfare. In the final analysis, every act of war was a gamble—a gamble with the universe in which all the odds were concealed, hidden away somewhere in that "universal maze of cause and effect."

The most a guy like Bolan could do would be to introduce the "cause" in his most skillful and persuasive form of argument.

The rest would be up to the court—that Supreme Needs Court of universal law—and the combatants would have to abide by that final "judgment in the wind."

Mack Bolan, in his own mind, was a living instrument of the universe—a sensory extension into that which was—as were, he believed, all living things.

He could only hope that the winds blowing across

central Jersey in this time and circumstance were winds of justice and high purpose.

In any other context, the Executioner was indeed involved in a damn-fool exercise.

21 IN THE WINDS

It was drawing onto two o'clock, and the previously sharp edge of the night was beginning to writhe in anticlimax.

Mike Talifero paced the small office of Boots and Bugle and squeezed his palms together behind his back.

Augie Marinello, the Invisible Second President of the United States, occupied the nearest approximation of a throne available, a luxuriously padded executive chair at the desk.

His two trusted "tagmen" (chief bodyguards) of long standing went right on standing, in his shadow, revolvers nervously exposed through the opened coats of two-hundred-dollar suits.

"Why doesn't he hit?" Talifero muttered, the tone of voice strongly belying the set smile of that face.

Marinello removed a long cigar from his teeth to observe calmly, "The guy comes at his convenience, Mike, not ours. You should've learned that by now."

"I was just talking to rattle my tongue," the gestapo chief said. "I know what the guy is doing."

"There's always the chance he won't come tonight

at all," the *capo* pointed out, for perhaps the twentieth time.

"You're forgetting Boston," Talifero said.

"I'll *never* forget Boston," Marinello assured him.

"The guy goes off his rocker when he finds a turkey. Look at what he did to Freddy, that time in New York. Over a dumb kid he hardly knew. How do you think he feels about *this* one? The guys were battlefield buddies in Vietnam. This guy worked with the surgeon who gave Bolan his new face, out in California."

"I know, I know."

"Well, what do you think this is doing to that guy's guts? He's crazy, I'm telling you, crazy for revenge. He's running around out there somewhere just crazy as hell, trying to come up with a way to hit us. I know that, and you know that, Augie."

"Don't get assy with me, Mike."

"You know I'm not . . ." Talifero halted his pacing and told the big boss, "I'm sorry, Augie. Bear with me through this, huh? This is a hell of a—"

"I know." Marinello's cigar had gone out. He frowned at it, then cast a reproachful glance at the nearest tagman. The guy leaned forward with the ever-present lighter and applied new heat to the five dollars' worth of hand-rolled tobacco leaves. The old man puffed new life into the cigar, then told his fair-haired boy, "You're taking this too personal, Mike. You're going to fool around and stub your toe again. You better back off some."

And that was a hell of a thing to say. Right out in the open, that way. Talifero shot an angry look in the general direction of the bodyguards. It had not been a thing to say to the hardarm of the whole damn world, not with underlings present.

Without looking at the boss, he quietly stated, "I have never stubbed my toe, Augie. You don't run an outfit like this with stubbed toes. You know that. Why are you needling me? At a time like this—"

"This is exactly the time," the old *capo* shot back. "I've been counting the score, Mike—me and some others. It's why I came down, myself, personal. You missed the guy at Miami. You missed him in Vegas —damn near permanently. Your brother is still a vegetable from that. You missed Bolan at Philly. And you've been missing him here in Jersey all week long. You can understand, I know, if we start wondering, Mike, just when you're going to start connecting."

"Well, what a hell of a time to . . ." The famous Talifero smile was absolutely plastered from one ear to the other. In a voice as calm as cold soup he recovered himself and told the boss of bosses, "That's not fair, Augie. I have never before had absolute control over any situation involving that bastard. You know that. I've always been called in to save a losing situation after most of it was lost. This time is different. This time the guy is dancing on *my* strings. I'm going to get that son-of-a-bitch this time, Augie, if I have to go out and do it on my own. I am going to get him alive . . . and I am going to keep him alive for a long, long time."

"That's exactly what's got me worried," Marinello quietly replied. "I think you got too much of your own ass in this thing."

"Then take me off."

"You know I won't do that, Mike. You're the best

there is. I just want to be sure you keep your own ass out of the way. Get the bastard, Mike. Roast his dick off in boiling oil if that's what you gotta do, but *get* 'im first. Any way you can. Forget the fancy horseshit. Just *get the guy!*"

"I fully intend to."

The *capo di tutti capi* arose abruptly from his chair. "And just in case you don't, I'm going back home."

"That could be a wise decision," the gestapo boss said icily. "But not for the reason given."

The two architects of human misery locked gazes, and the little flares deep within the wily old eyes of the man who had built an empire of it from nothing but nerve and determination clearly showed an awareness of and distaste for this other monster of his own creation.

"I made you, Mike," he reminded his hardarm. "I can unmake you just as easy."

"That would be at your pleasure, of course," Talifero replied stiffly, smiling the deadly smile.

"Just don't get any assy ideas, that's all. I put out a memo before I come down here. The council is going to review this whole setup. Just don't try anything assy in the meanwhile."

"That's an ultimatum, isn't it?"

"I'm not sure I know what that means, Mike. You college boys have it all over me in the word department. I'm just telling you to get this Bolan. If you can't get *him*, maybe we're not so sure about the way you might handle other things. You get me, Mike. You know what I'm saying."

"I know, Mr. Marinello. What I don't get is why

you're sp
fidence, not a k

"You're the boy w
just wanta make sure you k
that's all."

The *capo* swept out, a tagman at front a
He picked up another small group who were waiting just outside the office door, and the party from Manhattan moved swiftly toward the main exit.

Mike Talifero appeared in the doorway to call out instructions to his own troops. "Mount a convoy! See that our friends get back to their plane and off the ground safely!"

Marinello halted in mid-stride to throw back a counter-command. "Never mind that. We'll take care of our own selves our own way!"

This was not only an open slap in the face for Mike Talifero. It was also an open statement of mistrust by the boss of bosses in his commander-in-chief of the armed forces.

Mike himself knew that, even if every other man in the building did not.

The Marinello party moved on, and before it had even cleared the building, a Taliferi lieutenant burst in through a side entrance and hastened to the side of his boss.

"Okay, it's started," he announced tensely. "Charlie just stumbled on two of our boys down on the early line, necks broke, dead."

Mike Talifero chuckled and commented, "Well, well."

"You want me to stop Augie?" asked another lieutenant who had been standing by.

...ardarm of the world replied ... By no means whatever."

While outside, with a promising wind at his back, the Executioner was about to find his first great windfall of the long night.

22 INTO THE MAZE

Bolan had quietly withdrawn from his soft probe and returned to his temporary war wagon, with hardly a blade of grass disturbed to mark his transit through that enemy territory.

He sprang the arsenal from its storage in the luggage compartment and put together everything he could carry.

He would very probably not be coming back this way again.

In addition to the usual combat rig, he was now burdened with back and chest packs, loaded with the necessities of one-man warfare.

A one-man army had also to double as pack mule, from time to time, and this was clearly one of those times.

The packs featured quick-disengage buckles. He could come out of them in a flash, if necessary.

Fully engaged, he estimated that he was now carrying a load almost equal to own weight. He experimented with the tender leg and found just a bit too much demand imposed there. Regretfully he jettisoned several of the heavier munitions and went on. With all votes counted, he would need his own physical prowess more than a few items of hardware.

ing the edge of creation on this
rough. He was at the very center of it, and he had to clear a path as he advanced—a trail through a jungle of jumpy amateur warriors whose first loud alarm would mean Bolan's premature exposure, and undoubtedly a quick end to an unhappy night.

The object was to get in close, undetected; to make some sort of setup from where he could send war winging into several quarters at once; to induce confusion and panic, paralysis in the enemy, and, hopefully, full flight on the part of the ragtag street-corner bad guys who'd hired out their guns for a war they knew nothing about.

This would be a sort of victory in itself, but of course, this was not the primary objective of the night.

It was but a means to an end.

The end was Mike Talifero.

He meant to execute that guy, and leave him with a marksman's medal lying atop the wound.

Maybe someday other guys would get the message, deciding that the wages of command in this outfit were too poor for the risks involved.

At that moment, though, Bolan had to admit to himself that his objective of the night was but a forlorn desire, not a true and viable goal of the battle.

He would consider the mission a success if he could simply storm in there and rattle them, scatter them, scare the living hell out of them, and make them wonder why they'd come—destroy their smug pride and wipe that arrogant "lord-of-the-realm" sneer from their faces. And make them think twice

the next time around, when another helple[illegible]
of storm-trooper tactics lay at their mercy.

For the moment, he had to *sneak* in, and [illegible]
his progress with every wile of silent combat.

And twice during that quiet reentry he shrugged out of his mule packs and slithered in with the sighing wind, to silence quickly and efficiently a potential alarm post.

These two were his only obstacles, and he reached the eastern perimeter of the dumb line with his mission intact and with an angle of attack rather clearly formulated.

And, at that point, he received a bit of assistance from the enemy themselves.

A tri-mount of floodlights was emplaced at the front corner of the clubhouse, angled toward the parking area. These floods were lighted, had been throughout the long wait, and they were the only outside lights in use.

Bolan had pondered the fact on his earlier penetration, deciding finally after much weighing that this was a weak point in the enemy defenses; moreover, one which the enemy also recognized. The vehicles massed there presented a possible point of cover for an invader who might slip through to that point; also, they represented a potential weapon.

If a guy could get in there and spill some gasoline around, he could get one hell of a whomping jazz-bang going with all those exploding gas tanks.

They would not disperse the vehicles—not this outfit. Mack Bolan was not their only enemy. The boys always liked to have good wheels quickly available, should the ever-present threat of the law suddenly materialize.

At the same moment, they could not adequately defend such a motor pool against a determined aggressor—one like Bolan, for instance—so they simply lit it up and dared the bastard to come in.

While admitting that the motor pool jazz-bang would make a nice effect, Bolan had already written it off as too risky without sufficient payoff. He did not accept invitations to combat. He issued his own.

Still, he had seen a way to use the situation.

It was why he had come in at this particular angle to the dumb line. The defense perimeter had been emplaced on the low ground, below the knoll and surrounding it. Looking back toward the clubhouse from this particular point, a guy would be staring straight up into those blinding floods on a direct line of maximum effect.

Bolan himself did not intend to look into those lights.

He did, however, desire to persuade this particular sector of the dumb line to squint up there, if only for a few seconds—long enough to put the pupils of their eyes into sharp contraction and induce a moment or so of night blindness in the defensive line. It was a simple tactic, sure. But it should work. Well enough for a quiet shadow of the night to slip through that line and head for the high ground. From that moment on, the people behind him would never again see him. Each time they looked his way, they would see nothing but blinding floodlights.

And so it was that Bolan was preparing to breach the dumb line when the excitement up there in the vehicle area provided the distraction he was already planning.

Several men had run from the front of the building to the parking lot and were cranking the engines of three crew wagons.

Bolan was crouching in the grass, a frozen illusion of the night, about twenty yards out and dead center between two of the paired-men sets on the dumb line.

The dumb men had been quietly talking within their own sets until those engines up there fired. Then one of the guys just uprange from Bolan called down to the next set, "Hope they're not bailing out on us, man."

One of the guys down there chuckled nervously and called back, "You got paid in advance, didn't you, man?"

"Sure. But they never mentioned no death benefits."

"Or bail," another snickered.

This entire sector was now staring toward the hill.

Bolan, mule pack and all, made his penetration while a guy farther up the line was exclaiming, "That's that boss from New York!"

"Which one is that? They're all from New York."

"The old man. The big boss . . . What's-his-name."

"Manischewitz," someone offered.

"Naw, that's a wine."

"Same difference."

Bolan had missed none of it, and now he was moving swiftly along the base of the grassy knoll, in smooth golf-green now, swiftly seeking the most favorable spot in which to set up his fire base.

He found it about midway up the hill, amidst the

foundations of the signboard with the daring young lady and the leering fox, the lights of which were now prudently extinguished; and it was the sheerest of coincidences that this spot also provided excellent command of the driveway where it circled off the hilltop and dropped into the straightway toward the main gate.

Bolan had hardly touched down and shrugged away his packs when the first vehicle in the Marinello procession came whining into the descent.

This was a quick-reaction situation—an instant flicker of the instinctive combat sense—and Bolan the warrior did not even question the route that had brought him here. He simply sent an unformed thanks to the powers behind the winds and made a quick selection of weapons.

"Entrez-vous, Augie," he sighed as the second vehicle nosed into view.

Step into my *maze,* the spider should have said to the fly.

Yeah, and Bolan could feel that universal wind at his back for sure now.

Augie Marinello, boss of all the bosses, was a much riper plum than Mike and all his Taliferi combined.

The Executioner would make at least one positive statement on this night to top all nights in Jersey.

23 THE HIT

The limousines surged in beneath the driveway portico, and the Marinello party quickly embarked, the boss himself stepping into the sandwich vehicle with his two tagmen sliding in behind him to occupy the rear-facing jump seats in the center.

Another bodyguard leaped into the front beside the driver, and the procession moved out.

The haste was not entirely motivated by a desire to quit that bastion of Taliferi power, though that element was certainly present in the nervous departure.

The *capo di tutti capi* usually moved from point to point in this fashion, quick ins and outs, moving swiftly, with fully crewed escort wagons to front and rear.

In the home stand, Augie used a bulletproof vehicle that he often compared with that used by the President.

This trip was in an ordinary crew wagon, though one equipped with all the animal comforts and conveniences.

The possible presence of Mack Bolan in that particular area also undoubtedly influenced the emotions in this instance, but the conversation of the moment clearly pointed toward that other danger.

"Pardon me if I'm out of line, boss," the chief bodyguard said as he was settling into his seat, "but I don't like the smell of this place."

"Don't worry, me neither," Marinello muttered glumly. "I'll fix that when I get back, you better believe it."

They were facing each other across the rear deck.

Marinello flicked his again-dead cigar with thumb and forefinger. The tagman leaped to light it.

The radio up front crackled with a question. "To the airport, boss?"

The *capo* grabbed a mike from the armrest to reply, "Naw. Go on straight home, the turnpike. Let's not dick around here another minute."

The crew chief in the lead vehicle acknowledged the instructions as the procession picked up speed leaving the turnaround.

"Run close, but not too close," Marinello instructed his own wheelman as they swung into the descent.

The chief bodyguard was wondering about something else. "How 'bout Marty, boss? He'll be sitting down there with the plane all night."

"Call him when we get back. Not until."

"Right, sir, I getcha."

The Marinello vehicle was slowing for the final curve at the base of the hill when the electrifying event occurred.

Something crashed through the rear window directly between the boss and his tagmen and fell to the floorboards with an ominous thud.

The chief bodyguard still held the cigar lighter

in his hand. He dropped the lighter and lunged toward his boss in an instinctive defensive reaction; then he yelled, "God, it's a damned . . ." and began scrabbling along the floor with both hands.

Marinello was screaming, "Stop the car, stop!" when the whole wide world turned red before his eyes and his chief bodyguard was suddenly lifted toward the ceiling with a roll of flame beneath him.

The limousine did not take that final curve.

It lurched on in a straight line of travel, bounded across the graveled shoulder and along the bottom edge of the slope for about half a car length, then slowly teetered onto its side and on over into a wheels-up slide to the bottom.

Then it exploded again, this time from the rear, and the last thing to occupy the exploding consciousness of the boss of bosses was a question: Who did it? Who did this awful thing? Was it Mike, or was it Mack?

It was Mack, and he did it with a hand grenade, baseballed into the target with major-league precision, and he did not even take the time to assess the results.

Without consciously realizing that he was counting numbers, he had a flare round loaded and ready to fly, awaiting only the cover of the first explosion to launch it.

With that larger roar came the barely discernible *phut* of the launching which sent that silent streaker into the northern skies beyond the clubhouse.

During that second or two which separated the second explosion within the Marinello vehicle from the opening of that celestial floodlight, a group of hardmen from the front of the clubhouse had dashed over to the edge of the hill to gawk at the spectacle below.

Someone screamed, "That's Mr. Marinello down there! Get down there! You boys get down there and pull 'im out!"

But as that horrified command was being issued, the sizzling white light of the flare popped into brilliance and began settling across those back acres, and someone else yelled, "Twelve o'clock high! Watch the rear! You boys get back there and cover that rear!"

Another excited command blended with that one to direct the men on the rooftops: "Riflemen! Keep alert! Watch your sectors! It's a trick!"

So, okay. Quickly on the tail of that, the riflemen had other problems to ponder. From only God knew where, in all that yelling confusion, something very disconcerting came whizzing out of the darkness on a thin tail of fire. It struck the chimney atop the clubhouse and exploded in a shattering rain of shrapnel and flying chips of brick.

Pandemonium erupted up there, while back at ground level some of the men from the dumb line had surged in from the front perimeter to assist the Marinello people who were frantically trying to pull bodies from that flaming wreckage.

Another grenade dropped into their midst, out of nowhere, and the dumb men raced back to the edge of darkness.

Someone down there yelled, "Well, *fuck* it! I didn't sign up for *this!*"

Another shaky voice seconded that conclusion at about the same moment that the glass front of the clubhouse disintegrated in another shattering explosion.

A Taliferi lieutenant ran halfway down the hillside to shout into the night, "You boys get back here! Where the hell you think you're going?"

Anyone standing close enough and with mind enought left to perceive would have heard the deadly *phu-uut* of a silenced Beretta, and perhaps would have even discerned a slender pencil of flame emanating from the base structure of the club signboard at about the same instant that this same lieutenant sprouted a mushrooming hole in his face and toppled down the hill.

A voice out there in the darkness, a bit fainter now, yelled back, "We ain't going where you're at, man. Not for no five hundred bucks!"

And the battle had hardly begun.

Vehicles were lurching away from the motor pool and taking the scenic cross-country route to the gate, and the surviving Taliferi had given up trying to threaten and cajole the fainthearted troops to remain and give battle.

It was an understandable problem.

There is something particularly jarring to the psyche of even well-trained troops when high explosives begin thundering through the night, when friends and buddies erupt into frothing fountains of blood and die screaming, and especially when even the leadership becomes shaky and disorganized.

Green troops, never exposed to the hellish realities of honest-to-God warfare—nor even to the conditioning courses of the training fields—cannot be expected to stand firm through such an experience.

Bolan knew that. He had been counting on it.

But then something else occurred in the midst of that hell fire which Bolan would wonder about later.

From down around the Marinello wreckage, someone had yelled, "We need an ambulance."

Another voice replied, "Fuck that. Put 'em in your car and haul ass for Trenton."

"He's gonna die! Just lookit his legs! That old man's gonna die!"

"If you don't get moving, we're all gonna die! That fuckin' guy is right over there somewheres. Right under our noses!"

"Wanta try for the cars again? Think we can make it?"

Hearing, Bolan consigned Augie Marinello's aged fate to the needs of the universe. He sent a brief burst of chatter fire around their heels, then called down to them, "Is the old man alive?"

A startled voice came back muffled and about one beat off its numbers. "Yeah, just."

"Okay. I'll give you a white flag. For five seconds. Beat it!"

It was the first "white flag" Bolan had ever given in the heat of a Mafia war. He was to wonder about it later, and decide that it had been a small concession to the nobler instincts of the human animal.

He watched them scamper to the remaining vehicles, bearing their wounded into a hasty load and exit; then he turned back toward the jungle.

Those fleeing vehicles would only serve to deepen the battlefield trauma of those hired by the week.

Let them go, too.

Let all the weak bastards go.

He wanted the lords—the lords of this rotten jungle.

He checked his belt clips and filled in the blank spots with concussion grenades, heavy ones, swung the chatter pistol to the rear, and draped another belt across his shoulders.

Then he picked up the weapon of the night, the M-16/M-79 over-'n-under configuration, and went quietly up the hill.

24 HELL'S LAST DITCH

Mike Talifero had been pacing about the dining room, a pistol in each hand, since the first sounds of battle rent the night.

Two of his lieutenants and an edgy palace guard had stood by their posts at the windows and kept him informed on the developments that were discernible from their observation points.

"Can't see the cars, sir, but I guess he got 'em for sure. Flames are shooting up from down below, near the road I guess."

"Flare back here, sir! High one. 'Bout a hundred yards out."

And the asides:

"How's he hitting both sides at once?"

"Guess it's easy if you know how."

"Everything that bastard does is easy!"

"He just makes it look that way. Try it yourself once."

Then a Talifero bawl: "Shut up! You boys shut up! Look alive there!"

"Christ, sir . . ."

And a heavy *ba-looom* as something hit the roof, shaking the entire structure.

"What the hell was that? What was that?"

"You boys stay put! I'll shoot the first man to run!"

"Christ, sir, he's gonna burn it down!"

A lieutenant yelled, "Isn't anyone shooting back? What the hell are all those boys doing out there?"

"What d'ya shoot back *at*, sir? You can't shoot back at an *explosion!*"

As though to punctuate that remark, the glass-fronted entranceway disappeared with a roar. Flames huffed inside, carrying with them acrid smoke and a million flying slivers of shredded glass.

The lieutenant who had just complained reeled away from that with his face spurting blood like a shower head, clawing at his eyes and groaning. One of the other men grabbed him and steered him to a chair, while Mike Talifero watched with rounded eyes and an entirely sober face.

From outside he could hear one of his men shouting at deserters, and he knew that the tide had turned before the battle was even enjoined.

"Turn some tables over!" he yelled suddenly. "Stack them up at least three deep, and take cover! He'll be coming in! Get ready! Andy! Set up a crossfire to bracket the doorway! Two of you boys get over there and barricade the side door! *You,* what's your name, and *you!* Just barricade it and stand there! Go through it, and I'll chase you all the way to hell! Understand?"

The free-lancers understood.

Mike Talifero just wished that *he* did.

Just a few hours ago, *twelve fucking hours ago,* the guy had been as good as dead—grounded, hurting, just waiting for them to track him down and snuff him out.

And now, look.

Just look at this!

He could hear engines firing up in the parking lot, could sense their fleeing movements into the night.

How did you handle a thing like . . . ?

He withdrew a small manila envelope from his pocket, shook the little metal emblem out of there, and held it in his palm. Then he spat on it and threw it to the floor.

"Come on, baby," he said half-aloud. "Come on, come on. This is where it's at. Come on and *find* it!"

Bolan came up over the hill with an HE round in the breech of the M-79 and a belt load of alternates slung over his shoulder, including double-aught buckshot, flares, tear gas, and several more rounds of the high explosive powerhouse.

The M-16 riding atop that one-man light-artillery section handled thirty-round clips of 5.56mm. tumblers, deliverable at seven hundred rounds per minute.

A guy came running around the corner from the stables area, a Thompson cradled across his chest, and skidded about two feet into that confrontation with striding death.

Bolan swung the over-'n-under that way and gave the guy one second's worth of the M-16, and that target quit skidding and fell away zipped from groin to throat.

A group of five more who'd been right on his heels promptly tossed Thompsons and shotguns into a pile on the ground and showed the impressive figure in black how high their hands could stretch toward heaven.

He told them in words dropped from an icicle, "Okay, down the hill. Don't pause, and don't look back. Move it!"

They moved it, with vigor, and Bolan went on swiftly across the driveway circle. Some clown poked a light machine gun over the edge of the roof and began spraying slugs wildly into the ground across his route of advance.

Without breaking stride, Bolan angled his multi-weapon upward and squeezed into the pistol grip of the M-79.

A forty-millimeter HE round whizzed into that parapet with a thunderous impact and sent man, gun, and goodly portions of roof tumbling onto the portico.

He coolly inserted another round of high explosives into the slide breech and went on, beneath the portico and inexorably toward that shattered entranceway.

Now it was the Executioner who was smelling blood, and already he was sickening on the overdose.

But it was that kind of world, this Mafia jungle; better their blood than the altar sacrifices of goats both scaped and bled.

Mike Talifero was about four heartbeats removed from the judgment of the universe.

It was no time for the instrument of execution to falter.

He moved on up, kicked aside the twisted aluminum remains of the door casing, and went back into hell.

And it was almost pitiful, this climactic end to the great fox chase of central Jersey.

He was met by two batteries of stacked and overturned tables, one to either side of the doorway, with nary head nor weapon showing at any edge.

This hardsite had gone mighty soft mighty fast.

A scramble at the far side, accompanied by the angry swearing of Mike SuchIron somewhere in the murky interior, signaled the frantic departure of more battlefield deserters.

The place was filled with smoke, and a lot of heat was coming down from the ceiling area, but he could see a dude in the background, slumped over a table and covering it with blood.

Talifero gave away his position in the rear with an emotional scream, "Open fire! Shoot, shoot, damnit!"

The snout of a Thompson came hesitantly around the side of one of the table-turrets.

Bolan flipped a grenade into that one and dispatched forty millimeters from the M-79 into the other one.

Tables splintered and flew and rolled all over that place while men in both sectors screamed until Bolan's M-16 mop-up put an end to that agony.

Mike Talifero was yelling something in a strange tongue, and Bolan could dimly see him moving around back there in the smoke—coughing and stumbling about.

Then a door back there opened and closed, and the target of the night abruptly disappeared.

It just had to be.

Bolan knew precisely which door.

The maze had a way of turning back, folding in,

devouring those who played cruel games in her chambers.

He went on, slid in another round of HE, and let it fly into that door, then followed quickly with his own imposing figure.

It was the men's locker room, yeah.

He went in under the cover of his own smoke while selecting another round for the M-79, and he stalked the fox to his final burrow.

And the guy was standing there, in the only place left—in the corner of that shower with Bruno's blood darkly caked about his feet.

Those eyes were positively wild, and there was not a hint of a smile upon the face that had snickered at human agony lo these many years.

He had a gun in each hand, and certainly at least a fighting chance, unlike any he'd ever offered another poor bastard who screamed and pleaded only for death.

But he was frozen there—tongue-tied for probably the first time in his life—stammering something about strong men who die together; but there was nothing truly strong about this man about to die, nothing commendable or admirable.

He was just another cornered punk, alone and contemplating his own death and seeing nothing of value beyond.

Without a word, and from about six paces out, the Executioner squeezed the pistol grip of the M-79 to send a chewing pattern of double-aughts grinding in at chin level.

The pistols clattered to the floor, the body sagged in a flowing river from the shoulders, and a shredded head bounced off the back wall and rolled along the incline toward the drain.

"May his soul thank mine," the Executioner muttered.

He threw a marksman's medal into the gore; then he turned his back on that and walked away from there.

And it was a very short step out of hell.

EPILOGUE

He appropriated one of the few remaining vehicles at Boots and Bugle—ironically enough, a camper van—and calmly withdrew along that trail of tears, taking with him along those darkened Jersey roads new fodder for future nightmares along the river of blood, as well as some fond memories of tender moments agreeably spent.

He heard but did not see the approach of the federal task force screaming into that grim ex-encampment back there in the smoldering ashes of the night, and he mentally tipped his hat to Leo Turrin and Hal Brognola, a couple of true friends who, he was sure, would forever figure in his future—no matter how many lifetimes lay ahead.

He was leaving Jersey with himself in better shape than when he entered. All things considered, that should say something for the place. So he sent a quiet "thank-you" into that corner of quivering universal mold and apologized for all feelings harshly held—while at the same moment promising to return one day for a closer look at the nature of things there.

And when he arrived at the little airstrip "a few miles south" of the hardsite, he was already relaxing into that postcombative torpor and mellowness that characterize a hard campaign honorably met.

Waiting there at that quiet edge of the hell grounds was a sleek executive jet, of the type used by corporations to fly their executives around with style and efficiency. Another type of corporation and a decidedly different sort of executive had been calling the shots for this particular air vehicle; Bolan could think of no more fitting exit for himself from the late and not so great shadow of the Jersey guns.

A single "sentry" waited there, a Marinello hardman with more sand in his eyes than brains in his head; the guy's eyes flickered but briefly into an awakening one startled heartbeat ahead of the flying fist that sent him back into a deeper and perhaps a more peaceful sleep.

The pilot was lying in the aisleway of the cabin, fully dressed, a pillow propped beneath his head, feet crossed, sleeping like a baby.

The Executioner intruded into his dreams and brought him back to the hard world with an awesome black Beretta tickling the tip of his nose.

The guy's eyes flared into an awareness of that which was and must be, and his greeting to the man in black was a quiet, "Oh, hell."

"Let's fly," Bolan suggested, with ice cubes enclosing the words. "Like the birdies. South."

It was to be the sole exchange of dialogue until they reached the southern-flow altitude corridor for air traffic; then the pilot advised Bolan, "You'll have to give me a destination for an ATC clearance."

The man in the co-pilot seat replied, "Forget ATC. Just fly south. I'll tell you when and where to do different."

The pilot showed him a halfhearted smile and agreed, "It's a good night. I can fly visual."

Yes, it was a fairly good night. It had been good to Mack Bolan. And all but a few festering wounds had been expiated into that night.

He shrugged out of his combat rig and tossed it to the rear, then asked the pilot, "You know a fat ghoul they call Sal?"

"No, I—"

"A turkey doctor."

"Oh, hell no. I just fly these people, I don't—"

"When you get home, you pass the word. In the right places. There's a contract on Sal written deep into my guts. You pass that word. Sal is out of business. Or he'd better be."

"Sure, I . . . I'll see that the word gets around."

Bolan sighed, lowered his lids about halfway down those blood-wracked eyes, and settled into a light "combat sleep"—that divided state of consciousness which gave him rest yet kept him animally alert to the outside world.

The pilot was telling him, "Between you and me, Mr. Bolan . . . I mean, just between the two of us, I think you're an okay guy."

The animal side of the Executioner grinned.

Sure.

Sara was okay.

Bruno was okay.

And—for the moment, at least—that wild and woolly universe of Mack Bolan's was okay.

His soul stretched, seeking a shortcut through the maze, sending a gentle probe into that receding countryside down there, giving form to the thought:

Good-bye, Mother Sara. Stay hard.